"Elandra Albain," whispered a soft voice through the darkness.

Elandra stirred and sat up. An eerie green light filled her surroundings, and she saw herself sitting unclad and shivering upon a bench of stone. A figure came wading toward her through the glowing fog, a tall shadow, powerful with broad shoulders and muscular legs.

He walked like a warrior, graceful and strong. She strained to see the molding of his head and face. To see him more clearly . . . to gaze into his eyes . . . to feel the touch of his fingertips on her skin . . .

Her heart lifted and yearned. She knew him, had known him throughout the sands of time. He was for her, as she was for him. In the blink of a moment, the distance between them ended. They stood face to face, breathless and cloaked in the strange shadows.

"Elandra," he whispered, his voice striking like a bronze bell within her soul. *"I have found thee, my only love."*

REIGN
of
SHADOWS

DEBORAH CHESTER

ACE BOOKS, NEW YORK

REIGN OF SHADOWS

An Ace Book / published by arrangement with
the author

PRINTING HISTORY
Ace mass market edition / June 1996

Copyright © 1996 by Deborah Chester.
Cover art by Mary Jo Phallen.
Interior text design by Kristen del Rosario.

For information address: The Berkley Publishing Group,
a division of Penguin Group (USA) Inc.,
375 Hudson Street, New York, New York 10014.

ISBN: 0-441-01166-7

ACE®
Ace Books are published by The Berkley Publishing Group,
a division of Penguin Group (USA) Inc.,
375 Hudson Street, New York, New York 10014.
ACE and the "A" design
are trademarks belonging to Penguin Group (USA) Inc.

PRINTED IN THE UNITED STATES OF AMERICA

10 9 8 7 6 5 4 3 2

REIGN OF SHADOWS

prologue

IN THE BEGINNING OF TIME THERE AROSE A mighty warrior named Kostimon, who used the power of his arm and the cunning of his mind to make himself a king. Favored by the gods, he drove his army against the provinces, using sheer force, trickery, or raids to subjugate them. At last the provinces were joined together, and he stood as emperor over a united land. One by one, through choice or coercion, the warlords swore oaths of eternal allegiance to him.

When it came time to marry, he chose a red-haired and untamed bride, a beauty with the blood of warriors in her veins. Together, Kostimon and Fauvina ruled well and wisely, creating laws both fair and just for government. Religion flourished and unified into two state cults—the Vindicants and the Penestricans—balancing each other in perfect harmony.

Thus did the fledgling empire prosper. Through diplomacy and alliance its borders spread. When war assailed it, the empire prevailed. Fauvina bore sons, and the gods willed they grow straight and strong.

But as the years lengthened, Kostimon's ambitions soared ever higher. He saw his work unfinished and his dreams incomplete. His quarrelsome, impatient sons thought only of their own pleasures and never of the responsibilities of rule. Into Kostimon's mind came a most unholy plan. He turned unto darkness and petitioned for immortality. A fearsome bargain was struck, and Kostimon was promised life for one thousand years. Fauvina would not share his bargain and died at the fated end of her time, her soul consigned to the fertile earth from which it had come.

Slaying each successive generation of sons so they could not challenge his throne, Kostimon lived on, feeding on power and glory, lusting for new achievements, building impressive monuments to himself. Under his obligation to the shadow gods, Kostimon turned against the light and built temples to darkness. No longer did he tolerate his enemies. Those who spoke against him were destroyed, and when the Penestricans dared to criticize the injustices of his reign, they were reviled and driven from their place of counsel. Greed walked the streets of his cities. Corruption swelled in the halls of justice. And it came to pass that men ceased to obey laws and followed only the capricious will of their emperor. He became a legend, more than a man but less than a god, greater than any other mortal.

But prophecies tell true, and the gods forget no reckoning. Kostimon has reached his last century. His final years are running out like the last few coins in a spendthrift's purse. Kostimon has forgotten how to accept defeat; even now he struggles against his fate. Yet the shadow gods remain deaf to his entreaties. Again and again the Vindicant augurs have cast his future, but for the first time in a millennium his sign does not appear. Nor does the sign of his one living son. The heavens are silent; the gods send no answer. The lack of portents has made even the augurs afraid.

The empire waits with trepidation to see if the world will end with Kostimon. His enemies plot and circle, growing bolder as the sun of his empire sets. The shadow gods, released by the tolerance of his reign, wreak their own form of destruction on the hearts and souls of men. Yet Kostimon's subjects still hope for a successor. Many lift prayers to the gods of light; others send their appeals to the gods of darkness. All seek clues that will reveal the founder of the next dynasty.

Who—or what—will come?

PART ONE

one

BEYOND THE MARSHLANDS THE SUN WAS A ruddy orb sinking into the trees. Clouds scudding across the pale indigo sky turned gilded bellies to the west, reflecting the last rays of sunlight toward the frozen ground.

At the close of afternoon lessons, a silent line of novices walked solemnly across the courtyard of Rieschelhold, famed school for the healing arts. The line of first-termers was led by an older, gawky boy in the long, medium blue robe of a disciple. Sauntering at the very end of the line, Caelan E'non cast a wary eye around for proctors and lagged back until he could step behind a stack of cider kegs near the wall.

No one seemed to notice his disappearance. Grinning to himself, Caelan crouched low in his hiding place and waited impatiently for the courtyard to clear. The stone blocks at his back were very cold, and he had no cloak or mittens. Sucking in his breath, he tucked his hands in the wide sleeves of his grubby novice robe and felt content. This was freedom, tiny moments stolen at every opportunity to escape the tedium of his life here.

Tonight the serfs seemed slower than usual in finishing their chores. Drumming his fingers on his knees, Caelan listened to the cadenced sounds coming from the road outside the walls and mentally urged the serfs to hurry.

Finally the cobbles were swept clean of straw, mud, and leaves. The women hastened to finish gathering the laundry, and the carts holding apple baskets from the harvest were rowed up neatly along a wall. Even the well rope had to be coiled neatly over the crossbar. Nothing could be left undone or untidy, lest it attract the mischief of the wind spirits that blew at night.

Already the breeze was picking up, sweeping down even into Caelan's hiding place. Pine-scented and frosty, the air held a promise of snow.

He shivered and didn't care. The serfs were gathering the last of their tools and heading for the hall. From the tower, the Quarl Bell began to toll the first of its nine solemn counts, calling all inhabitants of Rieschelhold indoors to safety.

The sound of the bell made Caelan crouch forward.

Everyone would hurry now to get inside. It was the best part of the day. Besides, if his absence hadn't been noticed by now, it was unlikely to be. He had to stay after class so often for punishment drills that his fellow novices wouldn't even notice his failure to show for washing up.

He'd be inside by darkfall, and at the table for supper. The proctors counted heads at supper and made a bed check at lights out. The rules here were strict, but the ironclad routine made it easy to dodge most of what he really wanted to avoid. He just had to pick the right moments.

Like now.

Scooting past the cider kegs, he dashed for the steps leading up to the ramparts of the wall. Bending double, he scuttled along below the crenellations until he reached the open-topped lookout turret near the main gates.

Inside the circle of brick, he could not be seen from the courtyard.

Grinning broadly, Caelan flung himself at the sloped tip of a crenellation and balanced there on his stomach with his toes barely touching the ground.

From up here he had sweeping views of the surrounding marshlands and forest. A place of evil mists said to shelter wind spirits and the evil spawn of the shadow gods, the marshlands were mysterious and forbidden. Even now, a dank fog could be seen rising above them, gilded on top by the sunset. The sky was tinted a muted gold, with streaks of coral and indigo. Winter geese flew overhead in a ragged V formation, calling plaintively. The wind nipped bitterly at his uncovered ears and blew his hair into his eyes, but he didn't mind.

He was in time to see the soldiers.

All day he'd been obliged to do his chores and work at his lessons, while in the distance came a steady tramping of feet along the imperial road that passed beside Rieschelhold. Word had passed among all the boys—imperial troops were marching home from the border wars.

None of the masters would release classes even for a few minutes so the boys could see the army. Rieschelhold clung to its routine no matter what the rest of the world did. But alone of all the students, Caelan refused to miss this opportunity.

Now, at last, he saw them, and it was a sight worth the risk of lingering out here past the forbidden hour.

The fading sunlight reflected off the burnished spear tips of more men than Caelan could count.

His mouth dropped open at the sheer size of the army. They filled the road, as far as the eye could see in either direction, marching ten men abreast. Never in his life had he seen so many. And they had been marching by all day.

Caelan drew in a slow breath of wonder. It must be the entire eastern force—three legions at least, perhaps more. Eighteen thousand fighting men and their officers.

A force larger than the town population of nearby Meunch. Staring at the sight, Caelan's spirits slowly sank. Was the war over? As long as he could remember, his dream had been to join up and become a warrior in the service of the emperor. Right now the war involved fighting off the heathen Madruns who were overrunning the eastern borders of the empire. Caelan's fists clenched on the wall. The war just had to last until he could be a part of it.

But it couldn't be over. The bells would be ringing if there had been victory. And the standard-bearers on horseback still carried banners and legion emblems, so there hadn't been a defeat. These men must have been replaced with fresher troops, although none had marched east on this road.

Still, to see an entire army—even a small one—real and entire . . . Caelan leaned out farther over the edge of the wall, absorbing every detail of these men who were his heroes.

Silent and grim, the veterans looked battle-worn and tired. They trudged along, crusted with mud and frost. Some of them wore bloody bandages, but not many. He knew army regulations separated wounded men from sound troops.

All the foot soldiers wore winter-rusted mail and tattered cloaks. Few were clean-shaven. Besides the long spears, they were armed with two standard army daggers each—barbed blades that were nearly as long as Caelan's arm. A regiment of archers passed by next, clad in tunics of imperial red and winter fur leggings. These men were tall and mostly blond. Their longbows were slung over their shoulders, and each man carried four quivers.

Officers and cavalry, however, were the most flamboyant. They wore polished armor breastplates beneath their red cloaks and had leopard skin saddlecloths. Booted and spurred, with mail leggings and armored knee and elbow protectors fitted with wicked spikes, they wore mail

cowls, and their helmets dangled on straps from their sad-
dles. Their curved swords had crooked hilts for one-
handed fighting. War axes and spiked clubs also hung
from their belts. Their massive war chargers—also armored—made ordinary horses look like mere ponies.

The hoofbeats of the trotting chargers on the stone road
rumbled like constant thunder, a glorious sound that made
Caelan's heart beat faster.

At that moment he would have given anything to go
with them.

"Caelan! Here you are."

Startled, Caelan slid off the wall and turned around.

For a split second he saw only the long robe of a disciple, and with disgust he knew he was in for more demerits. Then the boy stepped out of shadow.

Caelan let out his breath in relief. "Oh, it's you. Well
met, Cousin Agel."

Black-haired and blue-eyed, Agel was a slim, handsome boy who always looked neat and well dressed. Unlike Caelan, he never slept in his robe. He never used it
to dust his room. He never knotted up stolen apples and
cheese in it, using it as a makeshift haversack on outings.

Agel was townbred, unlike Caelan who had grown up
in a country hold. His father was a merchant and a
wealthy man. As a result Agel possessed a level of so-
phistication Caelan had always envied. Agel was poised
and well mannered around adults, who thought him in-
capable of the pranks he could think up. When he
laughed, he had a pair of dimples and a charming twinkle
in his eye. He could sweet-talk any cook into slipping him
extra food for a growing boy.

But right now as he stood there with his fists on his
hips, he wore a frown instead of a smile. "Are you deaf
tonight?" he asked. "The Quarl Bell has rung."

Disappointment crashed into Caelan. He thought Agel
had come to share this moment with him like old times.

"Did you hear the bell?"

"Yes," Caelan said with a shrug. "What of it?"

Agel blinked. "You know very well—"

"Careful! You'd better run for hall before you get a mark and spoil your perfect record."

Agel's frown deepened. "I was upstairs in the hall of studies when I saw you sneak off. I came to bring you in before you ruin yourself. You can't risk another—"

"Never mind." Caelan grinned and beckoned. "You're in time. Come look."

Agel shook his head, but Caelan caught him by the front of his robe and pulled him over to the wall.

"Look at them!" Caelan said. "Did you ever see anything like it?"

Agel gave the troops a quick glance and turned away immediately. "They'll probably loot and burn Meunch on their way through."

"No, they won't!" Caelan said, disappointed in his reaction. "They're heroes. I've dreamed of the chance to see a fighting force this large."

"Well, now you have. Come, let's go before the proctors catch us."

Caelan sighed. His cousin used to be fun, always ready for mischief, eager to join in any adventure. But since coming here to study healing, Agel had turned into a dullard. It was as though he'd checked his sense of humor and fun at the gate when he took his matriculation oath. This term, he'd advanced a grade to disciple, and he was more pompous than ever before.

Hooking his elbows over the wall, Caelan turned his back to Agel. "Go on, then. Sit in hall and eat your stew while Master Umal delivers another boring lecture on philosophy. I'm staying out here until it's too dark to see anything."

"You're mad!" Agel said angrily. "It's too dangerous, especially in winter hours. The wind spirits—"

"Silly old superstitions," Caelan said, keeping his gaze stubbornly on the troops.

Agel slapped his back, and Caelan flinched and whirled around. "Don't!"

"You still have bruises from the last beating the proctors gave you," Agel said, glaring at him. "Why don't you ever learn?"

"Learn what?" Caelan retorted, angry now. "To fold my hands and practice *severance* until my eyes cross? To recite passages that are so dull I can't say them without yawning? What's the point of it?"

"You know," Agel said in a low, disapproving voice. "Or maybe you don't. You've acted like a child ever since you came here."

"I hate it here!" Caelan cried. "Last term you complained as much as I did."

"But I advanced, and you didn't. You're at the bottom of the novice class in ranking. For shame, cousin! You're already on academic probation. If you fail again, that will be the end of your studies here."

"Good," Caelan said stubbornly, hating this lecture. "Then I'll be free."

"How can you talk so? Rieschelhold offers the best training in the empire. To be a healer with any kind of reputation, you—"

Caelan scowled. "I don't want to be a healer."

"Nonsense. Of course you do."

"I don't!"

"You have to be!"

"Why?" Caelan shot back. "Because my father's one?"

"Of course."

Caelan spat over the wall in the soldier's way of insult, and Agel's eyes narrowed with disapproval.

"You don't mean any of this," Agel said. "It's time you grew up and started acting your age."

Caelan sighed. He would be seventeen next month, which meant he was one year short of being able to legally defy his father, one year short of residing under a roof of his own choosing, one year short of breaking his apprenticeship, one year short of taking himself out of school, one year short of living as and how he chose.

"I get enough lectures from the masters," Caelan said angrily. "I don't need any from you."

Agel glared back. "I've tried to let you walk your own path, but how can I call myself your friend and kinsman if I let you throw this away? This place is so pure, so special. It's—"

"It's smothering me!"

Consternation filled Agel's face. "You've known since childhood you would train here as your father trained, following in his footsteps. Why didn't you protest earlier if you really didn't want this?"

"I did. You know that."

Agel shook his head. "If you really want something else, you could have insisted. I did with my father, and he listened to me. Otherwise I'd be working in the counting house instead of studying here."

Caelan couldn't believe Agel was saying this. It was like he'd forgotten those summers when he'd visited E'nonhold. "You know Beva. He hears only what he wants to. Nothing I'd ever said has made the least difference to him."

"Well, if you told him you wanted to be a soldier I'm not surprised he ignored you."

Caelan bristled. "What's wrong with soldiering?"

Agel threw him a scornful look. "Spend your life tramping hundreds of miles and being bullied, for what? For the chance to be speared by a heathen wearing tattoos and a breechclout?"

"I would see the world," Caelan said, his dreams turning his gaze back to the ribbon of soldiers marching into the gloom. A trumpet sounded in the far distance, mournful and low. The sound made him shiver. "I would serve the emperor. I would have honor—"

"More honor in taking lives than in saving them?" Agel sounded genuinely horrified. "I thought you would

grow out of this foolishness, but you're worse than ever."
He threw out his arms, making his wide sleeves bell. "We
are in the very place most devoted to the preservation of
life, and all you can think about is killing. It's a defile-
ment—"

"Oh, shut up," Caelan growled. "You sound like Master Hierst. It's not like that. You're twisting everything."

"Am I? Or are you? How can you glorify a profession
devoted to slaughter? Yes, in the name of the emperor,"
he added scornfully as Caelan tried to protest. "And does
that justify it?"

"Careful," Caelan warned him stiffly. "You're close to
treason."

Agel sniffed. "Your father has dedicated his life to
helping people, to alleviating suffering, to saving lives
whenever possible. He has honored the gods who gave
him the gift of healing. What about you, Caelan? What
are you going to honor? Bloodshed and pillage?"

Caelan's face flamed hot. He had never heard Agel so
cutting, so contemptuous. "You sound like you'd rather
worship my father than the emperor."

"Uncle Beva is worthy of everyone's admiration,"
Agel said. "Yours most of all."

"I'm not like him!" Caelan cried. "I'm not *ever* going
to be like him. I used to think you understood that. Now
you sound just like everyone else."

"I've grown up," Agel said coldly. "You haven't."

His scorn hurt. Caelan glared at him, trying not to let
it show. "You used to be on my side," he said softly,
struggling to hold his voice steady.

"I still am. If I didn't care about you, I wouldn't be
out here now, risking a demerit to save you another beating."

Caelan snorted to himself, almost wanting to laugh except it hurt too much. "There was a time when you
wouldn't have cared about demerits."

"You're right," Agel said quietly, almost with pity. "I

wouldn't have cared. I would have probably raced you up here, and we could have stayed out until we froze in the cold, daring each other to risk an attack of the wind spirits.

Caelan laughed. "That's more like it."

"But I have enough sense these days to know that's stupid," Agel went on, still in that same quiet voice. "I have my future to think about, and the way I want to spend my life. I'm an adult now, not a boy. I want to be a healer, because it is good work and helpful work. It gives something back to the world. I admire Uncle Beva more than anyone else I know, and I'm grateful to his kindness in seeing that I was allowed to enroll here. I've had to work hard and prove myself worthy of that admittance, while you—you have it as a birthright. That's why it makes me so angry when I see you throwing your opportunity away."

"And it makes me angry when you refuse to see my side of things," Caelan answered. "I am not Beva. I will never be him, no matter how much everyone wants me to be. All my life I've had to follow around in his shadow, hearing about his skill, his gifts, his success, his fame. I'm sick of it!"

"Are you jealous of him?" Agel asked in astonishment.

"No! I'm just tired of being expected to measure up to what he is. As though anyone could ever come close to him."

"But he's the greatest healer in Trau."

Caelan shut his eyes.

"More than that. His fame spreads beyond this province," Agel said eagerly. "He could go all the way to Imperia if he chose. An appointment as court physician would be—"

"My father doesn't want that. He's only interested in living in *severance*," Caelan said bitterly. "No fame. No fortune."

"He is a good man."

"He's cold and unfeeling!" Caelan burst out. "Damn you, why have you started worshiping him like this? You used to think he was as strict as—"

"But since I started studying here, I understand *severance*." Agel folded his hands in his wide sleeves and hunched himself against the cold. It was nearly dark now, and the soldiers could only be heard on the road. They marched in unnerving silence—the brutal force of the emperor evident and thrilling. "It is a total philosophy of life," Agel said. "It is completion."

Caelan rolled his eyes. Everything angry and rebellious in him rose up, roaring inwardly against hearing any of it again. "It's not for me."

"You must learn to accept it if you are to heal."

"I don't want to heal," Caelan said in exasperation. "Why can't you accept that?"

"Because it's in you."

"It's in my father, not me!"

"But you have the gift. You are his blood. He tested you and said you could *sever*. I remember when he did it."

"The ability to do something doesn't mean it's my destiny," Caelan said. "I know they teach that here, but you don't have to believe everything they say."

"The ways that are taught here are good ways," Agel said.

"But they aren't the *only* ways," Caelan argued. He saw no change in Agel's expression and sighed. "What's the use? You've turned to stone, just like the masters here. You're becoming exactly like my father."

A smile dawned across Agel's face. "Really?" he asked in delight. "You really think so?"

Disgust filled Caelan. Without answering, he shouldered past Agel and headed down the steps to the courtyard.

Agel followed close on his heels, and in silence they hurried toward the hall.

In the gloom and quiet of evening, the courtyard had an eerie, deserted feel. Light glowed warm from the narrow window slits in the buildings, and the air smelled of peat smoke. The wind still blew sharp and bitterly cold, knocking old snow off the roofs in soft drifts of white.

No one was supposed to be abroad by the last stroke of the Quarl Bell. All residents of the hold had to be indoors before nightfall, safe within the warding keys and secured from the wind spirits that hunted during the long winter darkness. Which, Caelan thought to himself, was only an elaborate way of enforcing a strict curfew.

It seemed that everything at Rieschelhold was buried under an endless series of rules. Living here was like dying a slow death. Caelan hated the tall stone walls, hated the confinement, the serenity, the order, the iron routine that never varied. At home he could always find a way to escape his tutors. He lived for wild gallops across the glacier, his horse's mane whipping his face, the icy wind whistling in his ears. The mountains, the sweeping views of the top of the world, the endless sky. And at night, the breathtaking display of colors from the light spirits.

That was living.

But here, in the marshy lowlands, the winters were bleak and rainy and the summers were hot and insect-riddled. Beautiful days were wasted cramped inside classrooms. The joy of life, the urge, the passion were all driven away in favor of *severance*, which meant to be cold, aloof, detached, emotionless, and dead as far as he was concerned.

Caelan tipped back his head to look at the starry sky. His heart ached for freedom. But even if he sent for the scrivener and wrote another letter to his father, begging for release, it would be a waste of time. Beva E'non wanted his only son to be a healer; therefore, the son would be a healer. Close of subject.

Accept it, Caelan told himself as he and Agel crunched

across gravel, then reached the cobblestones. Grow up and do as you're told.

But even when he forced himself to concentrate and really tried to do his lessons, his heart wasn't in the work. He wasn't a scholar, never had been. And always in the back of his heart gnawed the question of what kind of healer he would be. How could he cure anyone? How could he reach the depth of empathy necessary to *sever* illness and suffering from the lives of his father's patients?

Ahead, from the side yard, a shadow suddenly emerged from the darkness. Long-robed and hooded in cerulean blue, it carried a long rod of yew carved with the faces of the four wind spirits. Its left hand was held aloft, and upon its palm glowed a pale blue flame not of fire. It saw the boys and paused, then headed toward them.

Dragging in a breath of exasperation, Caelan stopped so quickly Agel bumped into him from behind.

Agel's breath hissed audibly. "Gault have mercy on us."

Caelan turned his head. "Run," he whispered. "Take the passage by the stables and slip into the hall of studies through the side door. It's always open at this hour for Master Mygar."

Beside him, Agel was tense with alarm. "But the proctor—"

"Shut up and go! I have so many demerits another won't hurt me. Just go."

As he spoke, Caelan gave Agel a shove. Ducking his head, Agel shuffled away; then abruptly he broke into a run and vanished from sight.

The proctor veered that way and lifted its staff, but Caelan stepped into its path.

"I have permission to be out after Quarl Bell," he lied loudly.

Proctors did not split their attention well and tended to confront whatever was closest. Figuring this out had enabled Caelan to avoid them many times. But now he danced nervously across the path of the proctor a second time as it tried to look in the direction Agel had gone.

The proctor finally turned its hooded head back to Caelan and pointed its staff.

Caelan backed up warily. That staff could strike with lightning speed to enforce the hold's many rules. He had the bruises to prove it.

"Master Mygar released me from late drills for an errand," he said quickly. "I'm to report back to him after supper."

The proctor, its face unseen within the depths of its hood, stared at Caelan in grim silence. Extending its left hand, it cast the truth-light at him.

His heart sank, but he knew better than to flinch.

The light flowed over him from the top of his head and spread slowly down. Caelan scarcely breathed and kept his lie uppermost in his mind, visualizing old Master Mygar with his food-stained robe and toothless gums.

The pale blue light flowed over him in a shimmering glow. At first its color did not alter, indicating the truth had been told. Caelan began to hope he might get away with this.

Then the light faded to sickly yellow.

Caelan gulped but resigned himself. All this meant was a couple of stout blows and no supper tonight. The black mark would go on his record, and tomorrow he'd have extra drills from Master Mygar for lying. Unpleasant, but easy enough to endure when he had to.

The proctor stretched forth its left hand again, and the light spread from Caelan's feet, then gathered itself into a tight ball and returned to the proctor's palm. The proctor swept its rod aside, gesturing for Caelan to pass.

Disbelieving, for an instant Caelan thought he was being allowed to go. He grinned and hurried past the proctor, but a faint whistle in the air warned him of his mistake.

The blow slammed across his back with a force that

drove him to his knees. Streaks of black and red crossed his vision. He wheezed and could not draw in air. His back felt as though it had been broken in half. Wrapped in agony, Caelan sagged forward onto his palms.

The staff struck him again, knocking him flat. His cheek scraped on the cobblestones, a tiny flare of pain beneath the immense agony in his back. He coughed and choked, still unable to drag in any air.

Just when he began to panic, his lungs started working again. He drew in another breath, then another, although each one caused pain to stab through his back. It was too hard to get up so he lay there, fighting back tears, too angry and proud to let the proctor see how badly it had hurt him.

The proctor glided around him in a silent circle. From where he lay, Caelan could see that the proctor's feet did not quite touch the ground. Instead it floated ever so slightly in the air. Caelan swallowed hard and closed his eyes. He and another novice had a bet on whether the proctors walked. Right now, winning Ojer's quarterly allowance didn't seem very important. Caelan felt too gray and clammy to care about anything except that it was over. In a moment he'd manage to get to his feet, then he'd be confined to his quarters without supper. No loss, the way he felt right now.

The tip of the proctor's staff struck the ground a scant inch from the tip of his nose. Startled, Caelan jerked open his eyes.

The proctor bent over him. Truth-light rolled down the length of the staff, making it glow. Caelan thought he saw the carved faces of the wind spirits shift and grimace.

Gasping in alarm, he jerked himself up to a sitting position and winced with pain.

"You fear no wind spirits. You mock the rules of protection," the proctor said, its voice hollow and not quite real. "You meet wind spirits."

"No," Caelan said in growing unease. He held up his

hands and scrambled to his knees. "I've learned my lesson. Honest. Don't—"

"More lies," the proctor said sternly. It lifted the glowing staff over its head and swung it in a circle.

A gust of wind swirled around Caelan, dumping snow down his collar and making him shiver.

"Tonight you meet the wind. You learn."

The proctor turned, but Caelan reached out in desperation and gripped the hem of its robe.

The cloth was scorching hot. With a cry, Caelan released it and shook his singed fingers.

"You can't leave me outside all night," he said in protest. "I'll freeze to death."

"Then lesson will be learned." Without looking back, the proctor glided away and left him kneeling on the cold cobblestones.

two

BY THE TIME CAELAN MANAGED TO STAGGER
to his feet and lurch forward, the proctor had vanished
from sight.

Sharp pain stabbed through Caelan's left knee every
time he took a step. He could feel blood trickling down
his leg, and his leggings were ripped.

Fresh resentment washed over him, but he pushed it
away, determined to get inside the hall before the proctor
locked him out. He wasn't going to spend all night out
here. They had no right to do that to him.

Limping and gasping, he hobbled past the main hall
entry. The massive wooden doors with their elaborate
carvings were always bolted shut at the conclusion of
Quarl Bell. He didn't waste time trying to get in that way.
Instead, he limped around to the side door that he'd rec-
ommended to Agel.

It was locked.

He pushed on it with all his strength, then cursed and
kicked it.

He tried the larder.

Locked.

He checked the stables, but they were firmly bolted. He knocked as loudly as he dared, but no one came.

The storage barns, harvest shed, and cider press were all secured. He could not gain entry to the servants' quarters, and the only access to the tall stone building that housed the students was through the hall.

As for Elder Sobna's small house, tucked up against the low wall of the kitchen garden . . . impossible. He wasn't about to seek refuge there.

Darkness—bleak and terribly cold—closed in around him. The wind cut harshly through his clothing. Shivering, he tucked his numb hands into his armpits and tried to pull his robe up over his head to protect his aching ears. It wasn't enough.

They had to let him in, he kept reassuring himself. They couldn't let him die of exposure out here. How would they explain it to his father?

His mind's eye conjured up a scene of his father, grim and sorrowful, standing in Elder Sobna's study. The Elder would be stroking his beard and shaking his head.

"The boy was always in trouble. Lax and disobedient, always breaking rules designed for his own protection. No one knew he'd slipped outside again. The poor boy simply froze to death. An unfortunate accident."

Caelan's anger came surging up hot and fierce. He wasn't going to shiver out here, losing toes and the tips of his ears to frostbite. They thought he would pound on the doors and plead for forgiveness. They were trying to scare him into behaving.

But it wasn't going to work.

Furiously, he circled the infirmary and classrooms. All the windows were shuttered firmly. The doors were locked tight.

No refuge anywhere.

The wind blew stronger now, whipping his clothing and lashing his hair into his eyes. It cut straight through him, driving him into a corner of the wall. Gusting and shrieking around the eaves of the buildings, it seemed to sob and wail. For a moment he thought he saw a blurry shape forming in the air itself, long talons reaching out to rend him.

"No!" he shouted, and shoved himself out into the open again.

He wasn't going to give up, and he wasn't going to beg for forgiveness. There had to be another way, one he'd wanted for a long time.

He limped toward the main gates. It took four men to lift the stout crossbeam that lay across the brackets of the gates. But there was a smaller pass gate, also bolted from inside and guarded by a softly glowing warding key.

By day the key was only a crude triangle of hand-hammered bronze. But at night its powers awakened to guard against all creatures of the shadows, including wind spirits and the unnameable things that crept the earth in increasing numbers. Spell-forged by the mysterious, nomadic Choven, warding keys could be found on the gates of the largest holds in Trau, or on the doors of the humblest daub and wattle cottages.

Warding gloves were required to handle the keys, but those were locked away in the gatehouse along with the gatekeeper, who was probably spooning his supper and refusing to listen to any knocking on his door.

The glimmer of pale blue light in the distance made Caelan look up. He saw a proctor gliding along the upper ramparts of the wall.

Caelan shouted and waved, but the proctor did not glance in his direction. When it reached the corner of the wall, it descended the steps and vanished from sight among the working sheds.

Desperation had many sides. Caelan's resolution hardened. He'd rather be cursed now than to chase down a proctor and beg for mercy. He'd rather lose a hand from touching a warding key than endure another beating.

Everyone in Rieschelhold could go to Beloth, for all he cared.

He looked around, but as usual no tools had been left lying about. There was nothing he could use to pry the warding key off the gate.

Every time Caelan stepped too near, the key's glow brightened to a dazzling intensity, and the metal hummed with a force that vibrated through his skull.

He stepped back and scowled with growing determination. Beyond the gate lay freedom and hope. He could join the soldiers and shake the dust of Trau once and for all off his shoes.

Although most of the time Caelan daydreamed through his lessons, he had received some training in *severance* at home from his father. And the extra drills from Master Mygar had not all been worthless.

Caelan squared his shoulders and shut his eyes, forcing himself to concentrate. All his anger had to be gathered first. He visualized a chest with a lock. Placing his anger inside, he slammed shut the lid. He visualized another chest. Into it he shoved doubts, fear, cold, hunger, and thought.

It was harder to do out here in the brutal cold than in the classroom under Master Mygar's cynical eye. Caelan could feel himself wavering. A trickle of sweat beaded along his temples, and he gasped with the effort.

Focus, he told himself. *Focus hard*.

Then, for a wavering instant, he felt a surge of icy coldness go through him, a coldness that burned inside and cleared away everything. He seemed to stand in a frozen place of pure isolation. For a second he could see . . .

Now.

His hand reached out and plucked off the warding key. Heat blazed into his palm, but the pain was far away.

He tossed the key aside, and it clattered and spun on the cobblestones before going black.

Exultation roared through Caelan. He heard himself shout; then the world rushed back around him at its normal speed. He half stumbled forward, hit the gate with his shoulder, and shoved up the bar.

The gate swung open with a frozen creak of its hinges, and he went staggering through.

His hand ached intensely, but when he checked it there was no burn.

A feeling of wonder spread through him, but he had no time to think about what he'd done. Instead he spun around and shot a defiant gesture at the dark walls towering above him.

He was free at last of his prison.

With a laugh ringing in his throat, he stepped onto the smooth, stone-paved road and headed west at a trot, eager to catch up with the army he could still hear marching far ahead of him.

DEFIANCE WAS EASY ENOUGH IN THE HEAT of the act, but a far different thing when the path was dark, the trail long, and only cold and hunger marched by his shoulder.

Caelan gritted his teeth against fear, refusing to look too far to the left or right. The forest bordered the road in ominous quiet. Now and then he heard distant howls that might belong to wolves or worse. He kept quickening his pace, refusing to run, but going fast enough to be breathless. How had the rear of the army gotten so far ahead so quickly? All day he'd listened to them march by; now there was only the dreadful silence of the woods.

He thought he saw eyes gleaming off to one side. His mouth went dry and his heart quickened jerkily. But then the faint gleam vanished.

Caelan told himself he was seeing visions.

The gleam reappeared in the trees, brighter now although still distant. He heard a faint trace of sounds, an echo of laughter perhaps, and smelled food cooking. Pausing in the middle of the road, Caelan realized he was seeing the lights of a camp ahead. He'd found the army.

Relief washed over him. It was hard to believe his lifelong dream was finally in his grasp. At last he was going to live as he chose. All he had to do to enter the army was to lie about his age. He was tall and broad-shouldered. He thought he could convince the officers he was old enough to serve.

Squaring his shoulders and brushing quick hands down the front of his short novice robe, he practiced briefly what he would say, then strode toward the outskirts of the camp.

A shape barreled into him from nowhere and knocked him flat.

Half-stunned, Caelan slowly registered a foul stench; hard, heavy muscles; and a triumphant grunting. It was a lurker, and it had him.

Fear galvanized Caelan, and he yelled with all his might, flailing wildly with his arms to drive the creature off.

His resistance only seemed to excite the creature. It leaped atop him, ripping his robe into shreds. Lurker smell was nauseating, and Caelan gagged and choked. He had no weapon, not even a tinder strike or a coal box. Lurkers were skulkers, cowards who preyed on carrion and stragglers. Although vicious, they were easily frightened off by simple tactics such as armed resistance or even fire.

With regret Caelan thought of the knife he kept hidden in his clothes chest in his quarters. He'd bought it at the fair from a Neika tribesman last summer. It was forbidden, of course, and certainly not allowed at school. But he'd managed to keep the proctors from finding it during their periodic room searches. What he'd give to have the weapon at hand now.

Stupid to be caught like this. With the wide, paved road bordered on either side by deep ditches kept cleared by imperial order, he had felt safe. He hadn't even been thinking of lurkers this close to the hold or the nearby town.

Sniffing along Caelan's throat, the lurker laughed low. For a moment it sounded almost human.

Horrified, Caelan jabbed it in one eye with his thumb.

The creature reared back with a howl, and Caelan was able to scramble free. He gave it a kick that knocked it over, gained his feet, and ran for his life.

Shrieking, the lurker lunged after him, and the chase began in earnest. Caelan knew if it caught him it would tear him apart in its excitement, or else drag him off to feed a colony.

Lurkers were fearsome things, half human and half animal. Man-sized when grown, they could walk upright or drop to their knuckles. Hook-nosed and fanged, they had faces that looked semi-intelligent, and they were certainly cunning. Their skin was usually mottled or covered with warts. Long silver hair grew to their shoulders and hung in tangled locks filled with twigs and burrs. Said to be originally spawned of demons, they skulked the fringes of fields and hid in mountain passes. They preferred fresh meat, but they were also carrion eaters. If they were hungry enough, they would even prey on each other.

In springtime they were especially bold, seeking field-maids to force. If the villagers did not kill women who were attacked, often they killed themselves rather than give birth to such monsters.

Peasants slaughtered lurkers at every chance. Whenever the creatures ventured too near villages, the men formed hunting parties and rounded them up, driving them to their deaths over cliffs. But still the bestial creatures increased in number every year, migrating in from other regions.

The one coursing at Caelan's heels now was more than enough. Snuffling, it kept up with him easily. Caelan ran flat out, arms and legs pumping, straining to hold his short lead.

His cut knee began to twinge, then hurt. He ran anyway, ignoring it, but the pain intensified until every step brought a wrenching stab of agony.

The lurker was closer now, snuffling and grunting in excitement. It lunged at Caelan, and the graze of its claws on his back made him leap forward.

Howling, the lurker lunged again.

This time Caelan's leg buckled under him without warning. He went down hard, the lurker clawing his back with shrieks of triumph.

Mashed beneath it, Caelan felt it grip his neck to snap it. Fear convulsed him, but he was pinned and helpless.

The lurker squalled anew, uttering a bellow of triumph that changed to a weird, high-pitched sound and ended abruptly.

It fell across Caelan with a thud and did not stir.

Breathing hard, terror still running through him in waves, Caelan did not at first realize what had happened.

Then he heard running footsteps and voices. A light from a lantern shone in his eyes.

Dizzy with relief, Caelan raised his head. "Help me!" he cried. "Get it off."

The soldiers surrounded him and dragged off the lurker's dead body. Sitting up, Caelan saw the haft of a javelin sticking up from the lurker's back. One of the soldiers pulled out the weapon, and dark green blood dripped off the point.

A noxious stench rose up from the wound, driving the soldiers back with wrinkled noses.

"Break that javelin and throw it away," one of the men advised in slurred Lingua. "You'll never clean lurker stink off it."

The owner of the weapon grimaced, then cursed to the war god Faure. He snapped the javelin across his knee and tossed it in the ditch.

Caelan scrambled to his feet, filled with admiration. "That was as true a throw as anyone could hope for, sir," he said in flawless Lingua. "And in the dark, even finer. Thank you for saving my life."

The four soldiers exchanged glances and hooted with laughter.

Not understanding, Caelan stared up at them. His eagerness for acceptance burned brightly. It was hard to believe his dream was finally coming true. Already he felt a part of the group. He had survived danger and been rescued. His eyes drank in their mail and long daggers, gleaming in the lantern light. Scarred and tattooed with shocking symbols of blasphemy, their faces looked cruel and savage, but he didn't mind. To him, they were heroes.

"I thought you Traulanders were afraid of the dark," the tallest man said. He was swarthy with an evil-looking pagan tattoo on his cheek. Long plaits of braided hair hung to his shoulders, and a leather thong kept them back from his face. He wore a gold ring in one ear. "Comes dark, and the whole populace bolts indoors like rats into their holes."

"Not the dark," Caelan said earnestly. "It's the wind spirits that come in the darkness."

Two of the soldiers grinned, but one glanced around and fingered a small amulet hanging from his neck.

The tattooed man eyed Caelan a while, then shrugged. "You'd better get home, sprout. We've business, see?"

"But I want to join up," Caelan said.

The men laughed again, elbowing each other and shaking their heads.

Caelan grinned back, holding himself as straight and as tall as he could. "I'm old enough and strong," he said.

"Aye, big enough," the tattooed man agreed.

Another man leaned forward. "Best take him to the sergeant, then."

A third man slapped him hard on the shoulder. "You daft? Boy's run away. Sergeant won't join him up."

"Please," Caelan said anxiously. "It's all I've ever wanted to do."

The tattooed man was still looking him over. "Well-dressed boy. Good clothes. Warm and close-woven. You from the town?"

"Meunch? Yes," Caelan lied. He didn't want them to know he'd run away from school. With a yank he pulled off the torn remnants of his robe and tossed it away.

"Takes money to join up," the tattooed man said, fingering his earring. His eyes looked dark and intense over the jagged symbol of Mael on his cheek. "Seven hundred ducats for a kit."

Caelan's heart plummeted. It was a fortune. He had nothing but a few coppers in his pocket.

"Naw," the other one said scornfully. "That's officer's kit. This big, strapping lad ain't wanting none of that lot."

"Why not? He's well born."

"Take him to the sergeant," said the man holding the lantern. He spat near Caelan's foot, and Caelan flinched involuntarily.

"The sergeant won't take him."

Caelan frowned, trying to follow their argument. They were staring at him in a peculiar way he didn't much like. At some point they had spread out and formed a circle around him. He swallowed and felt suddenly alone and vulnerable.

"There must be something I can do," he said nervously, eying them. "I'm old enough to join and strong enough to march."

"And squalling like a baby for its mother when that lurker was after you."

The men roared with laughter. Caelan felt ashamed of his earlier fear now, but tried not to let it show.

"How much you got?" the tattooed man abruptly demanded.

"Sir?"

"How much money you got?"

Caelan looked up at their faces. "I—not much."

"You can't join without buying in," the man said gruffly. He stepped forward, and Caelan cringed back. "Hand it over."

Caelan shook his head. "I don't have any—"

They grabbed him then and lifted him bodily despite his struggles. Rough hands patted him down and turned out his pockets. The meager remnants of his allowance spilled onto the road and lay gleaming in the lantern light.

The men swore with disappointment and dropped him bodily onto the ground. One of them kicked him.

"Is this all he's got?"

"Pipsqueak!"

"Faure consume his liver!"

"Damn!"

They kicked him again. Caelan lay huddled face down on the road, clenching his fists and trying not to cry.

"Get up," growled the tattooed man.

Caelan heaved himself up to his hands and knees, but then with an oath the man seized him by the back of his shirt and hauled him to his feet.

"Where do you live in town?" he asked.

Caelan stared at him, seriously frightened now.

"Those ain't working hands you got, boy. Your da a rich man?"

Caelan swallowed hard. He shook his head.

"Leave him," said one of the others. "Let's go and see what better sport we can find."

"What about that fancy hold down the road a bit? Good pickings in there, I'll bet."

"No!" Caelan cried involuntarily. He thought of the gate he'd so carelessly left open, and his face flamed hot.

The tattooed man smiled. "So you're a schoolboy, eh?"

His eyes were terrible, pinning Caelan's and holding them. The obscene figure engraved on his cheek moved with every shift of his jaw. It was all Caelan could do not to stare at it.

"Yes, sir," Caelan finally said.

"I thought as much. You wearing that cute little school-boy robe no longer than your bottom."

The men all laughed again, and Caelan's blush intensified. He felt raw with humiliation.

"So what kind of school is it? And no more of your lying."

"It's a school for the healing arts," Caelan said.

They groaned.

"No money boxes in that kind of place."

The man with the tattoo narrowed his eyes. "Still want to join up?"

Caelan hesitated, then nodded warily.

Someone behind him snickered, but the tattooed man didn't smile.

"You're no good for it," he said, his voice cutting and contemptuous. "We've no use for such cowards."

Caelan flinched. "I'm not—"

"Aye, coward!" the man roared, silencing him. "A braggart and a fool, as well. You can't stick where you are now, so how will you do your job in the emperor's army? Eh?"

Without warning he struck Caelan across the mouth with the back of his hand.

Caelan reeled back and went sprawling on the ground. His head roared, and he thought he might pass out.

"Lying runaway!" the man bellowed at him. "I wouldn't bet my life on a scab like you holding your line position during a charge."

"But—"

"Shut up! You're going back where you belong."

Caelan scrambled to his feet in fresh defiance. "I won't! I—"

The man slapped him again. The pain seemed to burst Caelan's head. Panting with his hand pressed against his mouth, he barely managed to keep his feet this time.

"Leave it," one of the men urged. "Let's go find the town. There's better prey there than this."

"Better shut him up, though," warned another.

Their eyes held no mercy. Frightened, Caelan took a step back and dodged his way out of the circle.

"Coward!" one of them taunted him.

"Mama's boy!" another joined in.

Their teeth gleamed in the lantern light.

"Run, schoolboy. Run for mama."

The man with the tattoo pulled out a javelin and hefted it in his hand. His eyes narrowed, sizing up Caelan. Then he smiled a terrible, empty smile.

Fear congealed in Caelan's veins. For a moment he could only stare, caught like a rabbit before a snake; then he turned and ran for his life.

The wind whistled in his ears, and the light from the lantern dwindled quickly behind him. Darkness faced him, and the cold wind lashed his face as though trying to slow him down. All he could think of was his own exposed back and of how the lurker had died from a javelin throw.

Behind him the men shouted encouragement and called out bets.

They were laughing, and Caelan told himself they were only trying to scare him. Maybe they wouldn't really spear him in the back for sport. After all, they had saved his life.

He stumbled on his bad leg and glanced back just in time to see the man throw.

The javelin came, arcing perfectly through the air. Too late, Caelan tried to double his speed, tried to zigzag to dodge it.

Too late.

It hit his shoulder with a glancing blow, bringing a ripping flame across his back. The impact drove him down, and he was falling, falling in a tumbling dive that took him off the road and down into the ditch beyond it.

There were sticks and briars and stubble from where

the bank had been cleared. He rolled in a bruising tangle, unable to stop his impetus, and all the while there was the brutal fire in his back, unquenchable, driving him mad.

He landed at the bottom with a jolt. Numbed and shaken, he sank into stagnant mud and water that was freezing cold. With a groan, he tried once to lift himself, but the effort proved beyond his strength.

He groaned again, hurting so much he couldn't think. The darkness seemed to tilt and fold over him. He heard a strange rushing sound, and then there was nothing, nothing at all.

three

CAELAN AWAKENED IN A SHAFT OF SUNLIGHT
that streamed in over his cot. The air smelled warm and
aromatic with herbs. Dragging open his eyes, he blinked
slowly until the room began to make sense. It smelled like
the infirmary at school, only he was surrounded by screens
that blocked his view of the rest of the ward.

He felt strangely light-headed and lethargic. A warm
blanket of moag wool covered him, and a little brazier on
a stand flickered with a small fire that kept his area com-
fortable.

"You're awake."

The voice startled him. Caelan lifted his head slightly,
finding the effort exhausting, and smiled at his cousin's
serious face. "Agel," he said, his voice sounding thin.

Agel did not smile back. The sleeves of his robe were
rolled up above the elbow, and he was carrying a tray of
items that he set upon a small table next to Caelan's cot.
A lock of his dark hair had fallen over his forehead, and
his blue eyes were as cold as a winter lake.

In silence he set out a roll of bandages, small crocks
of ointment, and bronze scissors.

Frowning, Caelan tried to make sense of things. He had the feeling of time lost, and his memories all seemed hazy and confused. "How did I get here?" he asked. "What happened?"

"Sit up, please," Agel said coldly. "If you're too weak, I'll assist you."

Caelan levered himself slowly upright, finding himself absurdly weak. Pain flared across his back, making him suck in a sharp breath, and with it came clear recollection of his attempt to join the army, the soldiers who had robbed him and speared him, leaving him for dead in a ditch.

Meanwhile Agel had started undoing his dressings. Caelan tried to catch his cousin's eye.

"I remember," he said. "The soldiers tried to kill me."

Agel's hands went on working with gentle skill.

"How did I get back?" Caelan asked.

Agel said nothing.

Caelan sighed, then winced. At once Agel stopped and reached for a damp sponge to soak a place where the dressing had stuck to skin.

"I asked you a question," Caelan said.

Agel evaded his gaze and made no answer.

Footsteps outside the screen made both boys look up. Master Grigori entered with his hands tucked austerely inside his sleeves. His white robe was stained with blood splatters. His eyes held the cool blankness of *severance*.

Agel stepped aside, and in silence Master Grigori examined Caelan's back. His fingers were warm on Caelan's skin. His probing was gentle, pausing at each place when Caelan winced. His touch drew away the pain, leaving behind a gentle tingle. A sense of well-being seeped through Caelan. He felt stronger already.

Finally Master Grigori stepped back. "That will do," he said, glancing at Agel. "The wound is closed and will finish healing quickly in a day or two. Bandage him so he doesn't forget to protect the area, then arrange his release from the infirmary."

Agel bowed. "Yes."

"Thank you, Master Grigori," Caelan said, but the healer turned on his heel and left without another glance at Caelan.

"So it's to be the silent treatment, is it?" Caelan muttered angrily.

Saying nothing, Agel rebandaged him with quick efficiency. "Your clothes are in the basket," he said, pointing at the foot of the cot.

Resentfully Caelan flung off his blanket and dug out his clothing. He found a fresh shirt and leggings and a replacement novice robe, all clean items from his quarters.

He dressed while Agel stripped the bedding from the cot and removed it. By the time Agel returned, rolling down his sleeves, Caelan was ready.

In silence they left the infirmary and walked across the courtyard. The day held the warm golden light of mid-afternoon. Serfs were baking bread in the large, outdoor ovens. The fragrance of the loaves was intoxicating. Caelan closed his eyes and drank it in.

"I could swoon from hunger," he said. "How long have I been unconscious?"

Agel walked steadily beside him, not looking at him, not replying.

Caelan's anger flamed higher. He grabbed an apple from a basket and munched on it as they entered the hall, shadowy and silent, its vaulted ceiling soaring high above their heads.

Novices were arranging the long trestle tables and benches for the evening meal as part of after-class chores. Some of them looked up at Caelan with open mouths and astonished eyes. Others turned away with frowns.

At the entrance to the quarters stood a hooded proctor. Caelan tensed involuntarily, but the proctor let them pass without question. They climbed the broad staircase to the fourth floor and walked down the silent corridor. Agel pushed open the door to Caelan's room, and Caelan walked inside.

Agel started to shut the door on him without entering, but Caelan gripped him by the front of his robe and pulled him inside. Slamming the door with a bang that echoed down the corridor, Caelan released Agel and stood with his back to the door.

"Now you can talk," Caelan said, glaring at him. "How was I found? How long have I been unconscious?"

Agel compressed his lips, but Caelan strode over to him and gripped him by the arm. Agel jerked away from his touch, and the two boys glared at each other, nostrils flaring and eyes hot, for a long moment.

"Talk!" Caelan said.

"It's forbidden."

Caelan snorted and swung away. "So I'm to be shunned now by everyone. Even you."

Agel's face whitened with rage. "What you did was unforgivable."

Caelan shrugged, but doing so brought a faint twinge to his shoulder. "I ran away. What of it? Anything was better than freezing to death."

"Even now you have no shame, no remorse," Agel marveled. He sent Caelan a horrified look. "I thought I knew you. But your kind heart and decency are gone." Shaking his head, he stepped past Caelan. "There is nothing to say to you."

"Wait!" Caelan said, reaching for his sleeve.

Agel shoved him hard against the wall.

Pain shot a sickly web of yellow and gray across the world. Caelan caught his breath and sagged against the wall, trying to hide how much it hurt. The expression of contempt on Agel's face made it hurt even more.

"Agel," he said, making it a plea.

His cousin averted his eyes. "You have shamed your father," he whispered, his throat working. "You have shamed *me*. I cannot forgive you. No one can."

"But—"

Wrenching open the door, Agel stormed out and left Caelan there, too stunned and bewildered to go after him. Caelan rubbed his face with his hands and slowly straightened himself. Agel was only overreacting like everyone else around here. Running away was a worse offense than most, but it was hardly a calamity.

A faint rustle of sound made him look up. He saw a proctor standing in the open doorway.

Warily Caelan faced it. "What do *you* want?" he asked rudely.

The proctor said nothing, but only closed and bolted the door. The sound of the lock shooting home made Caelan bite his lip.

His temper heated up, and he paced slowly around his small room twice before plopping down on his cot. He didn't care what kind of punishment they handed out this time, he told himself. As soon as he got the chance, he was running away again. And this time he would be properly prepared.

IN THE MORNING CAELAN AWAKENED TO THE sound of silence. The usual dawn bell was not ringing. He listened a long while, his body attuned to the regimen of Rieschelhold.

Silence. No work in the courtyard. No shuffling of sleepy boys along to the washrooms. No bell of assembly. No smell of breakfast cooking.

Getting up, Caelan dressed and paced the floor hungrily. He felt stiff and sore this morning, but when he flexed his right shoulder there was no discomfort from his wound.

The continued quiet made him nervous and uneasy. So what were the proctors doing, punishing all the boys for his infraction?

Defiance and resentment hardened in Caelan. If they thought to make him penitent, they had misjudged him. Caelan could be persuaded, but he did not like to be pushed. The more they tried to break him, the more he vowed to defy them.

Outside in the corridor, he heard doors opening slowly, the hinges creaking with hesitation. Boys shuffled out, their queries to each other low and apprehensive.

Caelan listened at his door with derision. No bell, he thought. Without a bell to tell them what to do, the novices were stupid and helpless.

That's what the masters wanted them to be. But he wasn't ever going to become mindless and blindly obedient. Rote learning, cruelty, and fear were the tools of lazy teachers. They didn't want the novices to think or grow. They considered inquiring minds dangerous. Instead, the masters wanted trained monkeys, silent and respectful monkeys, who would heal only the simple cases and be baffled by anything requiring innovation.

He hated them, hated them all.

"Watch out! Proctor on the floor!" called someone in warning.

The voices and footsteps outside hushed immediately as though everyone had frozen in place. Caelan pressed his ear to his door gain.

"No bell. No breakfast," a proctor's hollow, unnatural voice said into the quiet.

Voices broke out in consternation and protest.

"Silence!" the proctor ordered, and they quieted at once. "No classes are held. You will remain in quarters until further notification. That is all."

There came the repeated slam of doors up and down the corridor. Caelan heard the bolt to his own door slide back, and he stepped away from it just as the door was pushed open.

Two proctors stood looking in, their faces hidden deep within their cerulean hoods.

One of them pointed at Caelan with his carved staff. "Come."

Wary, expecting a beating, Caelan made no move to obey.

"You have been summoned to the chambers of Elder Sobna. Come."

Caelan's mouth went dry, and for a moment he was frightened. He'd actually spoken to Elder Sobna only once, on the day he first came to be enrolled. The Elder had eyes like glaciers, a white beard, and a soft voice as quiet as falling snow. He had made a dry little speech about welcoming the son of Master Beva. Caelan, anxious to avoid favoritism, had said all the wrong things. Since then, the Elder had not acknowledged his presence again.

Caelan straightened his shoulders and told himself not to worry. There was no punishment worse than what he'd already faced. Maybe he was going to be expelled. But as soon as that hope was born in Caelan, it died. No one was ever disrobed from Rieschelhold. He'd probably have to poison a master or something.

Wearing defiance like a cloak, he swaggered out into the corridor with his silent escort.

It was strange walking down the staircase at that hour of morning to find the place still and empty. The air smelled of peat fires and wood polish. But not even the serfs were to be seen.

Caelan looked around. "Has everyone been confined to quarters?"

"All," said the proctor on his left.

The other glided stoically on his right, close by, his staff held out as though to steer Caelan.

"But why?" Caelan asked. He'd never expected to find himself grateful to be talking to proctors, but even they were better than no one. "What's going on?"

The proctor on his left turned slightly toward him. "None is to look upon a transgressor."

"But—"

The proctor on his right lifted its hand. "Silence."

They walked on, pausing only while the proctors unlocked the doors to the building without touching them. Outside, they paused again, and Caelan heard the bolts shoot home without being touched by the proctor's hand. He shivered, feeling spooked and increasingly nervous about this.

Caelan gazed up at a pewter-gray sky, then across the snow-draped expanse of garden and courtyard. The air lay still, not a whisper of wind stirring the quietness. The courtyard had been swept of the fresh snow that had fallen in the night, but it might have been twilight instead of day, for not a soul was to be seen anywhere.

I have vanished, Caelan thought with a shiver that had nothing to do with the cold sinking through his wool robe. *They can do anything to me now, and no one will ever know*.

With difficulty he forced his alarm away, drawing on his own anger for strength. This place thrived on fear, using it as a tool, a weapon to coerce the students into obedience. There was no joy here, no light. Dreams and ambitions faded into the mind-dulling miasma of hard work, stern threats, and punishment.

Caelan refused to let fear conquer him now. He had faced soldiers and lurkers and the unknown. He had even risked meeting a wind spirit. Yet somehow, the silence surrounding him now seemed far worse. For courage he sought memories of his home, E'nonhold, which shone like a refuge in his mind. He thought of days of unhampered freedom when he'd raced his pony up through the valley pass of the Cascades and climbed out on top of the glacier. He thought of the cold wind whipping his hair back from his face and the feathery soft feel of snowflakes on his eyelashes. He thought of hawking—his version of it, not the swift bloody sport of the rich. No, to reach out and share identity with the great predator bird. To feel the rush of wind through its wings. To feel the weightlessness of its body on the air currents, circling, circling, keen eyes alert. To dive in one great, swift, heady rush, the earth hurtling straight at him. Then pulling out seconds before the strike, earthbound and separate once again, gasping with the forbidden exhilaration of it.

Ah, *sevaisin*, the joining. So different from *severance*. So much fun, yet absolutely denied. It was supposed to take years of training among the Vindicants in order to learn the technique. Caelan didn't know how he did it, and he didn't care. It seemed to be as natural as breathing, unlike *severance*, which was a strain.

At that moment they passed near the gates. He saw no warding key hanging over the small pass gate. A momentary pang of guilt shot through him, yet at the same time he had to bite the inside of his lips to keep from grinning. Wonder what old Master Mygar thought of him now? Who said he couldn't *sever*? He could when he had to. He'd proven it.

With a swagger back in his step, Caelan entered the Elder's house. The entry was lined with the burled wood of Carpassian walnut, very rare and costly to import. No carving adorned it. The lovely grain of the wood was its only ornamentation. Large oil lamps of plain silver cast a steady illumination to supplement the weak morning light crawling in through the narrow windows.

A servant attired in a plain tunic of heavy fawn-colored wool with a narrow band of dark fur at collar and cuffs stood by to receive them. The servant was clean-shaven and old. His blue eyes regarded Caelan without expression.

In silence the servant led Caelan and the proctors up a staircase. Lamps hung from brackets on the walls, lighting their way.

On the second floor, the air hung heavy with the scents of snow-dampened wool, old carpets, and crushed borage. The same oppressive silence was to be found here as everywhere else. It seemed, as Caelan's feet moved soundlessly over the carpet running the full length of the hallway, that all he could hear was the loud *lub-dub* of his own heartbeat, growing louder and faster with every step.

He swallowed, but his mouth grew no less dry. His confidence wavered, but he forced himself to keep his shoulders straight and his head high. He was the son of a master healer without equal in all of Trauland, not some nobody they could frighten.

The servant tapped softly on a heavy door at the very end of the passage. Caelan heard no response, but the servant opened the door, then stepped aside. Caelan entered alone, the proctors and servant remaining outside. The door closed quietly behind him.

The Elder sat at his desk, writing on parchment. He did not look up at Caelan's entry.

Sighing, Caelan looked around. The walls of the office were smooth white plaster, very austere. Cold northern light from large windows on one side made the room seem even bleaker. A modest fire hissed and crackled on a small hearth. It failed to warm the room.

The Elder's desk, fashioned from plain native spruce-wood, held tidy scrolls of parchment rowed up on one side. His ink stand was carved simply from buta horn, as was his pen. On the other side of the desk, balancing the harmony, stood a small triangle, the symbol of *severance*.

Finally the Elder's pen stopped scratching across the parchment. He read what he had just written, sanded the ink to dry it, then shook the grains away into a small receptacle and rolled up the parchment.

Only then did he lift his gaze to Caelan. He quirked up one eyebrow, and Caelan walked forward.

The Elder was a thin, white-haired man. His robe was white, indicating the level of his powers as well as his rank. His face curved in a crescent, ending in a pointed chin made more prominent by his short white beard. His skin was very pale, translucent enough to show a faint tracery of veins pulsing at his temple.

It was said that any follower of *severance* eventually grew progressively paler throughout life, until the very ancient practitioners were practically transparent. They were said to die like beams of light, shining bright, then slowly fading as they finally achieved total *severance* from life.

"You do not answer my question, Novice Caelan E'non," the Elder said in a displeased voice.

Caelan blinked and realized he'd heard nothing. He flushed. "I'm sorry," he stammered. "I did not hear."

"It seems you make a habit of living with your mind unfocused."

Caelan lowered his gaze. He could not protest.

"You have caused much trouble since your arrival here last term."

Caelan kept his head bowed. So far, this wasn't too bad.

The Elder's pale thin hand fluttered over certain of the scrolls on his desk. "These are lists of your various transgressions, offenses, and errors. They have been compiled by the masters who have charge of you."

Caelan looked up. "I guess there's a lot of them."

The Elder's expression grew even more severe. "This is not a matter of amusement, Novice Caelan."

Caelan hastily rearranged his own expression. "No, sir."

"Nor pride."

"No, sir."

"You are from one of the finest Traulander families. You have been brought up according to principles of harmony and perfection. You have been taught *severance*, witnessed it practiced in your home. You have enjoyed the advantages of private tutors. You have never known want or lack. Is this true?"

Caelan shifted uneasily. He wasn't enjoying this. "It's true, Elder Sobna."

Harmony and perfection, he thought bitterly. Yes . . . if he made no noise, asked no questions, never ran or leaped or stretched, never sought independence, never searched for different answers. Private tutors like jailers, droning on and on, holding accounts like money changers, running to share the results with Beva, telling, tattling fools. No, Caelan had never known any lack at home, unless to crave love and understanding was a lack.

He could feel his emotions churning up, stinging his eyes. Furiously he held them back.

"Why did you run away?"

Caelan lifted his chin. He didn't answer.

"Have we mistreated you here, Novice Caelan?"

Caelan opened his mouth, then checked the hot words on his tongue.

When he said nothing, the Elder's gaze moved sharply to his. "Did you fail again to hear my question?"

"No, I heard it," Caelan said.

"Then give me your reply. Have we mistreated you here?"

Caelan set his jaw. There was no going back now. "I think so."

"You *think* so. You are not sure?"

Damn him. Caelan flushed. "I'm sure," he said curtly.

"Please go on."

"You know," Caelan said, struggling against his anger. "You probably have it on a list."

"You are impertinent, Novice Caelan. I am waiting for a reply to my question."

"Why?" Caelan burst out. "You know the answer. What I say isn't going to make any difference. You already have your mind made up."

The Elder's face might have been carved from stone. "Ah, so you have the ability to read minds, Novice Caelan. Interesting. What other talents do you possess?"

Seething at his cool mockery, Caelan glared at him and said nothing.

"Your failure to answer my question indicates you have no answer. Therefore, I can only conclude that you do not truly believe we have mistreated you."

"You want to see my bruises?" Caelan retorted.

The Elder raised his brows. "You have been disciplined, Novice Caelan, when you transgressed. You have been placed under a discipline conducive to study, no doubt for the first time in your life. You have fought that, as many wild or untamed creatures must fight at first. But neither have you learned."

Caelan glared at the floor, his ears roaring against this lecture he didn't want to hear.

"We are tolerant here," the Elder went on, "but tolerance has limits. Because of your father, we were willing to continue our efforts to train you, even allowing you to remain in the novice class for an unprecedented third term if necessary."

Caelan looked up in dismay. He should have known they wouldn't kick him out. His anger welled up anew. "I'll run away again."

"It will not be necessary."

Caelan caught his breath in hope.

"Boyish pranks and rebelliousness are an annoyance, nothing more. Endangering the entire hold is something else entirely."

Caelan thought about the destroyed warding key and dropped his gaze. He hadn't meant to put anyone in danger.

"How did you remove it?"

Caelan frowned and said nothing.

The Elder rose to his feet. "How?" he demanded.

"I—I just took it off."

A look of alarm crossed the Elder's face, then was gone. His eyes were bleak. "Impossible."

Caelan shrugged. "Then believe what you want."

The door behind him opened, and the proctors glided inside. Glancing at them, Caelan shifted uneasily on his feet. He didn't like the idea of them standing behind him, and both held truth-lights in their hands.

"How did you remove the warding key?" the Elder asked again.

There was something awful in his tone, something that compelled Caelan to answer. Casting a resentful glance at the proctors, he scowled and tucked his hands inside his sleeves. "I entered *severance* and pulled the key off the gate. I just wanted out."

"You were not injured from touching the key?"

Caelan shook his head. "My hand felt burned, but it really wasn't. That's the way *severance* is supposed to work, isn't it? So for once I did it right."

The Elder did not meet his gaze directly. "You show no remorse for this action."

"Oh. Well, I didn't mean to leave the hold unprotected. The soldiers could have come looting, I guess. But they didn't." As he spoke, he looked up with a question in his gaze.

"No, they didn't," the Elder said heavily. "We have nothing here which they would consider of value."

Caelan nodded. "So it worked out. Except for—" He broke off, remembering.

"Yes, except for the fact that you were attacked and nearly killed."

"I—" But there was nothing for Caelan to say. He thought about the soldiers who had jeered at him, robbed him, then tried to kill him for sport. Their laughter still rang in his ears. Humiliation still burned inside him, fueled by his shame.

"We are responsible for your life while you are entrusted to our care," the Elder said sternly. "We keep you inside our walls for a reason, to guarantee your safety."

"I'm not a baby," Caelan said. "I don't need—"

"Help?" the Elder said softly.

Caelan bit his lip and scuffed his toe against the floor. "I guess I did need some."

"We have warding keys for good reason. How you twisted the purity of *severance* to shatter the spell of a key is blasphemous enough."

"But—"

"You have done far worse. You left us vulnerable to attack, whether from this world or the other. You exposed our throats, and only by the grace of Gault were we not attacked."

Shame filled Caelan. "I'm sorry," he muttered. "I wasn't thinking about that."

"Running away to join the army," the Elder said, contempt like ice in his voice. "Wanting to become a butcher, a defiler, a taker of life. This is abhorrent to us and all we stand for."

"But I—"

The Elder lifted his hand for silence. "If you had died out there in the forest, what could we have said to your father? How could we explain our mistake in letting harm befall you?"

"It wasn't your responsibility," Caelan said. "I chose to leave. I took the risk, and I'll—"

"It *is* our responsibility. You are underage, and we are entrusted with your safety. You put us in an untenable position."

Feeling cornered, Caelan turned and pointed at the proctors. "Your proctor locked me outdoors for the night. What was I supposed to do, freeze or be clawed by wind spirits? I chose neither. Blame your proctors as much as me."

"You would not have been left outside all night," the Elder said dismissively.

"How was I to know that?"

"At Taul Bell your absence was discovered. Harmony was broken. Disorder filled the darkness. The serfs had to brave the night to search the hold for you. The proctors found the open gate. That told its own story, and by the quick wits of your cousin we were able to determine which direction you had fled."

The Elder came around his desk, frowning with daunting severity. He pointed his finger at Caelan. "Men risked their lives to find you in the dark forest. They searched all night, before at last you were found, half-dead of exposure and blood loss."

Remorse touched Caelan. "I didn't mean to put anyone at risk," he said softly. "I just wanted to get away."

"You were brought in at dawn. Master Grigori and Master Hierst labored hard within *severance* to save your life. Had anyone been lost to lurkers or worse out there, what could you have done to repay your debt to them?"

"I don't know," Caelan said miserably. "I'm sorry."

"Apology is not enough." The Elder beckoned to the proctors. "Cast the truth-light over him."

Caelan turned around in protest. "But I haven't been lying about any of this. I swear."

"It is not your words they will test. It is you."

The Elder nodded at the proctors. They glided forward and tossed the tiny balls of blue light at Caelan. Light burst against his forehead and sprayed down to his feet in a shimmer. It changed color from blue to yellow to green, then faded to white and seemed to vanish altogether.

"Enough!" the Elder said, sounding shaken.

The proctors stretched forth their hands, and the light flickered feebly back into existence at Caelan's feet. It surged away from him, split into two halves, then reformed itself into two tiny glowing balls of light.

"It is decided," the Elder said.

"What?" Caelan demanded, puzzled. "What's decided?"

The Elder gestured, and the proctors stepped back. "You, Caelan E'non, are in grave danger of losing your soul. You have deliberately sought the ways of shadow."

Caelan gasped in shock. "I haven't—"

"By your own confession you wrongfully used *severance*. You betrayed the safety of this hold. You willfully exposed every inhabitant to possible death or worse. That crime is attempted murder."

"But I didn't mean—"

The Elder held up his hand. "Rebellion is as much a gateway to the center of the soul as is obedience. By your actions, you prove you are becoming a vessel for that which is foul and otherworldly."

"No!"

"We want no part of you here among us, infecting the other boys."

"Fine!" Caelan said furiously. "Then let me leave."

"We have laid the matter before your father," the Elder said as though Caelan had not spoken. "He has asked us to purify you."

Caelan stared at him. He felt frozen with growing apprehension. "I don't believe you," he said through stiff lips.

"Do you understand purification?" the Elder asked. "It means to enter with the masters for forty days of fasting and surrender. They will *sever* you completely from everything, root out the evil from your mind and soul, and then allow you to return to your body."

Long ago, as a child, Caelan had heard the servants talk about someone possessed at another hold. Healers had been called in—not his father, but others—to cleanse and purify the man. The fellow had been quite mad when they finished. Nor did he ever regain his sanity. The healers said the possession was so strong it could not be driven from him. Others whispered that he had been *severed* too long and could not be made whole again.

A shudder ran through Caelan. He knew he wasn't evil. Not in the sense the Elder claimed. He'd never tried to harm anyone here. He wouldn't knowingly expose them to danger. Yes, he'd been foolish and selfish, thinking only of himself when he ran away, but his carelessness didn't warrant this. As for having Master Mygar—so cruel, so heartless—walking through his mind, reshaping him—

"No!" he cried. "I won't let you touch me, none of you! Not like that. You'll kill me, or make me insane. I'd rather you'd let me die in that ditch than face—"

"Enough," the Elder said icily. "You have made your refusal quite clear."

"Father didn't request this," Caelan went on. "I don't believe that. He wouldn't."

"Beva E'non was my star pupil," the Elder said, his voice as sharp and cold as the icicles hanging off the roof outside. "Aside from the principles of *severance* which teach us to place no man above another, I loved him as a son. For his sake, for the memory of how eagerly he took learning from me, I offer you this final chance to redeem yourself. Accept the purification, Caelan E'non, and remain with us as your father wishes."

Caelan's heart was pounding. Without hesitation he looked the Elder square in the eye. "Never," he said. "I don't want to remain here. I deny your charges. I refuse purification."

The Elder stared at him for several moments without speaking. The room grew still and oppressively quiet except for the fire hissing on the hearth.

"Master Beva wanted to teach you himself, but you were not a willing pupil at home. No doubt a father's love for his son has clouded his usually clear perceptions. He sent you to us with a father's pride and a father's hope, expressing special concern that we might be able to teach you where he had failed. He thought our discipline would be more effective than his own. We have also failed."

Caelan knew no way to make this old man understand. "It isn't Rieschelhold," he said. "It's me. I belong elsewhere, in another kind of life. I was not meant to be a healer."

"You were born," the Elder said gravely, "to be nothing else."

He waited, but Caelan faced him without flinching.

At last the Elder bowed his head. "Very well. I expel you now from Rieschelhold, that you can cause no more harm to the other novices by example or by deed, that you can spread your evil influence no longer within these walls, that you can never again commit blasphemous acts to disrupt our harmony. In this expulsion, I pity your father, for the son he has, for the son he must again deal with."

Caelan realized he'd been holding his breath. He let it out now, hardly able to believe his ears. Jubilation lifted like skyrockets. Was this all there was to expulsion? What a relief. He barely held back a grin.

The Elder picked up the scrolls from his desk and threw them on the fire. The parchment caught, sending up sparks and curling into black cinders as the fire ate through it eagerly.

He looked past Caelan at the proctors. "Prepare him."

The proctor opened the door. One of them beckoned to Caelan. He rushed out, grinning broadly now, almost skipping with joy. All he had to do now was gather his belongings. They were few enough. A pair of soft traveling boots, fur-lined for winter. His thick cloak. A book of music and his flute. A drawing made for him by his sister Lea. A smooth, fist-sized stone of marble which he'd gathered in Ornselag at the seashore when his mother still lived. These things had been taken by the purser upon his admittance, locked away for the day on which he would leave.

That day had finally come. He couldn't believe it.

But as he stepped out of Elder Sobna's office, he heard a bell start ringing, a deep somber bell he'd never heard before.

At the foot of the stairs, the same servant waited for

them. But instead of leading them to the door, the man pointed at a narrow hallway.

Caelan's high spirits dropped. "What now?" he asked suspiciously. "Where are you taking me? I just want to get my things, then go."

The proctors shoved him down the hallway and into a tiny room containing only a tin basin and a stool. There was no heat and no window. Only a small, face-sized hole cut high in the door provided any kind of dim illumination.

Caelan took in these details with one glance as he spun around. "But why do I—"

One of the proctors drove him back with its staff. "You will remain here until you are prepared."

"No!" Caelan shouted. "It's a trick! You won't purify me. Do you hear? You won't—"

But they slammed the door, bolting him into the gloom.

four

OUON BELL TOLLED OMINOUSLY OVER THE silent expanse of Rieschelhold, its deep, sonorous voice echoing across the courtyard, orchard, buildings, and snowy forest beyond. Ouon Bell rang seldom; it was the bell of death and tragedy. It began tolling at midday, when Caelan was led from the house of the Elder, and it did not stop.

The sky remained slate gray. Intermittent snowflakes fell. Ushered by the proctors, all the students assembled in somber silence in the courtyard. Big-eyed, the young novices in their short indigo robes stamped their feet and blew on their hands to keep warm. The taller disciples—gangly and awkward in their long cyan robes—looked frightened or grave. The most advanced, the healers, marched along in gray robes trimmed with pale fur, their expressions blank within *severance*. White-faced and nervous, the serfs clustered at the rear. The proctors moved back and forth among the assembly until not a sound could be heard, not a rustle, not a throat being cleared in the crowd. Only the soft sigh of the falling snow and the low peals of the bell broke the silence.

The masters, robed and cloaked in white, walked the ramparts, stopping at each corner of the walls to sprinkle cleansing herbs of rue, hyssop, borage, and camphor. Then they came down and took their places on the dais before the assembly. Pale figures in the falling snow, their faces might have been carved from stone. Their eyes held only *severance*.

Crushed in among other bodies, with someone's elbow in his ribs and another student almost standing on his heels, Agel sought the calming refuge of *severance* within himself. But his heart was beating too fast and his breath came short. For the first time in months, he could not find his concentration, now when he needed it most of all.

The bell rang like a dirge. He wanted to weep with anger and humiliation. How could Caelan have done such a risky, foolhardy thing? How could he have let his stupid temper get the better of his good sense? Agel could not forgive him for it. He felt betrayed by his cousin, betrayed and bereft. Agel had thought they would spend their lifetime together, working for a common good, sharing the same occupation and interests, but now there would be no more friendship, no more companionship.

Caelan had thrown his opportunities away. Whispered rumors said he had refused the Elder's generous offer of forgiveness.

The fool. Agel's hands clenched into fists inside his wide sleeves. What would become of Caelan now? No one had been disrobed at Rieschelhold for at least two decades. And now, for it to be the son of Beva E'non was incredible, unbelievable.

Agel's throat stung with embarrassment.

He saved you from a demerit, a small voice reminded him, but Agel brushed it angrily away. So he still had his perfect record thanks to Caelan. Did that excuse Caelan's own behavior?

A stir made everyone crane to look. Agel saw his cousin coming, flanked by an escort of six hooded proctors walking three on each side. The proctors in front and the proctors at the rear held their staffs crossed, thus creating a cage around Caelan.

The boy walked tall, with his shoulders straight and his chin high. He was a strapping lad, taller than nearly anyone else, still growing out of his clothes. His hair blew back from his forehead like ripe wheat tossed by the wind. There was no shame in his face, no regret. His blue eyes were eagle-keen, almost happy.

Agel felt his eyes sting, and he could have kicked Caelan then and there.

Didn't the idiot understand what disrobing meant? Once expelled by the masters, there was no coming back.

Agel watched his cousin stride through the parted center of the assembly, the bell tolling over him as though he had died in the ditch. Maybe it would have been better if he had. He had apparently learned nothing from his near fatal adventure.

Agel's vision blurred, and he struggled to hold back tears. It was not manly to weep, nor was it in accordance with *severance*. Besides, Agel knew the proctors were watching him. They would always watch him now, seeking any evidence of the taint that Caelan had shown, nay, flung in their faces. The masters would drive Agel harder, for he was now the sole heir to Beva E'non's great legacy.

Secret pride touched Agel, and unconsciously he straightened his own slim shoulders. As upset as he was over Caelan's failure, Agel could not help but see this as his chance to shine. The masters' attention would now center on him. And Agel wanted that challenge. He wanted to excel, to show everyone how good he could be.

Caelan was past Agel now, his gaze straight ahead, looking neither left nor right across the faces that stared at him. Agel swallowed hard. He did not think he would ever see Caelan again. Certainly it could never again be as it was, or with welcome and a glad heart.

Their fates, always entwined, were now separating into two different roads of life. Agel saw his as a path to accomplishment and success. His talent would support his ambitions. One day his fame would surpass that of Uncle Beva's. As for Caelan, his path had already grown stony and broken, heading for a life of disappointment and hard times.

Their childhood was finished.

CROSSING THE COURTYARD WITH HIS escort, Caelan could feel the eyes of the assembly burning into his back. He felt their curiosity and shock flooding over him in a collective mass of emotion that nearly made him stagger. Somehow, he managed to hold it off. This was no time for *sevaisin* to grip him.

The wind was bitterly cold, flicking sharp little snowflakes into his face. His breath steamed about his face, and he fought not to shiver. He intended to show no weakness. If the masters expected remorse or doubt from him, they would not get it.

All he felt now was impatience to get this over with. It would have been easier on everyone if the proctors had just handed him his cloak bag and put him through the gate. No fuss, no assembly, no scaring the first-termers.

But, no, they had to make a huge ordeal of this, make it bigger than it was. They'd even had to seize one final chance to frighten him by making him think they were going to purify him against his will.

But soon their games would be over, as far as he was concerned. He couldn't wait.

Reaching the dais, Caelan halted. The proctors parted from around him. Looking straight up into the stony eyes of Elder Sobna, Caelan felt defiance fill him like heat. He smiled.

Twin spots of color blazed in the Elder's pale cheeks.

The Elder's gaze burned into his; then the mask of *severance* returned like the slam of a door.

Caelan looked away, indifferent as the Elder lifted his arms and began to speak.

Much of it was in the old tongue, no longer used by edict of the emperor. Caelan understood none of it, and even when the Elder switched back to Lingua, Caelan barely listened.

With his money taken by the soldiers, he had no chance of heading out on his own. He would have to go home. There would be plenty of time on the journey to think of an explanation for his father.

His whole life suddenly spread before him, radiant with limitless possibilities.

"Caelan E'non," the Elder said loudly, startling him, "what is your answer?"

A hush lay over the assembly as though everyone had held their breath to hear. Even the bell stopped tolling. Caelan had no clue as to what the Elder had asked him.

It was worse than being caught daydreaming in class.

Embarrassment flooded him. He almost started to stammer something; then he caught himself short. This wasn't class. He was no longer obliged to do anything these men wanted.

Defiant again, he looked up at the Elder and said clearly, "I have no answer to make."

A gasp ran behind him, and even some of the masters looked disconcerted, but the Elder's expression did not change. With a nod he stepped aside and gestured at the masters.

One by one, they approached Caelan and touched him briefly on his left shoulder.

"I concur," each one said.

Master Mygar came last. Old and stooped, he limped forward, his white robes stained and smelly. His palsied lips made him appear to be mumbling to himself, but his rheumy eyes glittered as malevolently as ever when they met Caelan's.

He did not brush Caelan's shoulder with his fingertips as had the others, but instead gripped him hard.

"*Casna*," he whispered.

It was the word in the old tongue for "devil."

"You will break the world," the old man whispered, his eyes rolling back in his head. "You are destruction incarnate."

Blackness poured into Caelan through the old master's touch, burning him, defiling him. Such hatred, such decay . . . an evil rottenness like a stench in the soul.

Caelan jerked free of the old man's grasp. Shocked, he stood shuddering and blinking. A clammy sweat broke out across him, and for a moment he thought he would be sick.

He stared at Master Mygar. As the black worm of Mygar's emotions continued to twist through Caelan's veins, he saw the old man's flesh melt away. A bleached white skull stared back at him, and darkness—a living, horrible darkness—writhed and pulsed within the plates of bone, flickering at the edges of the eye sockets.

Appalled by what his inadvertent *sevaisin* had brought him, Caelan sought desperately inside himself for the patterns of good and harmony. He tried to weave them around the worm of blackness until it stopped twisting inside him and lay still, cocooned in what he had spun around it. Then it faded and was gone, like ashes in his soul.

Still sweating, his knees weak as though they would let him drop at any moment, Caelan managed to regain his breath.

Watching him, Mygar widened his gaze. "*Casna,*" he whispered again, then drew back. "I concur," he said loudly for the assembly to hear.

Elder Sobna stood in front of Caelan once more. His fingers brushed Caelan's right shoulder, and this time

Caelan flinched. No more emotions came to him, however.

"And I concur," the Elder intoned. "You are no longer eligible to be trained for the healing arts here or in any part of the empire."

Caelan blinked in surprise. He hadn't expected such sweeping finality. Still, he didn't believe they could enforce it. The masters here might be renowned, but they didn't run the world.

"You are no longer to wear the blue colors of our training. You may never return through our gates. You will never practice the arts which you have learned here. Our ways and our privileges are henceforth forever denied to you."

The Elder raised his hands. "Kneel for the disrobing."

Two proctors reached out to push Caelan to his knees.

"No!" he cried, his voice ringing out across the courtyard. "I'll never kneel to you, any of you! Here." He yanked off the novice robe and flung it on the ground at the Elder's feet. "I have disrobed myself. Now let me go from this place."

Despite the rule of silence, murmurs ran through the assembly. The masters looked shocked, and even the Elder lost his *severance* to fresh anger.

Blinking hard, his mouth clamped tight, the Elder pointed at the main gates in silence. They swung open.

The gathered proctors moved aside and Caelan strode out, breathing hard, barely restraining his eagerness.

The bell began to toll again, its dark tone lifting over the countryside.

Head high, Caelan walked through the gates and paused to glance back. He would have liked to have said goodbye to Agel. But the gates slammed behind him with a mighty thud, and the Ouon Bell stopped ringing. For Rieschelhold, he had ceased to exist.

Lightness filled him. Caelan flung his arms to the sky with a shout of relief. Crowing with laughter, he danced in a small circle, kicking up snow. He felt as though he could fly.

"I'm free. I'm free!" he said over and over. Right then it didn't matter that he had no money, no cloak, and no traveling boots. If he got himself into trouble again out here, no one would come to his rescue. But he didn't care.

Scooping up a double handful of snow, he flung it into the air and let it rain down on him. "I'm free!"

"Caelan."

Startled by that quiet word, Caelan lowered his arms and spun around.

A man cloaked in white fur stepped forward from the bushes. He led two white, shaggy mountain ponies by their reins. A pole with a healer's globed lantern was attached to one saddle.

The man was tall and handsome, with a fringe of straight brown hair showing across his forehead beneath his fur hood. His face held no expression at all, but his gray eyes were dark with the bleakest disappointment Caelan had ever seen.

For a second, everything in this man's heart lay exposed to the boy—a lifetime of hope, ambition, and plans for the future now in ruin. A dream of companionship, of working together for a mutual aim, now shattered.

Caelan dragged in an unsteady breath. All the lightness in him dimmed. The relief, the joy, the sense of unfurling like a warrior's banner, faded. He was once again a boy in trouble for his mischief, small and sorry, waiting head down for the word of scolding.

"Oh, Father," he said, his voice a mere whisper of sound in the falling snow.

Beva E'non drew in his pain, closing it behind the gates of his own will. In silence he turned away from Caelan and mounted his pony. The globe lantern bobbed and shook on its pole as he settled himself in the saddle.

Gazing down at Caelan, he held out the reins to the other pony without a word.

Equally silent, Caelan took them. A wool tunic and cloak lay across the saddle. Caelan shook snow off the garments and put them on, grateful for their warmth. He hesitated a moment, hating to be collected like this, hating to still be a child in a man's body. But at last he climbed into the cold, stiff saddle. It was his own, the stirrups shorter now than they'd been on his last visit home. He looked at his father's erect back. The white fur made Beva almost vanish into the snowy landscape.

The man had always sought to blend into his surroundings, to never stand out, to never insist that he be seen or heard. This inner stillness, this silence of manner, appearance, and word, only added to his great mystique.

But for Caelan, it made his father impossible to approach.

Worse, he had not expected Beva to know yet, much less come for him. Beva must have overheard everything in the ceremony. Everyone in Trau would soon know of Caelan's public disgrace, and it would mark the first failure of this famous man.

How to explain anything to the unyielding back riding in front of him?

Caelan sighed. He glanced over his shoulder at the immense walls of Rieschelhold, and still felt no remorse. His way lay elsewhere, even if he did not yet know what his life was to be. Perhaps now, at last, Beva would accept that.

Frowning, Caelan kicked his pony and followed his father home.

five

THE SNOW FELL HARDER THROUGH THE AF-
ternoon, the flakes large and wet. Caelan pulled up the
hood of his cloak and searched the saddle pockets until
he found a pair of gloves. His feet were freezing in their
thin leather shoes, but he made no complaint. Concentrating on the patterns of warmth and well-being, he tried
to make his toes warm. It didn't work very well.

Beva swung his mount onto the imperial road, and
Caelan followed. In silence they galloped along the empty
ribbon of stone, hoofbeats echoing against the wall of forest on either side beyond the ditch. Clipping past the place
where he'd been ambushed, Caelan found himself holding
his breath. But no lurkers were in evidence today. Even
the corpse had been dragged away, probably by wolves.
The soldiers of course were long gone, with no trace of
their passing except a series of fresh clearings off the road,
with blackened fire sites and raw stumps sticking up jag-
gedly.

After about a league, the forest thinned to marshland.
The imperial road rose up atop a levy, but a common road

of frozen mire branched off from it, skirting the marsh and heading south toward Meunch. At this spot stood an immense archway of imported granite. Although plain of any carving or ornamentation, its architecture was foreign, exotic. The speckled stone seemed to speak of other lands, other customs, calling to travelers to seek them out. Strange letters had been etched into the base of the arch— tall, spiky letters in a script as foreign as the stone.

Towering almost as high as the trees, the arch spanned the imperial road, testament to one of the emperor's greatest achievements. The roads spanned the length and breadth of the empire, making every corner of it accessible. As for the archway itself, its sheer massive size stood as silent testament to the emperor's power and long reach. Had the archway stood at the edge of a large town such as Ornselag, imperial troops would have maintained sentries and a checkpost.

Beva reined up beneath the arch and gave the ponies a breather. He watched the forest and sky with extra care and seemed reluctant to venture out into the open marshlands.

"What's wrong?" Caelan asked, thinking of the shadowy denizens said to inhabit the marshlands.

"We must gallop on," Beva said. "We dare not stay long in the open. Come."

"But—"

Beva spurred his mount, and the pony plunged off the paved road and down a short embankment to the crude track that led north. Caelan followed more cautiously, wondering why his father had not lit the healer's lantern bobbing on the pole. Normally it was a signal to all robbers that this was a man of good traveling on a mission of mercy, lacking money to steal. Most bandits respected the lantern, and Beva had never been attacked in all his years of traveling. For him not to light it now, especially if he suspected danger, made no sense unless it was the unworldly he feared.

Caelan wrapped his cloak tightly around his chest and kicked his own pony to catch up. They rode hard and fast, the ponies' breath steaming in long white plumes. Geese rose off the water with startled honking as they galloped by. More than once their path dipped into the semifrozen slush. The ponies leaped and plunged through it, kicking spray high behind them.

Beva never rode hard like this, but Caelan enjoyed it. Their pace was exhilarating. The sense of mysterious danger gave the adventure extra spice. He found himself watching land and sky as warily as his father was, his senses drinking in the cold outdoors that he'd missed while in school. The air was crisp and clean with scents of pine and spruce overlaying the bog smell. The snow stung his face and matted his eyelashes. It was glorious.

Finally forest curved ahead of them. Beva dove into the cover of trees and undergrowth and drew rein beneath the sweeping branches of a larch. Breathless, his heart pounding, Caelan stopped beside him and let his snorting pony drop its head. Both animals were heavily lathered. Steam rose off their wet bodies into the cold air.

Around them the forest lay still, with only the soft rattle of falling snow through the branches. Occasionally a jackdaw could be heard in the sky.

Beva finally blinked and seemed satisfied.

"What is it?" Caelan asked softly. "Can we return to the road?"

"No. Too dangerous. We must stay in the forest, where there is cover."

"But if we go this way, it will take twice as long to get home."

"Better to be safe than quick," Beva said, adjusting his gauntlets.

"If you're worried about robbers, light your lantern."

Beva shook his head. "Light will only call attention to us. We must take great care."

"From what?" Caelan asked in bewilderment. "What kind of robbers do you fear?"

"Not robbers."

Caelan waited for his father to continue, but Beva was looking into the forest, tight-lipped and plainly worried.

"I can't help if I don't understand," Caelan said in frustration. "Why the secrecy?"

Beva shot him a glance, his face unreadable. He hesitated, then said, "Imperial troops are being withdrawn from the eastern borders."

"Yes," Caelan said impatiently. "I know that. You aren't afraid of them, are you? What happened to me was just a—"

Beva glared at him. "Some of the auxiliary forces are comprised of Thyzarenes. With their release from service, they have begun raiding—sometimes as far as the northern rim."

Caelan's mouth fell open. Instinctively he ducked farther beneath the branches. "Thyzarenes!"

His mind churned with the thought of it. Thyzarenes were worse than devils. They were said to attack from the sky, riding huge winged monsters that breathed fire. They were merciless savages who pillaged and destroyed. There had been none in Trau in Caelan's lifetime.

"But—"

"Quick hunt-and-strike raids," Beva said grimly. "If the emperor wants to use them against his enemies, that is one thing, but he should not turn them loose on a peaceful and loyal populace."

"But why are they raiding us? Are you sure it's not just rumor to liven up winter days?" Caelan asked with a skeptical laugh.

"I have seen their work," Beva said. "Two holds burned so far and one village. People slaughtered or carried off. The few survivors are in no shape to bury the dead, and that of course brings the wolves." His mouth tightened with the little twist that always came when he failed to save a patient.

Caelan was ashamed now that he'd laughed. "But the army has moved on, hasn't it? I mean, when I saw them they were marching fast, not living off the land or raiding as they went. Wouldn't the Thyzarenes go with them?"

"Who is to say what such savages will do?" Beva asked. "Trau joined the empire for protection, not to be pillaged for sport."

"When we get home we'll have to open the arms room," Caelan said. "We need to make preparations to fight if necessary. Did you bring weapons today for protection?"

Beva stared at him in disapproval. "The idea of fighting pleases you."

"Well, I think we should defend ourselves, not—"

Beva turned his pony and rode on through the trees without another word.

Caelan scowled, feeling the dismissal as strongly as the blow of a proctor's staff. His words, his opinions were not worthy enough to be heard. To his father, he remained a child of no standing. Resentfully, Caelan sat a long while, reining his pony when it tried to follow the other one.

Finally, reluctantly, he kicked his mount forward.

Fuming, he glared at his father, who refused to face reality. Beva wasn't going to bend principle one tiny bit, not even to be practical. How could his father wander the forest unarmed and unprepared with these raiders bringing real danger to the area? How could Beva depend on inner harmony, on *severance* against barbarians who probably had never heard of such enlightened philosophies?

Maybe Beva wasn't as wise as he'd always thought. Maybe Beva didn't know everything. Maybe Beva was capable of making mistakes just like everyone else. It sure looked like his father was making some now.

When his pony caught up, Caelan glanced at his father's stern profile. "I'm sorry your opinion of me is so low. I'm sorry you don't want to hear what I have to say."

Beva tucked his chin deeper into the folds of his hood. "It is actions, not words, that speak truth."

Caelan frowned and tried to hold onto his temper. "Whether you approve of fighting or not, it doesn't change the fact that we may be forced to defend our hold. What can we do to protect ourselves?"

"We have the warding keys."

Astonished, Caelan couldn't believe what he was hearing. "They aren't enough!"

Beva glanced sideways at him. "They are from the old ways, yes. While I do not approve of them, they do work. Someday, when all men are enlightened into the paths of *severance*, we shall not need warding keys or weapons."

"But that day has not yet come," Caelan said impatiently. "And until it does, we have to be strong and defend what belongs to us."

Beva sighed. "I had hoped the school would tame this wild spirit inside you. This craving for excitement, for things beyond the ordinary. Why can you not understand that excitement equals danger, that danger destroys, that destruction takes away all that is good and harmonious, leaving only chaos and harm in its wake?"

"But, Father, when the danger comes to us, what are we to do? Just let it destroy us?"

"To admire danger is to summon it. You have been warned of this, boy."

Caelan frowned. "So are you saying the Thyzarenes are *my* fault, that I brought them here?"

"Rebellion opens the gateway to darkness," Beva said. "When enough hearts resist harmony, then darkness grows."

Caelan slammed his fist against the pommel of his saddle. "I don't believe this," he muttered furiously.

"Elder Sobna told me you ran away from Rieschelhold, choosing night as your ally. You found only danger in your search for excitement, did you not?" Beva's voice was cold, holding condemnation with no hint of concern. "You brought danger to others. The soldiers you admire proved their brutality by attacking you. Has this lesson taught you nothing? Fighting only brings more fighting, just as war begets war."

"But how can a person learn if he doesn't seek—"

"The search is inward, not outward. I have told you so many times."

Caelan frowned. "But to sit and meditate . . . I can't do that."

"Why?"

"I just can't."

"You mean you will not."

"All right, then, I won't!" Caelan admitted stubbornly. "I want to see new places, to travel, to have adventures. I want to see the world and all its wonders, not remain forever cooped up in a hold with my hands tucked inside my sleeves."

"The journey must follow an inner road," Beva said with a reproof. "Why do you resist this truth?"

Caelan gestured behind him. "And what of that imperial road, leading across the world?"

"Leading to ways of wickedness and error. This, you crave."

"I just want to see how other people live. I'm tired of listening to stories, old tales that may be false. How can I judge the truth from the lies if I don't see for myself?"

Beva bowed his head. "No change," he said quietly, as though to himself. "All these months away, and there is no change in you at all."

Caelan could feel his stubbornness growing, along with the anger. "That's right, Father," he said. "The masters failed to beat or starve my dreams from me. And now I'm going to live as I please. I tried to tell you I didn't want to be a healer, and you wouldn't listen to me."

"There is no other path for you," Beva said with equal

stubbornness. "I tested you and saw the gift in you."

"No, you saw what you wanted me to be," Caelan said resentfully. "You've never cared what I wanted. It's always been *your* plan, *your* wishes, *your* idea of how my life would be. Never mine."

"You were born to be a healer," Beva said. "As I was born to it. My blood is in you. My skill, waiting to be trained and guided."

"Well, that's over," Caelan said with a shrug. "No more training."

"How proudly you say it. You come home disrobed with the Ouon Bell rung over you. That means you are dead, boy, dead to all healers. You can never be one of us. You are outcast from the profession. Is this how you honor me? Is this how a son thanks his father? How am I to stand among my colleagues now? How do I point to my son with a father's pride?"

Caelan frowned. After a lifetime of watching his father spurn emotions, these admissions were doubly bewildering. Caelan's heart twisted. "You have no pride," he said coldly. "You say that pride is a false emotion and to be avoided."

Beva's face burned with color. His gloved hands were clenched hard on the reins. "A father's pride," he said softly, "lies in knowing he has sired a strong, upright son, a boy of talent and keen mind, a boy in whom he can see himself achieve even more, become even more complete within the pattern, walk even farther along the inner road. That is a father's pride."

"All you can see is yourself!" Caelan cried. "All you think of is yourself. Haven't you done enough, accomplished enough? You're the best healer in all of Trau. Can't that be enough for you? Why do you have to live through me, control me?"

"You—"

"Why can't I be myself? Live my own life? Walk my own road? Why must everything be done your way?"

"Because my way is best."

"For you, but not for me! Now it's over. Face it, Father. I'm never going to be a healer like you."

"Once you are purified, all will change," Beva said.

Caelan stared at him, the blood draining from his face in shock. "I refused that," he whispered.

"I have already made the preparations at home," Beva said as though he had not heard. "It would have been better had the masters performed it, but I will do what is necessary. When you have recovered, I will personally begin your training once again."

"No," Caelan said.

"Of course you will never be able to achieve the rank of master this way. After all, the Ouon Bell has been rung over you. But when I am finished, you will be a competent and able assistant, and you will have forgotten these foolish dreams of becoming a soldier."

"I said no," Caelan repeated.

Beva did not even glance at him or indicate he heard.

Caelan drew rein sharply, and after a few steps Beva stopped and glanced back.

"I'm not going home," Caelan said. "Not to that. I'd rather be carried off by Thyzarenes than face that."

"Your fear shows the love of darkness within you," Beva said. "Why else should you fear the enlightenment?"

"You want to *sever* me," Caelan said, looking at him with horror. "You would do this to your own son."

"I will do what is necessary," Beva said, "to save you."

"You would destroy me!"

"Only the shadows within you."

"The shadows are in *you*!" Caelan burst out. "You don't want me to find the truth. You want me to trot at your heels in blind obedience to a philosophy that's as stupid as it is unjust—"

The back of Beva's hand smacked against his jaw. Caught completely off guard, Caelan went tumbling out of the saddle and fell flat in the snow.

Stunned, he lay there a moment. Astonishment flattened him more than the actual blow. His father had never struck him before. Never. His father did not believe in violence. His father always said his hands were a gift from the gods, to be used to heal, not harm.

Beva must hate him for what he'd done. Bitterness welled up in Caelan. He'd spent his life loving his father, wanting so desperately to measure up to his father's high standards, yet torn by wanting to go his own way. Now he wondered why he had ever bothered to seek this man's affection.

Above the treetops, jackdaws wheeled in the sky with their raucous call. The ponies jangled their bits impatiently and stamped in the cold.

"Get up," Beva said at last. His voice had lost its anger. It sounded hollow and unlike him. "Get back on your horse. We have far to ride."

Caelan rose to his feet and brushed the snow from his clothing. Nothing dealt him at the school had been this humiliating; not even the treatment from the soldiers had equaled this. His head was on fire; the rest of his body felt cold and detached.

"I'm not going with you," he said.

"Don't be foolish. You ran away from school without adequate preparation and came to grief immediately. How long do you think you would last out here?"

"I won't go," Caelan said, refusing to acknowledge his father was right. "I won't go home to be purified. I won't do it."

Beva's eyes narrowed. They locked stares—Beva's cold and Caelan's hot. Finally it was Beva who looked away first.

"Get on your pony," he said in a voice like stone. "We shall settle the matter once we are home."

Resentfully, knowing he had little choice, Caelan mounted and they rode on. Neither of them spoke again through the long cold hours until dark, when they camped in an ice cave at the foothills of the Cascades. The air held the crisp scent of the glacier far above. Outside, beyond the edge of the forest, the aurora shimmered lights of green and pink and yellow in a dazzling display that filled the night sky. Caelan huddled at the mouth of the ice cave, far from the warmth of the tiny fire his father had kindled, shivering in his cloak and enraptured by the sight.

"Caelan," his father said finally, breaking the long silence between them. "Come back to the fire. You have seen enough of the light spirits at play."

Caelan said nothing. He did not move.

"Caelan!" his father said sharply. "Come here."

Caelan ignored him, his gaze still locked on the beauty of the sky. How magical it was, as though the gods opened the veil between heaven and earth just enough for mortals to enjoy this glimpse of their wondrous world far beyond reach.

"The light spirits can dazzle your wits and draw you outside if you're not careful. Don't tempt the wind spirits into preying here."

Caelan snorted to himself. He knew the aurora had nothing to do with the malevolence that flew on the winds during winter nights. His father didn't believe the old superstitions either, no matter what he might say.

But defiance had a way of diminishing Caelan's pleasure in the beautiful display. Abruptly he returned to the fire.

It was so small it hardly gave out any warmth. Ice caves ran deep into the Cascades. They were camping inside a long, tunnellike entry that was made more of stone than of ice. To build a fire deeper would be to start the ice walls melting. The ceiling could fall. But here they were safe enough, deep enough into the mountain to avoid detection by anything prowling the darkness, their fire glimmer further concealed by the branches pulled across the mouth of the cave.

Beyond the fire and their bedrolls, the ponies shifted restlessly. Their shaggy bodies gave out warmth in the narrow space to supplement what the fire provided. Overhead a few icicles dripped. Caelan shifted position to avoid them. He had already eaten, too hungry to refuse the rations his father offered.

Beva, as usual, ate only a tiny portion of the bread and cheese, picking at his food, tasting, nibbling, putting it down again. He studied Caelan, who pretended not to notice.

Gathering a handful of pebbles, Caelan tossed them one by one at the opposite wall.

"You have never learned to stand fast," Beva said finally. "Your will is like a river, winding along the easiest path. Yet, like the river, you resist change and will not allow the channel you follow to be altered. This is not the way, my son."

It wasn't an apology. Beva was simply trying another argument on the same old line. Caelan ached with disappointment, but even that was nothing new. He went on tossing pebbles at the wall.

"They also told me you used *severance* to remove a warding key from the gate," Beva said quietly. "That, more than anything else, shows me the strength of your talents. If you would just surrender to the true ways, you would surpass even what I have accomplished."

Caelan frowned, refusing to look at his father. He did not like what he heard in his father's voice. Admiration? Greed? Caelan shivered and said nothing.

All he'd ever asked for was simple affection, plain dealing, and freedom. All he'd ever received was cold isolation, lectures, riddles, and philosophy lessons. Now he wasn't sure exactly what his father wanted. All he knew was that the blow from his father had destroyed something necessary and vital between them.

Beva said something else, but Caelan didn't listen. He was busy planning his next course of action. As soon as he reached E'nonhold, he would persuade Old Farns to unlock the arms room. He would gather weapons, provisions, and adequate clothing. If necessary he would break into his father's strongbox and take his inheritance. He would see his little sister and give her a proper goodbye before he left her.

"Caelan," Beva said again, sharply enough to penetrate his thoughts this time.

Caelan looked up, keeping his expression blank and cold.

Beva sighed. "Very well. If we cannot have a discussion, I will bid you goodnight."

Caelan's heart still thrummed strongly with anger. He met his father's gaze, aware of all they would never have as father and son, all they would never share. His father had killed his love. It was finished.

"Goodnight," Caelan replied and turned away.

six

IN THE STILL GRAYNESS OF DAWN, THEY broke camp and and emerged cautiously from the cave where they'd sheltered for the night. Heavy snow had fallen during the night, and the ponies floundered their way through tall drifts. It was not snowing now, but as they followed the steep trail into the mountain pass, they entered the gray bellies of the clouds until all was dim mist and fog.

Caelan could barely see his father's back, although his pony crowded close to the heels of the other. Beva's white fur cloak and the white ponies looked ghostly in the gloom. Around them the hills rose steeply, rocks jutting, the trail growing ever steeper and more treacherous.

The fog was freezing in the cold, coating the world in thin ice. Whenever Caelan moved, it splintered and showered off his clothing like glass.

Then they were high above the world, up in the Cascades themselves, and despite the gloom, the beauty of this silent, frozen world made Caelan catch his breath in appreciation.

The mighty waterfall that gave the mountains their name was frozen, a vast sheet of ice hanging in midair. During warm months the waterfall thundered with a force that could be heard for miles, but now its voice was hushed. It was as though the gods had struck the river and stopped it, leaving it suspended until spring thaw when it would rush, gloriously cold and rapid, mist rising high to make rainbows in the air.

They rode up the trail beside it, then turned and passed behind the great sheet of ice. Caelan put out his hand and trailed his fingers across its surface for luck, the way he'd been doing since babyhood when his mother told him about the blessings of the Cascade River. It was she who first dipped his chubby fingers in the icy water. It was she who told him the river's father was the mighty glacier high above them on the top of the world, and that was why the water would always run cold. It was she who had told him legends and stories from the ancient times, filling his head with heroes and adventures, stirring curiosity into his blood. She had loved life and laughter. Even now, though his memory was dim, he could see her sitting on the rocks in the sunshine, her skirts spread around her, a long golden braid hanging over her right shoulder, her face merry and kind.

She had been the sun in his life to his father's moon. She had been the gentle pressure of a loving hand on his shoulder after his father's scolding. She had bustled around the hold, directing the housework and singing melodies, her voice as clear as birdsong.

He had been eight when she died giving birth to Lea. The grief was gone now, faded through the years, but he had never stopped missing her.

Homecoming was never quite the same without her at the hearth, waiting to greet him.

Always cautious, always taking the worst trails in order to keep under as much cover as possible, they rode all day through the mountains. They passed other, smaller waterfalls also hanging frozen. Natural springs that in summer would seep from the rock faces now lay dormant in the grip of winter.

Once Caelan spotted a band of lurkers high in the rocks overlooking a ravine, but they were too far away to be a problem.

By twilight when Caelan and Beva descended into the thick pine forests of the plateau, Caelan was saddle sore and weary. His wounded shoulder ached, and with each landmark they passed, he grew more eager for home.

Finally the forest cleared and there stood the white limestone walls. Thin spirals of peat smoke curled in the air—smelling homey, warm, and beckoning. Recognizing their stables, the weary ponies quickened their pace, and Caelan would have let his mount gallop in had his father not been there.

The watchman, Old Farns, called down from the walls, and Beva replied. His grave, even voice could not be mistaken. In minutes, the gates were being pushed open, and Caelan found himself being greeted by familiar, eager faces crowding around to see him.

Farns stood to one side, his hands swathed in the thick, clumsy warding gloves. He held the warding key while they came through.

"Just in time, Master Beva," he said, relief clear in his gruff voice. "It's almost nightfall."

Caelan did not hear his father's reply. The gates were pushed shut and locked, and Old Farns reset the key. People surrounded Caelan, clapping him on the back, asking questions, faces glowing with simple pleasure to see him again.

Happiness filled him. The servants were openly pleased at his return. Perhaps they did not yet know why he was home, but even then they would not care. Caelan grinned all around, glad of the welcome. It was good to be home, safe and loved, once again.

"Let's take you in to the fire," said Anya the house-

keeper. Plump and motherly, she clucked over both Caelan and Beva. "Worn through and half frozen alike. This
weather's no good for traveling."

"Any trouble?" Beva asked.

Old Farns shook his head, then looked up to study the
night sky. "Snow will be coming again. We expect a
storm, the way the wind's turned to come off the glacier."

"Good," Beva said curtly and handed his healer's kit
and saddlebags to his assistant.

Gunder was lanky and taciturn, a devout believer in
severance. He had come to E'nonhold years ago to serve
as an apprentice, but lacked sufficient talent to become a
healer. Instead, he seemed content to remain here forever,
humbly serving Beva in any capacity he was allowed.

"There are Neika in the hold," he said quietly. "One
with a broken leg that needs setting."

Beva nodded. "I will make my rounds presently."

Gunder bowed his balding head and strode away,
shoulders stooped against the wind.

"May be in for a long howler," Old Farns said, still
sniffing the wind. "We've not enough peat gathered."

"Then we'll have to be cold," Beva said. His voice was
short with fatigue. "There'll be no forays until we have
word the army is well beyond the borders of Trau. Is that
clear?"

Without waiting for a reply, he walked away.

The servants exchanged glances of consternation, then
streamed after him, chattering among themselves. Anya
snagged Caelan by the arm, snuggling him close to her
ample warmth and chucking him under the chin as she
had done when he was little.

"Still growing," she said. "You're head and shoulders
above Old Farns now. I'll vow you're hungry enough to
eat the walls."

Caelan smiled, nodding. "I could eat everything in your
kitchen."

She laughed. "There's venison stew and fresh baked

bread and cheese made this summer and apples baked for a pie and even browly cakes with seed tops, if a certain miss has kept out of them."

"Lea," Caelan said, his gaze yearning toward the house, which stood square and plain, lights shining golden at its windows. "Is she up?"

"Up?" Anya said with a snort. "I'd like to see her stay in bed, with you expected home at any hour."

"Caelan! Caelan!"

A little voice was shrieking his name. Lea came bursting from the door, dashing past her father and the others, her arms outstretched for one person only.

She barreled into his legs and clung tight. "Caelan, Caelan," she said over and over.

His heart squeezed tight. Caelan crouched down and hugged her until he thought she might break. Her blonde curls smelled of rosemary and lavender, fresh from her bath. She was small and sweet and tender. He loved her so much he ached with the joy of holding her in his arms again.

"I missed you, little one," he whispered.

"Missed you more!" she shot right back.

Laughing, he stood up and swung her high in the air, making her squeal. Only then did he realize she'd come running outside into the snow in her nightgown and houserobe, thin cloth slippers on her feet.

"Silly girl," he said, pretending to scold her. "You'll freeze into an icicle out here."

Still tossing and tickling her, he carried her into the house, where the warmth was like an oven, wonderful and fragrant with the smells of food and cleanliness. Caelan paused on the threshold only to briefly dip his fingers into the basin of Harmony that was set in a wall niche; then he was inside with Lea squirming merrily in his arms, squealing with mock protest as he kissed and tickled her.

Their happy voices made the walls ring, and from the corner of his eye he saw Beva wince. Anger stirred in

Caelan, but he ignored it right then, wanting nothing to spoil this moment with Lea.

Finally he set her down, but she continued to cling to him, still giggling, her face round and alight with an inner joy that could not be quelled.

Caelan was relieved that even his father had not yet quenched her merriment.

"I have a surprise for you," she said. "Want to see it now?"

"Caelan, you will bathe and warm those feet," Beva said sternly. "Anya has prepared your room."

"Yes, Father."

Lea was still tugging on his sleeve. "Come and see it now."

"In a minute," Caelan told her. "I'm chilled through. You don't want me to catch cold, do you?"

She pouted and stamped her little foot. "If you have a bath, it will take forever. Then you will be hungry, and you will eat forever. No one will let me wait that long. Come now before I have to go to bed."

"All right," he said, laughing. "I'll come now."

Grinning, she pulled him across the room by his sleeve.

As they reached the doorway, Beva straightened from the fire where he had been pulling off his boots. "Lea," he said, "will I get no home-greeting from you this night?"

She paused, her forehead wrinkling in dismay. In a flash, she ran to him and hugged him tight. "I'm glad you're home, Father. I'm glad you brought Caelan back to us. Goodnight."

Beva touched her golden curls briefly. "Goodnight, little one."

Then she was back, taking Caelan's hand and jumping up and down as she led him out. Her chatter was nonstop and only made him laugh. He did not look back at his father as they left. Beva had only his own coldness to blame if she gave him no more greeting than that.

Her sleeping room was a small, plain cube like all the others in the house. But Lea had stamped it with her own personality, filling it with hanks of flower bouquets picked last fall and now well withered, birds' nests, necklaces strung from wooden beads, crooked sticks with curly bark, and a makeshift tent fashioned from an old hide draped between her clothes chest and a chair.

Down into this she scrambled, beckoning for him to follow.

Caelan's tired, cold joints creaked as he got down on his knees and crawled into the tent beside her. He was too big for it. His head poked against the hide, and Lea's elbow jammed into his side as she turned around.

"Is this the surprise?" he asked.

"No, silly." She was busy rummaging among her collection of cloth dolls sewn from scraps by Anya's kind hands, with horn buttons for eyes and hair made from shawl yarn. "We have to wake up the dolls, I'm afraid. You were so late I had already put them to sleep."

He had a vision of having to greet each doll by name and kiss it or something. Caelan yawned and rubbed the back of his neck. He was too tired for this.

"Here!" Lea said triumphantly. She pulled out a slim, flat box and plunked it in his lap. "I have to hide it, you see, so I let my dolls guard it. No one would ever look for it under their bed."

"No, indeed," Caelan agreed solemnly. He picked up the box and wondered with an inward sigh if he would find dried worm remains or colored sand inside it. "What is it, then?"

Lea's face was round-eyed in the shadows. She tensed with excitement. "Open it," she whispered.

Gingerly, he flipped the small catch and raised the lid. Nine pebbles, each about the size of his thumb, lay jumbled inside. He tried not to sigh.

"Very nice," he said without interest and started to lay down the box. Some glimmer from the lamplight sparked a glint of green. Caelan frowned and picked up one of the pebbles. Squinting to see it better, he held it up to the light.

It was angular in shape, with crisp facets. The green surface was rough, yet as he slid his finger over it he knew it could be polished. Quickly he picked up another pebble, and another, examining them all.

Excitement started thudding in his chest. Suddenly he couldn't quite breathe normally. He looked at Lea's up-turned face. "Are these what I think they are?"

"I wanted you to tell me," she said. "After all, you would know for sure. Are they emeralds, Caelan?"

He held the stones in his hand, hefting them. "I think they are."

She giggled and leaned against his arm. "Good ones?"

He didn't know. They were certainly big enough to be extremely valuable. "Great Gault," he whispered, not caring for once if he swore in her presence. "Lea, where did you find them?"

"I'll show you tomorrow," she said. "I've been wishing and wishing for you to come home. And now you have. Maybe my talent is for shaping the thread of life."

He burst out laughing. "Where did you hear *that*?"

"I thought it up myself. Don't laugh at me."

Hastily he straightened his face. "I would never laugh at you."

"Yes, you are. Your eyes are still smiling."

He drew down his mouth and crossed his eyes in an awful grimace.

She crowed with laughter and punched him. "Silly!"

He put the emeralds back into the box and closed the lid with unsteady fingers. These stones represented a fortune.

More than enough to buy his way into the army.

The thought came unbidden, and swiftly he thrust it away. He wasn't going to steal his own sister's treasure, but perhaps he could find some of the precious stones for himself.

"Where did you find these?" he asked.

"In the ice caves. Where else?"

"You shouldn't be playing in places like that," he said automatically. "Especially in winter."

Sometimes lurkers made dens in ice caves. And some of the caves, especially the older ones, sang. It was a trick of wind blowing through cracks in the ice, some said. Others who believed in the old ways said the earth spirits sang to lure the unwary. Either way, the melodies rang out like crystal, hypnotic enough to draw the listener deeper into the caves, until there was no way out again.

Caelan had grown up exploring ice caves of all kinds. He'd fallen into the lures of the singing caves and barely made it out. Once he'd almost been attacked by a lurker. He'd had many narrow escapes, including cave-ins, not that any of them had stopped him from going back. But with Lea it was different. Protectiveness filled him.

"Ice caves are not safe," he said sternly. "You must be careful, little one."

"I always am," she said without concern for his warning. "Since you're so clever, can you guess which ice cave?"

He had to laugh at her sauciness. "There are hundreds."

She nodded. "But only one where the emeralds are."

"Will you show me?"

"Yes, tomorrow. I want you to find as many emeralds as I have, and if you don't, then I will share mine with you."

"You are a generous lady," he said, bowing to her. His love for this sweet child welled up again. Little did she know how much her offer meant to him, and his future.

Smoothing his hand across the lid of the box, he handed it back to her and watched as she hid it beneath her dolls. It was madness to suppose them safe in such a place, yet he wasn't about to take them away and lock them in Beva's strongbox.

By law, all precious stones gathered had to be tithed to the emperor's tax collector, just as all income was tithed. Caelan wasn't about to tell his little sister she had to give up part of her treasure to the emperor—a man at the other end of the earth whom they didn't know and would never see. If Beva learned of the emeralds, he would obey the law and tithe without question. Better to leave them here in the child's hands. Lea wouldn't lose them.

"You're wise to keep them a secret," Caelan said. "You've got quite a dowry for yourself now, little sister."

"Yes, I have," she said, sounding almost grown-up for a moment. "Which is a good thing because Father spares no attention for such matters."

Caelan grinned. "Now I know you've been listening to grown-up talk. Who said such a thing? Anya?"

Lea nodded. "She tells me much, even when she doesn't mean to. She says women have to stick together in this hold of feeble old men."

"She's right."

"Only you aren't old, and you've come back. I missed you terribly."

"I missed you just as much," he said, stroking her curls.

Her hand stole into his and gripped it hard. "It was a bad place, your school. Wasn't it?"

He nodded.

She sighed. "I knew it. Every night I think about you before I go to sleep. And sometimes I've dreamed about you running and running. There were creatures flying through the darkness after you, and men with big sticks trying to hurt you—"

"Hush," he said, catching her close in a hug. "Hush, little one. Don't talk about that."

"But I was so afraid for you—"

"I'm all right," he said to soothe her, feeling her tremble in his arms.

They had always been closer than thought. Females were not expected to possess talents, and they were never trained. Still, Caelan knew Lea was gifted. She could frequently guess what he meant to say before he spoke. If she wished for something hard enough, very often it did come to pass. And sometimes, she could pronounce the future. He had warned her to hide what she could do. Although Lea was only sunshine and good, her gifts were the kind that might be misunderstood by superstitious strangers. It was important she learn to be careful from an early age. Besides, in a year or two, she would be expected to put away her dolls and wear a shawl. She would start her training in the domestic arts. Then would come betrothal, and eventually marriage.

Caelan found himself praying she would be bonded to a decent man who would let her sing and laugh, who would see her gifts for what they were and not use her harshly. Worry added to his sense of protectiveness. He knew he should stay here and see to it himself. His father might not take enough care.

Lea struggled against him and pushed away. "You're hugging too tight," she told him breathlessly.

"Sorry," he said.

"What are you thinking?" she asked. "You've come home different, and I cannot tell what is in your heart."

"That's just as well," he said, trying to make his voice light.

"Why are you closed to me? I could always read you before. Now you are all tight and guarded, like Father."

The last thing he wanted was to be told he resembled Beva in anything. Caelan shifted angrily and crawled out of the tent.

She followed anxiously. "Caelan, what's wrong? What did I say?"

"Nothing."

Her eyes widened. "You have quarreled with Father. Don't, Caelan. You mustn't."

His mouth twisted into a bitter little smile. "Too late. I already have."

She flung her arms around his waist. "Please don't sound like that. I don't want you to fight with him." Tears streaked her face. "I don't want you to leave. Please!"

"I won't leave you, sweetness," he said, hugging her. But even as he said the words, he felt horrible for lying to her. His throat closed up into a knot. "In my heart I will never leave you."

She lifted her huge, tear-drenched eyes to his. "I don't want you to go"

"I haven't left yet—"

"Caelan!"

He sighed, trying to find an explanation, and couldn't. "You'd better get in bed."

She frowned and stamped her foot. "Don't treat me like a baby! You're keeping things from me. I don't like it."

He scooped her up and tucked her into her bed, smoothing the feather-filled coverlet.

She kicked at it. "I can make you stay. I can, if I wish it hard enough."

"Go to sleep."

"You and Father have to—"

"All Father and I want to do right now is eat our supper," he said, trying to soothe her. "If you don't go to sleep, we can't go look for emeralds tomorrow."

She was still frowning, but her eyes were growing heavy. "Tomorrow I'll learn your secrets," she said sleepily. "I'll make you promise to stay."

He kissed her forehead and turned the lamp down low, leaving only a glow burning beneath the wall disk of the goddess Merit, protector of small children. At the door he hesitated, filled with regrets, but then he closed the door soundlessly and left before her will could force him to give in.

seven

SUPPER WAS EATEN IN SILENCE, HE AND HIS
father spooning Anya's rich stew hungrily by the ruddy
light of the kitchen fire. The kitchen served as the common room. Central to the whole house, its large hearth
never went cold, and there was plenty of space beyond
the long trestle table of worn, well-scrubbed pine for the
other members of the household to gather.

Surva, Anya's elderly mother, worked her loom in one
corner. The rhythmic clack of the shuttle was a lulling
sound in the general quiet. Old Farns carved wood, the
shavings curling over his big, gnarled hands. Gunder
frowned over lists, grinding herbs to refill the medical
supplies. Raul, the groom, had dragged in a saddle to oil
it, and the aromatic scent of the leather mingled with the
smell of stew and hot bread. Anya hovered with her big
wooden spoon, ready to ladle out additional helpings of
food, while the young scullion Tisa scrubbed copper pots
with river sand and made them shine.

On the surface it looked like a content domestic scene,
but although Caelan was dying to ask dozens of questions

and catch up on all that had happened at the hold during his absence, he dared not break the silence. Beva did not permit chatter at mealtimes, saying it impeded digestion.

When at last Beva pushed his bowl away and shook his head at Anya's apple pie and browly cakes, Gunder was ready to show him the herbal lists for his approval.

Caelan went on eating although it was rude to continue when his father had left the table.

"Good," Anya whispered, slipping him a third piece of pie. "You're too thin. You eat all you want."

He grinned at her and munched away. Beva frowned at him, but Caelan pretended not to notice.

Finally Beva went out. Everyone seemed to relax. Caelan shoved his plate away with a feeling of satisfaction and joined Farns.

With a smile, the old watchman went on with his carving. "It is good to have all our family home and safe," he said.

Caelan longed to pour all his troubles into the old man's sympathetic ears, but he couldn't here in front of everyone. "I need to talk to you," he said softly.

Old Farns nodded wisely. "Talk. There is time while the master and Gunder are making rounds in the infirmary."

"Not here. Alone."

Farns sighed. "Very well."

Putting down his carving knife and the piece of wood, he got up stiffly off his stool and stretched his low back. He and Caelan left the kitchen, with the curious eyes of the others following.

As soon as they were in the passage, safely out of earshot, Caelan gripped Farns's sleeve. "The arms room," he said urgently. "I need the key to it."

Old Farns frowned and shook his head. "Now, it's too late at night for you to start that nonsense, young master."

"I must have the key," Caelan insisted.

"No use for it. No Thyzarenes'll be coming at night for to scorch us in our beds."

"Please."

The old man's gaze was steady.

Caelan sighed. "This is important. I need—"

Farns raised his calloused hand. "No need for any weapons tonight, now, is there, young master?"

"But—"

"Rules are rules. I can't give you the key. Not now."

Frustration built inside Caelan. "I want my bow and arrow and another dagger. You said you'd keep my things safe. I—"

"Aye," Old Farns said, glancing away. He frowned. "Not tonight."

"But I need them. Once I tell you what happened—"

"It's too late tonight, boy. I'm sorry, but I have to enforce the master's rules especially when he's home. You know that."

"Yes."

"So I can't take you to the arms room now. It's too dark to be abroad besides."

"I'm not asking you to take me," Caelan said impatiently. "Just give me the key. Father doesn't have to know."

Old Farns cocked one eyebrow. "Seems like you've been in more than enough trouble lately, young master, without going to look for more. Your father doesn't want you messing about there anyway."

"Of course he doesn't," Caelan said in exasperation. "He never has, but I need my belongings. I took my dagger to school, but I didn't get a chance to bring it home with me."

Old Farns made a *tsk*ing sound in his throat and shook his head. "There you are. Careless as usual."

"It wasn't like that. They expelled me."

Farns blinked.

Having blurted out the confession, Caelan found himself miserably forced to go on. "Yes, I've been disrobed. I can't go back."

Sympathy filled the old man's face. "That's bad, young master. That's an awful disgrace for the family."

"I know, but . . . well, it's done now. It's done," Caelan said with a frown. "Anyway, now Father's upset with me. He wants to purify me."

"Ah, no!" Farns said, then glanced around and lowered his voice. "Not for you, my boy. That's too harsh a way to deal with the itch of adventure in your blood."

"I've got to leave before he goes through with it," Caelan said grimly. "You understand, don't you? You do believe me?"

"Aye, of course I believe you," Old Farns said slowly, puzzling through it. "Belike he'll change his mind. He's not so harsh all the time."

The corner of Caelan's mouth was still sore from where Beva had struck him. "He means it, all right," Caelan said. "And he won't change his mind. Not about this. He's determined to make a healer of me, no matter what. I can't make him understand it isn't what I want."

"Reckon fathers don't much care what their sons want," Old Farns said. "For all of time it's been the father's decision to set the son's course of life."

"I don't care," Caelan said stubbornly. "I want something different, and I'm going to have it."

"Stubborn alike, you are, both of you," Old Farns said. "You've clashed like bull elk in the forest since the first. It be worse without your sainted mother to step in."

"It's never going to get better. Farns, please. I have to go. As long as I'm underage, he can make me do anything he wants. And I can't go through a purification. I won't!" Caelan sighed. "I have to strike out on my own now, while I still have a chance."

Farns gripped his shoulder. "The world's no place for a young boy not grown and set. There be wars about and hard times. It's winter and there's no food aside from what honest folk have put by in storage. You can't be going now."

"I have to. Don't you see? If I hang around, he's only going to force me—"

"Hush," Farns said in warning and glanced over his shoulder.

Anya came down the passage toward them. "What are the two of you whispering about out here?" she asked. "Caelan, your bathwater is heated and waiting for you. Better jump in it before it gets cold again."

"Yes, all right. Thank you," Caelan said. He shot Farns a pleading look. "Just leave the key under my door," he whispered. "No one has to know."

But Farns shook his head. "I can't do it. I'm sorry, but, no. It ain't right. You got to think this through. There's no rush."

But Caelan knew he had little time. Farns's idea of thinking things through was to sit through the entire winter until thaw. By then it would be too late.

He gripped Farns's wrist. "Please. For me?"

Troubled, Farns met his eyes for a moment, then looked down. "I got to do what's best," he said with apology in his voice. "This ain't right. You go and get your bath now. In the morning, things will look better."

Disappointed, Caelan trudged away, passing Anya's curious look without a word. In the morning, he would have less time than ever. His father wasn't going to relent. As soon as Beva caught up on his work and tended the patients who had come during his brief absence, he would begin his meditation in preparation for the purification. Caelan figured he had three days, more or less, of grace before he was *severed* into a compliant creature, shuffling along to do Beva's bidding like a simpleton.

The idea of it made Caelan shudder. He couldn't endure that. Just because he had a gift didn't mean Beva could dictate how he used it. Caelan didn't care what tradition said about fathers having the right to say what their sons would or would not be. He wasn't going to bow to this. He couldn't.

A nameless hope in the back of his mind sustained him during his bath. When he was warm and clean and dry, he put the cover on the copper bathtub and hastened along to his room in his houserobe.

No key lay under his door.

His hope died. Old Farns's soft heart was usually persuadable. But not, apparently, this time. Not even to save him from purification.

Caelan struggled to put away hard feelings toward Old Farns. The man couldn't help if it he had to serve his master first. It was Beva who paid and housed him, Beva to whom he owed his allegiance.

That meant everything was up to Caelan himself. Without further hesitation, he took off his houserobe and got dressed again.

He waited until the house grew quiet and settled for the night. Crouched by the door, with the lamp turned out so his light wouldn't shine beneath his door, Caelan heard his father's footsteps go down the passage, and a few minutes later return. His father always checked all the windows and doors last thing at night to make sure they were all secure. When Beva's door was shut, Caelan forced down his impatience and made himself wait another hour in the dark.

He yawned and grew sleepy, but angrily forced himself to stay awake. If he let fatigue rob him of this opportunity, he would be nothing more than a fool.

He knew his father meditated before sleep. Caelan wanted to take no risk of getting caught. So he rubbed his face and made his plans and fought his own weariness.

At last it was time. He drew on his cloak and eased from his room, taking care not to let his door hinges creak.

On silent feet he went down the dark passage like a ghost. In the kitchen he gazed around through the shadows until his eyes adjusted to the dim glow from the embers on the hearth. Everything was tidied and in its place. Old Farns kept his wood carving tools in a pinewood box beneath the wall bench.

Caelan opened the lid and took a mallet and two stout chisels. These he tucked in his pockets.

It was quickest to go down the passage leading past the servants' quarters and exit through the door at the rear of the house. But that meant taking a risk of being heard.

Instead, Caelan made his way to the front of the house, walking stealthily through the cold receiving room where guests were greeted. The room had an austere, forbidding aspect to it. It had never been a welcoming room, not even when his mother was alive to place fresh flowers on the table.

Double sets of doors on either side of a tiny vestibule led outside. The inner doors served as insulators during the cold months. Caelan grasped the bolt and tried to slide it back as slowly and as quietly as possible.

The doors rattled softly from a gust of wind outdoors. He could feel a cold draft of air leaking in around them. It would be easier to go back to his warm bed, but he wasn't going to let a bitter, snowy night stop him.

A movement whispering against his ankles made his heart shoot into his throat. Gasping, he turned and saw the green eyes of the cat glowing up at him in silent inquiry.

"You," he whispered, sagging in relief.

Purring, the cat butted its head against his leg and rubbed. Then it stared at the door.

"Go away," he said. "You can't go outside. You'll give me away."

The cat didn't budge. When he eased open the inner door, the cat shot over his leg before he could hold it back. Cursing under his breath, Caelan groped around the dimly illuminated vestibule, bumping his head into the collection of cloaks hanging on pegs, and finally grasped the cat's soft middle.

He scooped it up, although it twisted furiously, and thrust it back into the receiving room. It shot back into the vestibule before he could shut the door and let out an angry meow.

"Ssh!"

Its tail lashed back and forth angrily, and it planted itself at the outer doors.

Caelan sighed. He was going to lose this contest of wills. Besides, there were worse things to deal with than a cat on the prowl. He stared up at the warding key hanging on the outer doors. It was glowing and active.

Outside, the wind howled and shrieked against the corners of the house. Caelan shivered.

Pulling one of the chisels from his pocket, he reached up to pry the warding key off the door.

It was hot enough to nearly scorch him even without touching it.

Gritting his teeth, he touched it with the chisel. A horrible smell filled the air, and the chisel flew from his hand. It hit the wall and fell with a clatter on the floor.

Caelan froze a moment, listening, but no one stirred or raised an inquiry. He bent to pick up the chisel and saw that the thick steel blade had been melted and twisted into a new shape. It was completely ruined.

Caelan's heart sank. How was he going to explain this to Farns?

He wasn't. The chisel would be dropped down the well, never to be found. No explanation. No lies. Nothing at all.

The warding key had to be removed or he couldn't get outside. If he waited for daylight, he would be seen and his father would hear about it.

It was like being imprisoned. Caelan was tired of the fear every night that kept people locked indoors. He would just have to remove this key the same way he'd done it at Rieschelhold.

But trying to enter *severance* when he wasn't desperate

and wasn't angry did not seem to work. He concentrated without much luck and couldn't find a focus point.

Sighing, he leaned against the wall with the cat rubbing figure eights between his ankles and tried to pull himself together.

It had to be done. That was all.

Grimacing, he shut his eyes and focused on the warding key, channeling all his thoughts, fears, and frustrations toward it. He threw everything at it, hating it, wanting to drown it in all that he faced. If he could just find a center . . . he made the warding key his center until everything began to twist and rush through him in the altered state of *severance*.

When he felt the coldness sear through him, he opened his eyes and reached for the key.

When he gripped it, the key went dark and ceased to glow. There was no heat this time to burn his hand, yet Caelan released it almost immediately. It dropped onto a pile of cloaks he'd thrown on the floor for the purpose, and the cloth did not burn. Caelan knelt over it and picked up the triangular piece of metal gingerly.

His caution was unnecessary. The key lay quiet and cold on his palm, its spell gone.

Hoping he had not ruined it, Caelan tucked it in his pocket for safekeeping, then unbolted the doors. The cat scooted outside, and then he himself stood in the snow-lashed darkness, buffeted by a wind that howled and billowed through his clothes.

Dismayed, he gripped his cloak around him and instantly felt frozen through. He couldn't linger out in these conditions long. Squinting against the snow pelting his face, he ran around the house and across the courtyard, floundering at times in the drifts, hoping he didn't lose his sense of direction.

The arms room was really the second larder, a small stone chamber built partially in the ground. It was usually crammed with barrels of salted meat, ice packed in straw for summer use, baskets of earthy potatoes, plaits of onions hanging from the rafters. On one wall hung rows of rusty swords, a rack of javelins, and a few longbows with broken strings and rotting quivers of arrows. The whole lot was spun over with cobwebs and dust, neglected and falling to pieces. Every time he was allowed inside, he begged Old Farns to let him polish the weapons and replace the rotted leather. But Farns always refused.

Now, however, he flung himself under the narrow overhang and tugged at the lock. It didn't budge. With the wind howling at his back, he pulled out the remaining chisel and mallet and pried up the door's hinge pins.

Pulling open the door, he ducked inside and paused a moment to get his bearings. The air smelled of onions, very dank and not exactly pleasant.

From his pocket he drew out a tinderstrike and lit the lantern hanging on a peg by the door. The light spread out around him, driving back the shadows.

The room was empty.

Caelan's mouth fell open, and he stared in shock, lifting the lantern higher as though that would change the sight of a bare room swept clean from rafters to floor. Barrels and baskets were gone. The pegs that had once held the old weapons jutted forth in empty rows.

"Why?" he whispered, feeling slightly sick. "Oh, Father, *why?*"

Where had everything gone? Why had it been cleaned out?

Puzzled and astonished, Caelan turned around in a small circle, unable to believe it. No wonder Old Farns hadn't wanted to give him the key.

A host of questions filled Caelan's mind, but he didn't have to speculate long to guess that the room had been emptied by his father's order. Beva disapproved of weapons. He believed utterly in pacifism, as though by keeping oneself calm and detached all the world's problems would go away. Caelan snorted to himself. Did that make his father shortsighted or simply naive?

Scorn swept through Caelan. Angrily he blew out the lantern and hung it back on its peg. He pushed his way outside into the raging elements, gasping from the cold that took his very breath, and replaced the hinge pins. For the first time in his life he considered his father a fool. Beva's beliefs were placing everyone in the hold in jeopardy. Even if the threat of Thyzarene raiders seemed to be over, other hazards would come along in the future. To render the hold indefensible was so unwise Caelan could not believe it. Surely his father had only had the weapons moved to some other location. Surely he hadn't thrown them out like rubbish.

Caelan's anger grew with every step as he struggled against the wind. He floundered, found himself blown back, then bent low and forced his way forward again.

Barely able to see, he blundered straight into a bundled figure swathed in a hood and cloak. The figure gripped him by the arms, even as he flinched back.

"Boy!" shouted the figure. "Are you mad?"

Caelan squinted at the man's face. "Farns?"

The grip on his arms tightened. "Aye, and who's the bigger fool to be out here, me or you? Come on back, you crazy boy!"

It was impossible to ask his questions out here in this raging blizzard. Caelan jammed his shoulder against Farns's, and together they struggled back toward the house.

The wind was brutal, shrieking and raging around them. Within its roar, Caelan thought he heard a moaning cry. Instinctive fear crawled up his arms, but he shook it off, concentrating instead on getting to shelter before he froze.

Another shriek came, and this time he could not call it his imagination. Farns stumbled to a halt, calling out something, and Caelan looked up to see a white shape taking form in the air before them.

Swirling and reforming, it became an elongated body that ended in tatters of mist and nothing. Farns held up his hands, shouting, and Caelan stood rooted, unable to move or even think.

The wind spirit formed a face, one as white as a skull, a face that would haunt Caelan's nightmares for the rest of his life, a face fanged and narrow like a viper's. Eyes like red coals suddenly glowed at him. It shrieked again, and his name was somehow entangled in that hideous sound.

Reaching out with long white talons, it rushed at him and engulfed him before he could run.

It was all around him, swirling and intangible. It billowed through his clothes, slid across his skin, burning him with cold. Caelan beat at himself, wild with fear, trying to drive it away.

But how could he fight the wind? The demon had him. He felt its talons rake his shoulder, and he screamed again.

"Caelan!" Old Farns shouted and clutched his arm.

The wind raged around them. Caelan toppled over and felt himself being dragged across the ground. Then he was lifted bodily on the current of wind despite Farns's desperate attempt to hang onto him.

Fear congealed within Caelan. He realized it was taking him, carrying him off like prey.

Its screams drowned out his own.

He fought and struggled, his flailing arms hitting Farns instead of the wind spirit.

"Help me!" Caelan cried. "Farns, get help—"

At that moment a second wind spirit came boiling into the struggle, whirling like a miniature cyclone. It caught Farns and ripped him away from Caelan. The old man's screams rose into the night, and Caelan could not see him at all within the white, twisting column.

"No!" he cried. "No! Farns!"

He struggled with all his might, yet the spirit that had him could not be touched. One of Caelan's flailing hands struck something hard . . . a post. Realizing he was near the stables and had rolled into the railing where horses were tied for grooming, Caelan gripped the post with all his might, while the spirit buffeted and clawed him.

"Caaaaeeelaaaannnnn!" the spirit screamed.

It shrieked his name at him again and again, filling his mind, driving his consciousness down, hammering at him.

Sobbing with fear, Caelan hung onto the post, but his strength was failing fast. The wind yanked at him hard enough to break his grip. Dragged bodily, he went bouncing across the cobblestones, and heard something clang beneath him.

It was the warding key, still in his pocket.

Twisting around despite the wind that clawed him, he dug into his pocket and pulled out the key.

It was still cold and lifeless. Dismay rose in him. Why didn't it activate! Why didn't its spell work like it was supposed to?

"Caaaaeelaaannnn!"

The wind spirit lifted him off the ground. He found himself flying, his cloak sailing away, his clothes shredding and whipping in the wind, his hair blowing back and forth as though it would be yanked out by the roots. The demon's face reformed right in front of his, just inches away, close enough for him to inhale the frosty, lethal vapors it breathed out.

He choked, gagging on his own fear. His heart was hammering so fast he thought it would burst in his chest.

The spirit shrieked in triumph. Its eyes glowed red, and it opened its mouth wider and wider, until all Caelan could see was a whirling maelstrom. And he was being sucked straight into it.

Panic filled him. He held up the key with shaking hands and remembered that he'd *severed* it. Crying out to the gods for mercy, Caelan instinctively used *sevaisin*, the joining. He poured back all its fire and heat, all its fear-some power.

The key ignited with heat and light, an immediate re-sponse that shone across the wind spirit.

The spirit squalled and dropped Caelan.

He hit the ground with a jolting thud and dropped the key. The sound of metal hitting stone cobbles rang out loud and clear, cutting off the wind spirit's shrieks. It drew back, shredding into mist, then vanishing in a swirl of snow.

The key was shining now, bright enough to illuminate the courtyard. It drew on Caelan, fed on him.

He could feel the tremendous charge of its power. It was like inhaling fire. He was burning up with it, dying from it as though exploding from the inside out. No mor-tal was meant to feel such things.

Even as he arched his back, screaming, he heard Farns's feeble cry for help.

Consumed with heat, Caelan twisted about on the ground and saw the second wind spirit still raging several yards away. Dimly he remembered Farns, who had been captured by it.

Caelan knew he must somehow save the old man. It was his fault Farns was out here. His fault . . . *his fault.*

Groaning, Caelan reached out and picked up the key. The pain seared his hand and up his arm, shooting into his heart with a jolt that seemed to break him apart.

Barely conscious, he somehow hung onto the key and scrambled to his feet. Staggering forward, he drove him-self into a weaving, unsteady run, holding the key ahead of him, and thrust it straight into the midst of the white cyclone.

The second wind spirit shrieked in an agony unbeara-ble to hear. It vanished as though it had never been, and suddenly the courtyard was absolutely still and calm. Only a few snowflakes drifted down, sparkling in the radiant golden light of the warding key that Caelan still held aloft.

He could not drop it, could not separate himself. *Sevaisin* was complete. He was melting, becoming heat, radiating . . .

With one last desperate try, he reached for *severance*. Cold met heat in a collision that burst and flowed over him. He felt himself flung aside, falling, falling; then he heard the key hit the ground with a clatter. It broke into pieces. Caelan landed in a heap of snow, the blessedly cool snow, too weak to even lift his head or care.

People surrounded him, their voices a babble.

Then strong hands gripped him by the shoulders and lifted him. "My son," a voice said clearly.

Caelan could not see him. The world remained a swirl of color, light, and shadow. Pain was everywhere, seeping into his awareness at first, then rushing over him.

"Farns," he whispered, his voice a broken, feeble sound. Guilt filled him, riding the pain. "Old Farns—"

"Caelan," his father said urgently. "My son, answer me. Caelan!"

But the darkness came, extinguishing even the light from the torches and lanterns. Caelan faded into it without a struggle.

eight

fOR THREE DAYS CAELAN DID NOT SPEAK.

Revived by his father, whose healing gifts soothed the fever from his veins, took away the cuts and bruises from the wind spirit, and cooled the burn in his hand, Caelan lay in a strange lethargy, aware of his surroundings but apart from them.

The infirmary was quiet and plain. Kept very warm, it consisted of his father's study, the examination room, and the tiny ward with its shuttered windows and row of cots.

Caelan lay with Farns on one side and the injured Neika tribesman on the other. Farns was alive, but unconscious. The Neika man and his brother—barbaric in long blond braids and fur—spoke to each other in hushed, fearful voices. Caelan ignored them, ignored everything. He was aware of the activity around him, but without interest or response.

Lea, her little face tight with worry, came to see him frequently. She would chatter and stroke his forehead. She would smooth his blankets and tuck the fur robe more closely around him. She would show him her dolls and bring him something to drink, which he did not take.

He saw her, but as though she stood far away. Her voice was very soft, almost too faint to hear. When she stroked his face with her gentle fingers, he felt nothing.

After a short time, the adults would gently shoo her away.

Beva came every hour, peering into Caelan's eyes, changing the bandage and salve on his hand, pouring a measure of dark liquid down his throat.

Huddled in her shawl, Anya stood at Farns's side, holding the old man's hand. Her eyes, however, were for Caelan. "Master," she said softly, "is there any hope for him?"

"Of course there is hope," Beva said briskly. He pulled up Caelan's sleeve and counted his pulse.

"But it's said that when the wind spirits catch a person, if he's not killed outright he goes mad. Is our sweet boy driven mad, good master?"

Weakness suddenly shook through Caelan's legs and traveled upward through his whole body. He closed his eyes in wretchedness, then felt his father's warm, dry palm upon his brow. The trembling fit was driven back, and Caelan sighed in relief.

"He is not mad," Beva said.

"The gods be praised," Anya said, dabbing at her eyes with her shawl. "Why, then, won't he speak to us? Why does he look so far away?"

Beva replaced the blankets around Caelan. "He is deeply *severed*, Anya. It is a way to heal his mind and soul after what happened. When he is ready, he will rejoin us."

She tried to smile, without much success. "And Farns?" she whispered, stroking the old man's gray hair.

Beva paused, and for a moment his gaze did not look so sure. "Old Farns will rejoin us when he can."

Anya nodded and wiped her eyes again. She left to

return to her work, but Beva lingered to gaze down at Caelan.

Caelan saw worry show plainly in his father's eyes, as though to refute everything he had just said.

Caelan let his gaze wander away. He did not speak.

SUNSHINE AWAKENED HIM, BRIGHT AND warm on his face. He stirred and opened his eyes, only to squint against a blinding beam of light. Shifting on his pillow, Caelan looked around.

The man with the broken leg was gone. Old Farns slept, his chest rising and falling beneath the blanket.

The inner shutters on the ward windows had been folded back. Sunshine was coming in around the edges of the outer shutters. Everything seemed quiet and peaceful.

Caelan flung off his covers and climbed out of bed. His legs felt strange and shaky, but he managed to stagger over to the window. Unbolting the shutters, he pushed them open and looked out across the courtyard.

The snow was dazzling in the sunshine. Great drifts of the white stuff filled the corners of the courtyard. Lea, bundled up in a scarlet wool cloak, scampered about. She was rolling up huge balls of snow almost as big as herself. Caelan smiled to himself at the sight of her.

Across the way, a neat path had been shoveled to the stables. He saw Raul breaking ice on the watering trough and lifting out the chunks. They shattered and skidded across the cobblestones.

"Oh!" said a voice behind Caelan. "You're up."

Caelan turned around and saw Gunder standing in the doorway like a startled hare. Always ill at ease, Gunder turned beet red and hastened forward.

"Your eyes look back to normal," Gunder said. "Are you feeling better?"

"I'm starving," Caelan answered. His throat felt dry

and sore. His voice sounded like a rusty croak. "Is Anya still in the kitchen?"

As he spoke, he walked back toward his cot. One moment he felt fine; the next, his knees buckled.

Gunder caught him before he fell and made him sit on the bed. "Slowly," he said. His long fingers gripped Caelan's shoulder to steady him while he peered into Caelan's eyes. "Hmm."

"What is this?" Beva said sharply, entering the ward without warning. "Why is the window open? Cold air is pouring in."

Gunder stepped back from Caelan hastily and tucked his hands into his sleeves. He stared at the floor. "I think he may be better, Master Beva," he said diffidently. "He spoke."

"Ah." Beva shut the window with a bang. Dusting off his hands, he tilted up Caelan's chin to look at him.

Caelan pulled back. "I'm tired of being poked. I want to eat."

A rare smile lit Beva's face for an instant; then he glanced over his shoulder. "Thank you, Gunder. Go and tell the Neika he must not walk so much on his leg yet."

Gunder hastened out, mumbling something too low to hear.

Beva turned back to Caelan. "Your *severance* is ended. I am glad to see you so much better."

Confusion filled Caelan. He rarely saw tenderness in his father. He didn't know how to react.

"I'm hungry," he said again.

Beva smiled and nodded. "Very well. Growing boys think only of their stomachs, but you haven't eaten in three days. Let me cover you with the blanket, and Anya will come soon with a tray."

Caelan frowned and took a wobbly step away from the bed. "Why can't I go to the kitchen? I'm fine."

He tried to walk, but gave out by the time he reached the end of his bed. Beva steadied him, and Caelan found himself glad of his father's help. Beva made him sit on the bed.

"You must not tire yourself," Beva said sternly. "You are not yet ready for activity. Take things slowly."

While his father walked away to call for the housekeeper, Caelan looked over at Old Farns. The man's face was sunken and gray on the pillow. His breathing came in quick, shallow rasps.

"What happened to Old Farns? Is he ill too?"

Beva returned, his eyes watchful and curiously eager. "Don't you remember?"

"Remember what? He looks bad. He's going to be all right, isn't he?"

"Perhaps," Beva said, still watching him closely. "Winter is a hard time for old men. He was caught outside in a snowstorm, trying to cut peat for our supplies. Foolish and stubborn, our Farns."

Caelan rubbed back a yawn, then stared at the bandage on his hand. "What happened? Did I cut myself?"

"Frostbite," Beva said. He reached out and smoothed Caelan's hair. "Your hand will heal quickly."

Caelan picked at the bandage, trying to see beneath it. "It hurts when I flex my hand."

He flexed it again as he spoke. Something about the resultant pain stirred his thoughts. The snowstorm . . . yes, he remembered being outside at night, trying to get back to the house. Farns had been with him. . . .

"Caelan!" his father said sharply.

He looked up with a blink.

"I think you should lie down and rest now."

Beva pushed at Caelan's shoulder, but restlessly Caelan shrugged him off.

"I'm not tired. I'm not sick, either. Am I?"

"You have been. You should rest. I will make a potion that will help you sleep."

"No!" Caelan said. "I don't want it. I'm fine."

But he felt strange—hollow and somehow emptied in-

side, as though an important part of him was missing.
What had he and Farns been doing cutting peat at night
in a snowstorm? Had they been caught unexpectedly by
the weather? No . . . he remembered darkness and the
walls of the courtyard. They had been trying to hurry.
They had been afraid.

Caelan caught his breath sharply and looked at Old
Farns with fear. "Wind spirits," he whispered.

"No!" Beva said forcefully. He shook his head with
peculiar urgency. "No, Caelan. You are mistaken. There
were no wind spirits."

Caelan stared at his bandaged hand. The pain called to
him.

"Listen to me," Beva said harshly. His tone was like a
net, surrounding Caelan and drawing him in. "You have
frostbite in your hand. You forgot your gloves and stayed
outside too long. We feared lung sickness for you, but
you are better. That is all. There is nothing else to remember."

Beva went on talking, but Caelan felt as though he
were floating on the words. Strange, compelling words.
The ward shrank around him, becoming distant and small.
He could feel the cold rush of *severance*, cutting him off
from everything except his father's voice.

Caelan thrust out his hand and knocked it accidentally
against the bedpost.

Agony flared from his palm, and with a jolt he remembered holding the warding key. Wind shrieked around
him, sounding almost alive.

It *was* alive. And the key was burning his hand, burning the life from him. . . .

"No!" he shouted, jerking from his father's hold. Terror seized him, breaking a cold sweat across his skin. His
heart thudded, and he found himself on his feet, his
clenched fists held up as though to ward off an attack.
"No! Get it away! Get it away!"

"Caelan!" His father caught him and shook him hard.

"You're safe. Stay within *severance* and be safe. Hear my words, Caelan. Stay within *severance*."

Caelan closed his eyes, feeling the terror fade by degrees. His father was taking away the fear, taking away the memories one by one.

From a long distance, he heard Master Umal's dry, boring voice delivering a lecture within the hall of Rieschelhold: "Relinquish memories one by one. When they are gone, then knowledge will go, piece by piece, until there is nothing left. Only an emptied vessel, purified and waiting to be filled."

Caelan blinked and struggled to focus. He felt as though he were spinning on a string, suspended within his father's voice. And he was shrinking with every word Beva uttered, losing all that he knew. Losing all that he remembered.

"No," he said in a whimper, trying to draw back. "I don't—"

"Trust me," Beva said. He held Caelan's face between both hands. His eyes pinned Caelan's, digging deep. "Follow me into the *severance*, and I will make you worthy—"

"No!"

Caelan jerked back, breaking his father's hold. Gasping and shuddering, he dodged when Beva reached for him again and lurched across the ward on unsteady legs, staggering from bed to bed in an effort to reach the door.

Beva came after him. "Stop! You are not strong enough to—"

Caelan turned to him. "No!" he cried. "You are taking my strength. Get away from me."

Beva stopped, his face white. They glared at each other.

Caelan pulled his sore hand into a fist and began smacking it into his left palm, striking again and again, using the pain to break the awful webs of coldness his father had spun around him.

"I held the warding key," he whispered, struggling to regain his memory. "The wind spirit had me. Another spirit had Farns. I took the key from my pocket, and it came alive."

He could feel a flash of heat inside him. His hand began to ache in earnest, throbbing. "I used it to drive the spirits away," Caelan said.

Long shudders ran through him, and suddenly his mind felt sharp and clear. The hollowness inside him vanished, and he was whole again.

Gasping and blinking, drenched with sweat, he slowly lifted his gaze to his father's. Horrified certainty spread through him. "You tried to purify me," he whispered. "When I was hurt and couldn't defend myself, you tried to *sever* me and make me into a—a—" He choked, unable to say it.

Beva stepped back and drew himself up, very erect and austere in his white robes. His eyes might as well have been chips of stone. "I was wrong to try this alone," he said with plain disappointment. "You are stronger than I suspected."

Caelan's disappointment was crushing. Beva hadn't even bothered to deny it. "Why do you hate me so much?" he asked.

"Hate you?" Beva said with a blink. "I do not hate."

"You want to destroy me."

"If you are not turned from the path you walk, you will become something reprehensible. I am trying to save you, boy. Let me."

Caelan's eyes widened. He thought of how he had handled the warding key, and remembered he had somehow brought it back to life. Despite its awesome power, he had used it, directed it.

He started to shake again. "People die when they hold warding keys. What *am* I?"

Beva looked at him coldly, offering no comfort or sympathy. "It is said that in the west there are men who walk both worlds, using *severance* or *sevaisin* as they will without regard for the patterns of harmony they destroy. It is also said they are not truly men, that demon blood must run in their veins for them to have such unholy powers. They are welcomed in the west, put to use in the evil worked by the emperor and his court of blasphemers. Many join the order of Vindicants and perfect their mastery of the shadow arts."

Caelan listened to this with growing dismay. He did not want to believe what his father was saying. "But I'm not like that."

"Perhaps you are. Or will become so." Beva's harsh tone was like a slap.

Caelan frowned, wanting to deny it, wanting his father to deny it. "But I am your son. I have your blood. I'm no demon! Just because I won't obey you—"

"Rebellion is one gateway to the dark path," Beva quoted without mercy. He gestured at Farns's unconscious form. "You have endangered my watchman, a servant of long devotion. He will probably die of the madness because of you. What were you leading him to, Caelan?"

"Nothing," Caelan said, appalled by this newest accusation. "I was only trying to collect my bow from the—"

"Weapons are the handiwork of destruction," Beva said. "I have had all of them broken—"

"Yes, I saw," Caelan broke in angrily. "This hold now lies unprotected and vulnerable to anyone who chooses to attack it. How could you be so irresponsible? Thyzarenes don't believe in the pattern of harmony. If they come here, are we to drive them off with our bare hands?"

"The gods protect us because we live on the path of good," Beva said.

"The gods protect those who stand prepared to defend themselves," Caelan said in disgust.

Beva scowled. "I will not have disrespect in my house."

"Fine. I plan to leave your house."

Beva's head snapped up. He looked at Caelan with alarm.

"That's right. I'm going," Caelan told him.

"But you are my son," Beva said. "Your place is here, with me."

Grief, anger, and disillusionment twisted inside Caelan. "When I go to sleep tonight, will you try to purify me again? Make me a mindless, obedient slave? You've already called me a demon. As if the insult to my mother wasn't enough, I know you care nothing about me at all. Why should you want me?"

"You are my son."

"Your pride be damned!" Caelan shouted at him. "I don't want to be your son! I don't want anything to do with you!"

Color flamed in Beva's face. "You are not of age. You must obey me. You must take the apprenticeship I assign you. The law supports me in this. If you leave, I can summon you home. And I will do it."

"Disown me! Forget about me! It's Agel who wants to be a healer and work with you. Just leave me alone, because I will never give in. Never! And you won't trick me again."

Caelan swung away, but before he'd gone two steps his father called after him.

"You cannot go."

"Watch me," Caelan muttered, seething.

"You cannot go! My son, if you do not stop this rage that fills you . . . if you do not learn to submit to the inward path, you will become what I most fear."

Caelan stopped and looked back. "What?" he asked with deliberate insolence. "A free man?"

"No, a *donare*. An abhorrence. Son, it lies within you. It grows into a twisted evil. You must be stopped. You must be saved. If you cannot crush it within yourself, then let me *sever* it from you—"

"No!" Caelan said, his fear returning. He backed away from his father, fearing the fanaticism burning in Beva's face more than anything. "Stay away from me! I don't believe you. I don't—trust you."

With that break in his voice, he rushed from the ward. By the time he reached the passage connecting the infirmary to the house, he was staggering on weak, unsteady legs. Tears streamed down his face.

There was no love in Beva. There would never be.

A sob choked Caelan's throat, but he held it down. His father had called him a monster, one of the demon-blood, all because he wouldn't submit blindly to Beva's wishes.

Unfair, but so was all of life. He refused to feel sorry for himself. That way led to weakness, and he might even find himself crawling back like a shivering dog, willing to take whatever abuse Beva wanted to give in exchange for acceptance.

There was no question of ever pleasing his father. He never had. He never could.

And now . . . and now . . . he choked again, and wiped the tears from his face. He thought his father was half afraid of him.

Fear, not love.

Control, not compassion.

Hatred, not acceptance.

Why?

The question branded him, burning deep, never to be erased from his soul.

Had he been a changeling of some kind or even an orphan of mysterious origin adopted by his parents, he might understand what was happening to him. But there had been no fateful discovery of an infant son by Beva during his travels. There had been no unexpected arrival of an infant son at the hold gates, left by the spirits. There had been no secret trade of an infant son with the Choven who migrated through the Cascades during the summer months.

Caelan had been born in the bed where his father still slept, as Lea had been. He was an E'non, able to count his ancestors back for twelve generations. There was no strange or foreign blood in his veins, nothing to support his father's cruel accusations. No soothsayer in the towns of Meunch and Ornselag had ever decried his destiny on a street corner.

Yet he had held a warding key three times, and he still lived.

What did it mean?

What did Lea's unusual gifts mean?

Beva had more than the usual talent for healing. What talents had his bride possessed? What had the two of them created in their children?

Or was it all a growing madness in Beva's mind? Were his own talents and beliefs driving him too far? People thought him so wise and good. Why couldn't he show that wisdom and goodness to his own son? Why did he have to be so harsh and unyielding? What did he want?

Something Caelan could not give.

Safe in his room, Caelan slammed the door and slid down it to the floor.

There, in the quiet shadows, he sobbed.

nine

THE NEXT DAY BROUGHT CAELAN'S CHANCE for escape.

Strangers came to the hold, more Neika tribesmen to fetch the two who were already there. Clad in furs, their long blond hair braided at the temples, ice frozen in their thick mustaches, they carried axes in their belts and freedom in their eyes. The Neika entered warily, forever uneasy within the confines of hold walls. They stood knotted together in the courtyard, fingering their axe heads and mumbling beneath their mustaches until their comrades emerged from the infirmary—one rushing out in greeting, the other limping with a broad grin.

There was much shouting and back-slapping. Squatting in a large ring in the courtyard, they began to talk formally, using ritualized sign language to supplement it.

Everyone in the hold except Beva and Gunder found an excuse to venture by and stare at the newcomers.

The Neika spent winter months following the nordeer that migrated across the glacier. They also cut wood and sold it to craftsmen in the lower towns. Sometimes, in lean years when the nordeer were scarce, the Neika cut peat and brought it to holds in exchange for food. In the summer they cut ice, packed it in meadow grass, and brought it down through the Cascades to the towns on large skids drawn by tame nordeer.

Brawny and tall, the tribesmen looked fierce. In reality, however, most were shy. They rarely fought among themselves and were aggressive only in protecting their herds and families.

These men had been to E'raumhold while waiting for their brother's leg to mend. Now they were back, having successfully sold their bundles of beaver pelts and nordeer hides. And they had an order for stripped logs for the building of a new barn at E'raumhold. Red-cheeked with prosperity, they talked rapid-fire, hands flying with gestures as quick as their words.

When Anya came forth with a tray of apple cakes, they accepted with hesitant pleasure.

Caelan approached them cautiously and took the piece of cake Anya handed to him.

"Have you heard about any raids?" he asked them.

The oldest man of the group glanced up. "Naw," he said gruffly. "We been to and fro along the river all this moon. No raiders. None since E'ferhold was burned out."

Caelan and Anya exchanged a glance. The housekeeper looked relieved. Smiling, she gathered her empty tray and headed back into the house.

"No sightings of Thyzarenes anywhere?" Caelan persisted. "I guess that means the army is gone?"

"Um," the Neika said around a mouthful of cake. "Talk in E'raumhold full of it. Bad, they say. Bad to let army plunder loyal provinces. Will be more war if army does not go."

Caelan's ears perked up. Trying not to act too interested, he said, "So the army is still in Trau?"

"Um. Talk be of it. Army camped near Ornselag. Waiting for transport ships. Too many fighters for waiting. Much trouble."

The Neika exchanged solemn glances, grumbling beneath their mustaches.

"We stay far from towns. No trouble for Neika. Talk say, raiders eager to go. When thaw comes, they take the fire-breathers home for breeding. Have a big festival after thaw. Got to divide spoils. Got to let fire-breathers breed and the raider folk breed too."

He glanced around, his eyes as untamed as the woods beyond the hold, and brushed cake crumbs from his mustache.

Beva came out, slender and tall, his white healer robes immaculate, his gray eyes cool.

The tribesmen rose to their feet in nervous respect.

Beva held out a small pouch, which the injured man took warily. "Mix that into a weak tea and drink a cup of it with each meal. The leg is healing well, but this will keep fever away."

"Um." The tribesman who had answered Caelan's questions dug into his money purse for coins.

Beva accepted them without expression. "I have taken away his pain, but the leg will heal straighter if he does not walk on it much for another week." He held up his left hand, fingers spread wide. "This many days."

The tribesman nodded, and Beva walked back into the house.

"We go," the Neika said.

Almost in unison, they headed for the gates, braids swinging around their wide shoulders.

Caelan hurried after them. "Wait!" he said. "I want to barter."

They laughed above his head, strong teeth flashing in the sunshine.

"No barter," the tribesman said kindly. "All goods sold. We go back to camp."

"Wait. Please." Feeling breathless, Caelan looked up

into his blue eyes. "How much for an axe?"

The Neika's laughter faded abruptly. He set his hand protectively on his axe-head and frowned. "Axe is blessed. No sell, ever."

Caelan held up his hands. "Sorry. I didn't understand. What about a dagger?"

The man squinted thoughtfully with his head tilted to one side. "What healer need with fighting dagger?"

"I'm not a healer." Caelan glanced over his shoulder at the house. "My father has nothing to do with this. It's for me."

"Little warrior." The Neika laughed and said something in his own language that made the others laugh too.

It reminded Caelan of how the soldiers had laughed as they circled him. Anger steeled him, and he vowed to himself that he would become a man at whom no one laughed ever again. But for now, he needed a weapon if he was to make his plan work.

"What can I offer you?" he persisted. "Which of my possessions would most please the Neika?"

"You have bargained with our people before. This is good." Nodding, the man squatted.

Caelan crouched beside him while the others stood patiently. Caelan's heart quickened with excitement. Carefully, he tried to be polite and wait for the big man to think.

Lea, bright in her scarlet wool cloak, came running up. "Caelan!" she called, elbowing past the tribesmen. "Are you coming? You promised—"

Caelan frowned and shook his head at her, but she settled herself beside him anyway. "You promised," she said with more urgency.

"Soon," he told her. "Wait until I'm finished with this."

"What are you doing?"

"Hush."

The tribesman beside him drew a long dagger from his belt and laid it carefully on the cobblestones between them. It had a bronze blade decorated with intricate carving worn in places. The hilt was a plain cross, long and tapering, with a round brass knob on the end. Wrapped in fine wire, it looked very old and nothing at all like the weapons the Neika usually carried.

"You trade for this?" the Neika asked.

Caelan nodded.

Beside him, Lea tensed. He squeezed her hand to keep her quiet.

"You give . . . medicines for this dagger."

Caelan looked up in dismay. "But I can't—" He caught himself, breaking off in mid-sentence, and thought about it. His father's herbal cabinets were kept locked. No one but Gunder was allowed near them. Caelan thought about what his father had tried to do to him and hardened his heart.

He nodded. "Yes."

"Ah." Looking satisfied, the Neika rocked back on his heels. He stood up, leaving the dagger on the ground.

"But, Caelan—"

Caelan frowned at Lea. "Don't say anything. This is my business."

"But it's a bad thing—"

"Lea, either keep quiet or I'm not going with you."

She frowned, looking hurt, and marched away.

He stared after her, sorry to be so harsh, but he didn't need her pestering him right now.

He picked up the dagger and turned it over in his hands, running his fingertips along the flat of the blade. It didn't come close to the dagger he'd left behind at Rieschelhold, but it would do.

Holding it out to its owner, he said, "I'll bring the remedies as soon as I—"

"You keep. We have made bargain. We go outside walls."

Pleased by the man's trust, Caelan smiled and quickly

tucked the knife out of sight beneath his tunic. "Wait, and I'll bring them to you as soon as—"

"There is pine tree with fork in trunk," the Neika said. "Forty strides from gate. You know this tree?"

Caelan had climbed in it throughout his childhood. "Of course."

"You leave bundle there before nightfall. We get."

"Agreed."

The tribesmen gathered themselves and headed for the gates. Raul let them out.

Caelan stood there in the sun-drenched courtyard, glowing with pride. They had treated him like a man. Now all he had to do was figure out how to sneak into the storerooms of the infirmary and get what was needed without Gunder catching him.

A tug on his sleeve interrupted his thoughts. Lea had returned, and she was staring up at him with open disapproval. "Why do you want that horrible old knife?"

"I need it." Caelan cleared his throat. "Every man needs a dagger."

"You are hiding yourself from me again. You trust the Neika, but not me. And now you won't keep your promise."

He bent down and gripped her by the shoulders. "Of course I'm going to keep my promise. I need—I want to go to the ice caves with you. We're going this afternoon."

Her face lit up. "Really?"

"Yes. You tell Anya that we want to take our lunch with us. We'll needs lots of food because I'm really hungry."

"I will. Oh, Caelan, I can't wait. Why can't we go now?"

"Because I have to do some things. Run along and get ready."

He did his best to keep his voice light, but Lea was not easily fooled.

She stopped jumping up and down and gripped his

hand with both of hers. "Don't bring that dagger with you, promise?"

He shook his head. "I'm going to carry it all the time. It's a part of me now."

"Don't say that!" she cried in genuine distress. "It's bad; I can feel it. Long ago, it killed. The metal is tainted with—"

"Stop it," he said harshly, pulling free. "You're making this up."

"I'm not!" She stamped her foot. "You don't want to listen because you're angry at Father. You've changed inside. Since the wind spirits hurt you, you're different."

He frowned. "I've grown up, that's all."

She shook her head. "I'm just trying to help you. Throw the knife away."

"I need it."

"But it's bad—"

"Look," he said impatiently, "whatever it was used for in the past has nothing to do with what I'll use it for. Remember that pouch Anya made for you to keep your treasure in?"

Reluctantly Lea nodded.

"Remember I told you it needed a leather lacing threaded through the top so you could hang it around your neck?"

Again she nodded.

"So now I can cut one for you. Knives can be used for good purposes."

Her face cleared for an instant, then clouded again. "But it is going to make you steal, to pay for it. That's a bad thing, too."

She could always sting his conscience. Caelan wished she'd never witnessed his trade with the Neika.

"You're wrong," he said. "I have some money. I'll put it in Father's earnings box to pay for what I take. Fair enough?"

She thought this over. "I guess so. But shouldn't you ask him?"

"No. And make sure you don't mention this to anyone. It's my secret, my business. You have to keep quiet. Now promise."

Stubbornness entered her eyes, but finally she nodded. "I promise."

"Good. Now run along. I have things to do before we can go play."

She scampered off, her bright cloak swinging around her. Caelan snorted to himself and patted the dagger at his side. Bad luck indeed. He was making good luck for himself with the accomplishment of each small step in his plan.

STEALING THE HERBS WAS SURPRISINGLY easy. All he had to do was wait until Beva was outside the house, then saunter into the workroom where Gunder was busily inscribing recipes on parchment. He told Gunder that Beva wanted him to come at once.

Blinking and obedient, Gunder hurried away, leaving his pen still wet with ink and his work scattered on the table.

Most of the cabinets were unlocked. Pulling out a leather rucksack from beneath his tunic, Caelan made his selections quickly, pulling out small flasks from the rear of the rows where they were less likely to be missed.

He selected simple concoctions for common ailments such as fever, tooth pain, wart removal, wound cleanser, and some of the salves. Some of the supplies were low, as though Gunder and Beva had been busy with other matters. Caelan didn't care. Keeping a wary lookout in case either of the two came back, he worked as quickly as he could. When the rucksack was satisfactorily filled, he laced down the top and slung it over his shoulder.

True to his word, he paused by the earnings box and

tried to lift the lid. It was locked. Caelan's mouth twisted. Trust Gunder to guard it so zealously. As though anyone in the hold would steal.

But even as the thought crossed his mind, he felt the tug of temptation. Better to put his trust in money he could clench in his fist than in the hope of receiving a gift from the earth spirits.

Caelan hesitated, his thumb sliding across the heavy, iron-banded lid. He thought he could pry it open with the dagger.

The sound of approaching footsteps made him glance up.

Breathing an oath, he ducked outside and behind the open door just in time to avoid Gunder's return. Peering through the crack below the hinge, Caelan saw the assistant shaking his head in apparent puzzlement.

Caelan frowned at him. If Gunder had only stayed away five more minutes, Caelan's pockets would have been full. Yes, and he'd be a true thief as well, whispered an accusing voice in his head.

He hurried away on silent feet. Less than a half-hour later he had filled a second pack with warm layers of clothing, his warmest fur-lined traveling boots, a tinder-strike, a small cooking pot filched from the kitchen earlier, and a bundle of dried jerky taken from the larder stores. Glancing around his small, plain room for the last time, he felt a pang of homesickness already.

Half angrily he shook it off. This was no time to go soft.

From a tiny casket of rosewood that had belonged to his mother, he withdrew a round bronze mirror she had bought from the Choven many years before. It was spell-forged to conjure up anyone's likeness on command.

Mother, Caelan thought and watched the cloudy surface of the mirror slowly clear. Her face—so loving and kind—smiled at him briefly before fading away. He drew in a deep breath and slipped the mirror into his pocket.

He did not want to forget either his mother or little Lea, the two people he loved most. The other item in the casket was an old medallion of the goddess Merit, her round sunny features stamped into the worn metal. As a child he had worn the medallion around his neck on a thong.

He slipped it on now, breathing a small, surreptitious prayer to the goddess to protect him. Feeling half-reassured and half-embarrassed, he kissed the medallion and tucked it beneath his tunic. When she was alive, his mother would never let him outside the walls without wearing it. When he went to Rieschelhold he had left it behind, feeling too grown-up to need it. Now he knew better.

He put on a fur-lined tunic over his regular one, with the dagger belted on in between the layers. For once he didn't forget his gloves, which he tucked in the pocket of a capacious fur cloak. Settling the garment over his shoulders, he arranged the folds to conceal the packs and ventured outside with a fast beating heart and a mouth dry as dust.

This time, his escape wouldn't fail.

ten

DANCING UP AND DOWN WITH IMPATIENCE, Lea was waiting for him at the gate. A food basket stood at her feet with a canteen lying atop it.

When she saw Caelan coming, she began waving for him to hurry.

He wasn't about to do so and risk anyone glimpsing what he carried beneath his cloak. Feeling self-conscious, Caelan crossed the courtyard, pausing only at a barrel to take out a pair of apples for later. Slipping them into his pocket, he grinned at Lea.

"You took forever," she said. "It'll be dusk before we get there."

"Don't exaggerate. We've plenty of time."

He glanced past her at Raul, who was waiting to open the gates.

"You two be careful," the man warned. "Out mucking around in the forest. Ain't a time for being too far from the walls, for all what those Neika said."

"We'll be careful," Caelan said.

"And you be back well before twilight."

An involuntary shiver swept through Caelan. If all went well, he would never be back. He frowned, wishing he could tell Raul goodbye. This man had taught him how to ride, had saddled ponies for him, had shown him how to oil and mend tack during long winter afternoons.

Caelan wished he could tell all of them goodbye. Anya would never forgive him for leaving her without a word. As for Old Farns, still unconscious in the infirmary . . . Caelan bit his lip and stepped through the gates quickly before he could lose his nerve.

"Wait!" Lea called, struggling with the heavy food basket. She picked it up and dropped it, nearly spilling its contents. "Help me with this."

Caelan didn't pause. "You wanted a picnic. You bring it."

"Caelan!"

That time he did glance back and had to laugh at her dragging the food basket. It made a wavy furrow in the snow. Raul shut the gates with a casual wave, and Caelan's heart clenched inside him.

He waved back, but the gates were already closed and Raul didn't see.

Caelan's eyes stung a moment; then he steeled himself and hurried back to hand the rucksack containing the medicines to Lea. In exchange he picked up the food basket, flinging his cloak back over his left shoulder to free his arm.

At the designated tree, he took the rucksack from her and stuck it in the fork of the trunk for the Neika. Then he pulled up the hood of Lea's cloak and tied the strings for her. She had on fur-lined boots and gloves and looked like a tiny imp as she skipped and clapped her hands in excitement.

He wished he could take her with him, but that was not possible.

She tugged at his hand. "Come on, Caelan. Come on!"

The edge of the forest curved away from them in a

dark green line, a hundred yards away from the walls. Snow lay white and pure, dazzling in the sunshine.

"I'll race you to the larch tree," he said, pointing.

With a squeal, she broke free of his grip and ran with all her might, floundering quickly in the deep snow. Caelan gave her a head start, then followed. His pack and heavy clothing slowed him down, but he was able to catch up with her easily. He stayed on her heels, threatening to pass her every time she slowed down. She kept churning, short legs pumping hard, and he let her beat him to the larch.

Dashing into the undergrowth, he caught her by the tail of her cloak and flung her bodily into the soft fronds of a nearby spruce. Snow flew in all directions, and she bounced on the branches gleefully, her laughter ringing around them.

"I beat you! I beat you!" she boasted.

His breath steamed about his face. "Sure. I'm carrying everything like a pack mule."

She laughed. "I don't know why you wanted to bring so much. We won't starve before we—"

"Show me the cave quickly," he said, switching the subject. "We don't have all day."

She took him a different direction than he'd expected, to a part of the woods where he'd never found any ice caves in his own explorations.

Lea walked across a stream, her boots making the ice crack ominously. Caelan jumped it rather than trust his weight on its surface.

She ducked under a fallen log that lay across the shallow gorge and pointed. "Up there. See?"

Straightening beside her and combing twigs from his hair, Caelan saw the mouth of the cave ahead. The entrance was tucked into a tall bank along the frozen stream, where mossy rocks jutted from the earth in a ridge swathed with dead vines and undergrowth. Unlike most ice caves, which had rock entrances and tunnels leading to the ice hidden deep within, this one was frozen to its very mouth. Concealed in the shadows of the bank, it looked murky and cold.

Caelan's heart pumped faster. "Stay here," he whispered.

Lea elbowed ahead of him. "It's my cave. I'll show you—"

"No! I'll check it first. You wait until I say it's safe."

She glared at him. "It's safe—"

"Lurkers," he said in warning, and she subsided.

Cautiously he pushed ahead, his feet silent in the snow. He sniffed the air but smelled no den. Pausing, he collected a stout stick and brandished it. When he reached the cave, he saw where ice had flowed in half-melted slush from the mouth, then refrozen like a tongue. His senses alert, Caelan focused a moment to see if any animal or demon waited inside. He even dared use *sevaisin*, the joining.

Nothing.

He crept up to the mouth and peered in. The air inside the cave felt clammy cold. It smelled only of ice and damp, nothing else. He poked the stick inside and banged it on the ice-covered walls.

Nothing stirred, fled, or jumped out at him.

Relaxing, Caelan beckoned to Lea, who came hopping without the food basket.

"I told you it was safe," she said and ducked inside.

Annoyed by her lack of caution, Caelan shed his cloak and pack and followed her. "Lea, I should go first—"

"Hush." She gestured at him with equal annoyance. "You'll scare them."

"Who?"

"The earth spirits. Be quiet so they can know I'm here."

He crouched just inside the entrance, tucking his hands under his arms for extra warmth. Maybe he shouldn't have removed his cloak.

The cave was silent, gloomy, and cold. The inside was completely encased in ice. Even the floor offered a slippery surface.

Lea crept farther in, taking one careful step at a time to avoid slipping and falling.

"It's good," she said at last. "We're welcome here. Come on."

He scrambled up, almost slipping, and followed her with his hand on the wall for support. The farther in, the taller the cave became until Lea could stand upright. He hunched along, his hair brushing the icy ceiling.

"Not too far," he warned her. "I didn't bring a lamp."

"Silly," she said impatiently. "I've been here lots of times."

He sighed and abandoned the attempt to be responsible. She didn't want him cautioning her constantly.

"How far to the emeralds?" he asked.

"Hush. They're a gift. You can't demand them."

Hard not to do so when his need for them was so great. He glanced around him and wondered how he was supposed to appeal to the earth spirits.

"Well, do we look for them or do we—"

She stopped and glanced back at him. "Stop asking questions. We have to stay in the cave long enough for them to decide whether they will give us gifts or not. You're making everything harder."

Accepting her chastisement, he rolled his eyes. "I'll be quiet."

"Good."

Finally they emerged in a small chamber about the size of Lea's sleeping room. It was still too low for Caelan to stand upright, and icicles hung down from the ceiling, some flowing all the way to the floor in frozen forms and shapes that made him smile in wonder. Natural light filled the chamber, but although he looked around he never saw the opening.

"Isn't it pretty?" Lea asked, her face glowing. "The

cave itself is a treasure. The earth and ice spirits made this one special."

He nodded, enjoying her pleasure. No wonder the earth spirits had given her precious jewels. Who else could appreciate the natural beauty of this place except a child like Lea?

"This is my palace," she told him, shifting into her own land of pretend. She launched into a whole story then, telling him of all the imaginary rooms that lay beyond, and where her guards slept, and where her servants worked, and where her stables stood, and how many beautiful steeds she owned. She described fabulous white horses that could fly and carry her to any corner of the earth.

She had earlier gathered stones, twigs, and pieces of bark twisted into play cups and platters. These she brought out from behind the ice formations and served him a pretend feast as a welcome guest.

"Wait," Caelan said. "We brought food. Why not eat some of it now? We don't have to pretend."

The light momentarily faded from her face. "That food is for you to take when you leave us," she said sadly.

His heart turned over, and he realized he shouldn't have assumed he could keep such an important secret from her. "I'm sorry," he whispered and pulled her into his arms, hugging her tight. "I don't want to leave you."

"Take me with you."

He groaned a little and pushed her away. "I can't."

"Why not? Don't you love me?"

He struggled to master himself. "Of course," he said, and saw disbelief hot in her eyes. Dismay rose in him. How could he explain? "Lea, it has nothing to do with how much I love you. If I took you, Father would have to come after us. You belong to him by law until you are married."

She tossed her bright head. "I'm not going to be married."

"Well, even so. I'm going far away. It will be a hard, dangerous trip."

"You're going to join the army," she said, her eyes filling with tears. "That's why you bartered for the dagger that has killed men. You want to kill too."

Angrily he turned away from her. "Now you sound like Father."

"It is a bad thing, Caelan. You know it. We have been taught to respect all life, to honor it."

"I know," he said, staring at the floor. He sighed. "I know."

Silence fell between them, and he was grateful for it. He had no words to explain this to her. It was as though the world called him forth, drawing him through a gateway toward exploration and adventure. Overmastered by it, he could do nothing except obey.

"I will pray for you," Lea said at last, sounding far older than her age. She pulled a little pouch out from beneath her clothing and slipped its thong over her head. "You will need money, and since you did not rob Father's earnings box like you wanted to, I will give you my emeralds."

"No!" he said immediately, then saw her face and softened his tone. "Thank you, but they are yours. I cannot take them."

"But I want you to have them."

"No," he said gently, putting the loop back over her head and patting the small cloth pouch. "You will need them someday."

"But—"

"Not a man in a thousand comes across such a treasure in a lifetime. Your stones are a precious gift. You must honor that by keeping them for yourself. They are not for me. And how do you know I wanted to steal from the earnings box?"

She grinned, distracted by the question as he had intended. "You have no secrets from me!"

He caught her hands firmly in his and squeezed them. "But you must keep mine, promise? You will tell no one where I have gone, even if you guess it."

Grief darkened her blue eyes. Slowly she nodded. "I don't want you to go. You said you would never leave me."

"I have to." Her pain entered his own heart, and he kissed her hands.

Her tears fell onto their gripped hands, hot on their cold flesh.

"I'm sorry, little one," he said. "I cannot keep that promise."

She shivered and he straightened.

"Are you cold?"

She nodded and wiped her eyes with the back of her hand. "We've been here long enough. If they're going to give you any emeralds, they've had plenty of time. Look close as we go out."

His excitement rose again in spite of his own doubts. He was hardly worthy of any gifts from the spirits, but maybe worth had nothing to do with it. He followed her out, staring at the ground carefully.

He found nothing by the time he reached the mouth of the cave. Ruefully, he shook his head and crouched down. "Well, we tried," he said, swallowing his disappointment. It had been too much to hope for anyway. "I'm sorry we couldn't come back sooner while the earth spirits were in the giving mood."

"They have to be kind to you too," she said fretfully, disappointment sharp in her voice. She stamped her foot. "You're my brother. They have to like you just as much as me."

"Lea, we need to go. I have to get you home, and then I must start on my journey."

"Not yet." Bending over, she circled around him and headed back into the cave. "Don't give up so easily."

He waited, knowing this was just her tactic to keep him there as long as possible.

She searched, but found nothing. Finally she bumped against his side and sighed, looking tired. "Maybe it's my fault. I shouldn't have brought my stones. The spirits probably think I'm greedy."

"No, they know why you came back," he said gently, putting his hand on her curls.

"Go look one more time."

"Lea, it's no good."

"Please."

"Lea—"

"*Please.* Just one more time."

"All right," he said to humor her. "But then we must go."

The angle of light entering the cave had shifted since they first arrived. He could see better, and he knew the sun was lower in the sky. They had to go soon. He wanted no trouble either for himself or for Lea. He had to see that she was safely home; then he must put as much distance between himself and the hold as he could before darkness fell and he was forced to take sanctuary in an ice cave for the night.

When he reached the back chamber of the cave, the tunnel suddenly seemed too small around him. He stopped, frowning, and looked back. The air grew strangely warm and smelled of sweet fragrance as though flowers bloomed. A shiver ran through Caelan, and he felt the touch of something cool and ancient go through him.

Afraid, he remembered the horror of the wind spirits, but this was nothing like they had been. This was strange but not unpleasant. He sensed no malevolence, only a peaceful presence.

Then the fragrance faded, and the air grew cold again.

Caelan stumbled back as though released. He blinked and shook himself. Suddenly he wanted out of there.

Whirling around too fast, he slipped and fell with a

thud. The impact made him grunt. Stunned, he lay there a second in an effort to regain his breath.

As he levered himself to his hands and knees, his fingers knocked against something.

It skidded away across the ice.

Caelan's heart stopped. For a moment he dared not move; then he scrambled forward on his hands and knees, patting the ground with his hands, searching in the gloom.

He found one stone, rough and angular like Lea's. A short distance away he found a second. This one was smaller, no bigger than the nail on his little finger, but polished.

He turned them over and over in his hands, unable to believe his luck. It couldn't happen like this. It simply couldn't.

Yet it had.

Lea's good fortune had been extended to him.

His hand closed over the stones and he crawled forward, trying not to whoop with joy.

She was waiting outside. When he came scrambling out, her face lit up. "You found some!"

"Yes!" He showed them to her.

They bent over the stones and held them up to the light filtering through the trees.

"Emeralds," he said in satisfaction. He wanted to shout, to dance. "I can't believe it."

"The spirits here like you too," she said, skipping around him. "Look at how pretty the little one is."

"It's polished, almost cut like a jewel," he said in wonder. "A miracle."

"A special gift."

In sudden generosity, he held out his palm to her. "You didn't find any today. Take one of them, the one you like best, as your share."

Her mouth made a little O and she shook her head quickly. "I couldn't. They're yours."

"No, one for each of us."

"But, Caelan, I have mine," she said. "Nine is a complete number. Keep these. You must. They're for you."

He started to protest, but she pressed her fingers across his lips. "They're a pair, as we are. This is a special day, Caelan. You have been blessed in this. Don't let Father or your anger ever let you forget what you have been given here. Believe there is good, and that you are good, just as you have been given good today."

As she spoke, the sunlight shone down through the treetops and glowed upon her in a shining mantle. Her words seemed to vibrate in the air.

Caelan's heart nearly stopped. He felt humbled by this child, so wise beyond her years.

Without thought he knelt before her.

She folded his hand around the emeralds. "One is me and one is you. Now you have something to remember us always."

Her kindness spread over him like a balm. He loved her for it so much he thought his heart would burst. Somehow he held his emotions in. "How do I thank the earth spirits?" he whispered.

She smiled and touched his cheeks with her small hands. "They know."

He took her hands and squeezed them. "Then I will say my gratitude to you. Thank you for bringing me here, little one. If the spirits have favored me, it is only because of you."

"Now you cannot forget me, no matter how far away you go."

He kissed her forehead. "I will never forget you," he said, his voice rough. "I swear it."

She pulled a little cloth bag from her pocket and held it up. "Here's a pouch to keep them in. I had Anya make two because I knew you'd find treasure too."

Smiling, he tucked the emeralds into the bag. He strung it over his neck and tucked it beneath his tunics. The stones felt small and knobby against his chest, tiny talismen of his sister's love.

He gathered her into his arms and hugged her tight. "I love you, little sister."

She hugged him back, tender and small in his arms. She was crying. "Oh, Caelan—"

Through the quietness of the forest came the sound of distant thunder. Frowning, Caelan slowly straightened to his feet and turned his head to listen.

Another sound came, a rumbling bugle note unlike anything he had ever heard before. His breath stopped in his lungs, and he was suddenly afraid.

His heartbeat started pounding faster, harder. No, he thought. This could not be happening.

He heard the sound again, a trumpet call of disaster, eerie and ominous, closer than the first. He had never heard such a noise before, yet instinctively he recognized it. Old stories, told around the hearth, flashed through his mind.

"No," he said aloud.

Beside him, Lea looked up at the sky. "What is that noise?"

His paralysis fell away. Caelan grabbed her by the shoulders, swinging her bodily around. "Get inside the cave. Hide there, and don't come out."

She stared at him in bewilderment, making no move to obey. "But why—"

Gripping her arm, he ran back to the cave, pushing her as he went. He picked up the food basket and tossed it in the cave, along with his cloak and pack. "Hurry!" he said, fear ragged in his voice. "Don't ask questions. Just do as I say!"

He pushed her toward the cave too hard, making her stumble and fall. Her face puckered up, and tears filled her eyes. "What's wrong?"

The dragons trumpeted again. The sound filled Caelan

with panic. On a sudden shift of the wind, he smelled smoke.

"Gault above, can't you hear that?" he shouted at her. "The raiders have found the hold. I've got to help them—"

Lea's eyes widened. "Thyzarenes?"

"I think so." He was busy yanking off his heavy outer tunic. Wadding it up into a ball, he tossed it inside the cave and drew the dagger from his belt.

"No!" She flung herself against him, gripping hard. "Don't go. You mustn't go!"

He tried to pull away, but she was crying. Caelan hesitated, his mind tearing in all directions. He was afraid to go back to the hold, afraid of what he might find. His instincts were yelling at him to run for his life, run with Lea and hide deep in the safety of the forest.

And yet, how could he abandon the others, knowing they were defenseless and unprotected from an attack? The walls couldn't keep out dragons.

"I must help them," he said and gave his sister a shake. "Lea, listen to me. Listen! You must be brave now. Hide in the cave until it's safe. I'll come back for you."

She shook her head. "They're going to kill everyone—"

"No! I'll help them. I can fight, with this." He held up the dagger, his body thrumming with protectiveness. "Now stay here. You'll be safe as long as you hide."

Her lip quivered. She stared at him through her tears. "Don't go, Caelan. Don't go! I'll never see you again!"

He rose on his toes, listening to the strange noises. The forest had gone silent with alarm. He could feel it around him. There was no time to waste with a distraught child.

"Sweetness, be brave. I have to help Father."

"I can help them too!" she said, refusing to let go of his sleeve. "Let me go. I'll wish the raiders away."

"No, you're better off here."

Even as he said the words, he wondered. What was he

and one dagger against the savages? What if he couldn't come back for her? How could she fare out here at night in the forest, unprotected? Would she have enough sense to go to E'raumhold? Or would she perish of cold, starvation, and the wolves?

His resolve almost folded, but then he heard the hold bell ringing out an alarm. He gulped in air. "Get in the cave."

"But they're ringing the bell for us to come back."

All their lives they'd been told to come home at once if they heard the bell. She would have run, but he flung his arm across her chest and held her bodily.

"Not you."

"But, Caelan, they want us to come home. We have to—"

He picked her up and pushed her into the cave. She clung to him, screaming his name, but he pulled free.

"Promise me you'll stay here," he said sternly, knowing he must keep her from following him. "Promise me you won't go to the hold, not until the dragons are gone."

She was crying again, her eyes clinging to him, eating him up. Slowly, fearfully, she gave him a tiny nod.

"Hide and don't come out," he said. "If you run out of food, you follow the stream south. Watch the sun and you won't get lost. You follow it to E'raumhold."

"Aren't you going to come get me?"

"Yes," he said firmly. "I promise I will. Now hide."

Touching her curls one last time, he turned and started running.

"Caelan!" she screamed after him, but he didn't look back. There wasn't time.

eleven

NOW THE DEEP SNOW WASN'T PRETTY AND it wasn't fun. It held him back when he needed to run like the wind. Soon his breath was sawing in his lungs. He wasn't that far away from the hold, only a quarter of a mile, perhaps less, and yet the distance never seemed to close. The bell rang again, then abruptly stopped.

Ignoring the pain in his lungs, Caelan drove his aching legs onward until he reached the edge of the forest. There he stopped, concealed by pine branches. He gulped in deep lungfuls of air. It felt like razors in his lungs.

The pale walls of the hold reflected the sunlight. To the north, the mountains rose mightily, filling the world. And overhead circled black creatures from a nightmare, too many to count, their wingspans as huge as despair. Leathery wings beat a hum that filled the air. And when the wind shifted, Caelan caught a peculiar scorched scent that made his nostrils wrinkle.

The dragons' long serpentine necks ended in narrow, crested heads and fanged snouts. Their bodies were long and thin as well, with clawed limbs tucked up tight against their scaled undercarriages as they flew.

Directed by riders clinging to leather harnesses, the dragons bugled, whipping their long necks around as they sailed low over the hold. Flames shot from their gaping mouths, searing the rooftops within the hold. Smoke was already roiling skyward in a dark column.

The riders carried weapons that looked like spears, only the tips were as long as a man's arm with jagged edges, and the hafts were short—weapons for stabbing, not throwing.

Dragons dropped into the hold, only to lift again in a constant shifting of motion. The stabbing spears dripped red, and Caelan could hear screams.

Still breathing hard, he gripped his own dagger in his fist and felt fear like a wall around him.

The gates burst open, and Caelan could glimpse smoke and flames inside the courtyard.

A pair of wild-eyed ponies came plunging out, dodging and snorting. Both were badly burned, and the mane of one was smoking. One pony broke for the forest, but the other passed too close to a dragon that was landing.

Unfurling its wings, it whipped its head and struck the pony in the neck.

Screaming, the pony dropped to its knees, still fighting despite the crimson blood that spurted across the snow. With a fierce shake, the dragon ripped open the pony's throat and gulped down a chunk of meat.

The lifeless pony fell sprawling in the snow, and with roars of greed, other dragons broke off the attack to fall on the carcass. They ripped it apart and gulped hide and steaming flesh, ignoring the riders who beat at them and shouted commands.

Fresh screams came from inside the hold, whether from animals or people Caelan could not tell. Agonized, not sure what to do, he drove himself to think of something that would help. The people inside were helpless since Beva had destroyed all the weapons in the arms room. As for the warding keys, they'd been spell-forged to keep out malevolent spirits, not to prevent physical attack.

Caelan turned and went running through the trees, keeping as much to cover as he could, until he'd circled around to the rear wall of the hold. The standing rule was that all trees and undergrowth were to be kept cleared well away from the walls, but saplings sprouted and grew tall every summer. As Old Farns had aged, more and more chores slipped by without getting done. Raul had plenty of his own work to do and could not get to everything either.

As a result, Caelan found a sapling stout enough to shinny up. At its top, it swayed alarmingly beneath his weight, but he kicked out and managed to get his elbow hooked over the top of the wall. Grunting, he hung there a moment, then swung his legs up. From the sky, he was an obvious target. He knew he had only seconds to move before he was seen by one of the raiders circling over-head.

As though from nowhere, a dragon came hurtling over him, wings tucked, talons raking. It bellowed, giving Cae-lan a split-second of warning. He dived headlong, flinging himself onto the low roof of the larder, and vicious claws clutched only air where he'd been crouching just seconds before.

Roaring in fury, the dragon could not shift the angle of its descent in time. It passed over, and Caelan scram-bled back, yanking his dagger from his belt as he did so.

Another dragon arched its neck and blasted fire from its nostrils, raking the thatched roof of the stables, which were already on fire. The door to the stables stood open, and smoke boiled from inside. Several ponies were rush-ing about the courtyard in raw panic, an obvious danger to the people trying to dodge them as well as the attackers. Caelan could hear other ponies still trapped inside the burning building, their screams horrible.

More fire raked down from the sky, crossing the roof of the infirmary. It was made of slate, however, and the fire did no damage beyond scoring twin black marks across the surface.

The house also had a slate roof, but the kitchen at the back was thatched. It was also in flames. The stench of smoke and the dragons filled the air.

People burst from the buildings, running, shouting. Caelan saw Anya trying to help old Surva, who could barely hobble.

"No!" he shouted at them, waving his arms. "Stay inside!"

But they could not hear him in the general melee. Beva came running through the smoke, easy to see in his white robes. He was gesturing at the women, shouting something they did not heed.

A dragon passed over Caelan, not attacking him, intent instead on other prey.

It was close enough for him to see the sun glint off the scaly hide, close enough for him to see old battle scars, to see a sparse hank of hair hanging from its lower jaw like a beard. The man astride the dragon was swarthy and small, hardly bigger than Lea. At first Caelan thought he might be a boy, but the rider turned his head to reveal a gray-streaked beard. His teeth flashed at Caelan in laughter. He lifted his jagged spear in mock salute.

Infuriated, Caelan dragged in a breath and went skidding off the roof of the larder. Landing on the ground and staggering at the jolt to his ankles, Caelan looked around swiftly and plucked down the first warding key he came to.

It glowed in his hand, growing hot the moment his flesh touched it. Caelan focused on it in an effort to reach its full power. He'd been able to utilize the mysterious force within the metal once before in driving off the wind spirits. Perhaps it would strengthen him now.

Gritting his teeth, he tried even harder until sweat ran down his face and his hand was afire with pain.

He felt something within him leap, as though he drew

in a lungful of fire. Suddenly he was connected with the metal, which became a living, fluid thing in his hand. The power stirred, flowing into him until he was filled with it. His fear dropped away, and he knew only the hum of the Choven force that twisted and stirred within him. Across the courtyard, he saw a flash from the warding key hanging on the side door of the house. Another flash came from the gates, then another and another as all the keys came alive, glowing brightly enough to be seen even through the black smoke.

And Caelan was one with them, a part of the interwoven net of power and protection crisscrossing the hold. He rode it, letting *sevaisin* join him. Exhilaration swelled into his throat, and he wanted to laugh at the Thyzarenes and their monsters.

Brandishing both the key and his dagger, Caelan ran for the steps leading to the top of the walls. There, he paused and turned around, his clothes whipping in the air stirred up by the dragons' wings.

One of the raiders flew at him, but Caelan raised the warding key without fear. "We are protected here!" he shouted, his voice deep with the power thrumming through him. "Leave us! Gather your beasts and depart."

The Thyzarene stared at him in astonishment.

Caelan's confidence grew. He had defeated a wind spirit. And now he defied a raider. If this was to be his destiny, then he embraced it willingly. He laughed again.

"Fear this!" he cried, bathed in the glow from the warding key. "Go, and come no more to E'nonhold."

The raider was still staring. Then he threw back his head and bellowed with laughter.

It was scorn, mockery, and contempt all rolled together.

Surprised in turn, Caelan blinked, but he set his jaw and gripped the key harder as its fire raced through his veins. "You cannot harm us here while we have the protection of the Choven," he said fiercely. "Go!"

The Thyzarene was still laughing, holding his sides and lolling about until it seemed he might fall off his hovering mount.

"Barbarian!" Caelan shouted in fresh anger. "Respect what you do not understand. We are loyal subjects of the emperor, not enemies for you to plunder."

He tried to hurl the key's power at this laughing fool, but instead the burning force raged more strongly in himself. No matter what he did, he could not direct it against the other man.

Below in the courtyard, a woman screamed. Caelan whipped around in time to see Anya running for her life, her skirts gathered high and her plump legs churning in thick woolen stockings. Overhead a dragon chased her with little snorts of fire, driving her back and forth for the amusement of its rider. Tongues of flame caught the back of her gown. The wool cloth ignited and suddenly she was on fire, screaming and spinning around in panic. The flames raced up her back, then her hair was on fire.

"No!" Caelan screamed. He started for the steps, but he was too far away to save her.

Beva reached her and hurled her bodily to the ground, making her roll. He grabbed someone's cloak and threw it over her, trying to smother the flames.

Caelan felt sick. Anya had been like a second mother to him. She had cared for him all his life. He stared at her, rolled up and unmoving in the cloak, and prayed to the gods for her life.

The raider hovering before him laughed afresh. "We take what we please. You are nothing to us," he said in a taunting voice, his Lingua strangely accented. "How do you make us go from here, little spell master?"

Furious, Caelan lunged at him. "I'll drive you barbarians away with this—"

The dragon whipped its black head around to face Caelan's attack. The dragon's eyes were crimson, glowing fiercely against the black scales. It lifted its crest at him, and a narrow, forked tongue flickered from its mouth. Caelan nearly gagged on the hot, sulfurous stench of its breath. Then it roared, blasting him with sound, and he saw the rows of vicious teeth behind the fangs.

Holding the warding key as a shield, Caelan struck with his dagger, slashing the tip of the dragon's snout. Dark, viscous blood welled up. The dragon whipped back its head, squalling in pain. The rider also shouted, but the dragon struck back furiously, hitting Caelan's hand and knocking the warding key flying.

The triangle of metal sailed through the air, its glow dimming as it went, and it landed far below on the cobblestones. When it hit the ground, it shattered into pieces.

The connection to its power snapped in Caelan like an explosion in his chest. Doubling over, he cried out. Around the hold, in swift succession, the other keys also shattered into pieces.

The wounded dragon roared, making the walls shake, and was barely restrained by its rider.

"Keep your spells for demons," the Thyzarene shouted furiously, still struggling with his mount. "Stupid Traulander! I'll teach you a lesson for this."

"And I'll open your dragon's belly!" Caelan shot back. The blood on his dagger stank of sulfur and something worse.

"Ho, Kuvar!" the raider yelled. "Drive him down."

The dragon beat with its wings, lifting itself above Caelan. Then it came.

With talons raking the air above him, Caelan ducked back and stumbled. Pain ripped along his jaw, making him howl. He felt blood run down his neck, and that drove him to slash back. This time he managed to nick the dragon in the leg. Roaring, it drove him to a corner of the wall, beating its huge wings until Caelan was whipped and buffeted by wind.

When the dragon wheeled, one wing tip struck Caelan

and nearly swept him over the edge. Only a quick grab saved him from falling.

Heavy net dropped on him. Twisting around in a panic to fight it off, Caelan found himself hopelessly enmeshed.

The Thyzarene gave the net an expert yank, and Caelan was pulled off his feet. He landed hard with a grunt, and started hacking frantically at the net with his dagger.

The cords were made of some tough material that resisted his knife. He kept cutting, knowing he was done for, but too frightened to give up. Another cord reluctantly parted. Tugging at it, he sawed away.

The dragon extended its wings and lifted, beating powerfully at the air. Caelan felt a sharp yank; then he was flipped upside down.

His dagger slipped through the hole he'd managed to cut and was lost.

Caelan found himself suspended in midair, dangling and spinning in the net, which was fastened to the dragon's harness.

Sobbing for breath, his fingers gripping the net as the ground fell farther and farther beneath him, Caelan stared down at the burning hold until the dizzying spin of his view made him feel sick. He closed his eyes until an unexpected bump made him open them again.

He found himself on the ground, with the dragon settling itself beside him. In the air, the beast might have extraordinary grace and agility. On the ground, it looked ridiculous and awkward as it folded its enormous wings and balanced on short, stumpy legs. Its barbed tail lashed angrily back and forth, and as Caelan stared at the creature, it turned its head to glare at him with those vicious red eyes. Its crest flared upright, and it hissed with a frightening displaying of fangs.

Caelan didn't dare move, didn't dare breathe. His heart was bursting in his chest with fear, but he refused to let himself look away from that evil stare. Dragon fodder or not, he wasn't going to let this overgrown lizard see that he was afraid.

Dismounting, the Thyzarene stepped between the dragon and Caelan and inspected the dragon's bloody snout. He spoke to the creature in a low, soothing voice, taking out some salve that stank of rancid fats and something else impossible to identify. Smearing it on the wound, he cooed and crooned to the dragon until it swayed from side to side. Its crest folded flat against its skull, and the red eyes slitted half-closed with apparent contentment.

Disgusted, Caelan looked away.

It seemed the attack was over. More and more raiders landed outside the walls of the burning hold. The dragons formed a stinking, jostling, snapping horde that showed far too much interest in the scant remains of the pony carcass. Those that had eaten looked sluggish and sleepy. The rest sniffed and craned necks and snorted, but their riders chained them away from the food.

Two more Thyzarenes came along and dragged Caelan bodily across the trampled snow to where the rest of the prisoners huddled. Still wrapped in the net, Caelan found himself sending hopeless looks at his father. Beva sat impassive and calm in the midst of the others. Raul had an ugly burn across his shoulder. He kept trying to chew through the net swathing him, but his teeth were even less successful than Caelan's knife had been.

The gates of the hold stood wide open, showing flames and smoke still tearing down what had been E'nonhold.

His home. Caelan found his eyes stinging, and he struggled not to let his emotions get away from him. For once he wished he could take refuge in *severance* like his father. Then it wouldn't hurt like this.

Picking up a handful of snow, he pressed the wet stuff against his jaw. The cold numbed the pain, giving him relief, but he saw blood drip through his fingers and run down his wrist.

The Thyzarenes chattered and laughed among themselves as they came and went purposefully. They dragged out bulging tarps, which were flung on the ground. Looted contents spilled out for inspection.

They left nothing in the hold unexamined. Clothing, scrolls, herb jars were all rifled. The cooking pots were brought out. The barrels of food stores. Spoons, cloak pins, shaving razors, writing ink, chairs, even the beds were dragged about and scattered. The raiders pawed through the items, selecting and rejecting with grunts and arguments.

Helpless and enraged, Caelan watched them. This was a violation such as he had never known. Home had always been a place of security, of absolute and utter safety. He kept looking at the destroyed ruins, and he couldn't believe it. This wasn't supposed to happen. Imperial auxiliaries were not supposed to kill and pillage imperial citizens. How could the army commanders have turned these barbarians loose on the populace?

Caelan found himself confused, resentful, and angry. For the first time, his belief in imperial right was shaken. He prayed the gods would strike these savages down, but the heavens remained calm and uncaring above him. Were the Thyzarenes merely robbers, it would be bad enough, but they destroyed what they did not want with brutal callousness.

Beva's earnings chest and strongbox were both found and dragged outside, the men sweating to carry them. Locks were shattered with hammer and chisel and the lids flung back. Parchment scrolls—the deeds to this land— were ripped and flung to the winds. It was the coinage that made the raiders cry out in delight and crowd around.

Their leader drove them back with fierce commands; then he alone crouched over the chests, sifting the glinting coins through his fingers.

Within the strongbox was a small casket of rosewood similar to the one in Caelan's room. Its contents held a few baubles—an amber necklace, a ring, and a few hair jewels that winked in the fading sunlight.

Caelan kicked at the netting. "Those were my mother's, you dogs! You can't have them. They're for—"

A kick in his ribs shut him up. He collapsed in the snow, hurting and trying not to cry. The other prisoners looked away in sympathy, except for Beva.

When Caelan finally sat up, wincing, he saw his father's emotionless gaze on him.

"Father—"

"You, quiet!" It was the Thyzarene who had captured him. He cuffed Caelan's head and glared at him. "No talk."

Caelan glared back, but he made no further effort to talk to his father. Beva was a man of stone. He probably didn't even care what was happening. After all, he had *severance* to console him.

The jewels vanished quickly, shared out and tucked into the belts of the few who were favored. The man who had captured Caelan was one of the recipients. He glanced at Caelan and grinned with a flash of white teeth in his beard.

Beva's medicines were sniffed and poured out. Then the jars and bottles were smashed. Caelan could see his father's lantern still hanging over the gate, unlit and forlorn. The sign of a healer was supposed to be respected by thieves. Now it hung over the looters as a symbol of Beva's futile trust in decency and mercy.

Would it have made a difference if the holdspeople had had weapons with which to defend themselves? Probably not.

Caelan scowled to himself and pulled up his knees against his chest. He wanted to scream, and kick, and fight—anything except sit here and take what was happening.

Then they came and surrounded the prisoners. Raul drew in his breath with an audible hiss. Gunder was trembling, his eyes darting back and forth. Tisa had her face buried in her hands, probably crying. Anya, a burned thing swathed in Beva's cloak, had already been dragged out. She lay unmoving beside the healer, and now and then his hand touched her with the lightest possible touch, drawing off the agony with an effort that quivered in his face.

One of the raiders shoved Beva aside and bent over Anya. He drew his knife and struck cleanly.

Caelan jumped, and someone else cried out. Caelan closed his eyes, feeding on hate.

Surva and Old Farns were dragged out and dumped on the ground. Both were obviously dead.

With prods and kicks, the Thyzarenes gestured for the remaining prisoners to stand up. The netting was pulled off Caelan. He glanced around, but there was no possibility of escape.

Beva tried to speak to the raiders, but one of them slapped him. With blood trickling from a corner of his mouth, Beva made no further attempt to plead for mercy.

"They'll sell us," Raul whispered from the corner of his mouth, his gaze nowhere, everywhere. Beneath the grime streaking him, his face was as white as chalk. "Sell us to the slave market."

Caelan frowned at him. "But we're freeborn—"

"Don't matter to these dogs."

"It's illegal. The emperor has forbidden it."

Raul didn't appear to hear him. "They'll sell us. We're the youngest and the strongest. We'll bring a good price." He blinked, gazing at the others. "Some of us."

Caelan tried to go on breathing normally as the raiders examined each of them and argued among themselves, but his lungs were choked by growing fear. At least Lea was safe, he reassured himself.

But for how long? How long would she wait? She had food and shelter for now. When her food ran out, would she be able to follow the stream and find E'raumhold? He didn't think so. She was too little to be on her own in the dangers of the forest.

Besides, even if she made it to E'raumhold, what if it had been burned out too?

Caelan found himself praying, his lips moving soundlessly. He had promised her he would come back. But he couldn't. *Gault forgive me,* he prayed, knowing he had failed her.

Tisa began sobbing, each sound louder and more out of control. The men prodded her breasts, lifted her hair, looked at her teeth. She cringed away from them, screaming. One of them shook her hard, but that only increased her hysteria.

With an oath, the knife came out.

"No!" Caelan shouted.

But it had already struck. Tisa fell to the ground and was kicked aside, her lifeless body rolling across the snow with a bloody trail.

Raul moved closer to Caelan. "The fool," he whispered angrily, tears filling his eyes. "The stupid little fool."

Gunder bawled at that moment, and two of the Thyzarenes grabbed his arms. He was dragged away, fighting and yelling, then knocked down where he lay spitting and flailing in the snow. One raider sat on him while another trussed his arms and legs, fitting a collar around his throat. Gunder snapped like a wild dog, and almost managed to bite one of the raiders.

With a snarl the Thyzarene struck him across the face. Sobbing in the snow, Gunder lay there, his brief force spent as quickly as it had come, until they yanked him upright and led him away.

"The master's next," Raul whispered.

Caelan's throat constricted. He looked at his father, and for a moment he saw only a skeleton standing there, the bleached skull white in the sunshine, the robe flapping on exposed bones. A horrified shiver ran through Caelan, and the vision was gone.

He felt dizzy and cold. He didn't want to believe his vision. Let it be false, he prayed desperately. Let it not happen.

"A healer will bring a good price," Raul was saying.

Watching the Thyzarene walk toward Beva, Caelan barely heard Raul. "No," he whispered.

As though he sensed something, Beva turned his head and met Caelan's gaze. Father and son stared at each other, one expressionless, the other filled with what he could not utter.

In that moment the Thyzarene slashed Beva's throat.

Blood spurted. His head tipped back.

Screaming, Caelan lunged forward and caught Beva as he crumpled to the snow. His father's weight carried Caelan to the ground also. The Thyzarenes kicked Caelan back from the body, and he fought them, wild with grief and hatred, spewing obscenities, until his captor pinned him to the ground and slapped him repeatedly.

Head ringing, Caelan finally tumbled out of madness and lay still. Tears choked his throat, and his mind felt numbed with shock. Again and again, as though the scene would be forever frozen in his brain, he saw the slash of the blade, the flare of pain in his father's face, the brief surprise in those gray eyes. In spite of his philosophy, Beva had not been prepared for the ultimate *severance* after all.

The Thyzarene hauled Caelan to his feet and dusted him off. "Strong and young," he said proudly.

The leader of the band faced Caelan, looking him up and down. Caelan barely noticed. He was lost in the fire of his own emotions.

The leader asked a question in a language Caelan did not understand.

His captor translated it. "How old?"

Caelan said nothing. They struck him, but he didn't care.

"How old?"

There was blood in his mouth. It tasted thick and sweet. His cut face throbbed brutally. "Sixteen," he replied and felt sick. "Almost seventeen."

"Ah."

They discussed him in their own rapid-fire language.

His captor kept shaking his head and pointing to Caelan's face. "Battle wound," he announced. "Kuvar clawed him. The nick will heal fast."

The round of argument continued. Finally his captor grinned and turned to Caelan. "Forty ducats we will ask for you in the marketplace. I am a rich man."

Laughing, he clapped Caelan on the shoulder.

Another came forward and broke the thong of the medallion around Caelan's neck. Then he pulled out the pouch from beneath what remained of Caelan's tunic.

"No!" Caelan yelled in protest, but they ignored him.

Raging, he thought of Lea. She'd said the emeralds were to remind him of her always.

"In the name of the gods, don't take that too," he said in desperation. "It's only my amulet. I—"

The raiders opened the pouch, joking among themselves, and poured out the emeralds.

The fight died in Caelan. Everything was gone. He stared bleakly at nothing.

An exclamation of surprise made him look. Instead of emeralds, two brownish, ordinary pebbles rested on the leader's palm. The man frowned in disgust and tossed them down along with the pouch.

"Bah!"

As he walked away, trailed by the others, Caelan's new owner picked up the pouch and the two pebbles. He put the rocks back inside and returned the pouch to Caelan.

"Your amulet, you keep," he said kindly. "Stupid Traulander bring forty ducats. Me rich man soon."

Dumbfounded, Caelan took the pouch with nerveless fingers. He didn't know whether to be more astonished at the pebbles or at the man's unexpected generosity.

But how . . . what had happened? Was the miracle in the cave just an illusion? Had he and Lea only fooled themselves?

Heartsick, he dug into the pouch and felt the beveled sides of the small, polished emerald.

Astonished, he pulled it out. In the sunlight, it was only a brown pebble. He stared, unable to explain it, then dropped it back into the pouch. Peering inside, he could dimly see the outline of the two emeralds. A glint of green winked out at him.

Caelan opened his mouth, then closed it. Briefly he smelled the soft fragrance of warm earth and blossoms; then it was gone, obliterated by the stench of smoke and death.

The earth spirits were still with him, still protecting the gift they had given him. He did not know why, but he wasn't going to question it. Hope filtered back through his grief and despair. Only a tiny sliver of hope, but it was more than he'd had a moment before.

Then the Thyzarene put iron shackles on his wrists, and reality returned with all its grim implications. Caelan stared at the chains and could not imagine himself a slave.

His owner grinned at him with admiration. "Plenty tall. Plenty strong. Young. All good things. You best of all those captured. When I am rich, I shall pay dowry for good wife. Best quality wife. See? All good things happening."

Caelan looked at the forest. His heart ached for his little sister. Perhaps he should tell them about her. Alone, she would die. If taken captive, she would be enslaved and sold, but she would be alive.

"Not too young," the Thyzarene chattered on, gloating. He took out his smelly salve and began smearing it on Caelan's cuts. The wound in Caelan's face stopped throbbing, and suddenly the pain was bearable.

Caelan sucked in a deep breath and refused to feel grateful.

"Too young, go too cheap," the Thyzarene said. "No profit there. Always trouble with little ones. Easier when they die. You just right."

Caelan's throat closed off. He said nothing about Lea.

The Thyzarene yanked on Caelan's chains. "You come. Come! We have far to go."

Feeling the unaccustomed clanking weight of the shackles and all their shame, Caelan did as he was told. Following Raul and Gunder, who were also chained, Caelan walked past the dead, and looked down at their beloved faces for the last time. Anya and Tisa, Surva, Old Farns . . . his father.

He jerked to a stop. "My fault," he whispered, staring at his father's sightless eyes. "I—I'm sorry I wasn't the son you wanted—"

The Thyzarene pulled him onward. "Come. You come now!"

Bound and helpless, Caelan was taken to where the dragons milled and bugled, sniffing the air and snapping restlessly. His owner put him astride Kuvar and chained him to the beast's harness.

And when it lurched, lifting into the air with a mighty beating of its leathery wings, Caelan looked down at the forest where he had abandoned his sister. He should have ignored the desire to play hero and stayed with her. He knew that now. As long as he lived, he would live with the chains of that guilt on his soul.

Once again he could see her tear-stained face, could hear her desperate plea ringing in his ears. "Caelan!"

He shut his eyes and wept.

PART TWO

twelve

Four years later

FLAMES BURNED HIGH IN THE CENTRAL FIRE pit, throwing off intense heat. Hundreds of fat white candles blazed along shelves built high on each wall of the sanctum. The smell of melting wax mingled with the more pungent aroma of burning incense.

The gathered sisterhood of the Penestricans entered the sanctum in a double line. Their chanting rose and fell like the ocean tide. As they entered, the women parted in opposite directions to line the rough-hewn walls. Each sister stood veiled in black. Each held a skull in her hands. The tops of the skulls had been sawn off to form crucibles filled with a mixture of soil and female blood.

The chanting rose in intensity. At the entrance a woman robed in black appeared. Her pale narrow face revealed nothing except concentration. It was ageless, unlined, yet gaunt as though a lifetime of challenges had drawn her down to only the essentials.

She was the Magria, supreme mother within the sisterhood. Their chanting beat within her like her own pulse.

For three days she had fasted in preparation for the visioning. She had lain in the sweat chamber, forcing all impurities from her body. Now she stood emptied, ready. Her mind was clear. She had no hesitations.

Behind her, the deputy Anas untied the lacings of the Magria's robe and pulled it off her shoulders, leaving her naked. The intense heat struck her skin, and the Magria drew in a quick breath.

She walked forward to the sand pit that surrounded the fire. The sand was hot enough to burn the bare soles of her feet. The Magria did not flinch. In her state of heightened awareness, physical pain only served to clarify the visioning. She could have walked across live coals had it been necessary.

The chanting continued, rising in a frenzy around her. She could feel the collective force of the sisterhood around her, sustaining and strengthening her for what lay ahead.

She lifted her hands high in supplication to the stone image of the goddess mother in its niche on the opposite wall. The chanting ceased in abrupt unison, and all was silent. The Magria closed her eyes and reached into the stone box next to the fire pit.

"Within the power of the goddess mother, we call forth these children of the earth," she said. "Let them tell us their truth. Let us be worthy enough to understand it."

Her fingers entwined among the knot of writhing snakes inside the box, and she lifted them out. A dozen or more in number, they hissed and coiled about her wrists, but none of them struck her.

The Magria held them high for a moment, then tossed them upon the sand. "Truth-sayers, speak!" she called out.

Retreating from the sand pit, she climbed a tall dais overlooking it and seated herself on the stone chair.

The serpents writhed and slithered across the sand. They were active in the heat, hungry. But none of them made any effort to crawl out of the shallow pit.

Watching, her mind empty with anticipation, the Magria clutched the arms of her chair and waited in silence. She considered the lines drawn on the sand by the snakes, finding the pattern disturbingly clear.

As she had expected . . . but she must wait. It was not yet time for interpretation.

Without warning, crimson filled her vision, coating all that she saw. Blood . . . or the scarlet hue of rubies. The jewels blazed before her as though a hand had tossed a thousand of them across the sand. They reflected the firelight, glittering with life of their own. One of the snakes opened its mouth wide, fangs unfolding. It gulped down an egg-sized ruby, the jewel bulging through its length.

The Magria swayed in her chair and moaned.

Around her the walls ran with blood. It pooled on the floor, then ran in streams into the pit where the sand soaked it up.

Feeling the power, the Magria moaned again. Her heart pulsed stronger and stronger. The veiled sisters began to chant again, very soft and low, while the flames hissed and blazed.

The snake continued to eat the rubies, faster and faster, gorging itself on them until its length was swollen and lumpy. At last it lay still and sated, its mouth open. Another snake began to eat the jewels that remained.

The Magria swayed in her chair, biting her lip to hold back her cries. She must be strong. She must hold the vision until it was finished. But this one was very powerful, far more so than she had expected.

Fear lay on her like sweat. Around her blood puddled at her feet, welling up between her toes, staining her skin with its warmth. The wet, heavy scent of it filled her nostrils.

The second snake was still gobbling rubies. So few of the jewels remained unconsumed . . . so few.

Across the sand pit, the remaining serpents rolled themselves together into a writhing wad. When they abruptly separated and slithered apart, the Magria saw there were now only seven.

One was colored a rich green. Another was blue; another gold; and yet another black. The fifth was striped with crimson bands. The sixth was speckled gray and brown. The seventh was white, its skin loose, stretching. The Magria saw that it was shedding its skin. The others surrounded it, coiled and hissing, their forked tongues flickering in and out as they waited.

The Magria felt pain inside her chest as though anticipation had drawn it too tight. She forgot to breathe.

Then the gold-colored serpent moved away from the black snake that companioned it. The crimson-banded serpent approached the gold one, but it veered away. The green and blue snakes surrounded the gold one, but the black serpent intervened and drove the gold serpent back toward the one with crimson bands. Gold and crimson entwined themselves together, and the black serpent retreated. Green and blue faced each other, rearing high. The green shook rattles on its tail in warning. The blue flared out a hood. Swaying with mutual menace, they struck in battle, lashing and coiling about each other in a fury.

Meanwhile, the pale molting snake emerged wet and glistening. It was five times larger than any of the others. It looked like none of the others, white as death, an unholy thing that seemed to grow larger while the others fought.

Then the gold serpent, lying so still around the one with crimson bands, tightened its coils and began to squeeze. When the crimson-banded one struggled, the gold one struck at the vulnerable spot at the back of its head.

Pain speared the back of the Magria's skull. With a scream she threw herself back in her chair.

The gold serpent raced across the sand, pursued by the green and the blue. The black snake tried to follow but found itself cut off by the gray speckled one. The two fought furiously until at last the black twisted free. It reared up, seeking the gold serpent, but before the gold serpent was found the white snake of death uncoiled its mammoth, sluggish body. It rose up, stretching high above the dais itself. And it swallowed the Magria.

HOURS LATER, SHE AWAKENED ON THE stone of revival, the granite smooth and cool beneath her back. Around her stood the rough walls of the small, private chamber cut into the rock just beyond the sanctum. The air was cool and refreshing. She could feel dried sweat on her skin. Her body seemed weightless, as though only her spirit anchored her to the stone. Exhaustion had melted her bones to nothing.

Someone came to her and laid a cool cloth across her forehead. The Magria could smell restorative herbs scenting the water that had moistened the cloth. She closed her eyes to seek the multiple points of relaxation. Cool hands continued to minister to her. Soothing hands.

After a short time, the Magria opened her eyes and looked up into the face of her deputy.

She forced open her lips, felt them tremble. "Anas," she whispered.

"Gently," Anas soothed her. She spread a blanket across the Magria and smoothed its folds. Then she washed the Magria's face gently with cool clean linen. "Take your time. I have brought wine for you."

The Magria nodded, sitting up, and Anas brought the cup to her lips. The Magria drank deeply of the golden liquid. It was dry, yet rich with flavor, supremely restorative.

She sighed, feeling strength flow back into her veins. But her fear and disquiet did not lessen. Taking the cup, she gestured Anas away.

The deputy folded her hands within her sleeves and stepped back. Well trained, she waited with serene eyes.

The Magria pushed away the blanket and climbed off the revival stone. She leaned cautiously against it for a moment until she had tested the strength of her legs. She was drained entirely. She longed to sink back into oblivion and sleep for a thousand years.

Then with a blink, the Magria's memory returned. She recalled the vision and its terrible message. Her mouth went dry, and when she tried to sip more wine her teeth chattered against the cup.

"There is no hurry," Anas said. "Rest longer, Excellency, until you are stronger."

The Magria turned her head sharply to look at the deputy. "Did you see it?" she demanded. "Any of it?"

Anas hesitated, then lowered her gaze. "I saw blood," she admitted.

The Magria hissed and slammed down her cup. "Anything else?"

"No, Excellency."

The Magria glared at her and said nothing. After a moment Anas raised her eyes and met the Magria's steadily.

"You know the danger of that," the Magria said, deliberately letting anger fill her voice.

Anas did not flinch. "I could not withstand all of it. Blood seeped from the walls. It ran among us, filling the floor. The hems of the sisters' robes were soaked with it."

The Magria turned away to hide her own fresh rush of fear. "Did anyone else see this?"

"No. All remained veiled."

Relief steadied the Magria. That at least was a mercy. She was in no mood to conduct a purge. Not now when there was so much to do. "The sisterhood has grown lax," she said, keeping her voice harsh. The tone masked much, and she did not intend for Anas to know anything other than what she chose to reveal. It was not easy to come to terms with a vision of her own death. She needed time for that, time that she did not have.

When she turned back to the deputy, she was in command of herself again. Her gaze was icy, and this time when she raked it across Anas, she had the satisfaction of seeing her deputy frown.

"Forgive me, Excellency," Anas said. "I alone transgressed."

"You have been trained better than this."

"Yes."

The Magria studied her, critical and still angry, but finding new shades of meaning in what had transpired. Anas was making no excuses, no justifications. That meant there was no deceit involved.

"You did resist."

Anas nodded, looking troubled. "With all my strength. I know it is forbidden to share a vision. I know the dangers."

The Magria narrowed her eyes. Yes, Anas knew the dangers very well. Her predecessor had been a fool who let driving ambition overcome caution. She had interfered in several visionings, until the day one of them killed her. Watching a visioning occur unveiled, yet resisting the temptation to share in it, was the final stage of training for a deputy. Until a sister passed successfully, she could not be considered a true ally, or an eventual successor to the Magria.

Anas had always been levelheaded and intelligent. She let patience temper her ambitions, which was the foundation of wisdom. She had much potential, and the Magria liked her.

If Anas said she could not resist, then that meant she had tried very hard. She must be afraid, although she hid it well. The Magria studied the deputy and found the skin around her eyes a bit tighter than usual. Her serenity was impeccable, but proving hard to maintain.

Satisfied, the Magria ceased to blame Anas for the mistake. The vision had been extremely strong, and that meant they had little time in which to act.

She glanced at the exit that led back to the sanctum. "Are they waiting?"

Anas shook her head. "I dismissed them. You have been unconscious for nearly six hours."

"Ah." More evidence of the power of this vision. And its truth. The Magria walked back into the sanctum, feeling the grit stick to the salve that Anas had smeared on the burned soles of her feet.

Anas followed, carrying a robe folded neatly over her arm. The Magria ignored the unspoken hint. She was not yet ready to be clothed. Robes were artifice and concealment. She wanted to think without either restriction.

Climbing the dais on legs that remained weak, she sank onto the stone chair with a faint sigh and frowned at the sand pit below.

All lay quiet. The candles had burned out, leaving the sanctum plunged in shadow. Anas moved about without haste, lighting fresh ones. Only cold ashes remained of the fire. The serpents had been left in the sand pit. They were ordinary brown snakes again, restlessly seeking prey.

The Magria extended her hand, and a small pale mouse appeared on her palm.

She released it into the sand pit. The snakes sensed it at once and turned. The mouse scampered back and forth in increasing panic, then froze, whiskers quivering, as the first snake reached it.

We are mice, the Magria thought, turning her gaze away from the creature's destruction. Our time is dwindling quickly.

She stared at the mutilation scars on her arms, remembering the past when her old dugs had been firm and ripe, when her body had been strong and young, when she had felt the five powers coursing through her, sustaining her where she had no wisdom.

"Excellency," Anas said softly. That one quiet word revealed her worry.

The Magria turned to her. "No, I am not slipping back into the void," she said wearily. "Fear not."

"You are troubled."

The Magria pushed aside her emotions. "Stop hinting. I shall tell you soon enough. I must."

Anas betrayed herself with a tiny smile. She had always possessed poise beyond her experience. And now that the Magria had not reprimanded her for having shared in the visioning, it seemed her natural confidence was returning.

She said nothing else, but she was waiting. It was her place to be told first, ahead of the sisterhood. She would expect the whole truth, not just part of it. That was her right, as well as her responsibility, for being the deputy.

But the Magria had no intention of sharing everything. Until her fear was mastered, she did not dare.

"At last, I have been shown the future of our world," the Magria said. "The world approaches . . . chaos."

Anas blinked. "This is hardly unforeseen," she said impatiently. "Death is coming to the emperor. There are few in the world who have known anyone but him as its center."

"He will die soon. This final incarnation will not be as long as the others," the Magria said firmly.

"Then the rumors that say he will find the means to bargain anew for his life are false?"

"Yes."

Anas drew in a satisfied breath. "Ah."

"The laws of time have been bent as far as possible, and the shadow gods are impatient to end the bargain. They will claim him soon."

"He shall be glad to die," Anas said with a lack of mercy that made the Magria flinch. Anas stood straight and slender in her black robes. Her eyes were blue and clear. "A thousand years is enough. Most men would find it an intolerable burden."

"Most," the Magria agreed wearily. She sipped again

at the wine she had brought with her, needing its help. "But he is not like most."

"He will die in the arms of Beloth," Anas said fiercely. "He will find death ten times harder, to match the number of times he has cheated it."

"His death will come from the hand of one he trusts," the Magria said bleakly. She glanced up. "When does the bride arrive for our training?"

"Lord Albain has sent word. She comes to us in two weeks."

The Magria sipped her wine and let the silence grow.

Anas's eyes widened. "Our future empress will—"

The Magria lifted her hand in warning. "Much of that remains unclear," she said. But her mind was busy turning over the interpretation of her vision. The empress-elect would resist her training, would resist the emperor. As for the blue and the green . . . who were these men? Blue would be Prince Tirhin, but the green? No answer came to her. A mystery. The woman whom destiny had chosen as Kostimon's final empress would be embroiled in that mystery.

And I, thought the Magria, *will die when the emperor dies.*

Death she did not fear. Death at the hands of Beloth, god of destruction—yes, she feared that most implicitly.

"And the child we want from this union?" Anas asked, bringing the Magria's thoughts back to the present. "Was it foretold?"

"Unclear."

"How are we to train this bride if we do not know—"

"We have more to do than teach a girl how to become a queen," the Magria snapped. "Civil war is coming. The land will run bloody, and we will not be able to stand apart from what transpires."

"Are we in danger, then? All the Penestrican orders?"

"The gravest," the Magria said grimly. "Beloth has awakened."

Anas's eyes widened. "And . . . Mael?" She spoke the dreaded name very quietly. It was unwise to invoke the name of the goddess of destruction, that fearsome mate of Beloth. She walked clothed in famine and plague. With the distaff of suffering, she spun the fates of the doomed. The return of both was only a matter of time, thanks to Kostimon's opening of the gates.

The Magria shook her head. "I was shown much. I shall have to meditate long to understand it all."

"Will you try another visioning?"

The Magria did not answer.

Anas compressed her lips. "When will we have the answers we seek? Every delay only drives us farther away from power. How are we to train the bride if we do not understand the path that will be victorious for our purposes?"

There it was, the hunger and ambition that drove Anas, revealed for an instant like a flash of lightning at the window. The Magria tucked the knowledge into a pocket of her mind, satisfied that Anas had not yet completely mastered her emotions. Until then, she remained an ally, not a threat.

"What is to come is not yet determined. Destiny does not speak it. Another visioning will tell us no more than we know now." The Magria glanced up sharply. "Be assured the Vindicants know nothing more than we do. No one has the advantage right now."

Anas began to pace back and forth. Her black robes rustled about her, and in sudden impatience she untied her lacings and took off the garment. Leaving it beside the Magria's, she seemed freer and more at ease. She had the kind of body that pleased men, but she was not destined for such a purpose.

"What are your instructions?" Anas asked. "Do I change the bride's training?"

"Yes."

Anas stopped pacing. "Resta has prepared the usual course to teach the girl receptiveness to seduction and the arts of—"

"No," the Magria said sharply. She pressed together the scars that crisscrossed her palms, remembering their legacy. "I shall teach her myself."

"You!" Anas said in complete astonishment before she tried to master herself. "But—"

The Magria lifted her brows coolly. "You have objections?"

"No, of course not, but—it's just that you have taken no personal interest in the training of any of the imperial brides."

"Only the first," the Magria said softly. Her mind folded back to the memory of a tall, clear-eyed woman with a fiery temper and a will of iron. Fauvina came from a warrior family, a mob of squabbling warmongers who were finally defeated and tamed by Kostimon. Fauvina had been the object of truce, the bride, the settlement. She had gone to Kostimon's bed like a tigress, unwilling and furious. But genuine love had been born of their initial passion and hostility. With love came liking, and with liking came an alliance of both hearts and minds. As empress Fauvina had used her intellect well, fashioning many of the laws under which the empire still operated. She had been tough but fair. She often fought, but she could also listen. She had heeded the Magria's training, and under her sponsorship the Penestrican orders had spread and flourished. Women had known equality in the first century of the empire. They had owned property and could speak up for themselves.

"Kostimon loved her," the Magria said softly. "She believed in him, in what he could do. She took his dreams and made them hers. She gave him all the hope in her soul, and it strengthened his arm when he forged the provinces into an empire and changed the world forevermore. For that, he loved her."

"Fauvina refused his cup of immortality," Anas said flatly, appearing unimpressed by the sentiment of this recollection. "She lies as dust in her tomb, and we have an emperor who still seeks to cheat death."

Not until after her death had things changed. The purges under the Vindicants had been a horrible time. The Magria remembered sisters who had been burned alive, those who had been hunted and used by dreadots, moags, and worse for the entertainment of the new noble class. Some sisters had been tortured in ways far beyond physical torment by the inquisitors of the Vindicants.

This dark time of persecution and injustice had driven the Penestricans apart. A schism formed between those who wanted to cling to the true precepts of the goddess mother and those who wanted to forsake the gentle power of the earth for the vicious power of the goddess Mael. Finally they had broken apart, to be forever enemies, but the harm remained. Although through time the Penestricans had achieved some measure of trust again, they had never forgotten what Kostimon had allowed. And of late there had been a scattering of disturbances and incidents that warned that open persecution might return.

Now, however, after centuries of waiting, the Magria almost had the tool of her revenge in her hands. She thought again of her vision, aware that death awaited her. But, like Kostimon, she had lived a long time. It would be worth everything to see a woman of her training on the throne again. It would be worth everything to have some hand in the destiny of the new emperor who would follow Kostimon's reign.

"I shall train the bride," the Magria said firmly, lifting her head high. "No one else, not even you, will have the governing of her lessons until I am finished."

Anas still looked troubled. "Do we dare stir up old animosities?"

"If we don't act now, we shall never act! Don't be a

fool, Anas. I chose you as much for your courage as your intellect."

Color stained Anas's cheeks. She bowed her head. "Yes, Magria. As you say, so it shall be."

"Our banner shall once again fly with respect everywhere," the Magria said. "All the old wrongs shall be righted. And what Sien and his followers plan for us shall be thwarted." She smiled, and in her heart she drew a sword. "The revenge begins."

thirteen

UPSTAIRS, IN THE EAST WING OF LORD AL-
bain's stone palace, the tall windows stood wide open to
catch the cool breezes. Early morning sunlight spilled in,
bringing with it a warning of the intense heat to come.
Soon the muxa bugs would dry their dew-paralyzed wings
and come alive. The screens would have to be rolled down
over the windows for protection. Already, the jungle beyond the stalwart walls emitted screams and bird calls as
its day denizens awoke.

Within the suite of apartments belonging to Lady
Bixia, daughter of the house, all remained peaceful. The
sunshine glowed upon fine Ulinian carpets and walnut
chairs gracing the sitting room. Yesterday the room had
been complete chaos, piled high with scattered possessions, halfpacked trunks, and muslin packing cloths. Now
it had a stripped, empty feeling. The trunks had been carried away last night by the porters. The room stood bare
of Lady Bixia's favorite trinkets, music, sewing boxes,
and foot cushions. Only a trace of her scent lingered on
the air. Otherwise, it was as though she had not lived here

for eighteen years. Even the cages containing her parrot
and pet monkey had been swathed in traveling covers and
removed.

The double doors to Lady Bixia's bedchamber remained firmly closed, for although this was the grand day
of her departure, she never arose before noon.

Her servants had been up since before dawn, driven to
a frenzy of last-minute packing and preparations for the
comfort of their mistress.

Some servants had been up all night.

Crouching on the cool stone steps leading up to the
empty hearth, Elandra forced her sore and aching fingers
to keep stitching. She had to finish hemming this new
dressing robe so it could be packed. Only last night had
Bixia discovered the robe was too long. In a screaming
fit, she had ripped at the garment and flung it on the floor.
Elandra tried to clean it, and she'd been up all night sewing.

The stitches were not ordinary ones, but instead some
kind of intricate embroidery indicative of the finest hand-
work. It had taken hours to puzzle out the trick of the tiny
stitches.

Now Elandra was so tired her eyes would barely focus,
and she could not stop shivering from exhaustion. Glancing up for a moment and grimacing at the stiffness in her
neck, she realized the sunlight was finally brighter than
her little lamp. Leaning over, she blew out the flame and
sighed with her eyes closed.

If only she could rest for a moment.

But she dared not. Dragging her eyes open again, she
forced herself to regain her concentration. If she didn't
complete her task, it would be the switch for sure.

The needle jabbed into her finger, and she flinched.

Swiftly she stuck her bleeding finger into her mouth
and sucked at the wound. She couldn't afford to spill even
a tiny drop on the gorgeous white brocade fabric. It was
the finest cloth she'd ever touched, incredibly soft, and

beautifully cut by an expert seamstress. It was the only garment of Bixia's trousseau that Elandra had been allowed to see, much less handle, and its exquisiteness took her breath away. It did not deserve to be treated like a rag and flung about, even if it didn't fit the way Bixia wanted it to.

Quick footsteps approached the door to the sitting room, and it was shoved open without a knock.

Startled, Elandra looked up in dread, but it was only one of the maids hurrying in with her arms full of clothing freshly finished from the laundry downstairs.

Elandra sighed and relaxed. "Hello, Magan."

The woman looked surprised to see Elandra. "What are you doing in here?"

Elandra shrugged, although the taut muscles in her shoulders screamed from the movement. "I haven't finished with this yet."

Magan looked at the garment flowing from Elandra's lap, and her eyes widened. "Gods' mercy, what are you doing with *that*?"

"Mending it," Elandra said.

Magan's mouth opened, and she seemed about to say something before she changed her mind. "Give me that," she said with an apprehensive glance over her shoulder. "If the hag finds this, it'll be the end of you."

Elandra also looked at the doorway in apprehension. The threat was real enough. Hecati was a vicious taskmaster. Not the tiniest detail or omission ever escaped her vigilant eye.

"Come on, I say! There's no time to be lost."

"But I'm not finished," Elandra said. "I've got to or—"

"Don't be stupid. You can't be caught with this."

Elandra didn't argue further. The servants had protected her more than once. Folding the robe hastily to hide the unfinished hem, she gave it to Magan, who stuffed it quickly in between some of the other gowns.

"And the box it was in," the maid said. "Where's that?"

"I don't know. Bixia came out wearing it last night. That's when she found out it was too long and threw such a fit." Elandra frowned in growing consternation. "It's part of the trousseau, isn't it?"

"Never mind that. If we don't find the box, it's my back as well as yours."

"It might be in her bedchamber," Elandra suggested.

Magan made a face. "I'm not going in *there*. Let her get in trouble for once, playing with things such as this without a care for their importance." She clicked her tongue in disapproval.

The sound of voices in the corridor made both of them look. Elandra didn't hear Hecati's unmistakable tones, and relaxed again.

Magan shook her head. "The men are in the courtyard loading the elephants. I'll get these put in the last trunk to be carried downstairs, and we'll pray no one figures out what happened."

"Thank you, Magan," Elandra said. The maid had always treated her with kindness, and she was grateful.

Rolling her eyes, Magan sent Elandra a quick wink and hurried into the dressing room at the far side of the suite just as more maids hurried in with armloads of slippers and undergarments, looking excited in the general commotion.

Elandra watched them go by, and felt her own spirits rise. Bixia was being packed for her bridal journey, and good riddance as far as Elandra was concerned. In an hour her half-sister would be gone at last, and perhaps there would finally be peace in this house. If nothing else, Elandra was looking forward to having a life of her own without spoiled Bixia to fetch and carry for.

Elandra put away her needle case and tucked it in her pocket. She rose stiffly on legs that would barely support her. After sitting on the steps all night, she was so cramped and knotted she felt a hundred years old instead of seventeen. Yawning, she pushed her heavy tangle of hair back from her face and stretched with her hands on the small of her back. She wanted to fall into bed and sleep forever.

A whistling sound through the air was the only warning she had before pain stung her leg through her gown.

Elandra turned around in a fury, barely managing to hold her tongue. There stood Hecati, a thin, tiny woman who had a supple willow switch in her hands. Her plain face was pursed in its customary vinegary scowl, circled by a snowy white wimple that never looked creased or soiled no matter how hot and steamy the days got. Her eyes glared at Elandra with contempt.

Elandra glared back, resentful of this woman who had made her life a misery. *Be careful,* a small inner voice warned her. *Soon she'll be gone. You can hold yourself until then.* But it was hard to be prudent, especially now when freedom was so close.

"Idle good-for-nothing," Hecati scolded. "Everyone is working as fast as they can and you stand here like some great lady with no task to do."

"I just—"

"Silence! You haven't my leave to speak." Hecati's eyes narrowed suspiciously. "I've not seen you for hours. Where have you been? Hiding? Sleeping? Shirking?"

Alarm replaced Elandra's anger. Hecati still had plenty of time to punish her before the departure. Elandra moved back a half step. "No," she said in a low neutral voice. "I haven't been hiding. I've been hemming the—I mean, I've been doing some mending."

Hecati focused on her even more intently. "You're lying," she said. "What have you been doing?"

Elandra could have cursed her own hapless tongue. She was too tired to lie effectively. With Hecati she needed all her wits about her. "Nothing," she said resentfully.

"Exactly. Nothing. You are a lazy wretch." Hecati raised the willow switch threateningly. "Now tell me the truth!"

"I've done no wrong," Elandra insisted. How she wished this horrible woman would just go, but Hecati stood before her like a nightmare that never ended.

Hecati tapped her shoulder lightly with the switch, and Elandra flinched reflexively. Hecati permitted herself a tiny smile of satisfaction that made Elandra hate her even more. "I am still waiting for the truth, girl. Or do you want it beaten out of you?"

Elandra sighed. "I was just mending some of Bixia's—"

"That's Lady Bixia."

Elandra lowered her gaze to hide her resentment. "Some of Lady Bixia's old gowns that she wants to give to the servants as her departure gift."

"Lie! That work has already been done."

"Most of it," Elandra said hastily. "But there were a few items she found and—"

Hecati lifted her hand, and Elandra broke off her sentence. The woman considered the story, her hostile eyes staring implacably at Elandra.

She had always been a foe. From the first day Hecati arrived years ago to take charge of Bixia's upbringing, battle lines had been drawn between her and Elandra. She had made her favoritism plain, taking obvious pride in the fact that her sister had given birth to Bixia. At first she had tried to get rid of Elandra, shutting her away, refusing to let her play with Bixia. Lord Albain had put a stop to that. Then Hecati had tried to have Elandra sent away. Albain had refused that also. He wanted his daughters raised together. Beyond that, he let Hecati do as she pleased, and it pleased her to turn Elandra into Bixia's personal slave.

But you are leaving today, Elandra thought, clinging to her one hope. *You are leaving forever and taking Bixia with you.*

"Truth and lies," Hecati murmured, her gaze rolling upward. "Truth and lies. You have been sewing all night—"

"Yes," Elandra said quickly and held her breath. She tried to think of something that would distract Hecati. If Hecati even suspected part of what she'd done, Elandra knew she would—

Hecati struck her with the switch. "Wrong has been done! What do you conceal from me? Answer me!"

As she spoke, she hit Elandra again.

The switch stung like fire. Elandra backed away, although trying to dodge punishment only made Hecati whip harder. "I'm concealing nothing!" she cried.

More blows rained down on her. Each one stung viciously.

"Speak the truth or say nothing at all!" Hecati commanded. "How dare you practice your mischief on this of all days?"

Cornered against the wall, Elandra endured the whipping. The switch was an awful weapon, for although it hurt terribly it raised only temporary welts and never made any permanent damage. There was never any proof to carry to her father.

With each slash, Elandra bit her lip hard to keep herself from crying out. Her cheeks burned with rage and humiliation. Defiantly, however, she refused to let any tears spill from her brimming eyes. She wished the gods would strike Hecati dead of apoplexy. She wished she dared wrest the switch from Hecati's hands so she could hit her back. A corner of her mind knew this beating was Hecati's last chance of punishing her simply for her existence, but that did not lessen the humiliation of it.

Finally the whipping stopped. Hecati stepped back, letting the tip of her switch rest on the floor. She was breathing hard, and her eyes glowed as though she had enjoyed what she inflicted. "Well?" she demanded.

It was the old ritual, carried out again and again through the years.

Elandra's ears were roaring. She held her head very

high as she forced herself to straighten away from the wall and turn around. Her eyes swam with tears, but she blinked fiercely in an effort to hold them back. Sunshine from the window behind her blazed in across her shoulders, and its heat made the welts hurt more. Hating the old woman, Elandra bowed her head and knelt at Hecati's feet in a pool of sunlight. She took the hem of Hecati's starched linen gown with its sheer overlay of silk gauze and kissed it while resentment pounded through her with such force she felt dizzy.

If only I knew the forbidden ways, she thought to herself. *I would risk perdition gladly to pay this creature back for her cruelty.*

Hecati put her slippered foot on top of Elandra's head, forcing her face to the carpet. "I am the aunt of the future empress of the world. What are you?"

Elandra nearly choked, but she forced herself to utter the answer. *This is the last time*, she promised herself. "I am nothing," she replied as she had been taught so long ago.

"You have been punished."

"As I—I deserve," Elandra said.

For that little break in her voice, Hecati's foot pushed even harder. With her face mashed against the carpet, Elandra breathed in its dust and fibers and knew the choking helplessness of being entirely at another's mercy.

"Should I punish you again?"

Elandra gritted her teeth on the expected answer. *No!* her heart cried within her. Her hands curled into fists on the rug. "Yes," she finally whispered, although she shook against the temptation to grab the switch and give Hecati a taste of it. "I—I should be punished again."

Hecati removed her foot from Elandra's head. "I think perhaps you should. There is anger in your voice today. Yes, and defiance too. You have not answered my questions either."

Trying not to sob, Elandra pressed her face against the rug and dared not make a sound.

Finally, Hecati stepped back. "There is not time to deal with you suitably. I read your heart, girl. I know you are eager to see Lady Bixia and me go."

Crouched there, Elandra still seethed, but she tried to control herself. "Lady Bixia must go to her destiny," Elandra managed to say. "It is time for her life to change."

Hecati sniffed. "Yes, how eagerly you say it. You think that when we are gone you will be made into a lady, that you will run this palace, that you will even sit at your father's right hand during banquets. Oh, yes, I know what is in your devious heart. But you will have none of those honors. Bastards deserve to remain hidden away. Without us here, you'll be relegated to the lowest end of the servants' hall. You can spend your years scrubbing pots and killing beetles in the kitchen, for all I care."

Elandra lifted her face to Hecati. "He is not as cruel as you."

Hecati blinked at this defiance; then her eyes narrowed. "That tongue of yours should have been cut out at birth. Your father forgets your existence half the time. See if he remembers you at all when we are gone."

Elandra drew in a sharp breath, but before she could reply, Hecati gripped her by the arm and pulled her upright.

"Stand over there, out of the way, and wait until you are summoned to assist dressing Lady Bixia."

Shoving Elandra aside, Hecati opened the double doors leading into Bixia's bedchamber and went in.

A frown knotted Elandra's brow, and she let out her breath in a gusty sigh of relief. The whipping still hurt, but it was the humiliation that cut deepest. She leaned against the wall. Her eyes were stinging, and the tears spilled out before she could stop them. She brought up both hands and pressed them against her trembling lips, trying to pull herself back under control.

Before she succeeded, however, Hecati came storming out of Bixia's room with an elaborately carved box of walnut in her hands. Her face was livid.

"Here is the box!" she cried. "The special box for the bridal robe. Empty!" She dropped it onto a chair and glared at Elandra. "I knew you were up to some wickedness! What have you done with the bridal robe?"

"Nothing!" Elandra said. She slapped her tears from her cheeks and told herself she should have fled the room the minute Hecati was out of sight.

"You're lying," Hecati said. "Here is the box, its seal broken and its contents stolen. You're a thief as well as a liar. What have you done with it?"

Elandra tried desperately to think of an answer that would spare her another beating, but she was too tired to think. "I know nothing about that box. I did not open it."

Hecati advanced on her, and Elandra had to force herself not to shrink away. It was not her fault, she reminded herself. She must stick to the truth, no matter what.

"The bridal robe has been sewn under a special blessing," Hecati said furiously. "I packed it away in this special box for safekeeping with my own hands." Hecati's voice faded away and she glared at Elandra, her face turning redder with every passing second. She gripped Elandra by the arm, her fingers digging in like claws.

"You got it out, didn't you?" she accused. "You wanted to see it, knowing no hands must touch it until the wedding day. You wanted to ruin Lady Bixia's happiness in any way you could. You jealous little bitch!"

She slapped Elandra a hard, numbing blow, and would have hit her again, but Elandra wrenched free. Hecati lifted the switch to strike her. Elandra caught it and pulled it away from her.

The switch vanished in her grip as though it had never existed. Elandra gasped, and backed away in fear. "What magic is this?" she whispered, then ran for the door.

"Magan! Trina!" she called. "Send for a *jinja*—"

An invisible hand gripped her throat. Elandra stopped in her tracks and put her hands to her throat, where the pressure was choking her. It tightened, closing off her air until she writhed in desperation.

Then the pressure ceased, and she was free.

Gasping and coughing, Elandra dropped to her knees and gulped in lungfuls of air. Her throat burned with pain.

Fear grew inside her, a cold, numbing fear that made her legs feel as weak as water. Her heart was pounding as though she had run up the thousand steps of the palace. She shuddered and closed her eyes. But she could sense the magic in the room. Her hair tugged at her scalp as though it stood on end from static electricity. She could smell something very faint but unpleasantly scorched. She swallowed hard and refused to look at Hecati.

The old woman strode over to her with a swish of her long skirts. "You force my hand," she said in a low, furious voice. "Damn you!"

Elandra shook her head and lowered herself like a toad. "Please," she whispered. "*Please, don't*—"

"You have gone too far," Hecati told her. There was something horrible in her voice, a menace beyond mere anger. Elandra bit back a moan of fear and shivered. "Too far! I give you one last warning to tell me the truth now regarding the robe, or I'll carve open the back of your worthless skull with my fingertip."

She ran her fingernail over Elandra's head, and Elandra flinched. It was all she could do not to leap up in terror.

Instead, she crouched at Hecati's feet, hating and fearing her as never before. Her mind was blank. She was sweating in the rising heat. She felt like she would be sick, and yet she had to find an answer.

"Please," she whispered.

"Speak!"

The command made her jump in her skin. Her heart whammed harder. Elandra struggled to find her voice.

"Bixia took out the robe because she wanted to try it on. She—"

Hecati cried out in rage. "You'll regret this, you she-demon. Everything you've said is a slandering, scurrilous lie."

Elandra raised herself in desperation, hurling the naked truth now like a weapon. "Ask Bixia! How else would I be allowed to touch anything to do with the wedding? Ask her!"

"I will not disturb her precious sleep with such a trifle. Why should she defend *you*?"

Why indeed? Elandra thought bitterly. Bixia was certainly capable of lying when it was to her advantage.

"Fool!" Hecati paced back and forth, fuming. "You have ruined it. Where is it? Give it to me at once."

Guilt sprinkled over Elandra. Now it would be inspected. Hecati would find where it had been spot-cleaned. She would find the wrinkles. She would see the unfinished hemming. She would notice the practice stitches that Elandra had botched before she caught the knack of the difficult embroidery.

"I didn't know it was that special," Elandra said, trying to defend herself. "Lady Bixia tried it on and was angry that it was too long. She threw it on the floor and I—"

"Be silent. You have always tried to cause all the trouble you could, but this action is unpardonable. Even Albain cannot forgive this." Hecati threw Elandra a look that was almost triumphant. "This time, you have ruined yourself."

Turning away, Hecati clapped her hands sharply until Magan peered in through the doorway.

"Yes, mistress?" Magan asked warily.

Elandra had no doubt the servants had heard every word.

"The dressing robe for the bridal night. Bring it," Hecati commanded.

Magan cast Elandra an unreadable glance. Elandra

looked back and quickly shook her head, but the maid was already gone. Elandra sighed. If Magan was smart, she would flee while she had the chance.

Freedom had been so close, just an hour away. Elandra felt fresh tears well up in her eyes, but she fought them back. It was no good feeling sorry for herself. Finding out Hecati practiced the forbidden arts was enough of a shock. Elandra warned herself not to breathe, not to move. She must take care.

But why couldn't it be enough that Hecati had accomplished her life's work? Why couldn't she be generous and forgiving just once? Bixia was going to be the new bride of the emperor, living in honor and unimaginable glory for the rest of her days. Hecati would have a place at court. Anyone else would be merciful for a small transgression, but not Hecati.

The old witch got too much satisfaction from hurling out this last punishment.

Elandra stole a quick glance at her, beginning to feel fresh resentment now that her shock was fading.

"You're a fool," Hecati said scornfully. "You've let your jealousy go too far this time. But you won't get away with it. I promise you that."

Elandra started to plead with her once again, but choked on the words. She couldn't go on begging. Not when this wasn't her fault. "If you would only hear my side," she said instead. "I've done only what I was asked to do. I—"

The door to Bixia's bedchamber wrenched open, and the bride came out.

Sunshine blazed over her, highlighting the masses of golden curls tumbling down her back. Her nightgown had slipped down off one plump shoulder, revealing skin that was pale and rosy. She yawned hugely, lifting her arms in a stretch that let the sunshine strike transparently through her gown, revealing the buxom curves beneath it.

Hecati pinned on a bright smile in an abrupt change of

mood and rushed to her. "Good morning, my lady!" she said, her voice like honey. "The weather has dawned perfect today. Most auspicious for our journey."

Bixia yawned again and frowned at her. "It's already hot. Where's my fan bearer? Why isn't she stirring the air for my comfort? And why are you two caterwauling outside my door at this ungodly hour? Be quiet. I'm going back to bed."

"But, my lady, you must allow your attendants to dress you. We leave in a few minutes. Even now your father is downstairs, ready to bid you farewell."

Bixia's shrewd, cat-green eyes darted around. "I'm sure Father is eager to see the last of me. And eager to start counting his new wealth." Tossing her head, she strolled back into her bedchamber.

"My lady, do not, I beg you, crawl back into bed." Looking frustrated, Hecati started in after her, but turned back at the doorway and glared at Elandra.

"You are not dismissed," she said in a low, vicious voice. "We are not finished with this matter."

Elandra drew an unsteady breath and climbed to her feet. Her gaze went to the door. This time when she got the chance, she would run. She could find a place to hide, and she wasn't going to come out until Hecati was gone.

Hecati's eyes narrowed suspiciously. She lifted her hand, and the willow switch reappeared magically. It whistled through the air, and Elandra jumped back to dodge it.

"Lady Hecati," interrupted one of the attendants timidly.

Hecati whirled around. "Yes?"

The girl came forward, holding the crumpled white dressing robe in her hands.

With a cry, Hecati yanked it from her and held it up. The luxurious folds tumbled to the floor. In the clear light, all the wrinkles could be seen. The soil marks showed also, as well as the water rings where Elandra had tried to clean them away.

Hecati's horror mottled her neck and face with color. She threw the robe on the floor. "What did you do with this? Dust the furniture with it? It's ruined."

Elandra gathered it up. "It can be cleaned and pressed. I'll—"

"Take your filthy hands off it. You're not worthy to touch it."

Hecati seized one side of the robe and tried to yank it away from Elandra. The cloth ripped, and both of them stopped their struggle, equally aghast.

Elandra was the first to recover. She dropped the robe and backed away. Fear tasted sour in her mouth. She wasn't going to be blamed for this. She refused to be blamed for this.

She looked around for the attendant, but the girl had vanished. None of the servants were in sight, and even the background chatter in the dressing room had fallen silent, as though they were all listening . . . or hiding.

Hecati flung the robe down and turned on Elandra. Her mouth drew back in a grimace, and her eyes held such anger Elandra backed up yet farther.

"You have defiled this, the symbol of a sacred union. It took the woman of Mahira ten months to sew it. Every thread, every stitch was blessed. It was pressed in sacred steam and scented with rosemary and hyssop. It was locked in a box for safekeeping, not to be seen or handled until the wedding night. This is what you have destroyed."

Elandra's pulse pounded in her throat and temples. Dismay filled her with every word Hecati uttered. She had not known, for she wasn't allowed to participate in the trousseau preparations. She had seen none of the fabulous court gowns made for Bixia. Whenever something new was delivered from the dressmaker's, Elandra had been dismissed from the room by Hecati. Last night, when Bixia offered to model some of her new things for Elandra, it had seemed at last as though they were sisters. Elandra had been pleased by Bixia's generosity, at least until Bixia had one of her temper fits and ordered Elandra to re-hem the robe.

Had she known of its significance, Elandra would never have touched it. And indeed, she had done her best to save the ruin that Bixia had started and Hecati had finished.

Now Bixia appeared a second time. Her nightgown hung even lower off her shoulder, revealing the heavy top of one breast. She was still yawning. "What are you yelling about?"

Mutely Hecati pointed at the robe lying on the floor.

Bixia stared at it and nudged its folds with her toe. "That's my bridal robe."

"Yes, my lady," Hecati said in a hollow voice.

"It's ruined."

"Yes, my lady." Hecati's eyes stabbed into Elandra like pins. "Your half-sister is to blame."

"No!" Elandra said. She looked at Bixia in desperation. "Tell her that you asked me to shorten it for you. Tell her!"

Bixia's green eyes didn't even waver. "It's been torn to pieces. Why did you do such a thing? Don't you care that it's sacred?"

Her accusation left Elandra stunned. "But I—you tried it on and didn't like it. You—"

Flatly Bixia said. "Don't be ridiculous. I would never play with my sacred bridal robe. It's evil of you to lie."

Hecati's head lifted and she seemed to grow taller and larger, filled with vindication. A gleam of satisfaction entered her eyes.

Hurt punctured Elandra. She tried to fight it off, tried to deny all feeling. Bixia never told the truth when a lie served her better. Elandra should have known Bixia wouldn't risk getting into trouble.

Hecati rubbed her thin hands together. "Now," she

whispered, glaring intently at Elandra. "The time has
come to finish you."

Elandra drew back, desperately looking around the
room for something to fight back with. But how could she
fight the forbidden ways? Refusing to give up, she shoved
off her growing despair. If she could circle around and
reach the door . . .

"Girls!" Lord Albain bellowed from outside the suite.
"Enough dallying. Everything is loaded. The beasts aren't
going to be kept standing while you primp and fool
about."

The three women stood silent, frozen in place.

Elandra gasped aloud in relief and pressed her hands
to her mouth. "Father," she whispered.

The door to the suite swung open, and a slim, green-
skinned *jinja* slid inside. No taller than Elandra's waist,
the creature wore a sleeveless vest and wide trousers embroidered richly with gold thread and tiny jewels. It had
a triangular face, huge eyes, tiny vicious teeth, and
pointed ears. It made the motions of walking, although
most of the time its small feet did not really touch the
floor. As Elandra stared at it, it paused just inside the door
and sniffed the air. Then, quicker than the eye could follow, it darted about the room—here, there, and back
again, before pausing at the open window. Where the sunshine hit it, the *jinja's* green skin shimmered translucently,
like colored glass.

"All is safe to enter, master," the *jinja* called. "No poison. No assassin. No spells."

Elandra whipped her head around to look at it in
amazement. Couldn't it smell the magic that had been
used in the room? But her own nostrils no longer detected
the faint scorched scent of Hecati's spell. She realized
Hecati had been fooling the *jinja* for years. Elandra's fear
grew. Hecati must be powerful indeed. But even she
would not dare act openly in front of Lord Albain, who
could have her put to death.

"You stupid creature!" Hecati said sharply to the *jinja*. "Who would offer his lordship danger here?"

Ignoring her, the *jinja* licked the tips of its little fingers and began to clean its ears with them.

Gihaud Albain strode inside with his customary impatience, spurs jingling with every step.

He was a tall, broad man. Not fat but square, with massive shoulders and thick arms. His hair had once been fiery red, but had now faded to a rich gold. It was shaved off the front half of his skull and worn in a long warrior's ponytail. He was dressed in his ceremonial mail leggings and embossed armored breastplate. He carried his embroidered gauntlets in one hand, and his dress sword clanked at his side. With his scarred cheek and missing eye, he looked tough and gnarled even in his fancy regalia. Lord Albain was responsible for holding the south border of the empire against the barbarians, and he did his job very well. At present, there was peace, and he had been bored and restless all spring from the inactivity. But today he looked content, even proud, and he strode in with a vigor that seemed startling in the secluded surroundings of this womanly apartment.

The sight of Bixia in her nightgown made him frown. "Girl! You idle lazybones, get dressed! Are you daft, to be dawdling on a day like this? We can't keep the Penestricans waiting. Nor the imperial escort waiting down in the courtyard. They're already mounted."

Bixia tossed her head, oblivious to his shouting. "Let them wait," she said haughtily. "I am to be the next empress. I can take as much time as I want."

Bristling, Albain shook his thick forefinger at her. "Now, listen to me, you spoiled—"

"My lord," Hecati interceded hastily. "There is good reason why your daughter is not ready. Hear me, sir. She has been betrayed by one close to her. By one she trusted with all her heart. Yes, and worse than that, your lordship has been betrayed as well by this same fiend." Hecati's eyes flashed. "The entire marriage agreement between Lady Bixia and Emperor Kostimon now lies in jeopardy."

fourteen

ALBAIN LOWERED HIS HAND. "WHAT?" HE said blankly. "Jeopardy? Betrayal? Are you sure?"

"Yes, my lord." Hecati gestured mournfully at the robe lying on the floor. "The sacred bridal robe has been torn beyond repair. I'm sure your lordship knows the terrible omen this constitutes for Lady Bixia's wedded happiness."

"Superstition," Bixia said; then, under her father's steady glare, she hitched her nightgown up properly over both shoulders.

"I hope that was a joke, daughter," he said with severity.

Bixia swallowed and dropped her eyes. "Yes, father."

"Heresy, even in jest, is a bad habit. I doubt you'll have the freedom at court to speak your mind as freely as you do here."

Her head came up defiantly, but at the last moment she said nothing. Her gaze went to Elandra, and she shrugged.

Lord Albain scowled at the robe. "Isn't this the piece that cost me nearly nine hundred ducats?"

"Yes, my lord," Hecati said.

Elandra gasped, and even Bixia looked impressed.

Hecati's eyes narrowed to slits. She watched Elandra closely, like a cat eyeing its prey.

Albain looked a bit stunned, but he rallied. "Bixia's got other robes. One of them will have to do."

"But, Father!" Bixia wailed. "The others aren't blessed. I can't marry the emperor like a rag girl. I have to have a robe from Mahira. You know how important it is."

"No!" he said explosively. "Murdeth and Fury, girl. You'll make a pauper of me."

Tears welled up in Bixia's green eyes. "I can't go through with it. My bridal robe is ruined, and my marriage will be cursed forever."

"Enough of that!" he said roughly, but helplessness had entered his gaze. "Oh, hell's breath. Don't start that drizzling. We'll see what can be done."

"Oh, Father, thank you!" Bixia flung her arms around his neck, standing on tiptoe to kiss his scarred cheek. "You're so good to me. So kind and generous."

He patted her shoulder and cleared his throat with gratification. "We'll see. Now mind you, get dressed in a hurry."

Beaming, Bixia vanished back into her bedchamber with a slam of the door. Her gong rang, summoning attendants. One of Elandra's duties was to help her sister dress every morning. Right now, however, she scarcely dared breathe, and she did not move.

"What is to be done, my lord?" Hecati asked. "The wedding cannot proceed as planned—"

"It must!" he shouted, then grimaced and raised his hand in placation. "No delays," he said in a more reasonable tone of voice. "Damn it all, I won't insult the emperor all because of an accursed nightgown!"

"Your daughter must have the raiment that is her due."

"Hell's teeth, woman! I've spent a fortune already on her damned trousseau."

"That is not the issue," Hecati said coolly. "Brides of high lineage are traditionally sent to their marriage beds in Mahiran bridal robes. The blessing was to ensure a swift conception of an heir. If Lady Bixia fails in this duty, there will be—"

"Enough," he said heavily and wiped perspiration from his brow. "No need to spell out what I understand perfectly. All must go on as planned. I'll send word to Mahira about getting a replacement. Damnation! I could buy a new war mount for the cost. Or a trio of young elephants."

The *jinja* darted over to Elandra and swirled around her in a green blur before joining Albain. The baron draped a fond hand over the creature's narrow shoulder.

"Must this horrid thing remain in the room?" Hecati asked with visible uneasiness. She made a shooing motion, which it ignored. "All is proven safe. It does not need to linger here."

"Who was whipped, master?" the *jinja* asked with a wicked grin that showed its pointed teeth.

Albain ignored its question, but spots of color appeared on Hecati's cheeks.

Elandra watched them closely. Thus far they had ignored her. She eased one step away. Then another, hoping the *jinja* would be quiet about the whipping. She wanted no attention turned on her now. There would be time to explain the truth to her father later, when Hecati was gone.

But Hecati turned her head and looked straight at Elandra. "As for who did this ignominious—"

The *jinja* swirled around. "Lies in the room. Lies in the room."

"Hush," Albain admonished it.

Looking hurt, the *jinja* darted over to the window and crouched on the sill with a sulky face.

"Enough sly accusations," Elandra said, stepping forward. She looked at her father. "Lady Hecati blames me for what happened to the robe."

Albain's single eye met her gaze, and he frowned. She had his jaw, his temper, and his auburn hair. Her height and slender figure she'd gotten from her mother. Her mind was her own, and she'd fought tooth and nail all her life to get it educated.

She knew he had other illegitimate children besides herself. There were several stablehands running about with the Albain hair or the Albain jaw.

But she was the only highborn bastard in his progeny, her lineage proud on both sides. Why her mother had consorted with Albain, breaking her own marriage vows while her husband was away at war, had never been told. Why her mother had not kept Elandra, but instead sent her to Albain when she was four years old, was also unexplained. As long as Bixia's good-natured mother was alive, Elandra had been well treated and happy within the household. When Lady Ousia died trying to bear Albain's son, her sister Hecati came to take charge of the children.

"There, she admits her guilt to you, my lord," Hecati said now while Elandra faced her father's glare. "She has cost you nine hundred ducats—no, double that if the robe is to be replaced suitably. And all because she envies her half-sister's good fortune."

Elandra glanced at the *jinja*, but it was still pouting on the windowsill, gazing outside. It was a creature of whim. Its only allegiance was to her father. She couldn't depend on its help at all. Her heart sank.

Albain looked at her with disappointment. Her throat choked, but she refused to lower her proud chin even a fraction. All she'd ever wanted was his affection, but he was a busy man who spared scant time for family. She had been hoping that with Bixia and Hecati gone, she and her father might finally become companions.

It killed her for him to look at her this way now.

"I admit no wrongdoing," she said, her voice low with the effort not to cry. "I deny their accusations."

"Wicked girl!" Hecati said angrily. "Your defiance

does you no good. You hate and envy your half-sister. Admit your jealousy. You are a horrid, lying trouble-maker."

"Lady Hecati," Albain said sharply, "mind your tone."

Hecati bowed at once. "Forgive me, my lord. But this wretch—"

"—is my daughter."

Something unreadable crossed Hecati's face. She swallowed. "Yes, my lord. But as a bastard—"

He scowled. "Elandra's maternal side comes from one of the most venerable and ancient bloodlines in Gialta. My own lineage is equally faultless. The fact that she was born of a love union rather than a sacramented one does not give you leave to yell at her like a fishwife."

A tiny smile quivered on Elandra's lips. He filled her eyes, a hero. His fairness and justice was on her side to-day, and she gazed at him with love, pleased to have such a champion.

Hecati turned red. She curtsied. "Again, I beg my lord's forgiveness."

He grunted and turned back to his daughter. "Elandra, you will tell me the truth of this matter."

For a moment it all rushed up inside Elandra, the urge to tell him everything about the way she was treated, the trick Bixia had pulled with the bridal robe, the scuffle with Hecati that had torn it. But instinct warned her to take care. She felt danger around her, like a hot wind blowing across the plains. The *jinja* apparently did not sense it; perhaps it was only her imagination. But she had learned the hard way not to underestimate Hecati's menace. And if she lost her temper or grew shrill in what she said, her father would not listen to her. Experience had taught her that as well.

She could not accuse Bixia, his golden child. His sense of fairness would stretch only so far.

Swallowing hard, Elandra said, "Last night before she retired, Lady Bixia asked me to shorten one of her dressing robes because it was far too long for her."

"A lie!" Hecati broke in. "You took the robe from the box and deliberately ruined it—"

"No!" Elandra insisted, her eyes flashing. "I knew nothing about its special significance. I never saw any box." She turned her gaze to her father, who was frowning. "The robe dragged on the floor, and Bixia was very upset."

"Everything was made to exact measurements," Hecati said. "I do not understand why you persist in this false tale when anyone knows it's untrue."

Elandra picked up the robe off the floor and held it up. "Look," she said. "I worked all night to replace the hem. See where I didn't finish? See how long it is?"

She held it against her. "As it was, it would have fit me because I am much taller than Bixia. But it looked terrible on her. I really tried to help her, Father." She upended the garment and showed him the stitches she'd sewn. "See the embroidery? I tried very hard to replicate it. And all would have been well had I had another hour to finish it."

Her father took the white brocade in his broad, battle-scarred hands. "How came it to be ripped?"

Elandra's gaze shifted to Hecati, who opened her mouth, then pinched it together very tightly. Hecati's eyes were glittering with warning, but as frightened as she was, Elandra wasn't going to lie. In a faint voice, she answered her father's question: "I was trying to show Lady Hecati what I had done when she lost her temper and grabbed it from my hand."

Hecati's face drained of color. "You—you—"

Albain scowled, and Hecati choked on the rest of her sentence. "This work is very fine, daughter," he said. "I cannot tell where your stitches begin and the others leave off."

Elandra smiled at the praise. "Thank you, Father. I tried my best. I'm sorry I could not finish it. And now it's torn. If I'd known it had been blessed, I wouldn't have touched it. You must believe that."

He met her eyes, but his own gaze still held doubt. "How could you be ignorant of such an important part of your sister's trousseau? That is the weakness of your story, which makes me doubt the whole."

"But I haven't seen the trousseau, Father," Elandra said.

His brows drew together, and now he did look disbelieving. "What is this? Have you no interest in Bixia's good fortune? I did not raise you to be petty and jealous, Elandra."

Anger sparked in her. *You did not raise me at all,* she thought with resentment. *You gave me instead to this creature.*

"My lord," Hecati said nervously, keeping an eye on the *jinja.* "We have not encouraged Elandra to loiter about during the fittings and viewings. The child would have only been bored, and I didn't want her to feel envious or left out by seeing the sumptuous gowns which are so far above her own station."

Albain looked blank. "I'm sure Elandra has no cause to feel envy. Her own gowns are pretty enough. I've made sure of that. Except for this ugly rag she's wearing this morning."

Elandra stared at him and felt fresh emotions welling up inside her. How to explain that his gifts were locked away in the cupboard, to be worn only on rare important occasions when she and Bixia dined with him?

Hecati was sputtering, but her voice died away when Albain shot her a sharp glance.

"Or does my daughter have pretty gowns to wear? It seems that whenever I glimpse her running through the grounds or the palace, she is always dressed in dull garb like this. Dressed like a servant."

"Too many pretty things make a young girl vain," Hecati said. "Besides, Bixia must come first."

"Of course Bixia comes first," Albain said impatiently. "That does not mean Elandra is to be neglected. I have spoken to you about this before, Hecati. I thought the matter settled."

"Of course, my lord," Hecati said in a voice as smooth and brittle as glass.

"Elandra, have you anything to complain about?" Albain asked.

She drew in a sharp breath, ready to tell him everything, but Hecati cleared her throat in soft warning.

Involuntarily Elandra tensed. Since childhood she had been trained not to tell her father anything. She could not count how many whippings it had taken to make the habit of silence strong within her. Now she stood tongue-tied and afraid, despising herself for her own cowardice, yet unable to take the chance he offered her.

Albain swung away impatiently. "I do not like to hear of these disturbances," he said grouchily, tapping his gauntlets on his palm, his gaze already darting about the room. "It is unbecoming for ladies."

Elandra held back what she might have said. He hated arbitration, and household arguments usually made him furious. He had little patience with hearing both sides of a matter and often punished everyone involved rather than deal with the issue. She reminded herself that in a short while Hecati and Bixia would be gone. Her troubles would be over.

"No complaints, Father," she said quietly. "I know my place."

His brows lifted, but Hecati nodded. "Exactly," she said with approval. "The girl knows her place, which is to serve her sister."

Albain made no contradiction, and Hecati smiled with renewed boldness.

"Perhaps," she said with false generosity, "I have overreacted. While Elandra made a dreadful mistake in what she did, I see now that she was only trying to help her sister last night. Of course the poor misguided child should have asked me first before undertaking such a project. Much of the disaster could then have been averted. As it is, I'm afraid Elandra's mistake will prove to be a very expensive one for your lordship to remedy."

His frown deepened, and Elandra thought about the nine hundred ducats with a fresh pang of worry.

"I am sorry for the trouble I have caused, Father," she said softly. "How can I make amends for something so costly?"

As she spoke, she saw a tiny smile of satisfaction flit across Hecati's mouth. Elandra knew Hecati was pleased to be able to turn the blame onto her. If Albain came to think her a fool, or worse, someone who was too much trouble to keep around, what then would become of her? Her position in his household was tenuous. She had no rights of her own, and suddenly she had never been more aware of that. Her breath stilled in her lungs.

Albain cleared his throat. "It seems to me that the least part of the blame is yours, daughter."

Elandra looked up in surprise.

Hecati frowned.

He continued: "Bixia knew this garment was sacred and not to be touched. What was she doing prancing about in it? Even to show it off to you, Elandra, she had no business doing that."

Hecati tried to speak up, but he scowled at her.

"If it did not fit, and I do not see how it could, why didn't she inform you at once? Why demand that Elandra sit up all night in an effort to mend it? An insurmountable task, for all this child's impressive skill with a needle." His scowl deepened. "Small wonder she stands here looking dead tired, with dark circles under her eyes. This is not service. It's abuse. And why does Elandra submit to it? Because she's been trained to think that's her place? Who did that to her?"

His scowl aimed itself at Hecati, who raised both hands.

"Now, my lord. You must not misunderstand the situation. You requested that I raise Elandra in domestic training, and—"

"Aye, teach her how to supervise servants and manage a household," he said angrily. "Teach her grace and poise and accomplishments, not to run about in a patched gown a scullion would be ashamed to wear, with dirt on her cheek and her hair uncombed, and her spirit fair scared out of her."

"She's a headstrong, temperamental girl," Hecati replied with equal heat. "Hard to train and rebellious. Strong measures have been called for to teach her her place. If I've made her take a servant's role to Lady Bixia from time to time, it's only to make her understand that she is not Lady Bixia's equal."

"Isn't she?" he asked with an edge to his voice.

"Of course not. The factors of her birth—"

"Elandra's mother was better born than Bixia's!" he roared.

Hecati sniffed. "But not under lawful union with yourself, my lord."

"At our rank, what does that matter?" he said. "You have common ideas, woman. Aye, and common morals as well."

Reddening, Hecati drew herself up. "I can see my years of effort are unappreciated. Well, you'll soon learn for yourself what your baseborn daughter's really like when you're thrown into her company, my lord. Perhaps you will regret not heeding my warnings about her."

"Elandra is not to blame for what transpired between her mother and me," he said.

"Her very presence is an affront to Bixia and the memory of my dear sister Ousia!" Hecati cried.

"And so you punish Elandra because you cannot punish me?" he retorted, his voice very quiet and very, very angry now.

The room fell silent. Hecati looked tense and alarmed, as though she realized she had gone too far.

Albain turned to Elandra and stared at her hard.

It was a glare such as he gave his men during inspection. She felt reduced to a speck, insignificant and worthless. She had fallen short of his expectations somehow, and yet she did not see how she could have done better . . . unless it was to have avoided the traps Bixia set for her.

Elandra's mouth went dry. She was so tired. Her eyes felt like grit. Her wits were muddled. All she wanted was for him to dismiss her so that she could escape this room and this woman. But she dared not give way to tears or exhaustion. Albain despised weakness in anyone. The only way to keep his good favor was to be strong. She could not whimper. She could not sway. With all her willpower she forced herself to meet his gaze steadily, her chin high and her aching shoulders straight. It was a struggle to keep her mouth from trembling.

Albain snapped his fingers. "*Jinja*, here."

The creature darted to his side immediately.

Albain pointed at Elandra. "It is ended," he said angrily. "It has gone on long enough. Release her."

Before Elandra could even guess at what he meant, the *jinja* jumped at her. Its hands brushed across her face, and it was as though ice touched her skin.

A wave of dizziness passed through her. She swayed, blinking against a sudden blur in her vision. For a moment she felt strangely cold and empty. Her mind was blank. She opened her mouth, but could not speak.

Albain's arm steadied her. "Gently, my girl," he said with kindness. "It will pass quickly."

Even as he spoke, the dizziness faded. She blinked and felt stronger, more confident, somehow free. She could not explain it, and gazed at him in puzzlement.

Oddly enough, it was he who avoided her eyes now.

His gaze returned to Hecati, who still looked alarmed.

"You took much advantage of what has been commanded of us, sister-in-name. How will you treat her now?"

Hecati's nostrils flared a moment; then she seemed to rally. "She has always been difficult. What will she do now that you've unleashed her to act as she pleases? Let her tear down the palace?"

Elandra's puzzlement grew. She looked at first one and then the other. "I don't understand."

"Well," her father said uneasily. "Well, perhaps it is better some things are left unsaid." For a moment he studied her with an odd expression on his face. "You are a good girl, Elandra. A good daughter. You think I don't know what goes on in this household, that I've been blind to the way you've been treated, but that's not so. I let it happen."

Elandra's eyes widened. She stared at him with growing shock.

"Aye, I did. And hard it was, too. I stepped in sometimes, when Hecati was getting too harsh with you."

Her eyes filled with angry tears. He knew nothing about it, for all his boasting. He knew not a tenth of what she'd undergone. For an instant she felt larger than he, older than he, wiser than he. She saw that her hope of becoming his companion was doomed. It was too late for them. Too much had happened. Too little had happened.

Her silence seemed to disturb him.

"I had . . . advice as to how to raise you," he said, wriggling his blocky shoulders uneasily. "None of that matters now. I see you can stand up for yourself when you have to. But you're not vindictive or petty. You've got a generous heart, my girl. And I'm proud of you."

A few minutes ago his unexpected praise would have made her smile. She would have soaked it up like sunshine after long days of rain. Now she stared at him, unmoved. She felt as though she were being turned to stone, losing all feeling an inch at a time.

He took her hands in his and turned them over. His eyes flickered when he saw how work-roughened they were. Then his gaze turned misty and he pulled her into his arms for a hard, fierce hug that nearly crushed her.

"I'll miss you most of all," he whispered.

When he let her go, she stared at him in bewilderment. "But I'm staying here with you," she said. "I thought—" She broke off abruptly, fear piercing her anew.

He shook his head. "No, my child," he said gently. "I could not tell you before. You're going with Bixia."

Elandra's mouth fell open. Anger rushed over her, driving back the fear and the disappointment. So this was her future? To spend her life at the beck and call of Bixia? To mouse about with her head down and her back beaten, pledged in eternity to Bixia's service? She choked on what filled her throat.

Hecati stepped forward. "My lord, it's too generous of you, but really you do not need to send Elandra along as a companion to Lady Bixia. The time has come to separate the girls. Let each of them follow the paths of their far different lives."

Albain ignored her. His eyes remained on Elandra, who stood there frozen with fury and shock. "Go and put on one of your pretty gowns. Put up your hair as befits your rank. Have one of the maids pack your things. There isn't much time."

But she could not move. Her heart was thudding so hard she could scarcely hear him. Sent away. Her mother had sent her away, years ago. All her life she'd feared the day when her father would do the same thing. And now it was upon her. Kicked out. Unwanted.

Oh, he could call it a great honor if he wished. She knew some people would sell their souls for the chance to live at the imperial court. But she saw only the hurt.

Worse than that, it meant no escape from Hecati.

Elandra could not bear it. "Please let me stay," she whispered pleadingly. "I'll do anything, Father. I'll work day and night, run the household or scrub floors, in whatever capacity I can serve. Willingly I will do this. But let me stay."

He flinched. "Is this what you have been taught? To beg like this? Where is your pride, girl?"

Her lips trembled. If she had to kneel one more time and thank the hag for a whipping, she would die. She looked at her father, who refused to see what she could not tell him. "I have no pride in this matter," she said at last. "Let me stay."

"My lord, consider," Hecati spoke up. "This is Lady Bixia's ascension into greatness. After a lifetime of training and preparation for her ultimate station in life, she must look ahead to new friends and new companions—those more worthy of an empress."

Albain scratched his chin. "These protests are unworthy of you both. There is something you do not know, Hecati. Something Elandra does not know."

Elandra felt tears burn her eyes and frowned to hold them back. "I won't go," she said.

"Elandra," he said to her, "you have your own destiny."

She glared at him, too defiant at first to understand what he had said.

"Nonsense," Hecati said with a sniff. "How can your lordship speak of trivial matters when Lady Bixia's good fortune outshines everyone?"

"Bixia has no destiny, save what has been foretold to me about my own fate," Albain said flatly.

Hecati twisted her fingers. "But the girl is to marry the emperor. We have known that since her birth. It was—"

"My destiny says that my daughter shall marry the emperor. That is true."

Hecati nodded emphatically, looking relieved.

"I have worked long and hard to maintain the best relations with the imperial court so this could come about," Albain said. "But that has nothing to do with Elandra."

"And Elandra has nothing to do with Lady Bixia's future," Hecati said with thin impatience. "Nothing."

She glared at Elandra, who glared back.

"Father, thank you," Elandra said, her tone not grateful at all. "You mean to be kind, but I will not go with Bixia. Empress or not, I don't want to serve her anymore."

"Nevertheless, I am sending you to the Penestricans," he said and shot a warning look at Hecati. "Not as Bixia's servant, mind you. But as my daughter, to be trained in the House of Women, and to be married advantageously through their selection."

Again Elandra felt as though all the breath had been knocked from her. Her anger vanished, and complete astonishment took its place. Married? She didn't want to be married. She hadn't thought about it. In fact, she was sick of the whole idea after watching Bixia moon and plan and gloat for months.

"You're seventeen," Albain continued. "Old enough to make a good match."

Hecati was blinking as though shocked. "Sent to the Penestricans?" she repeated hollowly. "But that's for wellborn—"

"You're a fool," he broke in sharply.

Hecati flushed to the edge of her wimple. Anger filled her eyes, and the *jinja* positioned itself between her and Lord Albain with its sharp teeth bared.

All expression smoothed from her face, which remained white and pinched. "Forgive me," she said, although she sounded as though her lips were too stiff to utter the apology. "It's just that I am—surprised at so generous a gesture on behalf of your *natural* daughter."

The scorn in that one word was like a slash from the willow switch. Elandra flinched, then felt angry for letting either of them see she could still be affected by taunts. She had to outgrow such foolishness, she told herself. She had to learn to be impervious to the insults. Her mind turned to the possibilities of the future her father offered. She had never even allowed herself to dream of any kind of life such as other young women had. But if she did go and if she was married well . . .

"Unlike Bixia, Elandra has her *own* destiny," Albain said proudly. "It was read by the soothsayer in her mother's household at her birth."

Elandra and Hecati exchanged an involuntary glance. Elandra took a step forward. "I did not know this," she said, intrigued despite a wary sense that she might not like it. "Why have I never been told?"

He smiled at her. "Because of your mother's wisdom. She asked me not to tell you until you were grown. I was also requested, by another party, to let you be raised more roughly than Bixia, to test you for a purpose I do not know."

"But—"

"I did not like to keep such a secret at first, but as the two of you have grown up together, I have seen Bixia spoiled and fawned over by everyone until she's vain and puffed up with conceit. I see you, resilient and wary, expecting no favors."

"You cannot say that Elandra is better than Lady Bixia," Hecati said with quick jealousy. "She is too tall, too thin, all awkward elbows. That hair is a fright. It will never stay combed."

Albain smiled at Elandra. "your hair has the same auburn tint as mine. And today you make me think of the last time I saw Iaris."

"My mother," Elandra whispered. Her mother's name was never spoken. How she thirsted to hear it, how she longed for any detail of what her mother was like.

"Iaris was quite a beauty," he said, his eyes growing soft and distant with memory. "Not in the common way, but very fierce and reserved. When she sent me away, she looked much as you look today, all haughty and tense, with tears in her eyes she would not let fall. By the gods, it was not easy to win her heart at first. Nor would she be tamed. Nor could I keep her."

Elandra bit her lip, and her yearning was an ache that filled her entire being. "I long to hear more about her. All my life I've hoped that someday you would tell me."

"I know." Gently he touched her cheek. "This is not the time. You must go today with your sister, for training and preparation for marriage."

"But—"

He shook his head to still her protest. "We are not always given our choice in these matters, Elandra. Had I been given leave, I would have warned you of your future long ago. I would have given you a trousseau too. For you are as precious to me as Bixia."

"But who commands you, Father? Who has told you to raise me thus? Who has made you keep silent?" Elandra frowned at him. "My mother?"

He shook his head. "Give up this guessing game. I am not at liberty to tell you. I have defied them enough by taking off the spell of restraint."

"But—"

"Hush. You must learn to accept what destiny writes for you."

"And what is this destiny that has been foretold for her?" Hecati asked in a spiteful voice.

His gaze never wavered from Elandra's. "She is to marry a man whose name shall be known throughout the ages. Whether he is a warlord or a philosopher depends on the match the Penestricans will arrange according to their wisdom."

For a moment there was only silence in the room.

Elandra forgot to breathe as her mind turned over his words. In spite of herself she was pleased and flattered. It was the destiny of someone intended for greatness. Her life was not going to be dull or ordinary after all.

"Well?" Albain asked, breaking the silence.

Elandra drew in a breath, and her involuntary half-smile flickered into a frown. "Must my life hinge only on what kind of marriage I make?"

He looked startled by her reply.

"There, you see?" Hecati said scornfully. "All rebellion and hopeless ideas. What is to be done with a creature like her?"

Albain ignored Hecati and gave Elandra his complete attention. "What else would you have for yourself?"

She spun away and crossed the room to the window overlooking the lush jungles beyond the walls. Hugging herself, she gazed at the sky. A pair of wild parrots flew overhead, their crimson feathers bright. "I don't know exactly . . . only I think I would like to be a scholar or a teacher. I would like to explore the world and see its wonders. I would like to put my own mark on history, not just content myself with running a household and bearing a man's children."

Albain laughed. "What a silly child you are."

Elandra turned around sharply. "Am I?" she asked, hurt by his laughter. "Am I really foolish? Are my dreams wrong?"

He beckoned to her, still chuckling, and she crossed the room to him. He gave her shoulder a little pat, then pushed her away.

"You are ready indeed to go forth and forge a path for yourself," he said. "The Penestricans can do much with you, I think. I am pleased."

"Must I marry?" she asked again. "Could I join the order of Penestricans and find a different destiny for myself there?"

The amusement slowly faded in his face. He shook his head. "Some think a destiny is a curse. Others, like Bixia, consider it a blessing. Either way, you must walk the path it sets for you. Now, go and make yourself ready. There is little time."

"I want to stay."

"I know." His voice was firm. "But you cannot. The Penestricans tell me it is time. Today I must lose both my girls."

She heard the unhappiness in his voice. Her heart went out to him, and she reached for his hand. But with a scowl, he abruptly turned his back on her and left the room. She listened to the rapid jingling of his spurs and knew with a sinking heart that she would probably never see him again.

The *jinja* lingered a moment. Its dark, mischievous eyes stared up at Elandra in a strangely compelling manner. "Greatness," it whispered. Then it grinned and vanished.

Elandra would have rushed out of the room then, but Hecati blocked her path.

She handed Elandra a small key off her ring. "This will unlock the cupboard that contains your things. See that you hurry. Wash your face and do something about that hair. You will behave yourself. You will conduct yourself properly. You will do nothing to bring shame to Lady Bixia, is that clear?"

Elandra felt numb. There had been too many shocks, too many emotions. She wanted only to flee, to be alone until she could understand some part of what had happened.

She did not take the key, but Hecati forced it into her hand.

"Destiny indeed." Hecati sniffed. "You think you have won your father, but you haven't. He'll forget about you within ten minutes of our departure."

"I know," Elandra said softly.

"You got out of the punishment you deserve, but let me tell you this. Make no attempt to put on airs around Lady Bixia or me, my girl. We aren't interested in your destiny. It is nothing in comparison to her ladyship's. Nothing! For all we know, you'll marry a scoundrel who'll end up hanged from an imperial road arch."

Elandra turned slowly to look at the spiteful old woman. For the first time in her life she felt no fear. She wasn't sure if it was shock that made her reckless, or if the *jinja* had somehow changed her.

"Better to wed a bandit than a darkness-riddled old man who's afraid to die," she retorted in a quiet voice.

Hecati blanched; then fury filled her eyes. "You—you—"

The switch appeared, and Elandra lifted her hand quickly to block the blow. But it never landed.

The switch transformed itself into a thin black snake that writhed back toward Hecati. Shrieking, she flung it away.

The serpent struck the wall and vanished. The air smelled scorched and tainted.

Wrinkling her nose, Elandra stared at Hecati in amazement. The woman backed away from her with an expression of mingled fury and dread.

"The *jinja* has given me protection," Elandra said in amazement. Relief spread through her. For the first time in years she felt free and safe. "You'll never beat me again."

"Is that what you think?" Hecati retorted. She rubbed her hands together violently as though to brush away some taint. "Take care, bastard-girl. Take great care. I have plenty of tricks left."

Elandra backed up. "Leave me be!" she said vehemently. "I want nothing but to be left alone."

"Fool," Hecati said, sneering. "Do you think I believe that? You were born under the sign of mischief. Even now, you seek to diminish Lady Bixia's moment of glory."

"You're wrong."

"Do not try to stand in Lady Bixia's way."

"I have no interest in Bixia at all," Elandra said with a frown. "I've never wanted to interfere with her good fortune. I don't now."

"Stay away from us," Hecati said. "I warn you, I have other ways to protect my niece."

"I mean her no harm."

Hecati sniffed. "Oh, what lies you love to tell. You want revenge, my girl. That's plain enough. But you'll never get it."

Elandra stared at her, tired of her paranoia. "You heard Father. My destiny isn't even close to Bixia's."

"You were wise to keep silent before Albain. Mind that you continue to watch your tongue. I want no trouble from you. None at all." Hecati pointed her finger at Elandra. "Keep yourself apart from her. If she's in a room, depart from it. If she speaks, fall silent. If she is mentioned by others, show only respect. You will bring no notice to yourself, not during the journey and not among the Penestricans. I don't even want you to bring her a cup of water. Is that clear?"

Elandra drew in a deep breath, then another.

"I asked you a question, Elandra."

"Yes," Elandra replied, her voice flat and quick. "Everything is very clear."

"Then go! See that you are dressed, packed, and downstairs waiting by the time Lady Bixia is ready to depart."

Elandra started to speak, but Hecati raised her hand. Her eyes raked Elandra with contempt.

"Get out," she said.

And she shoved Elandra into the corridor with a slam of the door.

fifteen

LESS THAN AN HOUR AFTER HER FATHER HAD turned her life upside down, Elandra hurried through the vaulted entry of state with its polished marble floor and soaring columns.

Outside beyond the portico, the famous thousand steps of gleaming white limestone stretched down to an immense rectangular courtyard where normally her father's troops assembled for inspections or conducted precise cavalry drills.

Today, however, a full ten squadrons stood in silent formation on matched horses. Five squadrons wore the white and yellow surplices of Gialta over gilded mail armor. Turbaned and mustachioed, they were mounted on white horses. Curved scimitars hung at their belts, and the Albain coat of arms flew from thin banners affixed to their spears. The five squadrons of Imperial Guards wore polished breastplates and plumed helmets. They were mounted on tall, muscular war horses, all bays. Wearing vivid crimson cloaks that spread out over the rumps of their horses, they looked foreign and formidable. The double-eagle crest of the emperor glittered with pure gold, magnificent in the bright sunlight. Imperial banners flowed and unfurled in the humid breeze, flying above Albain's own coat of arms.

The elephants of the caravan stood lined up at the foot of the steps, placidly waving their big ears to fan themselves. Their handlers squatted beneath them, ivory goad sticks dangling from idle hands.

The elephants were beautifully plumed and caparisoned with embroidered harnesses. Bright red curtains fluttered from their palanquins. Even the pack elephants wore the ornate harness of state, and red pack cloths showed beneath their loads.

Catching her breath at the sight, Elandra paused beneath the portico amid the waiting courtiers and officials.

Several of them turned and bowed to her automatically, then drew back as they realized she was not Bixia.

But even those few acknowledgments were enough to fill Elandra's heart with an unfamiliar sensation. She had found Magan waiting in her tiny tower room, newly assigned to be her personal maid. Magan had bathed her and dressed her in a traveling gown of stiff blue linen with a veil that fluttered now in the hot, sticky breeze. With her hair coiffed in a complicated knot as befitted a lady, Elandra hardly recognized herself.

For all her initial reluctance to go, she now found her heart beating faster with growing excitement. A new life stretched ahead of her—one of uncertainty, yes, but also one filled with all kinds of possibilities.

She lifted her head high and carried herself proudly, determined to act worthy of the honor her father had bestowed on her today.

Still, she must not forget that the imperial troops were waiting for Bixia, not her. This parade was in her sister's honor. Elandra must not keep anyone waiting.

One of the porters had already taken her shabby trunk

and Magan's little cloth bag down to be loaded on the rear elephant.

"We must hurry," Elandra said to Magan and hurried outside into the blazing sunshine.

She started down the broad white steps, her veil streaming out around her.

Shouted commands rang out, and two hundred polished swords were drawn in unison. Sunlight blazed off the steel. The Gialtan troops stood in their stirrups, brandishing their scimitars. Each member of the Imperial Guard rested his sword on the shoulder of the man to his right.

A deafening roar rose up from the courtyard, hitting her with a wall of noise.

Startled, Elandra stopped in her tracks about halfway down the steps and stood there with growing dismay at this tremendous tribute. They had mistaken her for Bixia.

The cheering bounded and rebounded off the walls, growing louder and louder. Even the elephants lifted their trunks to bugle.

Elandra's face grew hot behind her veil. She raised her hands helplessly to stop them, then glanced back over her shoulder to see if Bixia was coming.

Her sister was nowhere in sight.

Elandra met Magan's amazed gaze. "They think I'm Bixia. How do I stop them?"

Magan grinned, her nut-brown face filled with deviltry. "She ought to be out here on time to get her cheers, oughtn't she?"

Elandra lifted her hands at the troops again, but the cheering only swelled louder.

Exasperated, she reached for her veil clip. "As soon as they see who I am, they'll stop."

"My lady, don't!" Magan said in alarm. "You can't unveil out here."

"But—"

"No! It isn't done."

Elandra glared at her. "I've gone without a veil all my life. I've been seen by my father's soldiers countless times. What difference—"

Magan gripped her hand, and her eyes were serious now with warning. "The difference is that your father has recognized you officially today. You are a lady now. You must act in the way of a lady."

"But I can't let this go on—"

"You cannot stop it now," Magan said. "That would embarrass everyone."

Biting her lip, Elandra ducked her head and hurried down the rest of the steps as quickly as she could. She could not believe the trick of fate that had made them mistake her for Bixia. Her father would be angry, and Hecati would be furious.

Breathless, she reached the elephants and glared at the bowing handlers.

Then a herald's trumpet rang out above the cheering, cutting it off abruptly.

Elandra whirled around and saw the standard bearers with her father's coat of arms emerging from the portico. More trumpets continued to ring out in a fanfare.

Then Albain appeared with a veiled Bixia on his arm. Her gown was of green silk gauze, fluttering and stirring in the wind. Her veil was sheer and long enough to be looped up over her golden hair and fastened there with jeweled pins that winked and flashed in the sunlight.

Elandra shrank back closer against the side of an elephant, wishing she could sink through the ground for her mistake. She dared not even look to see what the troops were doing.

But as the fanfare ended from the trumpets, commands rang out a second time across the courtyard. Elandra saw the troops draw their swords again, and again the cheers rose up.

But they were not as loud this time, not as heartfelt or vehement.

When Albain and Bixia reached the foot of the steps, the cheers cut off as though in relief.

Silence flooded the courtyard, in its way almost as grueling as the heat.

Elandra met Bixia's enraged green eyes briefly, then dropped her own. She dared not look at Hecati at all. Beneath her veil, she took short, shallow breaths and knew reprisals would come.

Albain's one good eye was squinting balefully. As the two generals dismounted and approached side by side, he gestured for them to step back.

Wooden-faced, they saluted and did so.

Bixia plucked at Albain's sleeve. "Father, you saw how they insulted me. I will not receive them."

He turned his glare on her. "You will," he growled in a low voice. "Or, by the gods, I'll take a strap to you. Soldiers will cheer whom they please, and you got plenty."

"But it wasn't the same. Not after she ruined everything." Bixia swung her gaze to Elandra. "You cheap schemer! How dare you come down before me. I'll—"

"Compose yourself," Albain broke in. "Hell's breath, Bixia, remember who you are."

"I am future empress," Bixia said snappishly. "I will not be demeaned by this bastard upstart of yours."

Elandra's face flamed hot with fresh embarrassment. She stepped forward to speak, but Bixia pointed at her.

"I shan't have her in my caravan. Scheming and conniving, who knows what she'll do next to embarrass me? Send her away, Father. I command it!"

Albain's face turned purple. "You command *me*?" he roared, forgetting the need for discretion. "Murdeth and Fury, I'll brook no such impertinence, not even from you!" Abruptly he lowered his tone. "You are not empress yet, girl. Until the crown sits on your head, see that you remember that."

Bixia stuck her nose in the air. "In two months I'll—"

"Go on as you are today, and I swear I'll break off the arrangement."

Bixia blinked and turned pale beneath her sheer veil. She stared at him a long while, as though to make sure he meant it. Then her gaze shifted to Elandra and filled with tears.

"Why do you favor her?" she asked. "Why are you so good to her and cruel to me? She has ruined today, ruined it."

Bixia started to snivel, but Albain gripped her wrist and drew her close to his side. "By the gods, you'll stop this and compose yourself. Now! Do you hear? Start acting like the empress you want to be. Straighten your sour face and receive these officers properly."

Bixia gulped and sniffed. "Why do you scold me? Elandra is the one who has spoiled everything."

"Elandra, at least, knows how to keep her poise and act properly in public," he growled back, making Bixia gasp.

Wide-eyed, she gulped and straightened her shoulders.

"That's better." Albain glared once again at Elandra, who hadn't dared move, then gestured at the two generals.

Both came forward impassively as though there had been no delay.

They were presented to Bixia, who received them aloofly, her voice cold with hauteur.

Still red-faced, Albain beckoned to Elandra. She came forward reluctantly, embarrassed and uncertain as to whether her father was furious with her or simply disappointed. Over to one side, Hecati threw her dagger looks.

"My natural daughter, Lady Elandra," Albain said to the commanders. "She also travels under your care, sirs, to be received and prepared for marriage by the Penestricans."

"We are doubly honored, Lord Albain," the general of

the Imperial Guard said. He spoke Lingua with an odd, flat accent.

Alud Handar, general of the Gialtan squadrons, bowed respectfully to Elandra. His eyes were warm and friendly in his stern face. "We shall guard these precious pearls of our lord and master with our lives."

"Then good journey," Albain said gruffly.

He took Bixia's hand and kissed it according to protocol. "Farewell, my daughter," he said formally. "I count the hours until I can bestow your hand in marriage."

"Goodbye, Father," Bixia said haughtily. "I await our reunion."

They glared at each other for a moment longer; then Albain turned to Elandra and clasped her hand in both of his big calloused ones. "Have courage to face what lies before you. My blessing to you, little daughter."

Over his shoulder, Elandra saw Bixia turn red with fresh anger. Albain had not given Bixia his blessing, but no doubt he was saving that honor for her wedding day. Still, it was another slight that Bixia would want revenge for.

Ruefully, Elandra curtsied to her father. She wished more than ever that she was still an unnoticed member of the household, keeping out of sight and out of trouble in the servants' passageways. Aside from Magan and perhaps General Handar, she had no allies to protect her away from Albain's direct influence.

"Thank you, Father," she said softly. She gazed up at him, her eyes full of apology.

His expression softened marginally. "Remember to keep your place," he said.

The chastisement was mild indeed, but it was enough to make Elandra draw in a sharp breath and drop her gaze.

Bixia sniffed with patent dissatisfaction.

Then they were being lifted into the palanquins and settled. The handlers perched themselves behind the head of the elephants.

The troops wheeled about in formation, imperial horses prancing skittishly around the elephants. The Gialtan barbs ignored the elephants and trotted smoothly forward.

Trumpets sounded again, and the tall gates swung open. With banners flying, they were on their way into the unknown.

BY NIGHTFALL, THEY HAD LEFT THE ROAD that paralleled the river for a rough track that led away from the irrigated fields and paddies into the jungle itself. The terrain was rough, and leafy branches brushed the sides of the palanquin frequently.

Elandra soon adjusted to the majestic sway of the elephant carrying her and Magan. Riding so high above the ground, she was able to see numerous monkeys. Wild parrots flew everywhere in brilliant profusion. Flowering vines looped down from the treetops above, perfuming the air with sweet fragrance that briefly overcame the damp, fetid scents of the jungle. Now and then she glimpsed a predator lying concealed among the mossy branches. The air was heavy and still, making the intense heat a clammy, smothering enemy.

She and Magan used the reed fans constantly, but by the time they stopped for camp, Elandra felt limp from the heat. She had no appetite for the food served to her. To her relief, Bixia and Hecati looked equally exhausted and did not even talk to her.

The soldiers were detailed into sentry units. The rest dispersed elsewhere, to make a second camp. Servants put up tents and cots, and Elandra found her quarters a tiny, airless, claustrophobic place.

The darkness pressed down, hot and still. She felt as though it were water, trying to drown her. Magan draped netting over her for protection against the stinging, vicious insects. It was like being wrapped in a shroud, but Elandra made no complaint.

Eventually she slept, but her slumber was light and restless.

"Elandra Albain," whispered a soft voice through the darkness.

Elandra stirred and sat up. The netting around her was gone. As she blinked, uncertain whether she'd heard her name spoken, the dark tent around her faded away like smoke. An eerie green light filled her surroundings, and she saw herself sitting unclad and shivering upon a bench of stone. In the distance stood a pair of mighty stone pillars, like sentinels.

The green light spilled from between them, spreading low across the ground like fog. It illuminated this strange dream place with a ghostly radiance. A figure came wading toward her through the glowing fog, a tall shadow, powerful with broad shoulders and muscular legs.

Elandra drew in her breath with a sharp sense of alarm. She tried to scramble off the bench, but found herself unable to move.

Her paralysis frightened her even more. Heart pounding, she struggled to control her own fear. *It's only a dream*, she tried to reassure herself without much success. Dream or not, it seemed far too vivid and real.

She found herself increasingly mesmerized by the shadow's easy, loping stride. Time compressed to stillness, unable to flow naturally. The man continued to come closer, yet he seemed quite a distance away. Too far for her to see his face, which remained concealed by the gloom.

Like her, he was clad only in darkness. Her skin flushed hot as though she'd been dipped in boiling water, yet the very top of her head felt icy cold. She found herself gripping the sides of her bench with all her strength, and she could not stop trembling. Her breathing deepened, and her back arched of its own volition.

Suddenly she was off the bench, standing tall. Her fear remained, yet it shielded an eagerness she had never known before. Something inside her seemed to recognize this half-seen stranger. He walked like a warrior, graceful and strong. She had never seen anyone as tall. His neck was like a column, straight and strong. She strained to see the molding of his head and face.

To see him more clearly . . . to gaze into his eyes . . . to feel the touch of his fingertips on her skin . . .

She stepped forward, walking to meet him halfway. Her heart lifted and yearned. She knew him, had known him throughout the sands of time. He was for her, as she was for him. Gladness burst through her, and she wanted to sing as she ran. Why had it taken so long to find him again?

In the blink of a moment, the distance between them ended. They stood face to face, breathless and cloaked in the strange shadows.

"Elandra," he whispered, his voice striking like a bronze bell within her soul.

The light was spreading, lifting around them. In moments she would see his face and know his name again, this man whom she had loved for all of time.

She lifted her arms to his neck and pressed herself close against warm skin and hard muscles.

"Elandra," he said again. *"I have found thee, my only love."*

His lips brushed against her trembling ones, even as she caught her breath for the kiss that would return her memory.

But from the corner of her eye she glimpsed a quick flash of yellow light, bright and foreign to the soft green light at their feet.

Distracted, Elandra turned her head to look, and her lover vanished like smoke.

"No!" she cried aloud. She looked in all directions, but he was gone.

Filled with a sense of loss, Elandra took a few aimless

steps. "Come back!" she called. "Please come back to me!"

She did not know his name, and her frustration grew. If she could call out his name, he would come back to her.

"Please," she whispered again.

He did not reappear, and she knew she could search forever through the shadows and not find him.

Angry, she turned toward the yellow light and stormed toward it. "Why?" she called. "Why couldn't you wait?"

The light tried to recede and wavered. That's when Elandra saw it was only a shield for a woman, motionless and watchful.

Slightly plump and middle-aged, she was garbed in a long black robe that covered her entirely from neck to wrist to feet.

"Who are you?" Elandra demanded. "Why did you interrupt? What are you doing here?"

The woman's eyes widened in astonishment that changed to alarm. Without a word, she gathered up her long skirts and abruptly ran.

But her flight only fanned Elandra's anger more. She ran after the watcher, pursuing her in a wild, zigzagging flight up and down hills and over boulder-strewn ground. The woman ran awkwardly and not very well. Soon, she slowed and began to glance over her shoulder more and more often. Elandra gritted her teeth and increased her stride.

You are an old gazelle, she thought, drawing on an old childhood game when she had been taught by the huntsman how to pursue quarry with her mind as well as her body. *I am the panther, swift and bold. I can catch you.*

With every stride, she gained on the older woman.

By the time they reached the stone pillars, Elandra was close enough to grab the back of the watcher's robe. She yanked hard, bringing the woman to a halt just short of the gateway.

The woman twisted in her hold, eyes filled with fear. "No," she said breathlessly. "You cannot exit with me. You cannot—"

"Tell me his name, watcher," Elandra said.

The woman's fearfulness grew. "Impossible!" she breathed. "You cannot see me. You are not—"

"I see you," Elandra said, twisting harder on the woman's robe. "I have caught you, watcher. Tell me his name!"

"Yes, tell," commanded another voice.

Startled, Elandra looked around and saw Hecati standing in the fog. The old witch stood cloaked in murkiness, as though smoke billowed around her. Elandra smelled a scent of something burning, and knew Hecati's magic was at work. Strangely, in her dream she did not fear.

"His name!" Hecati commanded.

The watcher tried to pull free of Elandra's hold. "No!" she said to Hecati, lifting one hand in a gesture of repudiation. "Begone, intruder. You have no place here!"

Hecati threw back her head in laughter, and Elandra stepped closer to her captive.

"Quickly," she whispered. "Explain to me why—"

Something invisible hit Elandra a stunning blow. She staggered back, unable to breathe or even see. The world spun around her and went entirely dark.

Then she could breathe again. With a gasp, she struggled up only to find her face and shoulders entangled in insect netting. Through the tent flap, bright moonlight shone over the camp and cast a shadow from the silhouette of the sentry who paced outside.

Elandra drew in an unsteady breath and shoved her hair back from her face. She was covered with perspiration and breathing hard. Her nightgown stuck to her damp skin.

Unlike the usual sort of dream that faded immediately, this one remained vivid in her mind, haunting her. Who was the woman who watched? Why had she been in Elandra's dream?

And who had been the man?

Remembering how she'd responded to him, Elandra blushed in the night. Was she mad to dream of her future husband like a silly field-hand girl? Hers would be a marriage of convenience and dynastic alliance. The union would strengthen her father's power as a warlord. It would provide her with a home, a name, and possibly children, but nothing more.

Love . . . how could she dream about it like that, as though she'd been molten candlewax poured into a new mold, pliant for whatever he willed, eager to give herself like . . .

Breathing hard with embarrassment, Elandra pressed her hands against her cheeks in an effort to calm herself. Perhaps the woman she'd chased was only a symbol of her conscience, standing as a witness. But why had she run? And what had Hecati been doing there?

Perhaps she'd been visited by a dream walker.

Even as the thought entered her mind, Elandra shivered with dread. Dream walkers were creatures who entered the dreams of the unsuspecting and shaped their minds while they slept. Creatures who stole dreams and twisted them into dark magic. Creatures who might do worse.

She flung off the netting and stood up in the dark tent, restless with alarm. The camp was protected with *jinjas*. No dream walker could reach her without an alarm being sounded.

But even as she tried to reassure herself, a tiny voice in the back of her mind reminded her that Hecati practiced small magic all the time, and the palace *jinja* never noticed.

Hugging herself against another shiver, Elandra paced slowly back and forth in the cramped confines of her tent. Outside, a predator screamed in the jungle, but the camp slept on peacefully. No alarms. Her dream was only a dream, nothing more

Still trying to convince herself, Elandra continued to shiver in the hot silence of the night. She did not return to her hard cot. There would be no more sleep tonight.

sixteen

IN THE MORNING, ELANDRA SAID NOTHING about her strange dream, not even to Magan. The world seemed filled with mystery and danger. Wary and nervous, she caught Hecati's speculative gaze on her more than once, and Elandra made certain she stayed as far from the witch as possible. If ever the gods granted her a secure home or wealth, she vowed she would never again travel without the protection of a *jinja* of her very own.

At nightfall, she found her dreams once again restless and troubling, but nothing like the one in which she had kissed the tall stranger.

On the following day, their trail began to climb. They left the steaming jungle for the foothills and wound slowly into a forbidding mountain range.

The trees thinned out, and the air grew progressively drier and cooler until a sharp wind blew constantly and the air felt thin and hard to breathe.

When they reached the top of the mountains, Elandra lifted weary eyes to the heavens and saw the stone walls of a stronghold rising up above the narrow road. Something about the architectural lines of the structure made her hair rise on the back of her neck. It looked extremely old and primitive.

Indeed, with the sheer walls of the cliff faces rising up around her, Elandra felt hemmed in and increasingly trapped. She could not explain her feelings; they were deep fears, primitive and inarticulate. The age of the place filled her with uneasiness. Carved into the cliffs were ancient symbols that seemed almost familiar, although Elandra was certain she had never seen them before. Whenever she stared at them too long, a sensation of dizziness would force her to turn her gaze away.

She told herself it was the thin air that made her feel so ill, but inside she was less sure.

Equally disturbing was the fact that they came to no village. The stronghold stood alone, completely isolated at the top of this long, treacherous road. Even then, when the road abruptly leveled out in a sort of clearing and stopped, the stronghold towered high above them. The only way to reach it was via a steep series of steps carved into the solid rock of the mountainside.

The Imperial Guard galloped ahead, banners streaming. Trumpets blared, sending up a summons that echoed loudly. The Gialtans circled the elephants, grouping them into a bunch. Thus, Elandra found her palanquin unexpectedly next to Bixia's.

The two half-sisters glared at each other.

Bixia leaned over and said, "This time you will not usurp the honors due me. You will wait. You will keep your place. Am I clear?"

Elandra looked down, feeling humiliation burn the back of her throat. She clenched her hands in her lap and nodded silently. She didn't trust her voice.

The trumpets blared again, and this time a gong was struck in the stronghold in reply.

Figures robed in black appeared on the ramparts, gazing down in silence. The absence of welcome and fanfare made a sharp contrast to the streaming banners and fluttering saddlecloths below.

Both generals dismounted. As they approached the steps, a single figure in black descended to meet them.

Elandra felt a chill shiver through her. She had chased such a black-robed woman in her dream. To her knowledge she had never seen a Penestrican before. Nor was she someone with the gift of foretelling. How had she known what these women would look like?

Servants scurried about the elephants, bringing ladders to help the passengers dismount.

Conscious of the need to avoid further mistakes, Elandra sat still, making no move at all until Bixia was safely on the ground. Then Elandra descended as quickly as possible. The wind plucked at her veil, sending it streaming out to one side. She found herself conscious of her travel-stained and very wrinkled gown. Her muscles ached, and her eyes were gritty from insufficient sleep. She felt wind-blasted and unkempt.

Hecati moved quickly around Bixia, straightening her gown and brushing away wrinkles. Magan did the same for Elandra, who gave the maid a tired smile of gratitude.

Then the generals, gleaming in burnished armor, swords clanking at their sides, returned from the steps.

Both bowed first to Bixia, then to Elandra.

General Handar, his plumed turban powdered with dust and his spurs jingling with every step, dropped to one knee before Bixia and bowed even more deeply with his hand over his heart.

"My lady," he said in his deep voice, "permit this servant to wish you all the blessings of the gods in your future. I have discharged my duty in bringing you safely to the hands of the Penestricans. With my honor have I guided you to this place. With my life have I protected you. May peace follow your name. I request of you my farewell."

It was a beautiful speech, spoken with all the honor

and sincerity the grizzled old soldier was capable of expressing. Watching as he knelt there at her half-sister's feet, Elandra felt sentimental tears sting her eyes. When Handar left them, it would cut their final tie to Gialta. Theirs was the fate of all women, to be sent forth from the shelter of their home, to make lives for themselves wherever Fate decreed, delivered like chattel and trade goods for the purposes for men.

Bixia gazed down at the commander with a smug gleam in her green eyes. "You have served well, General Handar," she said in a bored voice. Her gaze moved beyond him, to the steps where more women in black robes had appeared. "We thank you. Farewell."

It was a moment before he looked up. Something flickered in his eyes—disappointment or chagrin, perhaps—at her short reply. He rose to his feet and saluted. His dark face might have been carved from wood as he bowed quickly to Elandra and turned away.

As soon as he was remounted on his horse, he bawled out commands. The Gialtans galloped away, leaving a cloud of dust and the echoing thunder of hoofbeats behind.

Meanwhile, the general of the Imperial Guard was giving his arm to Bixia, who smiled and used her eyes to flirt above her veil. Together, they crossed the dusty clearing. Elandra tried to follow, but Hecati gripped her arm and held her back.

"No," she said in a low, sharp voice. Hecati's face was pale and marked by dark circles beneath her eyes as though the journey had been a terrible strain. Even now, with Bixia safely delivered, Hecati looked tense and nervous as she glared at Elandra. "You will wait outside with the servants until Lady Bixia is received by the Magria and properly welcomed in."

Elandra's cheeks burned beneath her veil, but she retreated obediently to the elephants. The handlers were still unloading baggage. Magan stood guarding Elandra's bag.

Without glancing at the maidservant, Elandra took a place beside her. Hecati hurried after her niece.

At the steps, the general and Bixia paused. There was a moment of silence, broken only by the snorting of the horses and the restless mumbling of the elephants, which were to continue to Imperia as part of Bixia's dowry gift to her future husband.

The Penestricans had been waiting quietly on the steps. Now, however, they descended to the bottom. One woman, young and beautiful, with pale straight hair flowing down her back, walked ahead of the others. A pair of gnarled old crones with terrible mutilation scars on their bare arms followed her. They carried tall wooden staffs. The rest of the sisterhood lined the steps on either side, holding burning candles that seemed odd in the bright sunshine.

The leader's eyes were a clear blue. Her gaze swept everyone, then fixed upon Bixia. "I am Anas," she said in a voice that carried easily.

It was almost as though the cliff walls surrounding them formed a natural amphitheater.

Anas's voice made Elandra think of crystal—melodic in a sharp, piercing away.

"I am deputy to her Excellency, the Magria. I bid you welcome."

The general bowed low enough to make his armor creak. "The Lady Bixia," he said by way of introduction. Frowning, he glanced around as though seeking Elandra, but Hecati gave him an impatient pinch and he faced the deputy again. "Also, the Lady Hecati, sister-in-law to Lord Albain, and Lady Bixia's aunt."

He seemed to have a ritualized speech prepared, but even as he opened his mouth, one of the Penestricans lifted her wooden staff with a sharp gesture and pointed it at the sky.

A streamer of dark cloud appeared to obscure the sun, as though it had been wiped away with a rag.

Elandra gazed upward in astonishment. She could have sworn a moment ago the sky had been cloudless. A shiver passed through her. It was said the Penestricans commanded many of the old ways. Did they govern the heavens as well as the earth and its growing things?

"Where is the other one?" Anas asked. "We were told, General, that both of Lord Albain's daughters would be brought to us."

Bixia tossed her head, but Hecati turned halfway around and snapped her fingers imperiously at Elandra.

"Come, girl!" she said. "Don't hang back and call undue attention to yourself. You delay the proceedings."

Elandra's resentment burned even hotter. She was tempted to stay where she was, but with everyone looking at her she had little choice but to walk forward. Hecati was making sure she got off on the wrong foot with the Penestricans, and there was little Elandra could do about it right now.

Although miserable, she walked with her head high. She did not pick up her skirts and run to join the others, although Hecati snapped her fingers again. Instead, Elandra kept her steps modest and graceful as befitting a lady. If it was the only way in which she could defy Hecati, then she would do it.

She came up behind Hecati and stopped, grateful for the veil that hid her burning face from Anas's clear blue eyes.

The deputy stared at her for a long moment without expression.

"May I also introduce the Lady Elandra," the general said into the awkward silence.

Anas inclined her head graciously. "You are also bid welcome to our walls, Lady Elandra."

Bixia began to fidget and sigh. "We've had a very long, uncomfortable journey. May we have refreshment?"

Behind her veil, Elandra gasped at Bixia's rudeness.

For once Hecati made no attempt to correct her charge or to smooth over the matter.

A flicker of something unreadable passed across Anas's face. "Of course," she said pleasantly. "Everything has been prepared for you." She shifted her gaze and smiled perfunctorily. "General, according to our rules, no man may step past this point."

He bowed hastily and moved back a step. "Yes, Deputy Anas."

"At the base of the mountain is plentiful grass for the horses and forage for the elephants. You will find excellent camping sites near the stream. Please do not allow your men to ascend the mountain again until it is time for these sisters to depart from us."

He bowed again. "As you wish."

Turning smartly on his heel, he strode away. Orders rang out. The elephants were unwilling to move, but with much shouting and noise they were turned about and the guardsmen headed down the road. The mound of luggage stood abandoned and forlorn.

"That will be seen to later," Anas said. Stepping aside, she gestured gracefully. "Come."

Bixia gathered up her skirts with an ill-natured huff. "Why didn't you lay out a carpet? These old steps are so rough they'll snag my slippers. Must we climb all these steps? I would prefer to be carried."

Again, Hecati made no effort to correct her. Elandra frowned at the woman, but Hecati seemed lost in thought. It was strange behavior for her. Usually she would be fawning and flattering, doing her best to make sure Bixia charmed everyone.

Anas seemed impervious to Bixia's rudeness. "There is no one to carry you. Come."

She started up with Bixia at her heels. Hecati was next and Elandra last.

The cloud still obscured the sun, and indeed it seemed darker than ever. The burning candles in the sisters' hands flickered and blazed, although the wind did not put them out.

The steps were very steep and worn. Halfway up some were broken, making the footing treacherous. Trying to get a better grip on her long skirts, which were billowing in the wind, Elandra tripped slightly on her hem and pitched forward. To save herself, she put her hand against the small of Hecati's back for just a second to regain her balance.

Hecati jumped as though startled, and two candles in the hands of the sisters on either side of her went out with loud pops. Hecati loosed a low, strange cry—almost a moan. The timbre of the sound made goosebumps stand up on Elandra's arms.

At the head of the line, Anas was already turning back. She pushed past Bixia without a word and came gliding swiftly down the steps. Her face was set implacably.

Elandra tried to back away from Hecati, who was still making that eerie sound like a cornered animal. But the two Penestricans with the wooden staffs stood behind Elandra, crossing their staffs to block the way down. Their faces were harsh and suddenly hostile.

Alarm ran through Elandra. Not understanding what was wrong, she looked about.

Another candle went out, and another. The sisters standing farther up the steps now crowded down as close to Elandra and Hecati as they could get.

A cry of accusation went up: "Witch! Witch! Witch!"

Anas's blue eyes were as bright as flames. She glared first at Elandra, then at Hecati. "Worshiper of Mael, you are unwelcome in this place of the goddess mother."

Hecati's face tensed into a knot. She flung an accusing finger at Elandra. "She is the witch!" Hecati cried in a shrill, ugly voice. "The betrayer has already been at work. She destroyed the sacred bridal robe—"

Anas turned up her palms. A blue globe of truth-light

appeared on each of them. She tossed one at Elandra and one at Hecati.

It was all happening too fast. Elandra opened her mouth to defend herself when the light struck her forehead and shimmered down the full length of her. It felt strange and prickly, but then it pooled at her feet. When it touched the ground it turned into a tiny garter snake that slithered quickly away from the toe of her slipper and vanished.

Hecati screamed and threw up both hands, crossing her wrists as a shield. The blue truth-light struck her arms and burst in a halo of swiftly changing colors—blue to indigo to purple. A black pool formed on the ground at her feet. Instead of turning into a snake, the black ooze widened, spreading quickly toward Elandra.

Crying out, she tried to back away, but the Penestricans with the staffs still blocked the steps behind her and would not budge. The stench of something burning filled the air, as always when Hecati worked one of her spells. Only this time, although her face was strained with effort, whatever she was trying to accomplish did not materialize.

Anas extended her hand toward the ooze, and it stopped spreading. Only a scant inch from Elandra's foot, the liquid immediately dried to an ugly scum that stained the steps.

"Mael worshiper," Anas said again, her gaze locked on Hecati. "Witch!"

The word was as sharp as a lash. Hecati flinched.

Anas gestured. "Begone from us, dark creature. Begone!"

"What are you saying?" Bixia demanded, trying to push closer without success. "My aunt isn't a witch. How dare you call her that. How dare you—"

Hecati glanced back and forth angrily. She made no effort to deny Anas's accusations. Instead she glared at Anas with a mad light in her eyes. "You pious fools, your days on this earth are over. A new era is dawning, one in which the dark pair shall stride the earth and crush it!"

"No," Elandra breathed, horrified by this blasphemy.

Hecati's terrible gaze turned on her. "As for you, already you dance in the arms of the shadow lord—"

"No!" Elandra cried. Fear ignited in her. The half-seen figure in her dreams, the unknown lover . . . it could not be. "No!" she cried again, denying it with every fiber of her being despite the doubts Hecati had awakened.

"Think of your destiny, fool," Hecati said. "You are doomed—"

"Enough," Anas broke in. "Go now, before we drive you into the dust whence you came."

"You can't send her away!" Bixia cried, still not understanding anything. "She's my aunt. You can't—"

"Go?" Hecati said, glaring at Anas. "You feeble creature. You dare mock the strength of She Whom I Serve. But you will regret it. We sent the Vindicants to destroy you once. They will do so again."

"We survived," Anas retorted, her jaw set. "We were not defeated. Our path continues, strong in the visionings, no matter how much blood you unleash on this land."

Hecati hissed with fury, and now that sound took on a new, far more terrible meaning to Elandra. That she had grown up in the care of this creature horrified her. Hecati represented unspeakable evil. Elandra could feel the taint on her, a cold rottenness, like touching a slimy, decaying piece of fungus in the jungle by mistake.

"Let her pass!" Anas commanded to the women holding the staffs.

They reluctantly stepped aside. "Deputy—"

Anas gestured furiously, and Hecati laughed.

"They want to kill me, Deputy," she mocked. "They want to spill my blood. Why don't you let them?"

Anas's blue eyes blazed. "Violence breeds violence. Spill your blood on these steps and let evil take hold practically within our gates? Let her go!"

Hecati circled around Elandra as though to take the

escape permitted her. Then she paused and stared deep into Elandra's eyes.

"No!" Bixia called, still unable to get through the press of Penestricans blocking her path. "Aunt Hecati, don't leave me! I need you. I *need* you! Please, please. I don't understand!"

Hecati did not even glance back. Her evil gaze went on boring into Elandra. "You think you've won," she whispered. "I would have gained entrance here if not for you. Oh, you're a clever girl. Clever. But the dark goddess will not forget your interference this day. No, she will not forget."

As she spoke, Hecati lifted her hand as though to slap Elandra.

Elandra flinched reflexively, but instead of a physical blow, an intense white light struck and blinded her. Then something else hit Elandra, knocking her into the wall with stunning force. She must have cried out in pain and shock, but she could hear nothing for the roaring blast around her. It was as though the cliffs had exploded.

The roaring went on and on until she wondered if it was the end of the world finally come upon them.

Then the roaring stopped, and feeling returned to her bit by bit. Her head stopped ringing, although it ached fiercely. She felt the hardness of the steps beneath her, stone edges digging into the side of her left breast and hip. She smelled dust and a scorched scent of magic and some kind of bitter herbs she could not identify. The wind was still blowing, and the women around her were chattering with a mixture of fury and consternation. She could even hear Bixia wailing in the distance.

But despite all that, Elandra could see nothing. Instead of the shifting shapes and colors of vision, she was surrounded by a strange, unsettling whiteness. Like fog, only bright, like the glare of sunshine off the white walls of her father's palace in summer. A painful, glaring whiteness. Not the usual dark of having her eyes closed. Not that.

Gentle hands lifted her and smoothed back her hair.

"Are you hurt?" It was the voice of Anas that spoke to her.

Elandra stared at nothing, her wits slowly returning, although what they had to face was too terrifying. She opened her mouth and could not find the words to speak. What would become of her now? How could she live her life, crippled in this way? Could anything be done?

"Get back. Give her air," Anas commanded. "The Magria must be informed. Resta, I shall deal with you soon. You were careless, allowing a Maelite so near to us."

"But, Deputy—"

"Hush! We cannot discuss it here. Come to my chambers later."

"Yes, Deputy."

Footsteps and more chatter. A cool hand on Elandra's brow was comforting, although nothing could remove her shock and rising panic.

"Are you hurt?" Anas persisted. "Can you answer, Elandra? The witch is gone. You will not be harmed by her again. I promise that."

A promise. Elandra swallowed back bitter laughter. Oh, a promise. She had already been harmed enough; what more did she have to fear from Hecati now? As for this self-pity flooding her, what good was it? Elandra found herself choking on the unwanted emotion, hating it.

She coughed, still supported by Anas's kind hands, and felt tears slip down her cheeks. "I—I—" Her mouth was too dry. She choked again and bowed her head.

Someone else came.

"Be gentle with her," Anas said quietly. "It is spell-shock. She cannot yet speak. Take her inside. No, carry her. Speak softly and make no sudden movements. We were careless, sisters. We were all careless, and see what it has cost us. The Magria will be most displeased."

No one answered that stinging rebuke. The fact that Anas's voice carried self-blame as well as censure made little difference to Elandra.

Two sisters carried her between them. Elandra let them do as they wished. Her mind was filled with memory and a gamut of tangled emotions. Hecati—hate-filled and vindictive—had had the last word as always. With sorcery, Hecati had taken her sight.

seventeen

SLAVE MARKETS WERE ALL MUCH THE SAME in smell, in noise, in procedure; only the locations changed from year to year.

Caelan E'non crouched on his haunches in one corner of his holding pen, idly gazing through the bars at the thronging crowd shopping in the marketplace while he flicked pebbles with his thumbnail. It was blazing hot, like sitting in the bottom of a brass cauldron. No breath of wind reached this corner. The only shade came from a narrow oblong cast by a tattered scrap of cloth tied over the top of the large pen next to his. Some of the occupants were huddled there, making themselves even hotter by their own proximity. But most strutted around restlessly, flexing their bulky muscles and eyeing each other with open hostility.

Grateful to be isolated, since numerous fights had broken out in the larger pens since last night, Caelan pretended to ignore everyone. But his senses were nervously alert.

Unlike a common auction in which slaves for trades

and housework were sold, this was a gladiator sale—held but once a year and always subject to great interest and speculation. Dealers from near and far had come with hand-picked merchandise, hoping to reap good profit from the violent, favorite sport of Imperia.

Caelan turned his head and let his gaze wander across the pens jammed with men who were tall, men who were muscular, men who were simply heavy and out of shape. Many bore horrific scars of old combats. Ears, eyes, fingers, even noses were missing. A few were young boys, lithe and clean-muscled. Several were old and grizzled; these were usually veterans of wars who couldn't adjust to civilian life and had been condemned to the games.

Word had already rustled through the pens: anyone not sold for the games would go cheap for hard labor. The emperor had ordered repair of the city walls, and his agents were waiting to pick up the rejects.

Caelan rose to his feet and stretched. He didn't want to break his back hauling stone, to work until his body broke down. As a boy he'd admired the imperial roads and impressive stoneworks. As a man, he'd seen the pathetic creatures who built such edifices. He knew now that imperial stones were laid with blood and suffering.

He swallowed hard and began to pace back and forth, aware of the distant rattle of chains and slamming of gates. The handlers were fetching the first lots for sale. Already the skilled patter of the auctioneer could be heard over the noise of the crowd.

Another fight started in the common pen, and was broken up with whips.

Ubin, his current owner, appeared. Breathless and excited, Ubin reached through the bars of Caelan's small cage and pulled off Caelan's jerkin.

"Stand close, boy."

Caelan obeyed, and Ubin began rubbing oil across his sun-bronzed chest and back. The stuff smelled rancid and made Caelan feel hotter than ever. His sweat beaded up through the oil, making the smell worse. Caelan shifted away, but Ubin swore at him.

"Remember," he said, looking Caelan over critically, "to look as fierce as you can. Don't bow your head and mince along meekly like a damned houseboy. Flex those muscles and look like you could tear someone apart barehanded. For once, would you please try not to look so bored?"

Caelan yawned, indifferent to Ubin's dreams. The old man had bought him two years ago, when he was starved and beaten, and paid very little for him. Ubin had fed him decent food and worked him hard, always careful to change him from one oar to another so he would develop his back and shoulder muscles evenly. From the first Caelan had been an investment, bought only for eventual resale to the gladiator market here in Imperia. Caelan had been smart enough not to mistake interest and good care for kindness. For all Ubin's fussing now, the moment the auctioneer struck the gavel and gold was counted into Ubin's palm, the old man wouldn't waste any time missing the property he left behind.

Caelan's price plus the sale of his owner's boat was to be Ubin's ticket to retirement. Then Ubin was going to buy a small house on the coast and live in modest luxury, never risking his neck in another dangerous ocean voyage. The good life, the easy life, with a couple of servants, a willing little maid for his bed, and plenty of inexpensive wine to make his days sweet. Ubin's ambitions, all tied up in Caelan's broad back and strong shoulders.

In the distance, a crowd roared and cheered. Ubin craned his old neck a moment, then shrugged. "The dealers will get the best prices," he said. "Damned bunch of thieves. They've rigged the sale already. I saw some of them talking. I know what they're about. Sticking together to drive up prices for themselves, then cutting the throats of any independent person trying to make a decent sale."

Caelan tuned him out. He'd listened to the old man's

fussing all the way to Imperia. They'd come in from the sea, and the city had glittered in the hot sunshine like diamonds spread on the sand. Built on cliffs overlooking the busy harbor, the city was larger than Caelan expected. Taller, too, with buildings of several stories, domed on top instead of flat or pitched. Archways spanned wide paved roads. No muddy tracks here like in the provinces. Houses remained hidden and secluded behind walls. Only the branches of trees growing inside fragrant gardens gave any clue as to what might be contained within those quiet enclaves.

The shops were endless. Merchants of every nationality and description stood outside their booths, bowing and inviting passersby to inspect their wares. The wealth and plenty were staggering, even in the lesser parts of the city where Ubin dragged Caelan along hurriedly down twisting streets to the slave market, chaining him inside the pen with a hasty promise to return in an hour with food.

Clutching his receipt, Ubin had left and not returned until daylight, apologetic and hung over.

It would be Ubin's own stupid fault, Caelan thought sourly, if no one wanted to pay good money for a hunger-stricken rower. As a slave he could make no complaint, although he glared at the old man whenever Ubin wasn't looking. Ubin was a brainless old fool half the time. But in this, at least, they both wanted the same thing.

Beneath Caelan's studied indifference, he was boiling with impatience. As a trained fighter, he would gain skills that would make him valuable anywhere. More importantly, it was said that gladiators entered in the games in Imperia had the chance to fight their way to freedom each season.

Freedom. Caelan rolled the word silently on his tongue. If he still believed in the gods, he would have prayed for it. As it was, he'd learned a man had only himself and his wits, nothing else in this world. Family could be lost. Security was a lie. Wealth could be stolen. Kindness was deception. The gods did not heed the misery on earth.

Caelan had no intention of going back to ordinary labor. He'd spent four years of his life enduring just about every degradation and humiliation possible. But even a man at the bottom could hope. His dreams had shrunk to one ambition—to make the games. They were his only chance of escape. To simply run away was to incur death. He did not intend to become an outlaw chased down by bounty hunters with a pack of dreadots. No, he had other plans.

The first step was to be bought by a trainer. The second step was to drive himself to excel. No matter what it took or cost, he would be the best. He would survive the arena, and he would win his freedom. By next thaw he intended to make his way back to the north country. He would search out the land of the Thyzarenes and strike hard at what they held most dear. He'd had four long years in which to plan his revenge. It was what kept him alive and above despair.

His father would not have approved of his desire for vengeance. But Caelan no longer listened to conscience. Only free men untouched by tragedy could afford to be merciful. He had seen what ideals brought. He wanted none of them.

Ubin hurriedly poured the last of the oil on Caelan's hair, sleeking its long shagginess back. He looked Caelan over and grinned, revealing several gaps in his teeth.

"Now you look like a proper barbarian," he said in approval. He ran his fingertips along the thin scar on Caelan's left jaw. "Good boy. Good boy."

Revulsion made Caelan jerk away, but with the handlers coming for more lots, Ubin was too distracted to retaliate. He darted off, fussing to an auction official who ignored him.

The next lot shambled by with chains clanking on their ankles, and in spite of himself Caelan stepped near the bars to stare.

These half-dozen brutes were of a caliber he'd never seen before. A collective *aah* murmured through the pens. Even the most restless men grew suddenly quiet as the six marched by.

Clad only in loincloths, shaved of all body hair, and oiled, they were perfectly matched in height and weight, each possessing impressive pectorals and deeply ridged serratus muscles. They had fearsome scars puckering their hides to tell of battles they had survived. Their hair was cropped close to their skulls, and one man had but a single eye.

Unlike the others who had preened and picked fights, these men were extremely quiet. But their awareness was like that of wolves—wary, predatory, and supremely dangerous. Just looking at them sent a chill through Caelan. For the first time, he realized what a true killer looked like.

"Champion team," murmured a man in the next pen. "See the gold belts they wear? Champions."

But they hadn't won their freedom. Caelan turned his back to them. "If they're so good, why are they in the auction?"

"You mean they should be in a special sale." The man with all the information nodded and spat. "Aye. The best are usually traded privately, not dragged down here like us." He grinned. "The gossip is they're Lord Vymaltin's own handpicked team."

"So?"

The man sneered, but he answered. "Lord Vymaltin has been dismissed from court. No longer an ambassador. His house is up for sale too, with his house slaves."

The man paused and glanced around before edging closer. "Word is Prince Tirhin has come to buy these fighters. Maybe he'll buy us as well."

Caelan snorted. "And maybe not."

But Ubin suddenly reappeared at the pen, rattling the

gate impatiently and gesturing for an auction attendant to unlock it.

Ubin reached in to seize Caelan's arm. "Come, come!" he said urgently. "Hurry. This is our chance."

Dubious, Caelan thought Ubin would only get himself thrown out of the auction altogether. Dealers had first chance at the block. By trying to jump ahead of turn, Ubin could ruin everything. Caelan started to tell him as much, but then he held his tongue. Advice from a slave was seldom well received, especially when an owner was hell-bent on a course of action.

So Caelan let himself be pushed down the aisle between the pens, stumbling on his leg chains, and ducked beneath a low archway only to find himself in a high-walled enclosure.

Bidders sat on stone benches high above the selling floor, holding fans with numbers painted on them. Slaves and attendants surrounded them. Hard-faced men in leather who must have been trainers were walking around Vymaltin's team, pinching muscle layers, checking teeth, and making notes on small scraps of parchment.

An auction official blocked Ubin's path, glaring with outrage. "Independent lots are sold at the end of the day."

"Good sir," Ubin began with his most obsequious smile. He slipped the man a bribe, and the official walked off with a shrug.

Ubin shoved Caelan forward, positioning him not quite on the block with the others, but close enough to be clearly seen.

The trainers finished their inspection, and the bidding opened. Just the sound of it awakened a tumult of hurtful memories in Caelan. He tried not to listen, tried not to let the shame seize him.

But the bidding was quick and lively. The prices caught Caelan's interest and he glanced up at the gallery, curious to see which bidder was the prince. Sunlight shone down into the well of the auction ring and made him squint. He glimpsed a figure in a rich blue tunic whose lazy hand flick raised the bid every time.

Compressing his lips, Caelan lowered his gaze. He didn't care whether a prince or a common man bought him, as long as he got his chance.

The bidding closed with a final bang of the gavel, and an attendant shout from the crowd.

"Sold, to Prince Tirhin!" the auctioneer said triumphantly. "For two thousand ducats."

"Now," Ubin said in Caelan's ear, giving him a push. "Get on the block. Quickly, boy. Quickly. You're the next lot."

Caelan walked forward, although the team was still on the block. Ubin gave him a harder shove that sent him stumbling inadvertently into the back of the last man in line.

Swearing, the gladiator whirled with a vicious swing of his fist.

He moved faster than any man Caelan had ever seen, faster than thought.

Startled, Caelan reacted instinctively, shifting to one side. The gladiator's fist missed him and crashed into Ubin's jaw.

The old man fell as though pole-axed.

Astonished silence dropped over the crowd; then a babble of voices and questions rose in a tumult.

Caelan ignored all of it, keeping a wary eye on the gladiator who was still glaring at him.

Trainers and handlers rushed up with whips and spears to separate them, but a clear voice called out, "Let them spar!"

The auctioneer wilted on his podium, but with visible resignation gestured for the space to be cleared.

Handlers unchained the last gladiator from the line, although he retained his leg shackles. The rest of the team was moved out and secured in the pens for sold goods. Men dragged the still-unconscious Ubin out of the way.

Caelan found himself breathing too fast, feeling suddenly alone and vulnerable as he faced the brute, who had begun to smile slowly and viciously. The man's eyes held absolutely nothing but a flat sort of pleasure.

He would enjoy killing Caelan, and he had training and efficiency on his side.

"Weapons?" asked the auctioneer.

"No weapons," said the trainer, who wore a dark blue chevron embroidered on his leather jerkin. His gaze shifted appraisingly from Caelan to the gladiator. "Quick sparring," he ordered. "Move!"

The gladiator reacted to the instructions by dropping to a half-crouch and circling Caelan, who nervously circled with him.

The chains on his feet were a problem. Caelan tripped himself and stumbled. Instantly the gladiator seized the moment and lunged.

It was like being rushed by a charging bull. Caelan had an overwhelming impression of size and strength. Fear gripped him, but he had faced worse in the past. Steeling himself, he managed to recover his balance in time to dodge at the last second.

The gladiator's lethal fists missed him, and the man's surprise was revealed in the lines of his shoulders as he skidded to a halt and swung around. Cheering went up, and bets began to be laid among the crowd.

Sweat poured into Caelan's eyes. He shifted lightly on the balls of his feet, his tattered amulet bag thumping against his chest, every sense painfully alert. He could fight with his fists, but his common sense told him he wouldn't have a chance against this man. All he could do was to keep dodging and pray he didn't trip.

This time when the gladiator charged, Caelan was ready for him. Only the man feinted one way, then shifted back. Caelan twisted desperately, too late to save himself from his mistake. A fist slammed into his ribs like a hammer blow.

Caelan grunted as the wind was driven from him. He went down hard, fighting off a rush of blackness. The man loomed over him, but Caelan reached desperately for *severance* just as a mighty kick connected with his side. He felt a rib snap, but *severance* blocked the pain.

Rolling, Caelan regained his feet just in time to avoid another blow. From a great distance he heard the crowd's amazement, but he was floating now in the coldness of separation. The gladiator didn't waste time on surprise of his own. A shift in his eyes warned Caelan, and Caelan surged in straight at the man, getting close enough to touch that mighty chest with his palm before he leapt back.

Using *sevaisin*, the joining, he learned what the gladiator's strategy was and moved to anticipate the gladiator's next attack.

This time he got in a dirty kick to the man's groin, half-connecting even as the gladiator caught his heel and flipped him upside down.

Caelan was rolling before he hit the ground. The gladiator didn't even come close to him that time. Regaining his feet, Caelan crouched, letting the coldness carry him farther and farther from any awareness save his opponent.

"Stop!"

The command came sharply, cutting across the battle haze. The gladiator, breathing hard and slick with sweat, paused immediately. It took longer for Caelan to adjust. He dropped abruptly out of *severance* and bit off a sharp gasp of pain. The broken rib felt like a knife stabbing him with every breath.

He refocused his gaze and realized the trainer's hand was gripping his shoulder. The man tipped back his head and checked his eyes, then forced a thumb into his mouth and felt of his teeth.

"How old?" the trainer asked him in Lingua.

Caelan glanced around for Ubin, but the old man was nowhere in sight. "I am one and twenty," he said.

A commotion from the crowd made him look, and even the trainer swung around quickly and bowed.

The prince appeared, oblivious to the stares and talk. He was perhaps a decade older than Caelan, slim and upright, with black hair and a narrow, very precisely trimmed chinstrap beard and mustache. A handsome man, this prince of the empire. He wore a linen tunic dyed a vibrant shade of blue, and sleek hose of patterned cloth. A modern dueling sword—thin and almost dainty had it not also been a deadly weapon—swung at his side, and his hands were strong and well shaped. A large square-cut sapphire glowed in his left ear.

He stared up at Caelan with one dark brow arching in visible admiration. "Impressive," he said without preamble. "This young giant moves quicker than thought itself. Quicker than his size should allow. Who owns him? What is his provenance?"

The auction officials stirred about and dragged forth a shaken Ubin, still fuzzy-eyed and confused.

"No provenance, sir," the trainer said with scorn. "Anyone can see he's green-trained, if that. A rower, by the look of his muscles."

"Yes," the prince murmured. "Rowers who are properly rotated develop the bodies of gods, and this one has a face to match."

Caelan eyed him warily. Excessive compliments could indicate the kind of interest he didn't like. Caelan had been sold to the galleys in the first place because he spurned his first owner.

The trainer snorted. "A Traulander by the look of him, and Traulanders don't fight."

Prince Tirhin's gaze ran over Caelan. "This one would, if he knew how. There's plenty of spirit in those blue eyes. Now, I just paid top price for a team of champion fighters, and the man got in only two strikes against this one. Either I have wasted my money, or this boy has potential. What say you, trainer?"

The trainer shook his head. "I don't like the looks of him, sir. And who has the time to train him from the ground up, with season starting in two months?"

"That is your problem," Prince Tirhin said. He stepped closer to Caelan and smiled. "Well, lad? Have you spirit enough to fight under my colors?"

Caelan felt hope and satisfaction rising in him. He kept his eyes lowered respectfully to hide he felt. "Yes, master," he said quietly.

"A dodger," the trainer grumbled, still frowning. "Could be the mark of a coward, when it comes to the pinch. All the fancy footwork in the world won't make a man fight if he hasn't the heart."

The prince's smile widened. "Then he'll be good practice fodder for the others. Buy him."

The trainer bowed. "Yes, sir."

As the prince walked away, Ubin lifted his hands in the air and crowed. "A *prince* has bought my slave. I am doubly honored. I am a rich man." Gloating openly, he grinned up at Caelan and clapped him on the shoulder. "Good boy. Good boy! Hah, you'll do fine now. Pampered on a rich man's team. Fed well and trained daily. Yes, yes."

An answering grin spread across Caelan's face.

The trainer, however, counted out twenty ducats into Ubin's palm, and even as Ubin's mouth opened to protest, the auctioneer snatched two of the coins for his commission.

"But, sir," Ubin sputtered wildly, "only twenty—"

"Be grateful for that," the trainer said with a sneer and set his hand on Caelan's broken rib.

The pain was instant and grinding. Caelan winced and sank to one knee.

"Damaged goods go cheaply in this ring," the trainer said. With a laugh, he hauled Caelan to his feet and shoved him forward.

Ubin trotted beside them, still protesting.

The trainer cut him off sharply. "Begone, old fool! Your former slave hasn't made any team I'm training. He'll go to the common arena, and if he survives that hellhole, we'll think about using him next season."

Consternation filled Caelan. He couldn't stop himself from looking back in protest. "But the prince said—"

"The prince has already forgotten your existence." The trainer shoved him through the archway into the maze of holding pens beyond. "Now step lively!"

eighteen

AT DUSK THE DELIVERY WAGON PAUSED AT a guarded checkpoint, then rolled through tall, spiked gates into a compound filled chiefly with low barracks-like buildings. The wagon stopped before a towering, octagonal-shaped building. Torches set into brackets flamed brightly on either side of the entrance.

A man appeared there, short and heavyset, with bullish shoulders that strained against his jerkin. His head was shaved bald and gleamed with oil in the ruddy torchlight. A dagger hung from his belt, and in his free hand he carried a short club fitted with varying lengths of knotted rope.

Climbing down from the wagon with the others, Caelan found himself eying the weapon warily. He knew what a cattail club was. He'd felt the vicious marks of one on his back more than once, and he never wanted to be punished that way again.

"Get in line!" A guard passed among the new fighters quickly, pushing and shoving them into a straggly row.

The bald man walked along them, his dark liquid eyes

making a rapid inspection. When he came to Caelan, he paused and frowned.

"This man is sick."

The driver from the auction spat and handed over a paper. "Injured while sparring on the block for one of the customers. It's marked, here, see?"

"Ah." The bald man held his torch higher while he peered at the paper. "Bought cheap enough." Then he loosed a low whistle. "Bought by the prince!"

He gave Caelan a second look, doubt more evident in his face than before. Grudgingly he nodded. "That'll be noted, and you'll get the better food the prince always specifies. Well, well. He hasn't sent anyone to me to be trained in months. Not since he hired that fancy private trainer."

Still nodding, he inked a mark on the paper and handed it back to the driver. "All accounted for. Drive on."

The wagon turned laboriously and headed out the gates, its slatted sides rattling. The darkness swallowed it, and soon even the tired plodding hoofbeats faded from hearing.

The bald man stepped back and glared at the line of fighters. "Welcome to the common arena," he said in a gruff, no-nonsense voice. "Otherwise known as the hell-hole. Those of you who are veterans, don't think you'll have it easy here. This is Imperia, and our arena is like no other in the world. As for you green ones, if you don't know one end of a sword from the other, you have two months to learn before season starts. After that, you'll fight or you'll die. It's that simple. I'm Orlo. My word is law. Disobey me, and you'll find there are worse things than death. Am I clear?"

No man answered.

Orlo squinted at them and finally nodded. "Guards! Take them to the delousing tank, then quarters."

The guards were wary, armed to the teeth, and quick.

They shoved the men forward with shouts and oaths designed to confuse and intimidate.

Thinking only of food and a pile of straw for sleep, Caelan followed at the end of the line a little slower than the others. He had his elbow pressed against his aching side for support, and he was almost tempted to ask for some etherd root to chew on to ease the pain. But he dared not make any request until he knew what manner of rules existed here.

Just as he passed Orlo, the trainer swung the cattail club viciously across Caelan's bare back. The blow drove him to his knees, and the pain from his rib robbed him of breath. His scream lay smothered in his throat, and for a blinding moment he was awash in crimson and sickly gray. His back burned as though on fire, and he thought he might never breathe again.

Orlo circled around in front of him and gripped his hair to pull up his head. "Are you mute, you big bastard?" he growled.

Tears and sweat streamed down Caelan's face. Somehow he found enough pride to answer. "No," he said through his teeth.

"Get up!"

Clamping his jaw, Caelan managed to stagger to his feet. He was a full head and shoulders taller than Orlo, but it was the shorter man who had the advantage.

"The arena is no place for cowards," Orlo said.

"I'm no coward—"

"Shut up!" Orlo raised the club again, and Caelan flinched back. Grinning, Orlo slowly lowered his hand.

Shame flooded Caelan. He knew in that instant he'd failed some kind of test.

"All Traulanders are cowards," Orlo said. "Big brutes who can't move and won't fight. I know your kind."

Caelan burned inside. *No, you don't,* he thought. *Not me.*

"If you were any good, the prince would have let his

fancy private trainer work with you. He wouldn't have sent you to me."

There was something ugly in the way Orlo said that, something resentful that flamed in his eyes. Seeing it, Caelan's heart sank.

"I am going to make you good," Orlo said. "I am going to make you fight. Or I'll kill you in the effort. You understand?"

"Yes," Caelan breathed. It was what he had prayed for while he waited for the auction. Now he wondered why he had ever thought he could do this.

"What is it you call your religion?" Orlo asked. "*Severing*?"

Caelan did not trust his voice. Cautiously he nodded.

Orlo raised the club with clear menace. "You try that nonsense around here, especially on any of my men, and you'll taste this. You understand?"

It was clear Orlo didn't understand what *severance* was, but his fear was dangerous. "I will obey," Caelan said. Any other response was unthinkable.

Orlo did not seem to believe him. With a sneer, he gripped the amulet pouch hanging around Caelan's neck and yanked it over his head. "You won't need this."

Miraculously over the years, Caelan's owners had respected the pouch and left it alone, although slaves weren't allowed possessions. Now Caelan felt dismay wash through him. "It is my amulet," he said hollowly, trying not to betray his concern. "I—"

"Liar!" Orlo said sharply. "Trau is a civilized province, not a pagan one. Your kind don't carry amulets."

That was true, but until now no one else had seemed to know it. Caelan stared at the little pouch with its precious contents and swallowed the lump in his throat. *Lea, forgive me*, he thought in despair.

"Please," he whispered, but with a scowl Orlo shoved him forward.

Thus it began, a rigorous nightmare that never seemed

to end. From dawn until dusk they were pounded, forced to run laps along a track of deep, foot-clogging sand while guards on horseback whipped them to keep going. Practice weapons were heavy, blunt scraps of metal with worn hilt wrappings that often left a man's hand blistered raw or cut open. Injuries passed untreated. Many a man moaned through the night with sprains, bruises, and lacerations. They were fed plentifully and cheaply, mostly barley grain and beans, twice a day. The one blessing was they could have all the water they wanted, and it was always fresh in the barrel.

The first night Caelan tore strips of cloth off his straw pallet and used it to bind his ribs. Even with that tight support, the next few days were an agony he thought he might not survive. Only *severance* enabled him to bear the pain. At night when he was allowed to collapse on his pallet, he sweated in the darkness and tried desperately to remember everything he had learned at Rieschelhold and from his father's teachings in an effort to heal himself. For the first time, he had to acknowledge that he'd been a fool of a boy, but there was no going back. That path was cut forever, and he remained, the only survivor of his family, the unworthy one, the rebel and troublemaker who had disobeyed and disrupted and who had lived. Where was the justice in that? Where was the mercy? Where was the rightness?

Truly the gods toyed with the lives of men.

In the first days he was inept and slow. He kept dropping the fake weapons. His footwork stumbled. The trainers swore at him and whipped him. Every time Orlo walked by, Caelan made a stupid mistake.

And Orlo would look both disgusted and satisfied at the same time. "Extra drills for the Traulander," he would say and walk on.

Increasingly frustrated, Caelan could not understand why he did not improve. Even as a boy in his father's hold he had never been clumsy. Any physical activity was easy for him. He wouldn't have longed to be a soldier in the first place if he hadn't felt himself capable of it. But now it seemed as though all his natural abilities had deserted him.

His rib healed quickly, whether through the mercy of the gods or through his limited efforts to speed its recovery. And although no one made any effort to treat him, Caelan noticed he wasn't assigned to any practice bouts until he was sound.

Already fit, with a deep chest and powerful shoulders, he found the tough conditioning work honed his body even more. He grew another inch, and his muscles hardened to the kind of definition the trainers called deeply cut. The drills gave him flexibility and a new awareness of his body's strength. Long hours under the merciless sun bronzed his skin to a dark honey color and bleached his hair nearly white. His muscles rippled powerfully beneath his skin when he moved. He was perhaps the tallest man in training, and the other fighters called him Giant. The trainers all agreed that in looks alone, he would make an intimidating presence in the ring, but they had already laid bets that he would die in the first round.

Caelan knew about the bet, of course, and it did nothing for his morale.

Although he hadn't prayed in years, now in the privacy of nighttime he lifted his heart to Gault, asking why this was denied him. He had sworn he would do everything in his power to excel, yet here he was at the bottom of the group. The humiliation of his failure gnawed at him constantly.

Training separately in their own advanced drills, the veterans paused to laugh and jeer every time Caelan walked by. Sooner or later all the trainers came by to watch him performing drills. Shaking their heads, they discussed him as though he couldn't understand what they were saying.

"Orlo said he bested one of Lord Vymaltin's champions at the auction."

"Never! Look at the clumsy oaf."

"I swear it's what everyone says. It's why Prince Tirhin bought him in the first place."

"The prince must have been too drunk to see."

Laughing, the trainers walked on.

Seething, Caelan focused everything he had on the lunge-and-feint drill he was practicing. He *could* focus his mind. He had once been able to direct a warding key, after all. He could do this.

Fresh sweat broke out on his face with the effort he expended, but all he accomplished was a sudden cramp in his leg that pitched him down, gasping hard while the other trainees stopped their drills and laughed.

"Silence!" Orlo shouted, swinging his club indiscriminately among them. "Get back to work."

Pushing his way through the chastened trainees, he came and stood over Caelan, who lay sprawled in the sand, gritting his teeth while he worked the spasm from his leg muscles.

"Get up," Orlo said.

"Yes," Caelan gasped out, trying. But the cramp wouldn't release.

A whistle of the knotted ropes through the air warned him. Caelan tried to dodge, but the cattails cracked across his shoulders. The fresh pain drove away all awareness of the cramp.

"Get up!" Orlo repeated.

Caelan scrambled to his feet and stood there, drenched with sweat and shame until he was almost shaking.

Pursing his lips, Orlo stared up at Caelan a long while without saying anything. Finally he beckoned and led Caelan over to a corner of the practice pit.

"What's the problem, Traulander?" he demanded. "Your religion getting in the way?"

"No, master," Caelan said quietly. He kept his gaze on

the ground to hide his shame and frustration.

"Why won't Traulanders fight?" Orlo asked.

Caelan clenched his fists. "I want to fight," he said.

"You don't act like it. I could whip you bloody and it wouldn't help."

"No, master," Caelan agreed miserably. His plan was dying in his heart.

"Perhaps you're trying too hard. Relax, you fool, and let it come naturally. The weapon is caressed, not throttled. Settle the hilt in your palm the way you would your woman's breast. Eh? Make sense to you?"

Caelan's face flamed, and he shifted his feet. Orlo knew how few women entered the life of a slave, if any. But whether advice or a taunt, what he said did make sense.

Orlo sighed and slid the club into his belt. "Assume stance."

Astonishment filling him, Caelan obeyed quickly. He couldn't believe his luck at this special attention, but he knew better than to spoil it with hesitation.

"Flex your knees more," Orlo instructed. "Keep your back straight but loose. Pay attention! Feel how tense you are. You must be a reed, swaying always, never still, never locked up. Lunge!"

Caelan sprang forward, and Orlo skipped out of the way just in time.

"Not too bad," he said, "for a lumbering ox. Imagine you are standing on a pane of glass. Do you know what glass is, Traulander?"

"Yes, master."

"Well, well, perhaps you're more civilized than I thought. Don't pound your feet. You're dancing on glass. Every footstep must be light. You are a reed, swaying, always moving. Lunge!"

And on it went, for the rest of the afternoon. By the time he finished, Caelan was dragging with exhaustion but heartened. The next morning, however, when he was as-

signed a veteran partner for practice bouts, the moment
he drew a work sword from the rack he dropped it.

"Hail the loser!" jeered his opponent.

Face aflame, Caelan bent and picked up the narrow
strip of blunt metal. The balance was clumsy. Try as he
might, he couldn't even imagine it as a real sword. They
were forbidden actual weapons until they entered the
arena. Sometimes he felt that if he could practice with the
real thing, he might do better. But he might as well wish
to walk the surface of the moon.

Many years before, in the previous century, it was said
gladiators practiced with real weapons and as many died
from sparring as in the ring. But there had been an upris-
ing, with the trainers and guards all massacred. Gladiators
had escaped the compound and run amok in the city, rap-
ing and pillaging until the army was called out to stop
them. Even then, some of them had escaped into the countryside, never to be found. The others were rounded up
and executed. Their heads had rotted on the walls of the
city for weeks.

Thereafter had come the arena reforms. Haggai—whatever they were—had been brought to live in the catacombs beneath the arena. Weapons were taken away
altogether and not put into the hand of a fighter until he
was actually secured in the ring. Guards were retrained to
a new standard of vigilance. Any sign of rebellion or un-
rest was punished swiftly with death. The veterans were
kept separated from the new trainees, except during su-
pervised practice bouts. And even the veterans were rotated among the barracks on a frequent basis, to keep
friendships from forming.

Not that many men grew close, especially knowing
everyone was a potential opponent during season. With
all fights to the death, it was smarter to keep comradeship
to a minimum. Trainees who didn't heed that piece of
advice died quickly in the ring, eyes wide and astonish-

ment frozen on their faces as the sword thrust through their guts.

Like the trainers who expected Caelan to fail, all the other fighters believed it too. They taunted him at every opportunity. Brawling was forbidden, so Caelan had to grit his teeth and take it. But every day he worked harder and harder, driving himself more than the trainers did. At night, he lay on his pallet and ran the drills through his mind, visualizing the footwork over and over until he could do it without thinking. During brief moments of rest, he watched the veterans working with each other and he took mental notes of their skills and advanced tactics. They had many tricks and shortcuts that he mulled over constantly. In the darkness, he tried to imagine himself wielding a sword with grace and skill. He thought of reeds rippling in the breeze across the marshes. Sometimes it felt so natural as he lay there imagining it. He could actually feel the heft of a sword hilt in his hand, the tension in his wrist. At such times he believed he could master the weapon.

But by day, even if his footwork improved, his ability to work with the fake weapons did not. It was as though some strange force blocked the messages from his brain to his arm. By concentrating extremely hard, he could finally get his wrist and arm into the correct rhythm and perform the drills correctly, but as soon as his opponent shifted or attacked, Caelan muffed the whole thing and ended up with the blunt end of his opponent's practice weapon rammed painfully against his breastbone or pressing hard against his neck.

"By the gods, I'd like to cut off your bloody head," swore Nux when their practice bout ended in the usual way. He held Caelan pinned for longer than was allowed, glaring into Caelan's eyes.

"I will cut it off tomorrow," he said. A brawny Serian with a flat broken nose and no front teeth, he was a veteran of the arena and had been here for two years, the longest of anyone.

He fought in a weird style unlike any of the others, and his taunts were the worst. Somehow he always seemed to know what his opponent secretly feared the most, and he preyed on that, laughing as he attacked. He had never been deemed good enough to make it to the private arenas, despite the fact that he'd survived four seasons in the last two years.

A season lasted three months, with three months' rest while new fighters were trained. That meant each year was supposed to have two seasons. However, when the common arena was at rest, many of the private arenas were in season. That meant any citizen of Imperia, providing he had the means and the access, could attend a gladiatorial contest any given day of the year.

It was a bloody madness, a public obsession at its worst here in the capital city. It used up men voraciously, with the dead piling up in a carnage nearly equal to that of a battlefield. While the war with Madrun continued, there were plenty of prisoners of war to be hauled in to supplement the ranks of fighters.

Many people in Imperia disapproved of the practice, and that disapproval was said to be slowly gaining popularity. Critics who dared speak out claimed the arena games were an outdated piece of savagery. The empire had grown and matured beyond such barbarism, and the arena should be left behind in the dim past of a less civilized era, where it belonged.

Of course to criticize the games was to criticize the emperor, who had organized them long, long ago in his first incarnation. It was even whispered that those who wanted the games banned and the arenas closed wanted the emperor to die that the world might go on into a modern age.

There were many discoveries, many practices of new knowledge supposedly banned by imperial decree. As the centuries had passed, the emperor seemed to want to cling to the old ways more and more. He resisted modern progress in every way possible. That's why the army was still organized into fighting legions, still armed with old-fashioned short swords for the infantry, still encumbered with ancient rituals while the officers rebelliously wore modern armor plate and carried more efficient weapons.

Now and then people were heard to say, "When Tirhin is emperor, things will change."

But they did not say such things often or very loudly, without first looking over their shoulders. It was still considered treason to utter such a statement. And officially Tirhin had not been named as successor.

The prince himself was apparently as avid a supporter of the arena as his father. It was the prince who had instigated private arenas and taken his teams out of the common combat. The nobles who could afford it followed suit. The result had left the common arena shabbier and bloodier, with half-trained gladiators hacking brutally at each other with little regard for rules of combat. The masses enjoyed the spectacle, but the nobles came to the common arena less and less. This embittered the trainers, like Orlo, who felt betrayed and abandoned.

It also meant the age-old rule that an arena survivor was rewarded by receiving his freedom did not really apply anymore. Only the privately owned gladiators had a chance of that reward. According to the word in the barracks, several arena champions had won their freedom but continued to fight for plump salaries and special privileges.

Thus, men like Nux were forgotten or ignored. Having survived, they faced only another grinding season, when any unguarded moment in the ring could mean destruction or maiming injury.

Nux knew Caelan was privately owned by the prince. They all did. And while Caelan's abilities seemed too poor to threaten anyone here, he at least had the nominal chance to leave, which they did not. Resentment flared hot in the practice bouts, and Caelan came out bruised and battered.

"Let him up, Nux!" roared Orlo now, seeing Caelan still pinned with the blunt practice sword on his neck. "Let him up!"

Nux slid the metal edge along Caelan's neck, pressing hard enough to hurt. His eyes blazed with hostility. "Tomorrow it will be real swords, Traulander. Tomorrow, when I do this, your pretty head will fall on the sand and the crowds will cheer my name."

He stepped back just as Orlo came striding up. Looking innocent, Nux slid his practice sword into the rack and walked away.

Orlo gave Caelan a kick. "Hopeless," he said. "I knew it from the first. The prince sent you here to humiliate me. Stupid Traulanders, afraid to fight, afraid of the dark, afraid, afraid, afraid. Bah!"

Still breathing hard from the bout, Caelan knelt on the sand and found himself at eye level with the hilt of Orlo's dagger. The hilt was wrapped with very fine copper wire and had a brass knob on the end. It reminded Caelan of the old dagger he had bought from the Neika tribesman the day the Thyzarenes attacked the hold.

Mesmerized by the sight of it, Caelan half closed his eyes and listened to the faint song of the metal. It was as though the weapon called to him in a low, nearly inaudible voice. He could almost understand it, and he wanted to hold it.

A swift whack of his outstretched hand recalled him to the present. Blinking, feeling dizzy, Caelan dodged another slap from Orlo and scrambled to his feet.

The trainer glared at him. "Try something that stupid again, and I'll cut off your hand."

Caelan tried not to look at the dagger and failed. It still sang somewhere deep within him. Try as he might, he could not shake it. "Your dagger looks very old and fine. Where did it come from?"

Orlo's mouth dropped open, as though he couldn't believe Caelan had dared ask a personal question.

Turning red, Orlo raised his cattail club. "Get to barracks! Wash your filthy hide!"

Caelan ducked his head and ran. Humiliation and rage at himself burned within him. He wouldn't have taken the dagger from Orlo. He wouldn't have attacked the man with it. He was simply curious. But slaves weren't allowed to explain. They were judged and punished.

Slaves weren't allowed to be curious either. No opinions. No conversation. No questions. No privileges.

It seemed he would never learn.

And now there was no more time. Tomorrow morning the games would commence.

As he jogged across the drilling field with the others, he glanced at the arena itself. Dozens of workers swarmed it, scrubbing steps and setting up railings to direct the crowd. Beyond the gates, concessioners congregated impatiently, with their wares and cooking grills stacked haphazardly. They were shouting offers at the guards, trying to bribe their way in early.

As yet, Caelan had not been inside it. He wondered what it would be like. Supposedly the ring was divided into six sections. In the first game, twelve gladiators were positioned, two to a section. The six victors then fought, until there were three. Then there would be a free-for-all among the three men, or lots would be tossed to see who fought first. Only one victor left the ring each day.

On the following day, the lone victor would again be a member of twelve gladiators. The same procedure would be followed. Usually the least trained men fought first, with the veterans coming in fresh on subsequent days. Each week was called a rotation. At the end of the seventh day, the survivors would draw lots to see which day of the next rotation they would fight. And so on, until the end of the season.

In Caelan's barracks, the trainees were quiet. Most looked frightened. Tomorrow was looming larger and larger. Word had gone round that this was the last day they would see the sun except in the arena itself until season ended. Tonight they would go into the catacombs beneath the arena, a dark mysterious place that the veterans seemed to dread.

And what was the initiation this afternoon? None of the veterans had mentioned it before, nor would they discuss it now, which was odd.

Caelan ignored the whispered worries of the others. Standing in the doorway of the barracks, he stared out at the sandy jogging track and the wall towering beyond it. The sun beat down on the dry earth, and only a slight ragged breeze stirred the dust.

He thought of the glacier of home, the ice-capped mountains, and fragrant pine forests. He thought of the dazzling lights in the winter sky, of the apple harvests and the smoky smell of peat. All that seemed a hundred years in the past. Now he stood here, in a place of death. The smell of it already lay in his nostrils, although combat would not commence until tomorrow. He felt cold and shivery as a strange feeling passed over him. Glancing over his shoulder, he took in his comrades. He had not troubled to learn most of their names, and now as he gazed at them he saw their flesh fade away. They were a collection of skeletons sitting, standing, lolling on their pallets in unexpected idleness. The vision faded, and Caelan wrenched his gaze back to the jogging track.

Breathing hard, he wiped clammy sweat from his forehead. He'd had such visions before. These men were doomed. They would die tomorrow, or the next day, or the next.

And him?

He did not know, but his own death seemed to be the most certain thing of all.

nineteen

THEY WERE FED A MIDDAY MEAL—AN
unheard-of luxury.

While they ate, Caelan heard a clamor outside. Half
the men went to the window to look. The rest, Caelan
included, took the chance to grab all the food available.
In minutes guards appeared at the door, yelling for them
to assemble outside.

Squinting in the glaring sunshine, they milled around
uncertainly while all the veterans filed out from their barracks as well.

"Form ranks!" Orlo shouted.

In the broiling sun, they divided themselves into two
lines. Veterans on one side, trainees on the other, facing
each other. The guards were extra vigilant today, keyed
up even more than the fighters.

Caelan felt increasingly nervous. His stomach knotted
up, and he wished he had not eaten so much. He kept
swallowing, trying to ease the dryness in his mouth. He
tried not to think of tomorrow, and yet it was impossible.

While they stood lined up, the gates to the compound

opened, and a procession of priests entered, swinging incense holders that burned with crimson smoke. The priests were chanting something unintelligible that sent eerie chills up Caelan's spine.

The priests wore long brown robes with leopard hides across their shoulders. Their heads and faces were shaven. Still chanting, they walked between the two long rows of fighters, then circled around and headed up the steps into the arena itself. Prodded by the guards, the fighters filed after them.

Caelan wasn't interested in what the priests were doing. Their incense stunk, and he tried to breathe as little of it as possible. Going up the steps, he felt his heartbeat quicken and his palms were suddenly damp. He glanced back once for a quick look—probably his last—of the compound.

The interior was cool and slightly dank, all dim and shadowy, with ramps leading up to the stone seats that circled the entire structure. To his surprise, Caelan found the arena was shaped like a bowl, with the fighting area at the bottom and the spectators ranged above. He had never seen such a place before, but he had no chance to study it, for the guards were shoving them along as quickly as possible.

The veterans branched off through an open door, leaving only the trainees to follow the priests along a dim passageway and finally down a broad flight of stone steps. In the near darkness the steps were treacherous, and the air smelled strange and unhealthy.

As the air gusted up into their faces, Caelan's nostrils wrinkled with revulsion. It was more than dank. It carried smells of oiled leather, mildew, blood, and death.

He shook his head, angry at his own vivid imagination. Nothing had died in here for at least three months. Corpses were cleared away immediately to hold down the chance of disease.

Still, there was something odd and unusual to the mingled scents in the air . . . something he could not identify, yet it sent involuntary shivers through him.

Caelan stopped, all his instincts warning him against descending farther.

A hand shoved him forward so hard he nearly fell. "Get on!" Orlo said angrily. "None of your Traulander nonsense about the dark here."

Given no chance to protest, Caelan was crowded down the steps along with the others.

At the bottom they found themselves pushed into a large, vaulted chamber lit by flaring torches. Stone columns carved in twists supported the ceiling at its highest point. Carved into the far wall was an enormous, tormented face of a demon. At first glance Caelan thought it was the fire spirit himself.

Caelan's blood congealed in his veins. He glanced around swiftly, trying to back out, but Orlo shoved him forward with the others. The door was slammed shut and bolted, sealing them in with the chanting priests.

Already the stench of incense was chokingly thick. Caelan smelled blood again, fresh and warm. But now he realized it wasn't his imagination. Across the room stood a stone altar flanked on either side by two vats of copper. Both held a thick, shimmering liquid that darkly reflected the torchlight.

The face of the fire spirit on the wall had a fire kindled inside the open hearth of its mouth. The flames burning there made the empty eyes of the horrifying visage glow, and every darting shift of the fire made the face appear to move and gaze back at the men.

Overhead, Caelan could see the snarling faces of wooden beasts carved into the support beams, shadowy and all the more menacing. The fire hissed and licked the stone lips of the fire spirit, and if Caelan closed his eyes he could hear unworldly sounds in the steady chanting from the priests, a whispering of vile blasphemies from the ways of antiquity.

From infancy Caelan had been taught the lessons of ancient times, when the world had been ruled by the shadow gods and their spirits of chaos, also called *shyrieas*. Then they had been sealed away and the world had been placed under the rule of mankind. Such unholy carvings as Caelan saw around him now were said to be small breaks in the seal, creating tiny gateways for evil to return.

Caelan's forehead was beaded with sweat. His uneasiness grew, and he backed up until he stood behind all the others at the very rear of the room. The door was stout wood, bound with iron straps and bolted from the outside. He had no way to escape from this place, and he felt as though he had entered hell itself.

The stone floor was black with ageless grime. The burning torches sent dark streaks of soot up the walls. The torches themselves smoked fearsomely, emitting fitful pops as though they'd been soaked in bad pitch.

The chanting stopped. In silence the priests arranged themselves behind the altar in a semicircle. One priest in a saffron robe stepped forward to the altar and raised his hands.

"Here in the halls of death stand condemned men, O Gault."

Caelan held back a gasp. He had never known the father-god to be worshiped like this.

Again, Caelan involuntarily glanced around for a way out. There was none.

"Their blood is your blood, our father. Their lives are forfeit by the will of their masters. By your will, we have come to prepare their souls for the journey into your hands. We are your avengers, O Gault."

"Avengers," the other priests chanted.

"We are your punishers, O Gault."

"Punishers."

"We are the chosen faithful, who lead others to your understanding, O Gault."

"Chosen."

"Vindicate us, oh great one, as we vindicate others."

The priest lowered his arms and picked up a plain copper bowl, which he dipped into one of the vats of fresh blood. Lifting it high so that the blood dripped onto the altar in small, dark spatters, the priest looked around him with bright, fanatic eyes.

"Who will be the first to come?"

No one moved.

Caelan had long heard it said by gossips that the emperor permitted perversions of all kinds to flourish in Imperia, that the emperor—in his own desperate search for immortality—had opened the gates to the dark spirits. But this was Caelan's first real encounter with any such practices. Of course he knew who the Vindicants were. He had heard his father and other men in the hold shake their heads over the most powerful faction of the priesthoods. There were almost no Vindicants in Trau, and scant tolerance of such rituals as this.

Disgust rose in Caelan. He scowled and planted his feet, crossing his arms over his chest. Whatever they intended, he wasn't going to participate.

The priest was speaking again, softly, cajolingly. Whether pushed by a guard or drawn forward by curiosity, one man stepped up to the altar and bowed.

"I am afraid to die," he whispered.

The priest smiled and put his hand on the man's head. He spoke something aloud, then put the bowl to the man's lips. "Drink," he commanded.

Caelan swallowed hard, his revulsion stronger than ever. It was forbidden to drink blood. By all he'd ever been raised to believe, such was not allowed.

The priest was not satisfied with merely a sip. He insisted until the man had swallowed the entire bowlful, gagging on it. Then the priest seized the man's wrist and made a swift cut with a copper knife. The man screamed and tried to twist away, but the priest held him with unexpected strength. Blood bubbled up from the man's wrist, and the priest collected several drops of it in a second bowl, chanting all the while.

"From fear is born obeisance. From despair is created belief. You have taken the blood of the god and given your blood in return. Such is your passage into the brotherhood of life-takers. Gault be praised."

Another priest bandaged the cut efficiently and gestured at the large face of the fire spirit. "Pass through the mouth of the god," he said, "and receive your blessing in the next room."

Miraculously the fire blazing inside the mouth of the carving died down as though by command. Hesitant, the man finally ducked low and stepped through, hopping over the glowing coals. As soon as he vanished from sight, the fire blazed up again. It was as though the god had consumed him.

Everyone waited, but no sound came from the other side—not a scream, not a whisper. It was as though the man had vanished forever.

Someone crowded next to Caelan, his face pale. "What in the name of the gods do you think is beyond that?" he whispered.

Caelan shook his hand, unwilling to utter a sound in this place of evil. He had never witnessed such blasphemy, such a twisting of the truth or the old ways. Even witnessing these acts made him feel unspeakably tainted. He wanted to cry out condemnation at what was being done, but he kept silent, afraid of punishment from the guards. His own fear shamed him.

One by one the trainees went forward, sweating and fearful, forced to the altar if necessary. Some drank the blood with bravado, pretending to enjoy it. Others spat and choked. Again and again the priest dipped the bowl for more. Not one trainee failed to flinch as his wrist was cut in turn. Bandaged, each man then stepped through the mouth of the fire spirit and vanished until there were only five men left, then three, then one.

Caelan stood alone, the last man, and he would not budge.

The guards sighed and gripped his arms. "Always causing trouble, you are," one murmured. "Come now, Giant. Move your big feet."

They force-marched him to the altar, with him planting his feet at every chance.

"Bow to Gault," the priest commanded.

Caelan glared at him, tight-lipped and defiant.

"Blasphemer! Bow to the father-god!"

"Gault is not worshiped this way," Caelan retorted. "I will not defile him with such evil."

Fury twisted the priest's face. He struck Caelan across the mouth before the guards could react.

"You dare defy us, slave! You are a condemned man. You have no choice but to serve as you are bidden."

"Go to the hell you serve," Caelan said.

The priest stepped back, glaring. He snapped his fingers, and the guards closed in on Caelan. One socked him in the stomach, doubling him over.

While Caelan was still gasping and choking, trying to draw in air, the other man twisted his left arm behind him and gripped him by the hair.

Caelan gritted his teeth with all his might, struggling and kicking, but with four guards on top of him even his strength was not enough. One of the guards pried open his jaws while the priest poured the blood down his throat.

Choking and drowning in the stuff, Caelan thought he would be sick. Gasping and shuddering, he was released and sank to the floor at their feet. The priest chanted grimly over him, then gestured. Caelan was kicked.

"Get up," the guards told him.

Slowly, resentfully, he rose to his feet and towered over the priest. The man lifted the copper knife, its tiny blade stained with the blood of all the others. At the last second, Caelan jerked his wrist so that only the skin was cut and not the vein. A few small beads of blood welled up, but not enough to be collected.

"Hold him," the priest said to the guards.

They grabbed Caelan's arms, but he lifted his feet and kicked at the altar, sending bowls and implements flying. Blood splashed across the robes of several priests. Their chanting stopped abruptly.

Still kicking and struggling, Caelan condemned them at the top of his lungs.

The chief priest glared at him while others knelt on the ground, hastily trying to scrape up the spilled blood. The man's face was taut with fury. Spots of color blazed in his cheeks.

"Gault's curse be on you!" he shouted. "Defiler, know now the true meaning of condemnation, for you shall face death without the protection of the gods. All blessing is stripped from you. Gault's face shall be turned from you, and when you die the *shyrieas* will shriek acclaim at another soul lost to all damnation."

Even the guards looked shaken.

But Caelan did not believe in the religion of the Vindicants, and he laughed scornfully at the curse. *"Teiserat huggen fieh ein selt ein fahrne teiseran!"* he shouted, using the old words spoken to drive wicked spirits away from the walls of hold, house, and hearth. It was the only ancient countermand he knew.

Whether the priests understood it or not, it had the effect of freezing them in their tracks.

The chief priest gestured at the guards. "Get him out of here. Quickly!"

The guards dragged Caelan over to the fire spirit and released him with a shove. "Pass through!"

The fire was still blazing in the mouth. Caelan hesitated.

Another guard kicked him. "Do it or we'll throw you on the fire."

The flames died down, and Caelan ducked through. As

he did so, he could feel the radiant heat from the coals beneath him. He hopped down to the floor on the other side and found himself alone in a small, featureless room. An open passageway led from it.

Surprised, Caelan stood there and glanced around. There was nothing in here to fear or fight.

Suddenly the walls seemed to tilt. He sank to his knees, feeling nauseous with shame. If his father walked the spirit world and could see him at this moment, he prayed Beva would understand the many failings of his son.

Caelan ran his fingers down his throat until he vomited up the blood.

Spitting and wiping his mouth, he moved to another, cleaner corner and leaned back on his haunches, bracing his shoulder against the wall. Bitterness lay sour in his mouth, and he found the old hatred rekindled in his heart. Perhaps it was a mercy to die on the morrow. He would certainly rather be dead than to continue like this.

But another part of him raged silently, demanding vengeance for all the degradations that he had known. He had to find a way to battle free of slavery. He had to live, and win, and survive.

The strange, frightening scent that he'd been unable to identify earlier now returned to the air.

Startled, Caelan lifted his head and gazed at the passageway. Only darkness lay inside it, a darkness he did not want to explore.

"Come," whispered a voice. It was strange and mysterious, raspy yet soft, and definitely female. "Come to me, man of violence, and let me give you power to win on the morrow."

The hair rose on the back of Caelan's neck. Wide-eyed and dry-mouthed, he stared at the passageway, trying to see what spoke to him from the shadows. He saw nothing, yet she was out there.

"Do not fear," she whispered. "I am given to you until the dawn."

His mind raced. A prostitute?

Everyone knew a man lost his prowess by indulging himself the night before combat. Like draining blood from men under the guise of initiation rites, this was another trick designed to see that the trainees failed.

Angry, Caelan jumped to his feet. "Go away," he said curtly. "I don't want you."

"You must come to me," she whispered, her voice sultry and enticing. "I have power to give you."

"You will steal my power," he retorted. "Begone from me!"

"You are wrong."

There was silence for a moment, and he thought she'd left. The fire still blazed in the mouth of the carving, cutting him off from leaving the way he'd entered. From the larger chamber beyond came the sounds of the guards talking. The priests filed out in silence, their footsteps walking in even cadence.

He thought that as soon as everyone had gone, he would find a way to scatter the fire or smother it. Then perhaps he could get out of this place.

A scraping sound, as though something heavy were being dragged, came from the passageway.

"I can approach no closer," she called softly, her voice sounding breathless and strained. "I cannot enter the light. Come to me, and I will share wonderful secrets with you. It will be a night to remember always. This I promise."

"I'm sure," he said grimly. "But I'm not interested."

"You are gruff and fierce," she replied as though amused. "But when does a man refuse pleasure?"

"I do," he said, although the more she talked, the more uncomfortable and uneasy he felt. "I said no."

She began to sing, softly and throatily. Despite his suspicions, life stirred in his groin. He frowned and tried to block out the sound, but for once he could not tune it out. Even an attempt to *sever* did not work. He could not say the sound was melodic or pleasing, and yet it sent swift ripples of desire through his muscles. He found himself turning in that direction, swaying in time with the song, his breath rasping in his throat.

"Come," she sang. "Come, for I am given to you to make you happy, to make you forget tomorrow. I am given to strengthen you and make you invincible. I am better than wine. Come to me, Caelan E'non. Come."

He was afraid of the spell she was weaving over him, and yet into his mind came an image of a woman with pale flowing hair. She was running naked through a meadow of alpine flowers, laughing, her arms outstretched as though she were flying. He wanted to run with her, to laugh with her, to catch her in his arms and swing her to the ground.

Before he realized it, he was walking across the small room, drawn by a force greater than his own will. Through a haze he wondered how she knew his name. Through a haze he wondered why she would not venture into the light. Through a haze he thought of how this was a mistake.

Yet what was one more mistake among a lifetime of them? He had no hope of success in the arena anyway. Why shouldn't he take this opportunity to enjoy himself?

He reached the mouth of the passageway and somehow managed to stop by clutching the frame with his hands. His body swayed toward her, yet his fingers dug in and held him in place.

"Come to me," she whispered.

Her scent rolled over him again. He snorted against it, finding it cloyingly sweet, exotic, and yet somehow rotten.

"What are you?" he struggled to say. His lips felt wooden and thick.

"I am a haggai," she replied. "How strong you are. How suspicious. Do not fear me. I am given to you. Come."

He took one step forward, his hands sliding down the wall and dragging free.

At that angle, with the firelight shining behind him to cast faint illumination into the mouth of the passageway, he saw her. Just a vague outline—the long mass of curling hair springing up and blowing as though in a breeze, the liquid gleam of her eyes watching him from the darkness, the pale curve of her ripe breasts. She seemed to be sitting on the floor, and yet the height was wrong for such a position.

Blinking against the haze in his brain, Caelan took another step forward, staggered, and bumped into the wall. Feeling dizzy and strange, he twisted to put his back against the wall.

As he did so, the faint firelight gleamed off something shiny and smooth coiled around her. She was sitting on it, but . . .

She leaned forward, reaching out her arms. "Caelan, come. I am here to give you ecstasy such as you have never known."

When she moved, he realized she wasn't sitting on the coils. Instead, they were a part of her. The lower half of her body wasn't human at all, but rather eellike and a sickly mottled gray color. Her hair wasn't hair either. There was no breeze blowing here to stir the tendrils on her head. Instead, a thick mass of tentacles grew from her scalp, stretching and reaching, constantly moving with life of their own.

Horrified, he stood frozen, his mouth agape.

"Caelan, I want you," she sang.

Even more to his horror, he felt himself moving forward, obeying the spell of her summons. Revulsion burned his throat, and with all his will he tried to fight, but it was as though his feet belonged to another. They would not obey him.

He walked right up to her, raging inside, fighting the spell she'd cast over him. She was a monster, something demonic and evil. He couldn't couple with *that*.

Her fingers stroked his arm. With shock he realized he

was suddenly close to her. She ducked her head and brushed his chest with the tentacles. They felt soft and warm, squirming against his flesh.

Desperately, he shut his eyes and reached for *severance*. With a snap, he was freezing cold as though he'd entered an ice cave.

She cried out something, but her voice was too far away to hear. She reached for him, but he stepped back slowly, oh so very slowly, feeling as though he were moving under water. Yet her grasp missed him and he was free, still stepping backward while she called and called his name.

When he came to his senses he was running for his life along the sandy jogging track, arms and legs pumping, his breath a desperate rattle in his throat. Something unnameable was chasing him. He could sense it, although dusk had fallen and he couldn't see much in the starlight.

Then he realized those were hoofbeats behind him. He heard the horse snorting and the oaths of the rider. Exhaustion plunged through Caelan. His legs were burning, and his heart was hammering out of control.

He stopped abruptly and dropped to his knees, dragging in deep, gulping breaths of air. Shudders ran through him, and he had no idea how he'd gotten out here.

The horse reined up beside him, and its rider jumped down.

"Traulander?" It was Orlo's voice, half exasperated and half afraid.

Caelan dragged in more air, lifting his hands to wipe the sweat drenching his face. "Yes, master."

"Great Gault above, are you mad?" Orlo shouted. "What in the name of hell are you doing out here? How did you get past the guards? How did you get out of the arena? What are you doing running like this? You crazy fool, you can't escape the compound."

"I wasn't trying." Still panting, Caelan found unwanted memories washing over him. He could not shut them out.

"That thing in there—the haggai—" His voice broke on him, and he shuddered.

"I see," Orlo said at last. "You fool, you destroyed the initiation rites and risked the wrath of the gods, and now you run from the arms of ecstasy. Truly, you are mad."

"I wish I were," Caelan muttered, closing his eyes. "That thing—the sight of it—what in the name of the gods is it?"

"You saw a haggai?" Orlo sounded disbelieving.

Caelan nodded. "I didn't want to go into the passageway when she—when it called to me. I figured I should preserve my strength the night before combat. But she—it cast some kind of spell on me. When I got close enough, I saw what it was."

Orlo sighed. "That's the whole point. You aren't supposed to see them. Men would go mad, which is what happened to you. Am I right?"

Caelan remembered the order forbidding him to *sever*. "Yes," he lied. "I went mad." And perhaps it wasn't a lie. He didn't like losing himself this way. It was why he'd resisted *severance* at Rieschelhold, resisted those lost gaps of time spent doing the bidding of the masters with little or no recollection afterward of what he'd done.

He threw himself at Orlo's feet, all pride gone. "Don't make me go back to that creature. In the name of the gods, have mercy on me."

"Hush." Orlo kicked him back, sending him sprawling. "I'd rather have you stiff-backed and causing trouble than sniveling like this. Do you have regrets now for what you've done? The priests cursed you, do you understand?"

"Yes, master." Caelan pulled himself to his feet, trying to regain his composure. "I didn't like the blasphemous service they forced on us."

"And who asked you whether your approval was needed? Gault above, you are more trouble than a ring full of Madrun prisoners of war. Aren't you afraid now of tomorrow?"

"No more than before."

"But you face the chance of death without the protection of the gods. You cannot enter the afterlife without—"

Orlo broke off his sentence as though realizing he was sounding too concerned. He cleared his throat and gave Caelan a shove. "Move! I've a dozen duties ahead of me tonight. No time to mess about with a superstitious Traulander who won't take a night of pleasant forgetfulness with a haggai witch."

Caelan faced him. "I will not go back to such a creature. If I am to be whipped for disobedience, then do so, because I will not—"

"Careful," Orlo warned him. "You are an insolent dog, but it is a privilege, a generous gift, that is provided to condemned men, not an obligation."

Some of the tension faded from Caelan. He let out a breath of relief.

"I do not bargain with slaves," Orlo said. "Do you understand me? I do not bargain. But if you will not tell anyone that you saw a haggai, no matter what tales of pleasure are shared with you on the morrow, then I will quarter you with the veterans where they do not venture."

Caelan was grateful but also surprised. "The veterans don't—"

"I didn't say that!" Orlo broke in irritably. "The veterans have their favorites. They go down deep into the catacombs when they wish, but it is by their choice. The haggai do not seduce or lure them. Only the new fighters, for the first time."

Caelan had more questions, but instinct told him he had pressed his luck far enough. "I am grateful for your mercy, master."

"Walk," Orlo said gruffly. "As stupid as you are, you'll be dead by the first round. Just mind that when you are killed, you do not choose to haunt me. Gault's mercy!" He made a swift gesture of supplication and glared at Caelan. "You should have taken the night of pleasure."

twenty

ELANDRA DID NOT KNOW EXACTLY HOW LONG she had remained blind among the Penestrican women, but she guessed approximately a month had passed.

It was a hard, silent time of loneliness and self-doubt. She had always heard that to be blind was to be in the dark, as though one's eyes could not open. But she saw no darkness. Only the unending, featureless, glaring white of Hecati's revenge. It was more disorienting than Elandra could have imagined; worse, she thought, than actual darkness. At least the dark was a familiar place. But this was not.

The Penestricans had been kind but aloof, making no effort to treat her. She had been given a room to herself, very small. Eight paces in both directions. That hardly mattered; she was used to nothing else. The walls were stone but rough. She had explored them by touch and knew they were natural rock, not dressed blocks. She suspected she was in a cave. It was very dry and warm, however. A small hole—too small to crawl through—cut high in one wall brought her fresh air from outside.

Thus, she could smell damp and know if it was raining outside. Warm, sun-freshened air meant daytime. Cool air meant evening.

She had a stool and small table, a narrow cot, and a shelf to hold a lamp she did not need. No one ever came to light it. Her only contact with other human beings was three times a day, when food and fresh water were brought and her necessity pail taken away for cleaning.

Everything was clean.

Three times a week, she was led down a narrow passageway, placed in a corner, and doused with water. Her attendant would then swathe her in a rough towel and dry her while she shivered and gasped. She would be led back to her cell. Nothing was ever said to her, even if she asked questions.

Her clothes had been taken away, reminding her strangely of her dream where she had kissed the mysterious lover and Hecati had walked in her dream. She had no dreams now, only her thoughts chasing endlessly around and around in her brain.

To be kept naked at first had seemed the greatest unkindness of all. She felt totally vulnerable and dependent, and she had hated them for treating her with this silent indifference.

In retaliation she had trained herself not to cringe or try to cover herself whenever someone came to her room. Finally indifference became a habit, not a pose. She stopped caring, almost, and it ceased to be a torture. After all, she was in a place entirely of women. There were never any male voices, never any male scents. Sometimes, in the stillness of what she assumed was night, she could hear far-distant chanting echoing through the passageways.

It was always faint, but some element in it disturbed her and made her restless. She would get up and pace, back and forth, counting her steps so as not to bump into the walls, until the chanting would finally fade away altogether.

Idleness and boredom were the hardest elements to endure. She found herself wishing Bixia would visit, even if only once, to tell her she'd not been forgotten. But it was a stupid wish, an absurd wish. Elandra was angry at herself for even hoping for something like that. Bixia was busy being trained and prepared. She probably had no time for anything else. Even so, Elandra knew Bixia was too selfish to come even if she had the opportunity.

Elandra tried to stay grateful to the Penestricans for not turning her out as a cripple. After all, she could not be married like this.

As always, Hecati had defeated her.

All her life Elandra had tried to bury her own dreams and ambitions, to never allow herself high expectations under the guise of being practical. Without expectations, disappointments hurt less. But for a few short days during her journey here, she had allowed herself to dream of what life might bring her. Never had she imagined this fate.

The shock in her lingered deep.

She had never been an introspective person, but her confinement forced herself to explore her own mind. She examined the kind of person she had been until now. She thought about the kind of person she was becoming.

Not a self-pitier. She still had enough pride to hold herself together.

Weakness and dependence were abhorrent to her. She wanted to ask the Penestricans to train her in some task she could do, to give her anything that had purpose again. But that chance had not yet come.

A sound at her door disturbed her thoughts. Ever wary, Elandra rose from her stool and faced the door. It was not yet time for food. She had had a bath yesterday. Trapped in the whiteness, she strained with her ears and her sense of smell to determine who was there.

The door swung open, creaking slightly on its hinges. Hope lifted in her. Was this a visitor? Would at last she have someone to talk to?

"Yes?" she asked eagerly. "Why have you come? Who is there?"

The woman entered the room without answering. Her footsteps were soft on the stone floor. Bare feet, Elandra thought. But unlike the usual attendant who hobbled as though old and who puffed when she walked, this person moved gracefully with a low, distinctive jingle of earrings. With her came a scent of herbs and musk, very faint but pleasing. There was something familiar yet elusive about her that teased at Elandra's mind. How maddening not to recognize what her senses seemed to be telling her.

In silence, the visitor took Elandra's hand and tugged.

Elandra resisted. "Where are you taking me?"

Not answering, the visitor tugged again.

Anger tangled with frustration inside Elandra. "I don't understand why I am treated so. Why won't you answer my questions? Must I be punished for having been spell-burned?"

The visitor tugged harder, pulling her forward.

Elandra gave up the useless questions and stumbled along. Tears burned her eyes, but she refused to let them fall. She wasn't going to let anyone see her hurt and confusion. Blind or not, she was still the daughter of Albain. She wouldn't beg for their mercy.

There were fourteen steps from Elandra's door left along a passageway, then a turn to the right and thirty-nine steps to the bathing room.

Today, however, they turned left twice. Suddenly Elandra was lost and disoriented.

She slowed down, using her free hand to feel along the wall. The woman leading her kept tugging at her to go faster. Elandra's uncertainty grew, and with it came fear.

Quickly she squelched that emotion. She must not let

them think she was scared. If anything, she must bide her time until she could figure out a way to get word to her father. No doubt the Penestricans had concealed her fate, fearing Albain's blame in the matter. But Elandra did not intend to stay here imprisoned and forgotten like some charity case, if she could help it.

"I wish to speak to the Magria," she said now. "If you are not permitted to speak to me, fine. Only have mercy on my plight and give my message to her. My father is Lord Albain. He will come for me and take me off your hands if only he is informed of what has happened. Will you tell the Magria this? Please?"

The woman said nothing, only tugged at her to hurry.

Sighing, Elandra bumped into the wall and righted herself. Where were they going?

They turned again. The floor was very rough and uneven beneath Elandra's bare feet; then its surface grew smoother. Strange scents came to her: pungent odors of herbs, cedar, and rodents. The air against her face grew progressively warmer and drier.

The woman escorting her stopped in front of her without warning. Elandra bumped into her and heard a hiss of anger. She was shoved back with a rough hand.

Before Elandra could react, her arm was gripped above the elbow, and she was pulled forward, then stopped.

Confused, Elandra hesitated. The same action was repeated. This time, her foot stumbled down a step. Understanding flooded her.

"Steps," she said aloud. "Very well."

Slowly she made her way down a whole series of steps, her hand on the woman's shoulder. "It would help," she said, "if you would tell me how many steps there are."

The woman said nothing.

Annoyed, Elandra clamped her lips together. This rule of silence was both cruel and absurd. She might be blind, but she wasn't deaf or stupid. She would not ask again.

They passed through a doorway and entered a place that was extremely hot.

The temperature made Elandra gasp. Perspiration broke out across her face, and she wiped her brow with the back of her hand. Already the heat seemed to be sapping her energy. She could not imagine where she was, unless it was a kitchen, yet she heard no sounds of activity and smelled no food cooking.

The woman pulled her up one shallow step, then along a smooth floor of cut stone. Only five steps; then the woman turned around to face her and pushed her shoulders until Elandra sat down.

Even the stone felt warm when she sat on it. The heat was intense, radiating into her from all sides. Wiping her face again, Elandra lifted her head, tilting it to catch any nuance of sound that might help her understand where she was and what was happening.

She smelled burning wood, and heard a low crackle of fire. There were many other scents she could not identify.

The woman circled her and left the way they'd come.

When the faint patter of her footfalls faded and there was only silence, Elandra frowned. She extended her arms and touched only air. For an instant she thought she heard a faint rustle, but she decided it was her imagination.

Still, she had the growing suspicion she was not alone. Was she being observed? It was unpleasant to think she might be entertaining some watcher with her gropings and explorations.

Frowning more deeply, she folded her hands in her lap and waited.

Nothing changed.

At last she rose to her feet, paused until she had her balance, and slid one foot forward.

The stone ended abruptly half a stride away. She swept her toes back and forth along the edge of the pavement, then made a quarter turn and slid her foot forward. Almost immediately she felt the edge.

She made another quarter turn and found no end to the stone. That had been the way she'd entered.

Another quarter turn, and she found a nearby edge.

Another quarter turn, and she was once again facing the direction in which the attendant had left her.

Elandra did not intend to step off blindly into thin air. She turned around and started back the way she'd come.

"Stop."

The voice seemed to come out of nowhere.

Startled, Elandra froze in place.

"You are not permitted to leave."

She looked up, placing the voice as coming from high above her. Elandra turned around to face it. Inside, she felt overwhelming relief. At last someone was talking to her.

"Who are you?" she asked.

The woman chuckled.

"Why have I been brought to you?" Elandra asked. "Can anything be done for my blindness? I have heard the Penestricans possess many powers, but I know nothing about your order. Forgive my ignorance, and tell me please if you can help me."

"So many questions," the woman said. Her voice sounded old yet vigorous. "You have been dealt many tests, yet your spirit is not broken. That is good."

Angrily Elandra gritted her teeth. She had no patience for this sort of nonsense. "Why should I be tested?" she asked. "For what purpose, unless it is for your amusement?"

"You are impertinent. You were sent here by your father for training, and that is what you have received."

"There's been no training!" Elandra cried impatiently. "No one has even spoken to me, until now. Besides, I cannot be married if I am blind. What good—"

"The platform ahead of you ends two strides from where you are standing now," the woman said. "Walk forward slowly and step off the platform onto the sand.

It is not a high distance. You do not have to jump, but take care not to fall."

Bewildered, Elandra responded to the clear, simple directions in spite of herself. She felt her way forward, then crouched to hold onto the edge of the stone while she slid one leg down. The platform was perhaps no more than knee height above the sand.

Her feet sank into the grainy substance. The sand was almost too hot for comfort, as though the sun had shone on it. She winced and hopped a little, turning back to the platform.

"No," said the woman. "Sit on the sand."

"It's too hot."

"Walk forward. You will find a pillow. Sit on that."

Gingerly, Elandra minced across the hot sand and stumbled over the pillow. It was a wide square cushion, big enough for her to sit on and curl her legs under her. She brushed the sand off her feet as quickly as possible.

"Excellent," the woman said. "Now do not move."

"Why?"

"Ask no questions. Obey."

"Why are you testing me?"

No answer.

Compressing her mouth stubbornly, Elandra sat there with growing resentment. The idea of being tested was infuriating. It made her wonder if they could do something to restore her sight. If they could, and they had not done so, then they were beyond cruel.

Her anger growing, she reached down to scoop some of the hot sand into her hand.

Something ropelike and sinuous slid across the back of her hand.

She flinched back instinctively, her heart quickening.

Suddenly she was aware of them. She could hear the faint rustling glide of scales across sand, could hear the hissing. Snakes surrounded her.

A visual image of their powerful, writhing bodies filled

her mind. Her mouth went dry, and she choked off all sound, forgetting even to breathe as she froze in place.

"You sense them?" the woman asked, her voice soft and intense.

Elandra could not speak. Jerkily she nodded.

"Do not move. You must accept their presence."

In spite of the heat Elandra felt clammy all over. She breathed in fear.

One of the snakes slithered across her ankle, and she nearly screamed. All her life she had feared snakes. Growing up in the hot humid jungles of Gialta, she considered the reptiles a way of life, but deadly nonetheless. Even in her father's palace, the servants were ever vigilant. Cats and tame mongooses roamed at will to help patrol the rooms. As a very young child, Elandra had witnessed her old *muimui,* her nurse, being bitten while pulling a snake from Elandra's crib. The old woman had swelled up horribly and died. Shortly thereafter, Elandra had gone to live with her father, but the memory had never left her.

Now her heart thudded inside her chest, and she drew in short, raspy breaths. A snake slid over her legs, and she started shaking. They were closer, hissing, their tongues flickering along her wrist in delicate little patterns of exploration.

Her body was freezing. She had tensed her muscles so tightly they ached. Filling her was the certainty that if she moved the slightest degree, or spoke, or even breathed too deeply, one of them would bite her.

Then she would convulse with agony, and would swell with poison, and would die, choking for air.

"There are forty serpents in the sand pit with you," the woman's voice said calmly. "The warmth makes them active, and they have found you. Do not move."

Simple hatred was not enough. Elandra clenched her eyes tightly shut, raging against the woman in her mind. Clammy perspiration trickled down her temples. With every thud of her heart, she felt the urge to run consuming her.

She couldn't stay here, waiting for one of them to bite her. She had to do something, had to flee, fight, get out of here.

Suddenly she was gasping for air, gulping it in with desperation. Panic shuddered through her. This was crazy. She didn't have to take this.

And yet something held her motionless. She forced the panic down, remembering her father's voice in her mind. *Never act in panic,* he always instructed his troops. *Panic in warfare is defeat. Panic is death.*

A moan rose in her throat, and she stifled it. Don't move, she told herself. *Don't move.* She could feel them now, sliding over and around her. Their sinuous bodies were warm and silky soft on her skin. Their tongues flickered across her, making her fight herself not to flinch. She was trembling with exhaustion. She did not know how much more of this she could endure. Then one curled around her throat, and panic flooded her anew.

The snake tightened its coils. It was going to choke her. She could feel its blunt snout moving through her hair. Its tail tickled along her shoulder blade. She shuddered again and clenched her fists in the sand. Her heart was hammering out of control. She could not stand this, could not.

"Its coils will tighten slowly," the woman said in a soft, expressionless voice. "It kills by crushing its prey. Of course this is a young one, very small. When they are fully grown, they encircle the body and crush the lungs of their victims. Do not move if you want to live. If you move you will startle it, and it will crush your throat instantly."

Elandra did not have to be told. She had seen grown men crushed to death in the rice marshes by giant anacondas.

Tears ran down her cheeks. Her consciousness shrank

to the strong bands encircling her throat. She believed what the woman had told her, yet the snake continued to slowly choke her. The constriction was becoming alarmingly tight. She opened her mouth, panting, and realized that whether she fought or waited passively she was going to die here in this rite she didn't understand.

Anger fired within her. She was the daughter of a warrior, and she wouldn't die tamely.

Lifting her hand, she tugged at the snake around her throat. Immediately it tightened its coils with a quick, reflexive action that made her gasp for air.

Her anger intensified. She found the snake's head, felt its tongue flicker against her palm, and closed her fingers around his neck. Then she squeezed with all her strength.

Its tail whipped against her shoulder, and it tightened its coils harder. She was gasping now, fighting for every breath of air. With her last shreds of consciousness, she twisted with both hands and snapped the snake's neck. A final reflexive shudder ran through its length; then it lay limp.

She unwound it from her throat and flung it as far from her as she could.

Still consumed by fury, she rose to her feet, shaking off the other snakes that had been crawling over her legs. None of them bit her. She lifted her head and faced where she thought the watcher might be.

"I defy you," she said loudly. "I will not submit to your tests again. Let me go."

"If you cross the sand, the snakes will strike," the woman warned her. "Most are poisonous."

"You put me here to die," Elandra said. "But I will do so by my choice, not by yours."

She oriented herself and stepped off the pillow onto the hot sand. It burned her feet as before, but this time she did not flinch. She strode out, driven by her anger and defiance, and counted the number of steps back to the stone platform.

Despite the woman's warning, nothing bit her. Elandra tossed her head with a feeling of triumph. So that had been another lie too. She bumped hard into the platform, bruising her thighs, and climbed onto it.

"Stop her!" the woman commanded.

Elandra heard quick footsteps approaching. Hands gripped her arms. Elandra swung out blindly and managed to hit the other woman's face. The attendant uttered a soft cry and lost her grip on Elandra, who gave her a strong shove.

Stumbling forward, Elandra almost managed to get past the attendant, but she grabbed Elandra from behind by her hair.

Sharp pain in Elandra's scalp made her yelp. Gritting her teeth, she elbowed the attendant in the stomach and wrenched free again. She tried to run but immediately stumbled down the steps she'd forgotten were at the other end of the platform.

She landed awkwardly, bruising her knees and hip, and cursed her blindness.

The attendant was on her in an instant, pulling her upright and shaking her. "You fool!" the woman cried. "You'll break your neck trying to run like that!"

It was Bixia's petulant voice who spoke to her. Bixia who had led her here. Bixia who fought with her now. Suddenly Elandra knew why the sound of her earrings and the smell of her perfume had seemed so familiar. None of the Penestricans wore such adornments. She should have guessed immediately.

Elandra gripped Bixia's arm. "Sister! I beg you to help me—"

There was an abrupt sound, as though a pair of hands clapped once. The glaring whiteness around Elandra vanished, making her stagger with surprise.

Blinking, she frowned and squinted at the gloom that surrounded her. Rubbing her eyes, she found herself able to focus on Bixia's face in front of her. Bixia was scowling at her.

Amazement spread through Elandra. "I can see," she whispered.

The shock of it was too sudden. Her knees went wobbly and she sat down without warning. She raised her hands and turned them over, ecstatically gazing at the lines of her palms and the texture of her own skin. She didn't know whether to laugh or cry.

The room itself was a huge cavern, lit only dimly by fat white candles and the fire blazing in the center of the sand pit.

Elandra glanced over her shoulder but saw no snakes writhing on the sand. Puzzled, she swung her gaze back to her half-sister.

Bixia was as naked as she, revealing a lush, sensuous body adorned with possibly every item of jewelry she had been given by their father. Bracelets were rowed up both arms, and several necklaces hung around her neck. Jewels swung from her ears. Her blonde hair flowed down her back, unkempt and full of tangles. Fury blazed in her green eyes.

"Is this part of your training too?" Elandra asked.

"No! You simpleton, don't pretend you don't know what's happening. You and your innocent airs make me sick!"

"But—"

"It's all your fault! I'll never forgive you for this. Never! I swear it from the bottom of my heart!"

"Silence!" commanded the woman behind them.

At once Bixia bit back the rest of what she might have said and bowed her head. She managed to keep glaring at Elandra, however, from beneath her tangle of hair.

Still puzzled, Elandra turned slowly back to face the sand pit. She saw a thin woman standing on a dais beside a stone chair. The unclothed Penestrican's hair was braided around her skull. Her bare arms and legs revealed a network of mutilation scars. On her right wrist she wore a simple bracelet in the shape of a snake.

When the woman beckoned, Elandra walked slowly around the sand pit to the bottom of the dais. She gazed up at the older woman, recognizing an air of authority that was unquestionable.

"Are you the Magria?" she asked.

The woman's slim brows rose. In silence she inclined her head. Her eyes were filled with intelligent scrutiny.

"Why is Bixia being treated like this?" Elandra asked. "As bride-elect of the emperor, she deserves respect and courtesy. Surely you do not blame her for what Hecati tried to do."

The Magria's eyes grew cold. "She has been raised by a witch. There is much to be held accountable—"

"But not by Bixia!" Elandra said sharply. "She didn't know—"

"But you did!" the Magria broke in.

Disconcerted, Elandra stared at her.

"Yes," the Magria insisted. "You knew about the witch. Answer!"

There was no denying it, not now when she finally understood what Hecati really was. "I knew," Elandra admitted.

"And you did nothing. You told no one. You did not denounce her, as is required by law!"

Elandra bit back the urge to defend herself. There was nothing to say without being clumsy, no way to justify her fear without admitting cowardice, no way to explain the intimidation and coercion Hecati had practiced on her through the years.

Besides, she had a suspicion the Magria might already know the full circumstances. Warily, Elandra kept quiet, saying nothing even when the Magria glared at her.

"Well?" the Magria demanded.

Still Elandra refused to answer. Two could play this game of silence, she thought.

A terrible look entered the Magria's face. "You are both fools. I waste my time with you."

"Then give us to the women who are supposed to train us for marriage," Elandra said with deliberate insolence. "Clothe us properly and treat us according to our different stations. Put an end to these games of yours."

"Games!" the Magria said sharply. "Games? There are no games here, girl. Everything that happens in the sand pit is truth."

Elandra faced her without saying anything.

The Magria slowly descended the steps of the dais until they stood face to face. Then the Penestrican circled Elandra, studying her openly.

"You are very like Fauvina," she whispered. "The auburn hair and white skin, the temper and the courage. Very like her. Yes, the cycle turns. It turns, and destiny is written."

Elandra frowned, but it was Bixia who stepped forward.

"No!" she cried. "You cannot take my privileges from me. *I* am to marry the emperor, not her! It was foretold, and you cannot change that."

While Elandra's bewilderment grew, the Magria turned a terrible smile of pity on Bixia. "You have no destiny. Those who have told you so all your life have done you a great disservice."

"I *do* have a destiny!" Bixia stamped her foot like a spoiled child. "I do! It says I am to marry the emperor, and you can't stop me!"

"Father was told," Elandra said in agreement. "The prophecy was clear."

The Magria's eyes pinned her. "Speak the prophecy."

Bixia sighed, but Elandra said in a clear, precise voice: "The daughter of Albain shall marry the emperor."

"Yes," the Magria said. "That is correct."

"*I* am his daughter!" Bixia said hotly.

"So is Elandra."

"No!" Bixia cried. "She is a bastard, a worthless embarrassment. She doesn't belong here. Father was wrong to even send her with me."

"The prophecy does not lie," the Magria said.

"You make a lie of it! You are evil and a—"

The Magria lifted her hand, and Bixia's sentence choked off. Bixia clutched her throat, writhing and turning blue. Alarmed, Elandra realized she was in the presence of powers she did not understand. Were these women also witches?

"We are not witches," the Magria said severely.

Uneasiness crawled through Elandra. So they read minds as well. Surely they were indeed possessed of dark powers.

"No," the Magria said sharply. "Do not judge what you do not understand. You have met one real witch. Was she like us?"

"I—I do not yet know," Elandra said.

The Magria's mouth twisted. "We serve the goddess-mother of all creation, the earth itself. With education you will come to share our love and worship. You will walk our way."

Bixia was still being choked by the Magria's will. Elandra swallowed and made herself face the Magria.

"I will not walk your way," she said defiantly. "Call your powers what you will. They are not for me."

"We live with the five natural powers—that of the earth, in which all life grows; that of water, which nourishes life; that of the moon and her mysteries; that of blood, which is life; that of a woman's womb, which gives her power over men as she both takes their force and gives back sons in exchange. We do not consort with demons. We do not walk in shadows."

Elandra was only half listening. She took a half step toward her tortured sister, then stopped herself from intervening.

"Wise," the Magria murmured and lowered her hand.

The invisible force choking Bixia released her. Gasping and crying, Bixia sagged to her knees and coughed.

Elandra went to her, but Bixia fought her off. "Leave me alone! I hate you!" she croaked, and fell into another coughing fit.

Angrily Elandra turned on the Magria, but the woman stopped her with a quelling look.

"Do not waste your effort defending her. She does not want your pity. Disappointment is a bitter cup. Let her drink it unhindered."

"I don't understand," Elandra said.

The Magria's eyes were clear and very wise. "Yes, you do."

"But I can't be the bride-elect," Elandra said in bewilderment. "I have no birth—"

"Your lineage is above hers. Your mother Iaris was the daughter of Lord Cernal, holder of most of Gialta west of the river, as your father holds most of the eastern bank. Lord Cernal descends from the same line as the Empress Fauvina. You, Elandra, not your half-sister, carry imperial blood. You, Elandra, not your half-sister, had a prophecy told over you at your birth."

Elandra's heart began to beat very fast. Feeling breathless, she whispered, "I am to marry a man whose name shall be known throughout the ages." She blinked, unable to believe it. "But . . . not Emperor Kostimon!"

Bixia, still kneeling on the ground, began to cry.

"It can't be," Elandra said blankly. "I don't believe it."

"The Fates cannot be denied," the Magria told her. "You were raised as a servant in your father's house, yes?"

Elandra frowned but gave her a tiny nod.

"Yet you carry yourself with pride and the demeanor of a lady. You were persecuted by the Maelite witch, were you not?"

Elandra's frown deepened. She said nothing.

"Was she not cruel to you? Deeply, heartlessly cruel?"

"Yes."

"Yet you survived her cruelty. You did not let her break your spirit. Is this true?"

"Yes."

"On the day of your departure, the soldiers cheered you instead of Bixia."

Elandra's mouth fell open. "How did you know—" She cut herself off, knowing the question was foolish in the circumstances.

"When we drove the witch from our premises—that fiend who would dare to defile this place of the goddess-mother—it was not Bixia whom the witch attacked, but you, Elandra. You, the future empress of our world."

"But—"

"Why should she strike you down? If you were as insignificant as you believe, why should she waste her efforts on you? Why not destroy Bixia?"

It occurred to Elandra that Hecati would have enjoyed opportunities to do much mischief from her position behind the throne, but she said nothing.

"The witch struck you with deadly intent, yet you did not die."

"Blindness is a kind of death," Elandra murmured bitterly, awash with memories.

"Nonsense. Don't pity yourself now. That is past."

Elandra faced her, chin held high, eyes direct. "You could have restored my sight immediately, yet you didn't."

"I did not restore your sight," the Magria said, equally direct. "You did."

"How—"

"We have tried to bend your spirit and find that adversity merely strengthens you. I have looked on you with sight, and I know you cannot be coerced. Neither will you work in ignorance, nor will you obey without question what you do not understand. You have the qualities for leadership and position which your half-sister lacks entirely. Bixia also walked the sand pit," the Magria said, her voice soft but relentless over the sound of Bixia's weeping. "She failed the test of the serpents."

Elandra shot her sister a swift look of consternation, but all she saw was Bixia's bowed head.

"But you, Elandra, did not fail," the Magria continued. "You were given a paradox with conflicting solutions. The only possible means of success was to create a third solution, which you did. You fought and defeated the snake. You are truly the daughter of a warlord. Even blinded and at a terrible disadvantage, you did not allow your disability or your emotions to overcome your wits. You have not been pampered and spoiled. You have no conceit or vanity. Your mind is keen and ready to be educated. You are ambitious and courageous. Your strength will not fail you in the challenges ahead."

She took Elandra's cold hands in hers, and smiled. "You are our next empress, child. Destiny has called you, and it is my honor to train you to meet it."

Conflicting feelings raced through Elandra. This seemed so impossible, and yet she could not deny what the Magria was saying. *What about the man in my dream?* she started to say, then held it back with instinctive caution. In her heart, she wanted to believe he was the man she was destined to marry, not some debauched old man.

Instead, she skirted the question uppermost in her mind with another. "Why did you send dream walkers to haunt me?"

Something unreadable crossed the Magria's face. She hesitated visibly. "That is another matter, which we will discuss at the proper time."

"And my father?" Elandra said, frowning. "What has he to say to this change?"

"For your father, the alliance and its advantages remain the same. He will be informed."

Elandra's mouth was dry. She swallowed, but it did not help. "And . . . and the emperor?"

The Magria stroked Elandra's hair. "My child, the emperor will be besotted when he sees his lost Fauvina restored to him."

Elandra drew back sharply from her caress. "I am not this woman you speak of. I am myself!"

"Of course. But it will help win his heart."

Fresh doubts crowded Elandra's mind. For the first time some of the implications began to sink in. The emperor was as old as time, or nearly so. The emperor was said to consort with demons and those of the shadow world. The emperor had murdered all his children save one, the current prince. The emperor was a ruthless tyrant, whose word was absolute law. Invoke his displeasure, even once, and a person's life was forfeit. And she was to belong to him? She was to pleasure him? Obey his every whim? Fetch and fawn for him? Wait for him to die? And then what would happen to her?

Elandra began to tremble. It was not what she wanted. All the glory in the world could not make up for the risk. For Bixia, so vain and spoiled and pretty, it had been ideal. Bixia was shallow enough to smile and flutter and flirt. She would despise him secretly and dream of lovers. She would be ruthless and capricious and grasping. Bixia could survive such a life, even thrive on it.

But Elandra was not made like her sister. Elandra wanted a man she could respect and honor. She had never asked for much in her life, and now overwhelming bounty was being showered on her. While a part of her was dazzled by the thought of sitting next to the most powerful man on earth—a man some claimed was almost a god himself—the rest of her was afraid. She had not been made to lie and pretend. He would hate her on sight, and she would die.

The Magria gazed at her as though she could read Elandra's mind. "No," she said softly. "Do not decide before you fully understand. You were prepared to enter a marriage of convenience based on our selection and your father's agreement. How is this any different?"

Elandra opened her mouth, but she had no reply.

"We offer you a marriage of tremendous consequence. Do you really wish to refuse this chance to be queen?"

"He has seen Bixia's portrait," Elandra said, digging into hurts that lay deep. "He chose her willingly for her beauty. I do not have any allure for men, like Bixia does. I never have."

"You will be trained in the arts of pleasing a man."

Heat flamed in Elandra's face. To hide her own embarrassment she grew angry. "Will I learn to cast a spell over him?"

"Silence!" the Magria said sharply, eyes blazing. "You fool!"

Abashed, Elandra dropped her gaze and stood quietly, her heart pounding beneath her breast.

"Were not so much at stake, I would fling you out—both of you! Foolish, impertinent girl, mouthing off beyond your limited comprehension. You have no choice here. None!"

Glaring at Elandra, the Magria finally seemed to pull herself back under steely control. "Fear and emotional upheaval have made your tongue unruly," she said at last. "For that I will forgive this display. But only once. Am I clear?"

"Yes," Elandra whispered, still looking at the floor.

"There is opportunity for you beyond your wildest dreams. You wanted to see the world, and you will. You wanted knowledge, and you will have it. You wanted love, and it will come. Put your fear aside."

She turned away, gesturing for Elandra to come with her, but Elandra hesitated, gazing down at her weeping sister.

"What happens to Bixia?" she asked.

"That remains to be seen. Come."

"No," Elandra said, then tried to temper her discourtesy. "I—I mean, yes, of course I will come, but first please let me have a moment with her, alone. There is so much to consider."

The Magria's expression revealed nothing, but after a moment's hesitation she acquiesced. "Very well. It will avail nothing, but you may have the time you request. A sister will be waiting outside to conduct you to my chambers when you are ready."

She glided away without a sound and vanished into the gloom.

In the flickering candlelight, Elandra knelt beside Bixia and tried to put her arms around her.

But Bixia jerked away. "No!" she said, flinging back her hair. Her green eyes were puffy with tears. Wildly she glared at Elandra. "You want me to tell you I'm happy for you? You want me to forgive you for what you've stolen from me?"

Elandra sighed. "I just want—"

"I won't forgive you! And someday I'll make you regret the way you have betrayed me."

"But I—"

"Don't play innocent with me. You've planned this from the first. You and your special prophecies. How you must have laughed when you ripped apart my bridal robe. How you must have gloated when the soldiers cheered you. How you must be enjoying yourself now, at my expense."

"No, you're wrong," Elandra said in dismay. She had known Bixia would take everything the wrong way. "Please listen to me."

Bixia scrambled to her feet. "Get away from me! It wasn't enough that you always had Father's affection. It wasn't enough that you humiliated my mother and made her cry in secret every time she saw you. No! You couldn't be satisfied until you robbed me of all that was promised. Scheming and—"

"I didn't scheme for it. I just—"

"You're a liar and a thief!" Bixia screamed at her.

"They'll never let me near you again, and that's good because if I could I'd cut out your black heart!"

"Please don't be like this. It's not the end of the world. You'll still marry—"

"Who? Some paltry nobleman with a backwater palace in a forgotten, underfunded province?" Bixia laughed scornfully and tossed her golden head. "I'd sooner die than take your leavings. You think you're rid of me and Aunt Hecati, but you're not."

"It's Hecati who caused the trouble in the first place," Elandra said hotly.

"And she'll cause more. Plenty more!" Bixia's eyes narrowed, and her face held only spite. "Enjoy your pretty gowns and fancy jewels as quickly as you can. You won't have them long. The emperor will take one look at your long face and die of horror."

"Perhaps he'll be relieved to be married to someone with a mind for a change, instead of another pretty slut," Elandra retorted.

Bixia went white.

At once Elandra was ashamed of herself. This was no time to be petty, not when she'd robbed Bixia of her life's ambition.

"I'm sorry," she said softly, holding out her hand.

Bixia slapped it away. Tight-lipped and trembling, she glared at Elandra like someone possessed. "I hate you," she whispered. "I shall always hate you. Count yourself warned, for if there is any harm I can bring you or those you love, I shall do it! I swear this in the name of Mael."

Shocked, Elandra backed away from her. She started to say something, started to plead with Bixia to deny what she'd just uttered, but Bixia had become a stranger—enraged and violent, nearly insane with hatred.

"Get out!" Bixia said with loathing. "Get out! Get out! Get *out!*"

Clapping her hands over her ears to shut out Bixia's screams, Elandra turned and ran.

Outside in the passageway, she ran full tilt into some-one in a black robe, someone plump and motherly who held her close when Elandra would have fought free.

"No!" Elandra said, choking on her tears. "No, I—*please*."

"Hush," the woman soothed her. "Hush, now. All will be well."

And suddenly Elandra found herself clinging to this gentle stranger, weeping as though her heart would break.

"Greatness is born of pain, little one," the woman mur-mured, stroking her hair. "Let the tears fall. Let the tears cleanse you, little wife of the emperor who is and the mother of the emperor who will be. All will be well with you. All will be well."

twenty-one

AfTER ALL THE ANTICIPATION, CAELAN DID not fight on the first day of the season. Locked in with the veterans, it seemed he was forgotten. No one came for him the first day or the next. The gladiators paced about or played with dice, locked in the gloomy quarters beneath the arena. The thunder of the crowd rolled incessantly from noon until dusk, day after day.

On the third rotation, guards came with a small wooden pail. Without being told, the gladiators lined up against the wall. Caelan took his place at the far end, watching to see what to do so he wouldn't have to ask. Each man drew out a small bronze tag with a number engraved on it.

The guards swept the litter of their game off the crude wooden table and shook out a pair of dice three times. "Numbers three, twelve, and eight. You go in tomorrow."

One guard made notations on a tablet while the other collected the bronze tags and put them back in the pail.

Caelan's number had been four. He loosed a sigh of relief, and the tight knot in his stomach eased a little.

Nux had drawn number three. He scowled at Caelan with his small beady eyes and grunted. But Nux left him alone.

At the end of the following day, only Nux returned. Soaked with sweat and blood that apparently wasn't his, he shrugged off his leather harness and stripped down to his dirty hide to climb into a big stone tub of water in the corner. There, by lamplight, he splashed and scrubbed and soaked out his tired muscles.

Caelan watched him and wondered what he felt, being the victor yet again.

The guards came in for the drawing of lots. Excluding Nux, they passed down the line, then threw the dice seven times. Seven men were selected. Caelan's number was not among them.

This time dirty looks were cast his way. When the guards left, Nux climbed out of the tub and dripped his way across the room. Belting on a tunic, he glared at Caelan.

"What's your nick?" he asked.

Caelan put down the dice he'd been rolling idly and sat very still on his stool, trying not to betray his tension. "My what?"

"Your nick with the guards. What is it?"

Caelan shook his head. "Just luck."

"Naw. You got put with us, you! Green as grass, you are. Now you've missed two draws. What's your nick?"

"I'm telling you," Caelan said warily, never letting his eyes off Nux for a moment. "Just luck."

"Get off, Nux," called one of the other men. "You saw how they pounded him in training. It's luck."

"Better be. But why's he here with us? Don't deserve it."

Grins broke out around the room. "Why, the trainers are just giving us the privilege of killing him instead. Right?"

They laughed, and Nux moved away. Caelan sagged

on his stool and wiped sweat from his forehead. Another moment gained, but he knew it was only a matter of time.

The guards didn't return until the following week. Caelan knew they had been drawing veterans from another room. The next draw missed him again. He began to wonder at his luck just like the others. They muttered and glared.

"Midway through season already, and him left," Nux complained to the guards.

"Shut up!" one of the guards retorted. "What's it to you?"

They left with a slam of the door.

Nux stood up and came over to where Caelan was standing. His eyes glared over his broken nose, and his teeth were bared. "You ain't being saved, not you. I'm going to—"

"Better save yourself for tomorrow," Caelan said quickly, tensing himself on the balls of his feet in readiness for attack. "If you use up your strength on me, then you'll die in the arena."

Nux drew back with a frown, looking momentarily frightened. "Gault's blood!" he swore. "You putting a curse on me?"

The other men exchanged looks. "Giant put a curse on Nux."

"A curse."

They murmured and shifted back.

"It's not a curse," Caelan said, although if they wanted to think so he wasn't going to try too hard to talk them out of it. "Just a prediction. You jump me, and I won't go down easy."

Nux lifted his hands and took a step back as though agreeing.

Caelan relaxed and straightened.

At that moment Nux attacked with a roar, driving him back against the wall with a thud. Nux's fists were like battering rams, pummeling him. Caelan drew in his elbows and blocked the blows as best he could, then struck back, catching Nux in the jaw and sending him staggering.

Nux crashed into the table, breaking it like kindling, and lay sprawled there, shaking his head and blinking.

Someone helped him up, but the fight was over. Blowing on his aching knuckles, Caelan slowly eased away from the wall and kept a sharp watch on the others.

Nux kept touching his jaw and wagging it back and forth. He glared at Caelan, and the hostility in the room was thick enough to cut. Caelan steeled himself, but Nux finally swung away and pounded on the door.

When a guard opened it, he said, "Take me to the haggai."

He returned just before dawn, bleary-eyed and smug, looking well satisfied with himself. Then he and five others went out to fight. That night, however, Nux did not come back.

None of them could believe it.

"The guards said he lost an arm," Bulot said. "You know what happens to a man without his arm."

"Bleeding like a stuck pig," another contributed. "Great gouts of it shooting across the tunnel. He died before he got to the surgeon."

"Nux dead?" Bulot kept saying over and over. He was a short, wiry man, quick and agile. "I can't believe Nux is dead. He was too good. The best in the arena. He can't be dead."

"If he lost his arm, like the guards said, then he's a dead man."

Another man spat on the floor. "It's the giant's curse what's to blame." He pointed at Caelan. "He hit Nux, hurt him somehow."

Caelan wanted to tell them it was probably Nux's visit to the haggai that had sapped his strength, but he held his tongue. They were all like rats in a cage that seemed to shrink daily. Caelan was feeling crazy from being cooped up in the gloom all the time. He needed exercise and sunlight, not just halfhearted drills in a stinking, half-lit tunnel where the guards took them twice a day.

That night when the lots were drawn, Caelan was missed again. No one spoke a word as the guards noted names and numbers, but the fighters' eyes lingered on him with clear hostility.

He sweated through the night, afraid to sleep, certain they meant to throttle him in his bunk. But no one moved against him. In the morning, they huddled together in a conference that he pretended to ignore, but he could not relax. Not this time, not when they blamed him irrationally for Nux's death.

The lock turned with a noisy rattle, and the door was slammed open. "On your feet!" bawled a guard with a list. "Bulot, Mingin, Hortn, Rethe, Chul. Move it, now!"

The named men shuffled for the door, yawning and stretching and scratching. But the others were up as well. They closed in on Caelan and shoved him forward.

"He goes too!"

"What?" The guards frowned. "Not unless he's on the list."

"He's on today's list," someone insisted. "Let him take Chul's place. He ain't fought once this—"

"Neither have you, Lum," the guard retorted.

The spokesman turned red but he didn't back down. "Let the giant take Chul's place. He don't belong in here with us. He ought to have been fighting with the other trainees, days ago."

The guard's frown deepened. He peered at Caelan. "I don't know you. Name?"

"Caelan."

"You're no veteran."

"No."

"Never fought!" someone yelled gleefully. "Never even held a sword in his pinkies!"

They roared with laughter.

The guard was looking very stern indeed. "What in hell's name are you doing in here?"

Caelan shrugged. "I was put here."

"Don't get cute." The guard glanced over his shoulder at his companion. "You heard of any special orders about this one?"

"No."

"Let him fight!" the gladiators cried. "Let him fight!"

The guard hesitated, then shoved Chul back into the room. He jerked his head at Caelan. "Come on, then, if you're so eager. Move!"

Suddenly it was happening. Caelan's ears roared, and his head seemed to be floating above his body.

He found himself pushed down a tunnel lit by torches. He felt hungry, but he knew it was nervousness that gnawed in his belly. Sweat broke out across his body. His clothes felt too tight. His eyes were burning, and he couldn't see well. His hearing was even worse.

Somewhere, they were stopped in a gloomy chamber with the rest. Twelve men who might have practiced and eaten together the day before, but who now avoided each other's eyes, conscious of what was to come.

In silence, they stripped off their clothes and put on minimal loincloths. Little flasks of oil stood rowed on shelves. The men smeared the greasy stuff over every inch of themselves, and Caelan followed suit, aware that the oil would make him harder to hold and therefore harder to kill in a clinch.

The door banged open, and Caelan jumped about a foot, his heart hammering foolishly. One of the fighters noticed his reaction. He nudged someone else, and they chuckled softly together.

The sound had an evil, hostile quality that made Caelan swallow hard.

Orlo came in, flanked by four other trainers. Bald and burly, he stood with the cattail club in one hand, his feet braced wide and his other fist on his hip. He glared at each of them in turn.

When he saw Caelan, he blinked and dropped his jaw. In that instant, explanation was revealed in his face. He had clearly forgotten about putting Caelan in with the veterans. It was as simple as that.

Then he recovered his composure and cleared his throat. "We have a good crowd today," he said sternly. "You will give them their money's worth in entertainment. Any man shirking or trying to save himself will be speared by the guards. Am I clear?"

As he spoke, he glared straight at Caelan.

"You'll fight your unworthy guts out today. You're a miserable lot, this pick. But you'll fight like champions, each and every one of you! The emperor is here today. Aye, here to see your blood spilled."

The fighters exchanged looks. Caelan felt both confused and excited. Outside he could hear the crowd roaring thunderously. Something elemental and primitive in the sound made his blood charge. He wiped his sweating palms on his thighs and wished his heart would not beat so fast.

Orlo gestured, and the other trainers passed out leather fighting harnesses. Caelan's fingers fumbled with the unfamiliar buckles; then his hands were pushed aside.

Orlo stood beside him, stripping off the harness and fetching another one. It looked old. One strap had been mended. But the leather was well oiled and cared for. Caelan noticed the straps were dyed blue, even as Orlo let it out a notch, then another, then another in order to buckle it across his chest.

"Breathe," he commanded.

Caelan obeyed.

"Too tight?"

Caelan felt the restriction and nodded.

With a grunt Orlo used the point of his dagger to make an additional hole and loosened the harness. "Aye, that fits right. Were you worth it, you'd wear a custom-made one."

Caelan fingered the leather, remembering his disrobing so long ago when the masters had forbidden him to wear blue. Then, blue had represented life. Now it stood for the taking of it.

He swallowed. "Does blue show who owns me?"

"Aye." Orlo stepped back and looked him over critically. "Although you'll be a humiliation for the prince quick enough." He showed his teeth in a mirthless grin. "Perhaps it'll be worth it, just to see his face. Hah!"

The fighters filed out and marched double-time up a ramp. The cheering was louder now, deafening as it echoed through the stone. With every step, Caelan felt his blood stirring. He opened his mouth to suck in lungfuls of fresh air. He could smell sun-baked earth as well as roasted goat and sweetmeats.

They stopped, half-hidden in the shadows. Beyond an archway flanked by soldiers in full armor, dazzling sunlight streamed down. A breeze blew in, bringing heat to the dank coolness.

Orlo walked ahead, pacing back and forth in the archway as though he were about to enter the ring himself. Another trainer passed down the row of twelve men with lots for them to draw.

Muscles tight, Caelan drew his bronze tag. His thumb traced over the number. He would go in ring six. Handlers moved among them, pushing and shoving them into the correct pairs. Caelan eyed his opponent, a grizzled heavyset man he had never practiced with before. He was relieved it was none of the men he'd been quartered with lately. His opponent refused to look at him at all and kept his gaze stubbornly on the floor.

Irrational hope rose in Caelan as he noticed the gray in the man's hair and the slight flabbiness of his muscles. Perhaps he would have a chance after all. Youth and quickness must count for some advantage. But to temper his growing optimism he reminded himself that experience outweighed almost everything else.

The first pair was pushed forward to a spot at the top of the ramp just short of the archway. The armored soldiers there hastily crossed their spears across the archway, but the gladiators ignored them.

Caelan heard a creaking noise, and the pair for ring one disappeared into the floor. He stared, mouth open, and could not believe it.

A few seconds later, the second pair were positioned on the same spot, and they also sank from sight.

As the line moved forward, Caelan saw that a section of the floor was really a platform that was lowered into the bowels of the catacombs beneath the ramp. He relaxed, ashamed of his own amazement. No sorcery was at work here, just simple mechanical devices.

When it came his own turn to descend through the floor, he watched with curiosity and saw sweating slaves hard at work on the pulley ropes that lowered and raised the platform. Down here beneath the ramp, he could see the framework of heavy beams and timbers supporting it.

"Move along," a guard shouted, and Caelan had to jog along a curving passageway with his opponent at his shoulder.

Halfway around, the man started puffing, and he ran as though his knees hurt him. Caelan filed the information away. He was determined not to go down in the first round.

The inside wall of the passageway was built of thick boards with bolted doors set into it periodically. At the sixth door, the arena guards stopped Caelan and his opponent. The door was opened, and they stepped through into total darkness. A piece of cloth was flung over Caelan's head. Instinctively he started to fight it, then held himself still as a weapon was pressed into his hand.

It felt heavy and thick. The haft of it was wood. When he ran his other hand along its length, he discovered it was only a club. Disappointment crashed through him. Was this to be his fate, bludgeoned to a pulp like a dumb animal?

"Go," said the guard and pushed him up a ramp.

At the top he stumbled through a doorway, guided by another guard who yanked off the cloth as he passed. Caelan found himself stumbling outside in dazzling sunlight. Squinting, his eyes watering, he staggered around in deep sand. His opponent came jogging out after him and lifted his arms to the crowd, which was already roaring in excitement.

It was impossible not to gawk at the stone bleachers of spectators rising up on every side, impossible not to be stunned by the enormity of the sound, impossible not to be distracted by the burning sand under his bare feet and the heat itself that radiated up furnace-hot in the bottom of the arena.

His opponent might be old and out of shape, but he was arena-seasoned, and in those first few critical seconds he reached Caelan and swung his own club into Caelan's kidney.

The blow drove Caelan to his knees with a yell of pain that was drowned out by the crowd, already surging to their feet and cheering with bloodlust.

From somewhere through the haze of agony, Caelan could hear Orlo's exasperated voice: "There are no rules in the arena! Remember that, you blockheaded fool, or you'll be dead in the first five seconds."

The opponent swung again, and Caelan somehow wrenched himself around in time. The club thudded deep into the sand beside him. Caelan rolled and kicked, knocking his opponent's feet out from under him. The man should have fallen but he didn't. Miraculously, he kept his balance and went staggering over to one side.

Wincing, Caelan climbed to his feet, grateful for the momentary respite that gave him time to reset himself. He didn't deserve this second chance. He knew that. Already he was berating himself sharply for his initial mistake. If they had been equipped with swords instead of clubs, he'd be dead by now.

He couldn't afford to make another mistake. Most certainly he would not underestimate his opponent again.

Warily, they circled each other in the heat. The walls that confined them thudded occasionally from the impact of combat in the adjacent ring. The crowd went on screaming in waves and surges of sound, now on their feet, now sitting down again, calling out encouragement and curses alike.

The opponent moved like a crab, low to the ground, well centered, his eyes steady on Caelan. He dragged the tip of his club on the sand as he moved, conserving every bit of his strength.

But while Caelan noted his tactics, the younger man was also aware that not keeping a weapon high and poised meant wasting precious seconds of time to get it into position.

He attacked, yelling Trau cheers at the top of his lungs, and caught the opponent fractionally off guard. As he expected, it took the man a small amount of time to dodge and lift his club. Still he managed it, blocking Caelan's swing so that the two clubs struck each other with a sharp crack of sound.

The impact jolted into Caelan's wrist, and he nearly dropped his weapon. Desperately he changed to a two-handed grip and swung again just in time to block the opponent's attack.

They blocked and swung furiously for several moments, then retreated to circle again, each catching his breath while looking dangerous for the crowd.

Caelan was learning fast how to provide entertainment while staying alive. He also knew that the longer this conflict lasted, the more spent he would be. And there were still five more opponents ahead of him, providing he survived this one.

As though sensing Caelan's momentary lapse of concentration, the opponent attacked. Some piece of Orlo's instructions filtered through Caelan's mind. Instead of dodging back, Caelan rushed forward, stepping inside the man's lunge. With the club whistling over his shoulder, Caelan jabbed his own weapon like a dagger, thrusting it deep into the man's solar plexus. The opponent's face turned pale. He staggered back. Caelan could hear Orlo's voice shouting in his mind to drive hard.

Swinging short, Caelan caught the man in the ribs. The opponent fell to one knee, still trying to bring up his own club. Caelan knocked it from his grip. Cheering rose in the air, and Caelan felt something inside him cry out even as he swung his club one last time.

It bounced off the man's skull with a sickening thud. The opponent's eyes rolled back in his head, and he crumpled to the ground.

Breathing hard, Caelan straightened up and turned around. Sand clung to his sweaty arms and legs. He wiped his face with the back of his hand, then remembered to raise his weapon in a victory salute to the cheering crowd. Most people weren't even looking in his direction, but he did it anyway.

Then he saw the door had opened to his ring, and a guard was gesturing at him impatiently.

Obediently, he circled the fallen man and went inside, where the cloth was immediately thrown over his head and the club ripped from his hand.

He was hustled down the dark ramp and out into the circular passageway to a nearby stone tub of water.

"Climb in," the guard told him.

Still panting, Caelan immersed himself in the cold water. It acted like a shock to his system, cooling him off rapidly. Blowing water from his face, he shook back his dripping hair and stood up just as his opponent's body was carried by on a stretcher of leather webbing. He wanted to ask if the man was dead or merely stunned, but he knew better than to ask. It was considered bad luck in the ring to know until the fighting was finished.

Sobered, Caelan watched them until they were out of sight; then the guards put him in a holding cell, where he drank liberally from a water pail and waited until the other victors came in. They in turn looked drained, excited, or bored with the whole business.

Caelan did not think he would ever be bored. Right or wrong, killing was nothing to be indifferent about.

When there were six of them present, the door slammed open and they again drew lots. This time Caelan's opponent was Bulot. His momentary confidence faded, and he counseled himself to take care. Bulot hated him and would be a far more dangerous opponent than the first man.

They filed out, paired off as before. Orlo stood in the passageway, and when he saw Caelan he blinked in approval but said nothing.

Caelan's chin lifted a bit higher and he squared his shoulders. Inside, he tried to make himself quiet and ready.

Back around to a door, back into the darkness and the ramp that led upward. At the top, a short sword was pressed into his hand and the blindfold whipped off as he was pushed out into the sand of ring three.

This time, Caelan kept his eyes squinted to protect them while they adjusted to the sunlight. He jogged forward and spun around quickly, expecting Bulot to charge him straight out of the door, which the man did.

Wiry and strong, Bulot was far different from Caelan's first opponent and twice as dangerous. He skipped over the sand, small but light-footed. His quickness was disconcerting, and he was utterly familiar with a sword, which Caelan was only now holding for the first time.

Bulot swung, lunging hard. Caelan stumbled back, momentarily forgetting his training. He defended himself clumsily, and felt a razor-sharp sting of pain slash his arm.

Looking down, he saw a cut already dripping blood. It wasn't deep, but it hurt. The sight of his own blood soaking into the sand was mesmerizing.

But Bulot was already charging again. Regaining his concentration, Caelan forced himself to spring aside. Again, he was driven back under Bulot's expert charge, getting no chance to set himself or find his rhythm. Bulot's eyes were flat with menace and deadly purpose. Yet as he met their gaze, Caelan felt a shiver pass through him.

Although he was not actually touching the man, Caelan experienced a jolt of *sevaisin*. The joining was quick, momentary, and yet suddenly Caelan understood what Bulot was thinking, the pattern of his strategy, and his whole plan of attack.

Caelan shifted aside a split second before Bulot struck. Surprise flashed across Bulot's face. Again, Caelan anticipated him, but this time Caelan did so with a feint of his own, and only Bulot's own quickness saved him from being spitted on the end of Caelan's sword.

The blade began to hum as though the metal was warming, coming alive. At first Caelan thought he was imagining things. It was a trick of acoustics, something in the roar of the crowd, but this time when he raised his sword in a quick parry and the two blades crashed together, Caelan's sword sang shrilly.

The sound was for his ears alone, and it vibrated through the length of him. He was deep in *sevaisin*, joined with the weapon in a way he had never experienced before. Not only did he know what Bulot intended, but now his sword was telling him secrets of its previous victories in the hands of others. How to pause, how to move, how to parry and thrust, the correct angle of the swing—back and forth—in deadly rhythm.

Now he understood the footwork and the arm action, how the two worked in deadly concert. For the first time it all made sense. He had found the language of fighting, and nothing Bulot tried fooled him. Caelan's own body, his muscles and heart and blood all sang with the sword, harmonizing effortlessly.

Bulot began to tire. His attacks grew more desperate, his risks bigger. Again he barely managed to fling himself back from Caelan's sword, but this time he stumbled and nearly tripped over his own feet.

Caelan sprang, seeing the opportunity, and sank his sword deep into Bulot's side. The impact shocked him; then death agony washed over him in a tide that sent him staggering back. He left the sword in Bulot's side, his own hand tingling with a fire he could not flex out.

In his madness, he had forgotten to *sever* the joining. Bulot's death seemed to extinguish him as well. The sky went dark. His vision left him. He could hear nothing. There was only a brutal pain in his heart, as though the organ had stopped.

Then somehow he found a breath, then another. His heart started thudding again, and his sight returned. A second later he heard the crowd screaming and chanting, "Kill! Kill! Kill!"

The door to his ring was open, and a guard was gesturing furiously. Caelan stared at him stupidly a long while before he finally understood.

Slowly he returned to Bulot and drew out the sword. Blood gushed with it, leaving a dark stain in the sand. Bulot's eyes stared sightlessly at the heavens. Feeling sick, Caelan raised his bloody sword high in the victor's salute.

Across the arena, he saw the emperor's box this time. Unmistakable, with its flying banners of the imperial two-headed eagle, the box was filled with people in expensive dress. Servants moved about constantly, bringing fresh drinks on trays while others held up sunshades against the relentless light. Still others fanned and kept flies shooed away. Caelan squinted, but he could not make out the emperor's features. The man leaned over and said something behind his hand to his companion, a younger, dark-haired man in blue.

The prince was holding a tube to his eye and staring in Caelan's direction. Conscious of ownership, Caelan raised his sword again, although he wasn't sure whether the prince was actually looking at him or doing something else.

This time the crowd at least had noticed Caelan's victory. Clapping and throwing him kisses, some people even tossed flowers his way.

He turned his back on them and walked into the darkness.

It was a repeat of the previous routine. The sword was wrested immediately from him. At the bottom of the ramp, he climbed into the tub of water again, washing off the grime and blood—although what could wash his heart?

Numb, he walked with heavy footsteps into the holding cell. Another man waited there before him, a lithe individual with a handsome face and skin the color of soot. Their gazes met briefly, then broke.

Sighing, Caelan seated himself on a stool and closed his eyes. His father's face floated in his mind, stern and disappointed. His first kill. And all he could feel was shame.

It was as though something important inside him had suddenly crumbled to ashes. Even during the long years of uncertainty and grief since he'd been taken from home and sold into slavery, he had always been intact inside. He might grieve and he might mourn, but he had never been broken. Now he wondered why he should feel so flat and empty within. He wanted to go back, to reclaim what he had lost, but he knew it was impossible to do so.

This, then, must have been what his father knew, all those years ago. Beva had tried to warn him against becoming a soldier. Agel even had understood what it meant to take life. But Caelan hadn't listened. He had been so full of his boyhood dreams and ambitions, so eager for glory.

Was this glory now? To win? To hear the crowd cheer approval? To have flowers tossed at him?

Was it a suitable tribute for the blood on his hands?

Caelan's hands were trembling. He sat on them so the other man would not see, and told himself to stop this. He could not tear himself apart every time, not if he was to survive this ordeal.

It was the fault of *sevaisin*. If he'd only remembered to break the joining before he thrust the final blow, it wouldn't have been so bad.

Even now, he thought he could hear an echo of the sword, still calling to him, still singing in his blood. Beneath his wretchedness, he knew something even more alarming: he had been born to battle. The weapons knew it. That's why they had called to him so strongly all his life.

What am I? he wondered.

He had no answer to that question, but he understood why he could not do well with the fake weapons in practice. They were not real. They could not speak to him.

The third victor came in, breathing hard and looking exhausted. He drank water, but scarcely had he dropped the dipper back into the pail than the door opened and the guards entered with the final lots.

"No free-for-all?" the black man asked. His voice was smooth and deep. He alone seemed completely fresh.

"Not today. The emperor doesn't like them."

Caelan reached in the tub. His tag was numbered three.

"One and two, step lively."

The black man and the one who'd just arrived went out. The door was slammed shut for what seemed like forever.

An hour passed, perhaps an eternity. Finally the guards came for Caelan and took him up the dark ramp for the last time. He did not know who his opponent was to be until the door opened and he was shoved out into the sunlight. He saw the black man holding both a dagger and a broadsword, waiting some distance away in the center of the largest ring.

Caelan had the same weapons. He could not handle both at once, so he tucked the dagger into the waist of his loincloth and settled a two-handed grip on the broadsword. The weapon was incredibly heavy and long. Blunt-tipped, it was made for hacking, not thrusting. Not until he tried to lift it into readiness did Caelan realize how exhausted his shoulders were. His arms felt leaden.

But the weapons were already hot and alive. He could feel them against his skin, humming with purpose. But to enter *sevaisin* again was too draining. It took tremendous amounts of energy. He was not used to so much contact. He did not believe he could protect himself if he needed to.

He crossed the ring while the crowd roared and stamped its feet. They were crying, "Amarouk! Amarouk!" over and over. Caelan realized that must be his opponent's name.

The black man's eyes were steady and alert. His muscles rippled beneath his skin as he raised the broadsword, but he let Caelan come to him.

Caelan knew this meant he would have no time to get set. He knew also that it was Amarouk's right. The man was already the favorite, marked as today's victor. Knowledge of that shone in Amarouk's face, but he was far from cocky.

He crouched slightly, settling his haunches the way a great cat might before springing.

Caelan stopped in his tracks, slightly too far away for combat, and heard the cheers change to boos. Caelan barely heeded them. Something felt wrong to him. A broadsword was a weapon of war, requiring a shield or heavy armor for protection. Two seminaked men hacking at each other would cut each other to ribbons. What was the dagger for? To finish off the business?

Orlo had not trained him for this. The weapons were both humming, but not in harmony. They did not belong together. He could not do this.

Abruptly, Caelan turned and flung his broadsword away. It went spinning through the air, sunlight flashing along its blade as it landed with a thud and little puff of dust at the far side of the ring.

A hush fell over the crowd, broken by chatter here and there. People were gripping each other's arms and pointing.

Even Amarouk's eyes widened in surprise.

Caelan didn't care. His own doubts were spinning in his mind, calling him a madman and worse. He closed everything away and sought *severance*. With a snap, everything was cut off. He entered the coldness, isolating himself, and waited for Amarouk to strike first.

The black man didn't like it. His expression changed from surprise to annoyance, then to fleeting satisfaction. Circling, he closed in on Caelan, who circled with him, dagger held loose but firmly, wrist taut.

With a yell, Amarouk lifted the broadsword with both hands, swinging it in an arc as he lifted, the whole motion smooth and correct. He was clearly a master of the weapon, but even as he swung Caelan's senses were alert and prepared.

The sword's motion grew slower and slower. Caelan ducked and lunged, coming up under Amarouk's arm. His dagger thrust hard, but Amarouk shifted away barely in time.

The dagger tip skidded through hide, slicing along a rib without doing any real damage.

But the blood splattered red on the sand just the same. The crowd shouted and groaned, all in the same breath.

Fury flared in Amarouk's eyes. He swung again, and again Caelan dodged the broadsword, dancing too quickly for it to reach him. With an oath, Amarouk tossed the unwieldy weapon away, eliciting a cheer from the crowd.

He drew his own dagger, and Caelan's grew hot in his fist. The blade was suddenly screaming through him, driving *severance* away just as Amarouk came at him with a bloodcurdling yell.

Caught half off-guard by the changes inside himself, Caelan barely met Amarouk's charge. They slashed and parried and circled. Amarouk leaped, kicking at Caelan's head. When Caelan dodged, Amarouk drove his dagger at Caelan's chest. Caelan twisted and blocked with his own weapon. The two blades locked, and they were straining against each other with all their strength, feet digging deep into the sand, arms trembling between them.

Then Amarouk reached out and gripped Caelan's hair.

The physical contact brought *sevaisin* with a jolt that enabled Caelan to thrust him back. Amarouk went sprawling, still clutching a plug of Caelan's blond hair in his fist.

Caelan, acting without thought, broke one of the principal rules of short knife fighting: he flung his dagger at Amarouk.

The blade hit its target and went through the meaty part of Amarouk's arm, pinning it to the ground. The black man screamed and writhed over, pulling out the dagger with a grunt of agony. Blood ran down his arm in a crimson stream, and he raised the dagger in his other hand.

Caelan ran for the nearest broadsword and scooped it up just as the dagger flew past him harmlessly and thunked into the wooden wall.

Caelan left it quivering there and swung the sword around just as the second dagger came at his head. In *severance*, Caelan danced in the coldness, watching the dagger slow in midair as his senses heightened. He swung the sword and deflected the dagger. It went spinning harmlessly aside and landed on the ground.

Now Amarouk was weaponless and hurt. Pressing his injured arm to his side, blood still streaming, the man backed up from Caelan's advance, looking from side to side as he tried to locate the remaining sword.

Caelan charged him, but Amarouk dodged and scrambled on his hands and knees to grab the sword. Lifting it just in time, sand flying from the blade, he blocked Caelan's swing. Steel rang against steel, sliding until their grips locked.

They strained against each other, well matched in strength; then Amarouk twisted and managed to sling Caelan around into the wall.

Caelan's shoulder ached from the impact, but rather than try to regain his balance, he slid down into a crouch and slashed at Amarouk's legs.

The man danced back, but not fast enough. The blade sliced through meat and tendon, and suddenly Amarouk was down. The thews in his neck corded up like ropes as he tried to heave himself back up. He made it, kneeling with blood streaming around him, and screamed obscenities at Caelan.

Their swords clashed with a jolt that traveled up Caelan's wrists. Caelan's own flesh wound had reopened, and the blood and sweat trickling down his arm made the hilt slippery. He broke first, stepping back on his rear foot, then swung again. Now he did at last find the rhythm of the weighty sword. But even on his knees Amarouk refused to give up. He met blow for blow, the sword blades ringing out mightily again and again.

"Kill!" the crowd roared, on its feet now, fists shaking, voices screaming. "Kill! Kill! Kill!"

And as he fought the valiant Amarouk, a corner of Caelan's mind went back long ago to something his father had once said when trying to teach him a lesson in healing.

Opening his kit, Beva withdrew a copper scalpel and held it up so the firelight could flash along the burnished blade. "This is a tool with which to heal. It can assist life. It can also take life. Sometimes I must cut away that which is diseased and damaged in order to save life. Sometimes I must take life in order to grant mercy."

He ran his finger along the blunt edge of the blade. "Safety."

Then he ran his finger along the sharp edge. Blood welled across his fingertip, and he flicked it at the wall, leaving tiny crimson splatters. "Danger. Everything in the universe has two sides, the *aul* and the *zin*, the brightness and the shadow, the good and the evil. That is how balance is maintained."

Caelan sighed. He had no desire to listen to one of his father's lectures.

"It is not necessary to walk among evil, boy, in order to fully understand good. By looking into good, you will find the evil. Do not go seeking more."

Caelan frowned. As usual when talking to his father, he felt there were more riddles than answers. "So you're saying that with every wrong committed, good is lost. Until one day the balance shifts and it cannot be regained at all."

It was Beva's turn to sigh. "No, boy. That is not what I'm saying."

"I don't understand."

"In healing, sometimes we take the disease and turn it upon itself. It will kill itself when properly guided. There are many ways to the desired end. Many journeys, none of them more right than another, but all the same in result if needed."

Within the vision, Caelan frowned. This no longer felt like a memory. They had never had this conversation. His father had not said these words, yet Beva's face hung suspended in his mind. Beva's voice rang in his thoughts.

"You're saying I must kill this man," Caelan said, far away from the battle his body still fought with Amarouk. "*You*, Father? The peace lover?"

"Ultimate *severance*," Beva whispered. "The taking with the mind. The creation of balance by first walking through shadows and out again into the light."

Caelan felt split inside, as though he were losing his reason. The coldness was more pervasive than any he'd ever felt before, as though he'd become frozen to the marrow. His consciousness was gone. What was he doing? Fighting? Dying? He was lost to everything except this moment before his father.

"Don't make me a saint, boy," Beva said. "I have touched evil and walked with it. I have dipped my hands in it. I have drunk from the shadow, then left it, returning to the light of reason and sanity, back to doing good for humanity, back to life and the saving of it."

"No," Caelan whispered, horrified. If it were true, that made his father's cruelty even less understandable than before. "No, you can't be telling the truth. If you did that, you would have understood me. You would know why I wanted to go my own way."

"Your way is toward death. You stand there now, boy. Just as I warned you."

"But I am here because of you!" Caelan cried. "You left us defenseless. You and your ideals—"

"No! Listen now and share my understanding!" Beva said sharply. "Share it, or you will die by the other's hand. He is possessed by the taint of his own gods, and will not surrender to you. Why are you so fearful of my way, boy? Why do you close yourself against me?"

"Because you will not let me be who I am," Caelan said.

"All men are the same!" Beva said. "You and I are the same. See it, Caelan. Understand the pattern of harmony."

"No!"

"You walk now in the same darkness as I did. You must accept that, then leave it. Look into the darkness, Caelan, and admit that you like taking life. You like the power. You want it now. The craving grows inside you. Face it, boy! Admit it."

Caelan was shaking. Horrified, he knew his father was speaking the truth. He did want it, the glory and strength, and yet he didn't. The ultimate power, one life over another . . . he could see a dark mist looming over him, gathering force around him and his father. He shivered and was afraid.

"You take, boy," Beva said, drawing closer. "In healing, you take away pain and suffering. You take away disease. You take away madness and fits. You take away wrong intentions. You take what is necessary. You take the life force itself if it will help you. You take in order to work long hours without rest or food. You take in order to receive the deference and acclaim that is due you. You take in order to achieve your goals."

"And what do you give?" Caelan asked softly.

"Give?" Beva said as though he did not know the word's meaning. "There is no give. The pattern restores balance after you have taken. No void is left. If men with their foolish minds wish to say you have bestowed on them health or happiness or restoration or riches of the heart, that is their choice of sayings."

Caelan could barely look at him. His fear kept growing like the dark mist, like the coldness spreading so deeply into his soul. "All your goodness is a lie," Caelan said. "Like a piece of clothing you put on for the day."

"In *severance* I take," Beva said, unmoved. "If goodness restores order behind me, I will take the credit for it."

"Why did you teach me differently?" Caelan asked in anguish. "When I was a boy, why did you pretend?"

"Why should I give you the truth?" Beva retorted. "You do not like it, now that you have it. Like all gifts, it is spurned. Truth should be earned. It should be sought. Yet have you not come seeking, by entering true *severance* at last? You seek me here. Will you remain blind?"

Frustration filled Caelan. He was left again, as in all his father's lessons, derided and scorned, his failure to understand and agree like ashes at his feet. As always, Beva spoke truth and lies, so tangled together there was no dividing them.

"I did not come seeking you," Caelan said bitterly.

Beva, fading in and out as the mist shaped itself around him, did not change expression. "But I am what you found. I am your guide into true *severance*." He swept out his arm, where the darkness lay cold and waiting. "Enter, boy."

The coldness inside Caelan was painful now, burning and intense. He stepped back, shaking his head, putting as much distance between him and his father as possible. Yet it was as though he had not moved at all. Beva was still just as close as he had been before, but Caelan had the sense of a gate shutting between them.

What did it mean?

Wasn't the ultimate *severance* death?

He thought it must be, if he needed a spirit guide across a bridge into another life.

Shivering, Caelan drew back only to bump into a wall of clear ice. Turning, he pressed himself against its cold smoothness, feeling its surface melt slightly beneath the warmth of his breath. He could see through it, a distorted picture of the arena with him circling and fighting the tireless Amarouk, still bleeding but valiant, refusing to surrender or go down. Amarouk had somehow regained his feet, although he was limping and slow. Yet the black man's arms were like steel.

"Stay with me and learn," Beva said. "Stay with me and become what you were meant to be."

Still watching the battle, Caelan realized what Amarouk intended to do. Ignoring Beva's summons, Caelan hurled himself at the wall of ice, desperate to return to himself. He had to warn himself, had to—

With a snap, Caelan blinked and staggered back, finding himself back in the merciless heat of the arena. The sand was burning his feet. His shoulders screamed with exhaustion, and his arms were trembling. Amarouk sank down on one knee as though finally weakened by his wounds.

The crowd surged up, waving fists and screaming, the noise so loud it was incomprehensible.

Caelan saw Amarouk's free hand scoop up a fistful of sand and fling it at his face even as Amarouk's sword arm drew back.

The sand hit Caelan's face, but he closed his eyes and twisted his body to one side so that the flat of Amarouk's sword slid harmlessly past his belly. Caelan lifted his own sword with an effort that wrung a grunt from him and brought it down.

Amarouk's head went spinning across the sand, spraying blood as it tumbled. His headless body continued to kneel there for a second longer; then it toppled over slowly and crashed at Caelan's feet.

Only then did Caelan realize he had won. Gradually he became conscious of his sweat-burned eyes, the desperate sawing in his lungs, his pounding heart, and the deep burn of fatigue in his muscles.

He staggered back, and somehow managed not to drop his sword.

The crowd was cheering, "Victor! Victor!"

They did not know his name.

Caelan dragged his forearm across his face, then faced the emperor's box and found enough strength to lift the heavy sword in wavering salute.

Someday, perhaps by tomorrow, the crowd would know his name. He had achieved the first step toward winning his freedom. One victory, despite his doubts, despite his strange talents that he did not fully understand, despite the haunting of his father.

He swallowed, conscious of burning thirst, and let the sword fall from nerveless fingers.

The guards came running out, hustling him out of the ring back into the darkness of the ramp. They did not praise him. Instead they looked shocked, as though they had lost wagers because of his upset.

At the bottom, Orlo was waiting for him with a strange look on his face. He said nothing, however, and turned Caelan away from the tub of water to hustle him on.

"Hurry!" he said. "Step lively."

Caelan's legs were weak and trembly now that it was over. He found himself still struggling to believe it had actually happened.

"Don't let your head swell from this," Orlo said, stopping him next to a wide ramp that led up into the stands themselves. Guards stood everywhere, arena men mixed with soldiers in crimson uniforms. "Mind your manners and try not to act like the barbarian you are."

Caelan frowned, feeling bewildered. "I don't understand. What do you—"

"Your owner wants to give you the victory crown personally," Orlo said in a mixture of exasperation and pride. "Understand now?"

"Oh."

"Bow. Don't look the emperor in the eye. Don't speak unless you're spoken to. Don't linger. Don't forget you're nothing but a gladiator and have another day's battles ahead of you on the morrow."

After all the yelling and doubt, at last Orlo himself had called Caelan a gladiator. Caelan's heart swelled with a fullness he could not express. No compliment could be higher than the one he'd just received.

He looked into Orlo's eyes, struggling to thank him, but the trainer only smiled. "I guess Traulanders can fight after all," he said, then held out the amulet pouch.

Wordlessly, his heart too full, Caelan took it. "I—"

Orlo clapped him on the shoulder. "Hurry!"

Shoved forward, Caelan found himself flanked by imperial soldiers. He walked up the ramp, too stunned to take it in, yet beginning to feel dazzled by all that was happening so quickly. He emerged into the fading sunshine, and slicked back his long, sweat-soaked hair from his eyes.

He was met by a wall of sound. People were grinning and cheering him as well as Prince Tirhin. Caelan found it inexplicable, this sudden popularity, and warned himself none of it could be real or lasting. They had been cheering Amarouk only a short time before.

A tap on his shoulder made him turn. He climbed to the emperor's box and found himself sweating anew. As a child he had dreamed of someday seeing this man from afar. Even his own imagination had never brought him to the point of actually meeting the ruler of all the world.

Feeling dizzy from the way his heart was pounding, Caelan kept his eyes down respectfully and moved where the soldiers pointed.

He glimpsed a flash of blue; then the prince was standing before him.

"Well, well," Prince Tirhin said. "It seems I have found my missing property again. Thanks to you, my popularity with the common man has just jumped tenfold. That could cost me my head should my father decide to take offense."

Caelan stared at him, unsure how to respond to his mocking words.

"What is your name?"

"Caelan, my lord."

"I am not addressed as lord," the prince corrected, but with a smile. "You may call me sir."

"Yes, sir."

"Come."

Pulling Caelan by the shoulder, the prince escorted him across the box where courtiers and their ladies stared openly or made comments behind their hands. There were court musicians present, lyres idle in their hands, and concubines with painted faces and heavy perfume. Then he was at the front, before the throne. A haggard, gray-haired man in the polished armor of the emperor's protector stood behind it, his keen eyes missing nothing. The emperor himself was sitting on the splendor of crimson silk, sipping from a wine cup and smacking his lips appreciatively.

This was the man said to be immortal. This was the man who had dared to bargain with the gods to cheat death. This was the man who had molded a ragtag army into an invincible fighting force, the man who had proclaimed himself king, then emperor as he forged a united state of provinces that spanned the known borders of the world. This was Kostimon the Great—a legend beyond all comprehension.

"The victor at last," he said in a gruff, amused voice. "The unknown fighter who made a mess of all my wages and confounded the touts. Hah! Come here."

Even Caelan knew this honor was practically unheard of. He hurried forward and knelt at the emperor's feet. The man wore soft boots of purple leather. Caelan dared not look higher. He couldn't breathe. He couldn't think. He felt as though he were dreaming.

"You're a barbarian," the emperor said.

Despite his instructions, Caelan lifted his face and met the man's gaze squarely. "If it please the emperor," he said softly, his mouth so dry at his own daring it nearly choked him, "I am from the loyal province of Trau and was born free to good family. We are loyal to your imperial majesty, sworn to allegiance, and require no standing army to guarantee our obedience."

An uproar rose in the box. The protector moved quickly, smacking him across the back with the flat of his sword and bending him low. "Dog!" the protector shouted. "His imperial majesty needs no lesson in civics from you!"

"Let him up, Hovet," the emperor said, chuckling. "The wretch has spirit."

"He has foul manners," Tirhin said angrily.

"He's a fighter, a scrapper, like I was once. I like him. Get back, Hovet. Leave him be."

The protector stepped away, sheathing his sword with an ill-tempered snick of the blade.

The emperor snapped his fingers. "Well, victor, look at me again. Look!"

Slowly, Caelan straightened his aching back and met the emperor's gaze. Legend or not, he looked to be a man like nearly any other. Kostimon had been handsome once, but his face was now weathered and creased. Dissipation had carved unfriendly lines around his mouth and eyes. His hair was white and thick. It sprang back from his forehead in unruly curls. His eyes were yellow like a reptile's and frightening somehow, for all the amusement alight in them just now.

"Not many would dare correct me, much less in public," the emperor said softly.

Caelan's face burned and he bit his lip, wondering how it was he still lived. Would he never learn?

"Trau *is* loyal to me, as I recall. I have not been there in years. A rude, stiff-necked people not much given to hospitality."

People chuckled around them. Caelan gathered the emperor had made a joke, but he dared not smile.

"Do you have a name?"

"Caelan E'non."

The emperor sipped wine and settled back in his chair. "Well, Caelan E'non, you have pleased me today. You're a terrible fighter, nothing consistent about your form at all, but you've courage and heart and the guts to use them. I'll grant you a reward. What do you want?"

Tirhin frowned and looked disgruntled. Many of the others grinned and exchanged glances.

Caelan hesitated very little. "I want the chance to train with a champion team, so I can fight for my freedom."

The emperor sat bolt upright and hurled his cup away.

"Damnation! What kind of request is that? Why not ask for your freedom outright?"

Even now the temptation to do that was choking Caelan. But according to barracks tales, slaves who asked the emperor for freedom were always killed. It was said to be the emperor's favorite irony, in that death was the only genuine freedom a slave could ever know.

Caelan struggled to answer well: "Majesty, how can I ask such a request when I am not your property?"

Standing behind the throne, Tirhin relaxed visibly and even began to smile. The protector ran his hand suddenly across his mouth.

The emperor's yellow eyes smoldered. Glaring at Caelan, he leaned forward and gave him a little kick. "You have the slick tongue of a courtier, arena dog! How did you come to be a slave?"

Caelan's brows knotted with the old rage, checked just in time by his own prudence. Fighting down the emotion, he lowered his gaze. "The answer would displease your majesty."

"Hell's garden, I'm displeased now as it is! Give me your answer!"

Caelan's own temper rose to meet his. Setting his jaw, Caelan looked the old man in the eye. "Thyzarene raiders burned my home and sold me into slavery, majesty. Thyzarene raiders assigned to your eastern army, but set free to plunder loyal subjects as though we were enemies—"

"Enough!" the protector shouted.

Abashed, Caelan bowed low. Silence hung over the box, and during it Caelan dared not move.

"Well, Tirhin," the emperor said at last, snappishly. "He's your property, as he's had the stupidity to point out. What say you to his request to train for a championship?"

"I am not opposed to it. He's an ill-bred dog, but he does have potential. My trainer—"

Caelan looked up sharply, but just in time managed to curb his tongue.

Still, the emperor noticed. He sighed and raised his brows at Caelan. "Truly you are a fool. Do you have an objection?"

Again the courtiers laughed, but Caelan treated the question as though it were literal.

"If it please your imperial majesty and your imperial highness," he said breathlessly, "I would prefer to be trained by Orlo."

Tirhin snorted, and the emperor slammed his hand down on the arm of his throne.

"By the gods, I've not seen the like in years! Not only does he dare to correct me, but now he has specific instructions in how he'd like his request to be honored."

"He needs his tongue barbered," Hovet muttered darkly.

"Perhaps," the emperor said, eyeing Caelan with displeasure. "Were I not in such a good mood, I might have you cut into dog meat to feed my hounds." He snapped his fingers, and a slave put a victor's crown of ivy into his hand.

Leaning forward, the emperor squashed it onto Caelan's head. It was scratchy and smelled pungently where some of the leaves had been crushed.

"Hail, victor," the emperor said, suddenly sounding bored. "Take your wretched property away, Tirhin. I'm tired of the fellow."

Caelan somehow managed to swallow the knot of disappointment in his throat. He had gambled and lost. He tried to remind himself that today had been far from a failure. He would somehow persevere.

Standing up, he backed awkwardly away from the emperor.

Tirhin and the emperor exchanged a brief conversation in low voices, and Tirhin flushed.

Frowning, the prince exited the box without looking

back. Caelan followed, with the soldiers flanking him
again as though he might suddenly go mad and spring at
one of the concubines who tittered at him.

Out of sight of the crowd, nearly halfway down the
ramp, Tirhin suddenly stopped and turned around. His
eyes held something unreadable.

"Are you worth the trouble of defying my father?" he
asked aloud.

Caelan stared at him, not understanding what he meant
and knowing he wasn't supposed to.

Tirhin rubbed his chin thoughtfully. "Perhaps," he said.
"Perhaps. He wants me to sell you to him for his own
team."

Caelan held his breath.

After a pause Tirhin laughed unpleasantly and gestured
at an arena guard. "You, there. Have Orlo brought to me."

In moments the trainer came running, still carrying his
cattail club, his head bowed respectfully, his eyes shifting
up in quick, furious glimpses at Caelan. "Yes, sir?"

"I have decided to take my property home to my own
arena," Tirhin said loftily.

"Yes, sir." Again Orlo glanced at Caelan. His gaze
could have frozen meat.

"My trainer doesn't have time for additional men, especially new recruits as raw as this one. Yet I have seen
courage today, and my property has acquitted himself
well."

"He fought better than I expected, sir."

"I ask you to rejoin my service, Orlo," the prince said.
"To work as an assistant in my arena, but chiefly to train
new recruits such as this, who need hours of basic drills.
Will you consider it?"

Orlo bowed low, his face expressionless. "Your highness honors me," he said in a toneless voice. "I will consider it."

"Your answer tonight, or nothing," the prince said.

Giving them a general nod, Tirhin walked away with the imperial soldiers behind him.

As soon as he was out of sight, Orlo moved Caelan down the ramp and shoved him over into a corner out of everyone's way.

"Are you mad?" he asked furiously. "What did you ask for?"

Caelan said, "To fight where I could win my freedom."

Orlo's anger didn't soften. "Gault, you have the nerve. It's a wonder the protector didn't cut out your tongue."

"It's what I want," Caelan said simply.

"A sane man would have asked for money or a dancing girl."

Caelan raised his brows. "In a place like this, where would I put either?"

"Why your stupid games during training?" Orlo asked, with a rapid change of subject. "Why the fooling about, pretending you couldn't fight? Did you think it would deceive your opponents?"

"I—" Caelan found himself without an answer he thought this man would understand, or accept. Since his beliefs were forbidden, it was impossible to explain.

"No, don't tell me it was because I took your amulet away. I'll never believe *that*." Orlo snorted. "Your ruse worked, but don't count on it again. Rumor spreads fast. They may not see the conflicts, those locked below, but they hear about them. You understand? Great Gault! You killed Amarouk, the best man in my barracks. The best! Do you know where that ranks you now?"

"Yes," Caelan said.

Orlo glared at him. "And me? Why me? Why the hell, after all this time, does Tirhin ask me to serve him again?" Orlo paced back and forth, fuming. "Why does his sublime highness think I'd want to go back to wearing his colors? You tell me that!"

"Because I asked for you to be my trainer," Caelan said.

Orlo swung around to face him, his mouth open. "You?" he said, his voice almost squeaking. "You *asked*?"

"Yes."

Orlo flung his hands up in the air. "I do not believe this. You are mad. Truly."

"They asked what I wanted."

"And you mentioned me," Orlo said. "Before the emperor and before the prince. You mentioned *me*."

"Yes."

Orlo stared at him. "Do you know what lies between me and the prince? What have you been told?"

"Nothing," Caelan answered honestly.

Orlo turned half away from him and stared into space, oblivious to the bustle passing them. The arena still had to shut down. The crowds were leaving now, and there were fighters to be fed and secured for the night, the arena to be cleaned, a thousand tasks requiring supervision.

But Orlo stood there and stared at nothing, his jaw working in time with his thoughts.

"I do not know that I can go back," Orlo said softly. "But for him to give me the chance . . . it is a peace offering and a great honor. I owe you for this, Giant."

He faced Caelan again, frowning as though he did not know what to think.

Caelan met his gaze squarely, feeling hope rising once again. "Then help us both," he said and dared to hold out his hand.

Orlo hesitated, glancing over his shoulder to make sure no one saw. Then slowly he gripped Caelan's hand in the shadows.

"It is a bargain," he said. "If you want to be a champion, I'll take you the farthest I can. Just make sure you don't get yourself killed before I make my fortune with you."

It was Caelan's turn to stare into the distance, into the future. What lay before him, he did not yet know. He only understood that since this afternoon, everything had changed. By breaking through the ice wall in his vision with his father, he had crossed some threshold or passed some test that he did not as yet fully comprehend. He suspected, although he did not know how or why, that there were other tests still to come.

"Did you hear me?" Orlo said sharply, bringing him back to the here and now. "You've got to learn to concentrate, otherwise you really will find yourself bleeding on the sand."

Caelan shook his head with a faint smile. "That is not in my plans," he said softly.

The Sword, The Ring, and The Chalice

THE BESTSELLING TRILOGY BY

Deborah Chester

"Entertaining" —*Starlog*

"Mesmerizing." —*Romantic Times*

The Sword   0-441-00702-3

The Ring   0-441-00757-0

The Chalice   0-441-00796-1

**Available wherever books are sold or
to order call 1-800-788-6262**